THE HAUNTED WIND

Ross Griffin

Dedication

To my wife, Elaine, who introduced me to the Burren.

To the Burren... that introduced me to this story

Acknowledgements

I would like to thank and acknowledge the team at Booksgosocial.com for all their work and assistance in getting this book launched. Without their help, I may never have gotten this story published! I would also like to thank Elaine, Patricia, Mick, Mary, John, Carol, Michael and Elizabeth for all their help too. Without the time, I could not have written this!

Prologue

2019 - The West of Ireland

Adrien Guirado swallowed a mouthful of fresh air. He had reached the peak of Eagle Rock. In front of him, the sea was wild with sea horses. To his right, Ballyvaughan was hemmed in by tall grey hills of limestone. Bulbous white clouds raced along the crest of the hills. A beaming blue sky finished the picture. From grey, to white, to blue. Stunning. The scenery here was like a living piece of art.

Adrien turned around, took off his hiking bag and began to root through it. He found his map and unravelled it. As he examined his position, he dipped the map slightly and something caught his eye in the distance. Through squinting eyes he noticed two large stone slabs, a few metres apart, standing vertical in the ground. In between them, a larger stone slab was leaning diagonally. One end touched the top of the left standing stone while the other end slanted downwards to the base of the right standing stone.

Adrien realised that the structure was a dolmen and the capstone must have slid off somehow.

He raised his map back up. As he leaned to his right to retrieve his compass from his shorts side pocket, he noticed a person near the Dolmen. It was… a woman… with white hair… wearing a long black dress of some sort.

A strong wind suddenly snapped the map out of Adrien's hand. He swivelled round and tried to catch it, but it fluttered and twisted in the wind, before finally sailing over the cliff edge.

Out on the ocean, Adrien could see thick grey storm clouds rolling in. A huge flash of lightning erupted from them.

He turned back around, looking back for the woman, but she had disappeared. A clap of thunder growled in the air around him.

As Adrien picked up his bag, another strong wind whipped the glasses from his face. He thought he could just make out the blurry area where they landed. Crouching down, he fumbled with his hands and found them. As he put them on, a wave of anxiety went through him. His heart skipped a beat. He was dangerously close to the cliff edge.

Adrien stood and turned to leave, when another howling wind struck him. It brought him off his feet. Lying on his front now, he was slow to react. He felt himself being pushed closer to the edge and began to grasp at anything he could, until his hands found the sanctuary of a crevice. His feet scrambled to find a hold but as he turned his head, he quickly realised that his feet were already over the cliff edge. He let out a small cry of shock.

Adrien drew a breath. He composed himself, and pulled.

As he tried to reach another crevice with his right hand, the wind shot his arm violently backwards. He screamed, but the wind screamed louder. His legs were kicking, his eyes bulged, and his mouth was agape. He watched in horror as the little finger on his left hand was pushed upwards. Then the one beside it. “NO!” he begged.

Adrien’s hand was torn from the crevice. He plummeted down the 300 metre drop. The shriek he gave came from the pit of his soul, but the wind swallowed up that sound. He landed head first, his head exploding on the rock below.

Something in the wind above gave a slow cackle, but no one heard.

Chapter 1

December 2018- The Brazilian Rainforest

The mist danced upon the small morning waves. Neha Laogo recalled an elder telling him that the mist contained the souls of the dead. It was most vibrant before the dawn or at dusk; trapped between worlds maybe.

Neha held his net tightly, as did the other men on the boats, as they circled a section of water. His boat rocked gently from side to side and but for the sound of the waves lapping against it, all was peaceful. He was thankful for that. Only the smell of diesel disturbed him slightly.

He couldn't understand why these 'diesel engines' were necessary. Every boat seemed to use them now. The engines churned up too much water while the diesel continuously leaked from the engines, into the river. Why could they not simply use the oars!? The fishermen said the engines made their boats fast and helped them to access better fishing grounds. But maybe they were not supposed to access these places.

His son, Paka, agreed with the fishermen. He said the engines were 'practical'.

He recalled that strange word being used when their Chief decided that they should walk out of the forest all those years ago. Large strange yellow creatures had come. They moved on large black spinning disks. They would puff smoke and make strange noises before attacking the trees.

The men who controlled these yellow creatures told Neha and his tribe that they owned their land. They waved strange rectangular white leaves at them which also contained many small black symbols. Neha's tribe fought them with their spears and arrows. But many of their tribe were killed. The men controlling the yellow creatures left but then other men came. They seemed more respectful. These men offered them strange food, objects and clothing.

Neha's Chief went with these men for some time. When he returned, he told them not to worry but they were leaving the forest. He promised them shelter, food and a better life than they or their ancestors had ever lived. The elders were reluctant, but most of the tribe obeyed their Chief anyway. That was eighteen years ago. Neha had been the Shaman of the tribe. Now he wore strange clothing and pulled nets onto boats, most days. As for their Chief, well, he had taken to a substance called 'alcohol'.

The mist dissipated around the boat as the morning sunshine lit up his surrounds. Neha could see more of the trees on the far riverbank. They stood tall. They stood steady. They stood together. They were the greatest tribe of the Amazon.

Neha looked down at the water beside him, staring at his rippling reflection. It was him… but not the person he remembered he thought he was. Could a reflection show his past? Would it show him the person he had been so long ago? He wondered if he stared long enough, would he see someone different. Somebody he used to be…

The small diesel engine on the boat sputtered to life behind Neha. He half jumped as it pierced his thoughts. He had never really gotten used to the sound. The lead fisherman controlling the engine behind Neha shouted. Some of the men in the boats began to beat the water with their paddles. The lead fisherman shouted again, and the boats slowly tightened the circle. As some fish began to sporadically jump out of the water, Neha pulled his net closed as tightly as he could.

There was a frenzy in the water as trapped fish began to thrash about. Another shout came and the men began to pull the bulging nets up. Neha and another man now tried to get their heavy load on board their slender, ten foot wooden boat, when Neha noticed a strange ripple of bubbles beside the net. There was something else there.

Suddenly, a great grey fish leapt from the water. It got itself atop the net and flopped into the boat. Its great jaw, filled with needle sharp white teeth, began to bite and snap. The teeth seemed as long as a man's fingers. It had an arched, protruded head and was nearly as long as the boat itself. It had large circular eyes. Its tail fin thrashed back and forth, wildly.

The other man who hauled the nets with Neha was in front of the creature's snapping jaws. The fish reached the man's ankle and bit down… the man gave a blood curdling scream of pain. The tips of the fish's lower fangs protruded through the top of the man's ankle. Neha counted himself lucky that he was at the tail end of the creature.

Neha noticed that since the creature had bitten through the man's ankle it was not thrashing its tail fin as much. He waited… until it stopped moving its tail, then quickly reached for the point where the tail fin met the back of the fish's lower body and pinched the fish as hard as he could. It immediately swiped its tail at him, but it also opened its vice like jaws. The man at the other end got his ankle free and recoiled. Neha moved as far back as he could, away from the now thrashing predator. But the lead fisherman of their party simply shouted at Neha and pushed him forward. Anger infused Neha's body at that push, but he had no time and needed to act fast.

The fish was now trying to turn its head towards him. He had faced tricky situations with caiman and boar in the past. Neha quickly made the hunters move. He parried towards the fish's head on the left, before scuttling past it on the right side of the boat, dipping and snatching up one of the oars as he passed. He turned and jumped both feet up on the sides of the boat.

As the fish swerved wildly back to its right, Neha brought the butt of the oar down on its head. The fish hardly seemed to react to the first blow, but Neha kept pumping the oar down, harder and harder, onto its head. The creature stopped moving. Neha let out a guttural shout as he brought the oar down upon its head one more time. He saw the pupil of the fish's eye was dilated and frozen. Satisfied that the animal was not playing dead, he stopped. The low rumble of the diesel engines was the only sound now. The men on the boats around him were silent, as was the man who was clutching his ankle.

Neha, breathing heavily, looked about him. The lead fisherman's mouth was agape as were most of the others in the group. He stared at Neha. Neha held his gaze and slowed his breathing. The lead fisherman broke off and looked around. He shouted towards something akin to a sand spit or mud flat one hundred feet away. The group started to move their boats in that direction. They sped up as they got closer and the boats wedged themselves onto the sloping muddy bank.

Neha leapt off with the grey fish propped over his shoulder. He landed up to his calves in mud but slogged up to the solid sand ahead. Paka made it to his father and congratulated him. Neha dropped the fish beside him. It landed with a heavy thud.

The other men jumped out of their boats and attended to the nets. Some others carried the injured man ashore and set him down. The lead fisherman soon arrived on the sand but instead of heading towards the injured fisherman, he trudged straight to the dead fish in front of Neha. He bent down and reached out to touch it with his right hand. Neha grabbed his wrist and yanked it away.

The lead fisherman stood and delivered a set of Portuguese expletives to Neha. Two other men walked over. One stood just behind the right shoulder of the lead fisherman, the other stood just behind his other shoulder. Paka stood to the left side of his father. The lead fisherman carried on his tirade while waving his hands about him. Neha slapped the fish forcibly with his left hand and quickly slapped his chest with his right. Paka moved in front of his father and began to tell the lead fisherman in Portuguese that this was his father's fish. Neha placed his right foot upon it.

An eagle suddenly burst through the wall of rainforest at the lead fisherman's back. It made a loud call as it darted past them, moving over the river at speed. All the men were startled by this and went quiet. They stared at the wall of trees behind them, but then the fighting resumed. But Neha had not broken off his stare. He shoved past the lead fisherman and his two lackeys and stopped. The leaves and branches moved slightly and a woman came into view.

She wore nothing but a small tunic at her thin waist. She was carrying something… a baby. She was covered in a strange blue hue and took no notice of the crowd of men on the river bank. Suddenly four others stepped out of the green wall; two other women and two younger boys who carried spears, bows and arrows. They were all covered in that strange blue hue. The woman in front, carrying the baby, collapsed forward onto her knees. Neha turned and gave Paka a look and Paka strode forward to the woman. The fishermen all started to murmur and shared confused expressions.

Neha was just starting to follow Paka when another man appeared before them. Like the others he was covered in a blue hue and was emaciated. He wore a light green tunic, a necklace, and had a small hat of yellow feathers on his head. He carried a spear, or the spear appeared to carry him. As he wobbled, he locked eyes with Neha.

Cold realisation swept through Neha and his mouth fell open. This man was from another place, another time. The ghostly figure moved toward Neha and collapsed just as he reached him. Neha caught him and bent down, holding the man's head on his left forearm.

"Neha!" his brother uttered through a weak wheezing sigh.

Before his brother had finished his exhale a strong wind broke through the jungle wall in front of them. The trees swayed violently and the bushes shook uncontrollably. The wind struck the fishermen and one or two were forced backwards. They began exchanging shouts, but the roaring wind soon drowned them out. Neha held his brother and stood slowly. Just before he raised him over his shoulders, he heard his brother say two distinct, panicked words.

"Wind… Death!"

Chapter 2

December 2018 - York, England

Edward Marshall awoke with something between a gasp and a cough, with no idea where he was. As his bloodshot eyes took in the room, realisation dawned that he was in his rented bedroom in York. Absolute doom engulfed him as he raised his left forearm to his eyes. He made himself look for his phone, which he located on the ground to the right of his bed. It was beside what looked like last night's kebab and judging from the state of his carpet, either he or a wild animal had tackled it.

He looked at his phone and dropped it with despair. It was 3 p.m. He moaned. He would have to be up tomorrow at 5 a.m., for the monotonous and awful factory job. He had known this but went on the lash anyway and spent money he did not have. He remembered leaving the nightclub and then being cajoled into another late bar. Who was he kidding… he had been a willing follower and 'endorser' of that plan.

Ed knew how his day would go. He would try to get up and barely manage the toilet. He would then stay in bed for at least another two hours. Then get up and order a pizza. Watch television until midnight. Not sleep until all hours of the morning and be absolutely shattered when his alarm went off. He groaned.

Fuck!! He suddenly remembered that the meeting with the professor was today, in a bloody hour! He leapt out of bed and nearly fell over. He managed to throw on his tracksuit pants and hoodie and fumble his feet into his runners.

Ed stepped out of his lair and passed Lenny's room. Heavy snoring. Lenny was out last night too and would probably not be up until 4 or 5 p.m. But it didn't matter for him. Lenny was long term unemployed… and loving it. He was unemployed around five years, forty next year and he and the benefits system seemed to be in a very happy marriage. Lenny had tried to get jobs initially, but none of them came through, then none of them 'suited', then trying was 'pointless'. He essentially now just did back to work courses to convince the system, and his parents, that he was doing everything he could. Lenny's main shift now was down in the Fox pub. Ed took some solace in the fact that his life had not ground to a complete halt yet.

Ed moved down the stairs like something akin to a zombie in an old horror movie. A kind of stunted moving. He made a coffee and pounded two paracetamols, found his car keys, grabbed his jacket and headed out to his car.

He nearly collapsed into the driver's seat. He barely broke into third gear for most of the journey. Once he parked at York University, he felt slightly better. Nevertheless, he eased out of his car with the slow grace of a ninety something year old with two hip replacements on board.

Ed walked under the main triangular arch near the entrance and stopped, flipping a cigarette into his mouth. As he burned it to life and took a drag, all his problems drifted away in the smoke.

He looked up and noticed long strands of hanging ivy just over his head. They seemed to grasp at him like tentacles. The weather over the last few months had been kind to York, but the overgrown ivy needed the attention of the grounds-keeping team. He suddenly realised he was judging the upkeep of the campus as if it were his own abode. In truth, it had felt like that for the last four years.

After his redundancy, he knew another office experience was not for him. So he tried something completely different. He found out that some University courses offered government subsidized grants and had chosen Archaeology. The course was not exactly geared towards the economy of today, but he had really enjoyed it.

He had taken the course seriously from the off. This had been an outdoor job and sun, rain or snow, he had put in a massive shift. By year three, he was taking year one tutorials for Professor Barnes. He enthusiastically volunteered for most 'digs', mindless searches in fields, and had driven to countless museums assisting the professor in his curation work. By year four he was surprised to learn that there might be an actual job on offer.

He stared at the Archaeology building. It was a great square bulking lump of concrete with sharp edges. It was cold and forbidding. It lacked colour, windows… or soul. One of the last dilapidated tributes to Soviet Union architecture perhaps. But those thick walls had insulated him from the real world for some time, and he was thankful for that.

Ed's right hand drifted down to his jacket pocket. He felt the square envelope. He was shocked when it arrived at his parent's house. At best, it was a pointless gesture.

He took one more drag of his cigarette and then flicked it away with his thumb and forefinger. It landed in the duck pond nearby. It didn't really matter as there was no one around.

But that's what made the professor's text all the more ominous. Sunday was a strange time to do this.

A gust of wind raced through the archway. He checked the time and started to head towards the Archaeology building. Reaching the front door, he found it locked and walked around to the back of the building. Bingo! The emergency exit at the back had a small box keeping it open. Professor Barnes' private entrance. Ed walked down the corridor to the professor's office and knocked.

"Come in!"

The professor, hands spread on his desk, greeted Ed with a beaming smile. "Ed!" he half shouted, as if Ed were a guest joining a chat show. "Great to see you!"

His smile quickly evaporated as he looked Ed up and down.

"You look fresh today," the professor offered with a hint of sarcasm.

Ed responded with a grunt and shrugged, only realising now that the tracksuit pants, hoodie, unshaven face and bloodshot eyes probably screamed hangover. He looked over the professor's head at the giant picture of Stonehenge hanging on the wall. The style of the professor's office seemed a tribute to that ancient site; towers of dusty books and folders made up much of the space.

Ed sat into the chair in front of the professor's desk. He leant forward, placing his elbows onto the desk top. He clasped his hands into a fist and frowned. It was Ed's way of dealing with 'the desk', that silly symbol of authority.

"You look stern, Ed."

"Perfectly good," Ed responded sharply. "You called me here for a meeting?"

Ed reckoned if someone was going to stick a knife in you, make them look you in the eye first.

"Yes, I did," responded the professor in a haughty tone. "Tea, Ed?"

The professor had known Ed for four years and knew perfectly well that Ed didn't drink tea. A stubborn silence now gripped the room. The professor raised his owl like eyebrows up, indicating he expected a response.

Ed dragged up mock laughter. "When have I ever drank bloody tea?"

The Professor's eyes bulged. "We have given the Assistant Professor job to Lisa," he said loudly.

Ed let out a grunt followed by a hissing sigh. She was probably ten years younger than Ed. She was good, but surely not in his league. He tried to digest this shit sandwich… but couldn't.

"My thesis was top class… my interview and presentation with the Board was flawless."

The Professor stared down at his desk and replied coolly, "The Board felt she was the best candidate." He looked up at Ed. "And so did I."

Ed felt a cold sense of betrayal. He was furious.

"You encouraged me to apply for this – remember!?"

The professor's face went red. Ed wondered if that was a reaction to guilt or anger.

"Lisa is an investment in the future, Ed."

"As if I have anywhere to go?" Ed did not realise that was a problem for himself and not for the professor.

"Ed, it is not as simple as–"

"I applied myself, took your tutorials, attended the digs all over the place and went the extra mile. She seems smart, but is *she* practically smart? How many digs did *she* attend? How many fields did *she* cross on her hands and knees?" Ed's voice nearly lost control at the last part.

"She achieved a very high grade, Ed," responded the professor sternly.

"So wha–"

"It was higher than yours."

Ed gritted his teeth for an instant. "But what let you pick a twenty-five year old young one. She's a book worm!"

Ed realised that this was his hangover doing the talking. An incoherent defence to a decision already taken.

The professor leant forward in his chair, nodding his head side to side, and held up his hand. That was enough.

"Damn it!" shouted Ed, as he slowly rubbed his hands up and down his face. His charge of the light brigade had ended.

As hostilities ceased, a few moments silence broke out.

"How about a coffee, Ed?"

Ed looked at him. Feeling calmer, he responded in a tone of acceptance, "Yeah… go on."

The professor made him a coffee and handed it to him.

The mood in the office changed. They both took a nice sip of their respective drinks. The axe had now fallen between the executed and executioner.

A forced chit-chat ensued before the professor asked the delicate question. “What will you do now, Ed?”

Ed began to speak but responded slowly as if he was considering that point himself.

“Probably go home, figure things out… time to leave York in any case.”

The professor leaned forward, placing his elbows onto the desk and cupped his hands together. “Well, I’m glad you mentioned that as I have a suggestion for you. Have you ever heard of the Burren, Ed?”

The professor proceeded to turn his computer monitor towards Ed. The image Ed saw was a landscape of grey scattered rock.

“Is that Greenland? Iceland?”

“No, Ed, much closer to home… it’s in the West of Ireland. It’s called the Burren National Park. It’s a treasure trove of geological wonders and various archaeological sites.”

Ed raised his eyebrows and shrugged.

The professor gave an exasperated sigh.

“The Irish Archaeological Association are stuck, and they need someone to do an audit of that park. It was last done in the 1950s, but that report is well out of date. They need a fresh report as they look to tackle tourist footfall and climate change.”

“Don’t they have anyone from Ireland?” replied Ed.

“They can’t get anyone. All of their youth are jet setting to placements abroad.”

Ed let out a yawn.

The professor continued, “It’s paid, Ed, you have two years to complete it and the first year will be rent free – not the Ritz, mind you.” The professor chuckled at that.

Ed still didn't bite.

"If we are going to do this, it had better be soon, Ed. They mightn't have anyone in Ireland, but I know a colleague of mine in Sweden has mentioned that she could have someone for the role early this week coming."

The professor's mobile suddenly rang. He turned in his chair slightly as he answered it. "Hello, Alice."

As the coffee kicked in, Ed's brain began to chew all of this. Why should he take this job… that no one else probably wanted? Maybe the person in Sweden was simply a 'Desperado' like him.

"Yes, dear, I have his present."

Ed felt completely indifferent to the west of Ireland. Nothing new there really.

"I will collect the cake."

Was this all the professor could offer him for his hard work? An audit of a barren looking park?

"Yes, I will be on time."

The professor ended the call and turned in his chair to face Ed. "My grandson's fifth birthday," he said with a wide smile. He checked the time on his watch. "Well, Ed, what's it to be?"

Ed slowly realised that this wasn't the certainty he had chased but it was his last option. That or the repetitive 5 a.m. starts for the factory job, or worse, joining Lenny down in the Fox.

He locked eyes with the professor. "I'll do it!"

"Great decision, Ed. This will get you launched!"

The professor immediately rang Deirdre O'Connor from the Irish Archaeology Association. She answered and he put the call on speaker so the three could chat. But they could hardly hear her due to the noise of the wind at the other end. The professor roared, "Hello, Deirdre," four times but she couldn't hear. Then they heard what sounded like a car door shutting. The conversation started properly.

Deirdre was delighted to hear the professor had found someone for her. "Thank God!" she said loudly.

Ed tried to briefly give some of his credentials and experience, but Deirdre cut across him. "Ed, we'll discuss more about the role when you get as far as Dublin. Consider yourself hired. I'll have to get you a few authorisations and licences. They may take a month or two. I'll forward more information by email."

They booked an estimated date for him to come over. Deirdre said she had to end the call. She was up in Mayo at a dig. She hung up.

The professor and Ed shared a smile. Ed stood and shook hands with the professor, said "Good luck," and turned to leave. The professor answered in kind.

*****

The professor watched as Ed closed the door behind him. He was delighted the stench of alcohol and cigarettes was out of his office. He swivelled in his chair and looked out the small window to his right, pressed his chin to his clasped hands and closed his eyes for a moment.

He took out a file from the right drawer of his desk, opened it and looked at the news article. It was dated a month earlier. '*Aine O'Sullivan still missing. Gardaí to resume search tomorrow…*'

Indeed, Deirdre's report indicated that the girl was never found. But before that, the report said Aine had complained of some unusual events in the cottage. The report also indicated that Aine said she had made a significant archaeological 'find'. With quote, '*artefacts never seen before*'.

He ran through the logic of what he had told Ed, or what he hadn't told him. Ed was robust but not a pure academic. He was good at the practical but lacked the academic attention to detail necessary for the Assistant Professor job. The professor reminded himself that he also owed Deirdre a big favour.

Although Ed had been right about one thing, Lisa was a bookworm. But she had confronted him in his office last week. She had threatened to tell his wife everything. The professor concluded, that just like Ed, he too was out of options!

'Yappy' was what the children of the tribe called the animal, for it was always barking. Neha did not see the sense in naming the creature.

He raised a hand briefly to shoo the animal away but thought against it. It had been a long day for everyone.

Once Neha reached the trees, he trod carefully for he needed to listen for the hatzy birds. After a few minutes he heard them. He went underneath their tree and using his feet, began to carefully search the foliage on the ground. The yapping creature was not far behind, sniffing at something.

Neha stopped searching the ground and shook his head. He could see no eggs here. The yapping creature barked behind him. Neha turned, and saw the animal staring at him. Neha was surprised by the colour of its eyes. They were green, with flecks of gold around the iris. Strange colouring for an animal. But there was definitely an intelligence behind those eyes, although there was an intelligence behind most creatures' eyes, if people chose to look.

Neha noticed something at the animal's feet, something yellow. He walked over and crouched down – it was some discarded hatzy eggs! He picked them up and carefully placed them into his pouch. The yapping creature walked behind him.

As Neha stood, he noticed the light was dwindling fast. He needed to find a Felnas tree soon. He turned to call the yapping creature to him but it was not there. Neha's lips parted slightly as he strained his eyes to see any signs of it. He made a clicking noise and snapped his fingers, but it did not come to him. The children of the village would not be happy if the creature did not return with him.

Neha stood perfectly still and almost stopped breathing as he listened intently. He heard a slight snapping to his left. He waited. Now he heard a distant rustling. He slowly moved towards the sound. As he got closer, he could hear sniffing and panting.

As Neha walked around the large bark of a Cupuaça tree, he saw the yapping creature urinating on another tree close by. He shouted at the creature and moved to pick it up but it darted to its left and moved into the brush. Neha let out a curse, he didn't have time for this!

Neha moved over to the tree where the creature had urinated and sighed as he leant one arm up against it. Neha's brow creased, as he examined the tree further with both hands now. He smirked as he realised this was a Felnas. He walked around it briefly and in the dark could see the lowest branch was ideal. The flowers on its sides were just blooming. The branch was just another man's height above him.

Neha threw the pouch around the far side of the trunk and held the straps with his hands. He wrapped his legs around the trunk, leant back slightly, and began to slowly use his legs to climb up. He reached the branch; the smell of the blooming white flowers was welcome. He took his knife from his waist and began to cut the branch where it looked weakest. It snapped and he let it fall to the ground. He shimmied down the tree and landed softly.

Neha began to walk back to his village. As he cleared the trees, he noticed the yapping creature beside him. Neha was beginning to hold a begrudging respect for it. He found himself patting it on the head.

As Neha walked into the village, he saw that a great fire had been lit in the centre. The pig must now have been cooked. He moved towards the fire. His tribe were gathered there, on the small log seats spread out around it. They were sharing the pig and talking. There was no sign of the tribe's people they had rescued.

As Neha reached the edge of the circle he paused briefly to examine the inside of his pouch. People looked to him but said nothing.

Neha moved directly towards the pig, which was mounted on a spit to the right of the fire. He grabbed a bowl nearby, placed it under the pig and let fat drip down into it. He picked off bits of the meat and threw them into the bowl.

Neha then crouched down and retrieved the hatzy eggs from his pouch. He began breaking each of the eggs and emptied their contents into the bowl. Next, he took out the Felnas branch, plucked off three of the white flowers and threw them into the bowl also.

Neha then placed the Felnas branch on the ground. He took his knife and slowly began to cut down the middle of the branch from end to end. He placed one end of the branch to his mouth and the other into the bowl. He started blowing. Amber gel began to roll out of the branch into the mixture. Finally, with a cooking stick, Neha stirred and ground the materials up until they were an edible mash.

Neha was reluctant to stand. How long had it been since he had done this? How long since he had contacted the sky spirits?

He stood and placed himself in front of the roaring fire. The eyes of the sky spirits twinkled in the night above. He slowly raised the bowl above his head, closed his eyes and began the low incantation.

An elderly woman on the edge of the fire noticed Neha standing there. Above the drone of people, she could hear his words. She grabbed the wrist of her daughter and pointed at Neha. Some others in the circle saw her do this and looked to where she was pointing. The talking amongst the tribe began to die down.

Neha's chanting began to get louder. He sang from his stomach. He kept his eyes closed as he began to slowly walk around the fire. Neha felt… others… with him now.

The tribespeople watched as Neha began to hop and skip around the fire. He held the bowl under one arm as his other seemed to lash out at the night sky. Some knew the words he sang and slowly began to help him. The fire snapped and crackled as Neha's deliberate dance carried on. Wisps of smoke appeared to chase and tangle at his feet.

Neha stopped rigidly, faced the fire, and raised the bowl above his head once more. He brought the bowl to his mouth and took a taste. He stopped singing and stood there until he felt released. He turned and opened his eyes. All the tribespeople were looking at him.

Neha walked out of the circle with the bowl under his arm. The sound of the crackling fire filled the night, but the tribe were silent. The elderly woman who had spotted Neha at the start of his incantation broke the silence.

"It is him," she said placing a hand to her heart. "Our Shaman… has returned."

Chapter 4

The seagull hung in the air. It neither moved forward nor back but judged the wind current perfectly. The seagull had found a balance. Neither here nor there. Perfect. Ed appreciated that as he raised his cigarette to his mouth, inhaling a healthy mixture of sea air and nicotine.

Ed was in Holyhead in Wales and had driven down from his parents' place in Yorkshire. A tough drive, but he couldn't part with his trusty Honda Civic. Besides, he would need it where he was going. He had finished up the factory job but got a nice couple of quid into his back pocket. He had left Lenny to it, parted ways with a handshake and not much else.

Ed moved back to his parents' house at Christmas. He had a chance meeting with his uncle over the holiday that resulted in his uncle asking if Ed could help him during the lambing season.

His uncle's farm was on the edge of the Yorkshire Dales and Ed knew his uncle could use all the help he could get. So Ed agreed to help. Gathering and finding the ewes was the first challenge. The snow had come as well, which made it all the more difficult.

Ed was up at 5 a.m. in freezing cold conditions. Porridge in, gear on and out the door to darkness. Quick cup of tea and a sambo at eleven. Then work until four. Pile in a heated casserole. A cup of tea, slice of cake, and then bed. It was rinse, wash, repeat for two months, but in early March he had to stop. He needed to get to the Emerald Isle. His uncle was grateful for the dig out and paid Ed well for the work. It was a nice surprise and a bit more cash in his pocket. It was also a nice connection to his home before he took this mental leap over the Irish Sea.

As he finished his cigarette, he causally dropped it on the ground and stubbed it to death with his foot. So satisfying. Yes, he was slowly killing himself, yes, he was doing something bad for the environment, but this was therapy. That's what all the 'do gooders' didn't understand.

In the past, outside his office, he often dropped the cigarette stubs on the ground. His colleagues gave him plenty of dirty looks for not putting the stubs in the ash bin. Surprised them too as he was their Compliance Officer. But you needed to show people that side of you.

In Compliance, you were the glorified hall monitor. You needed an edge or the 'business beast' would eat you. He had worked in finance since he graduated from college. Compliance had taken off and the CEO looked for volunteers. Ed cared then and he put his hand up.

Within months, he had fallen out with half the office as he had tried to install a watered down version of UK/EU compliance into their daily working lives. The regulators wanted everything implemented and they were simply living in a dream. Much of the legislation was too heavy, broad, and open to too much interpretation.

The regulators did not understand the world of business, clients or commercial deadlines. A business was designed to make money. These days, that in itself was some sort of crime.

Ed had spent his time trying to take the horses to water in the job. Some of them drank; the ones who didn't stood in the fields, and openly laughed. Some old stallions saw this compliance thing as a joke; it simply wasn't in their day. A rock and a hard place did not adequately describe the difficulties of the gig. Then why did he do it for so long?

Ed heard a honking car or two and saw that the ferry had lowered its bridge door. The long line of impatient cars slowly started to move on. He stopped leaning on the metal pole fence on the dock side. As he did, his right hand reached inside his jacket pocket looking for his ferry ticket. His hand instead produced the wedding invite.

'Penny & Bob's Big Wedding. R.S.V.P. by March 31st'

He had met Penny when she joined their company through a merger. She had been the lone Compliance Officer in her company too so they both got on like a house on fire when they realised they would not be the only ones carrying the cross anymore. They shared their nerdy in jokes and tackled the 'business beast' together. A few office nights out and one thing led to another. Two years on and they had moved in together.

Bob then joined the company to assume the role of Head of Compliance from the CEO. Ed and Penny would now report to him. Bob was mates with the CEO, married with two kids and seemed like a decent bloke.

He was a breath of fresh air at first and all three had gotten on very well. They had been a united team.

But then the option of attending compliance conferences in various locations around Europe opened up. Two people could go. Bob wanted Penny to go initially and Ed to mind the 'mad house'. As the conferences became more regular, Ed argued that he and Penny should go but Bob always seemed to have a good reason for Ed to stay in the office. He was needed there at 'base camp'.

Ed remembered when his relationship with Penny began to break down. It was after she attended one of the compliance conferences with Bob… in Rome. She seemed tired, slightly distant. "Rome wasn't a big deal," was all she could say.

Then midweek, Penny started going out with 'friends' after work quite regularly. She didn't always come home. One morning, when she walked in the door, Ed had had enough. He confronted her at the door, and they had an almighty argument. She wouldn't answer anything and accused Ed of all sorts. Ed's fury shouted the place down. Penny packed her stuff and left.

The mood in the office was cold then but not just with Penny. Bob wouldn't make eye contact and their communication was through emails only. Bob was giving Ed only the barest information necessary to do his job. All of Ed's fears were realised when others in the office saw Penny and Bob holding hands and getting into a taxi together after a night out. Ed was furious the next day but there was no sign of either of them.

Bob and Penny appeared though, in the afternoon, for their quarterly meeting with senior management of the business. Ed waited until a question was directed at him and he let loose direct and obvious sarcasm towards Bob, "Did ya score last night Bob? Heard you bailed into a taxi with another lass!" Ed finished the sentence while glaring at Penny. She wouldn't look at him and stormed out of the meeting. Bob went white at first, stuttered over his words. Then a massive row broke out. Ed of course went too far. He got out of his chair, Bob stood up and they had to be kept apart by other members of the meeting. Ed was sent home. The story, of course, went around the office like wildfire.

The CEO called him for a meeting Monday afternoon. They met in a local café. He stayed away from the incident entirely on Friday and instead quickly explained that the company wasn't doing as well as hoped and that redundancies would soon be on offer. He told Ed a figure. Ed responded with a slightly higher one. The CEO agreed. Ed accepted then and there. He never even cleaned out his desk.

The seagull above him let out a loud cry.

"Too right," said Ed as he threw the wedding invite into the choppy water in front of him.

He watched as the invite melted away beneath the waves.

"R.S.V.P. me hole," he muttered.

The seagull above made for a new destination. Ed decided to do the same and moved towards his car.

His car was the last one over the ferry bridge. As he watched the ferry door close in his rear view mirror, Ed felt content that he was finally leaving some ghosts behind him.

Chapter 5

Neha found each of the blue tribe's people and administered the potion. They coughed and spluttered but he made sure they ingested it. He last went to his hut to do the same for Karo. When he went in, he had to check Karo's chest with his ear as Karo didn't look like he was breathing. He managed to administer the potion through more spluttering.

Neha was exhausted. He gathered some clothes and a blanket and lay down on his makeshift bedding. He was soon asleep.

Neha awoke. He was somewhere in the deep forest, standing. It was probably daytime but the canopy above blocked most of the light.

Now he was moving. He looked down. His appearance seemed different. He wore nothing but a small red tunic at his waist. He felt different too.

Neha carried on walking, but he did not know why. He could hear shouts in the distance. He started to creep forward now. Strange, why would he do that? Was he hunting?

His heart began to beat faster. He felt sweat running down his brow.

Neha began to see that the trees were becoming less dense ahead. He heard chanting now. He crept up behind a large tree and looked around.

Two lines of tribesmen, around two metres apart, appeared to be facing each other. They wore masks and red feather caps. They chanted and stamped the ground with their feet. They held spears in their left hands and stamped them on the ground. Was this some kind of tribal ceremony?

Ahead was a strange structure. It was widest at the base and appeared to be made of blocks of stone. It went up around ten levels, with each layer of stone becoming smaller. At the top there appeared to be a stone structure… a table?

Neha went behind the tree again. Why did he do that? He peeked out from behind the trunk.

A man, no, a boy, was being dragged out of a hut by four masked men. They each held an arm or a leg as they carried him, shouting and writhing in their hands.

Neha looked up as a woman appeared. All the men below except the men carrying the boy bowed on one knee. The men carrying the boy reached the base of the structure and began to climb. The boy was still shouting but Neha could not understand the words.

The woman wore a black cloak. She had long black hair and red painted circles around her eyes. Those eyes, even from this distance seemed large and distinctive. They were an intense green… but were there tiny flecks of yellow or gold there too?

The men carrying the boy reached the top of the structure. They placed the writhing boy on the table… no, the alter. They held him down firmly.

The woman moved forward and eyed the boy. Her eyes bulged and she gave a small smirk. She held a firm hand on the boy's upper chest. She produced a knife… a golden knife. The boy began to shout and shout. Neha understood the words now, "I worship! I worship!" The woman brought the point of the knife down to the boy's belly and looked at the boy with a face of glee as she slowly stuck the knife into him. The boy was begging her to stop.

As she methodically cut the boy open, she reached her hand down and brought out certain parts of his entrails and innards. The screaming, the shrieking, the crying was something Neha hoped he would never hear again. Even through the firm grip of the men holding him, the boy's body shook and convulsed.

The woman brought the knife up to his chest and stabbed it down to make another cut. She reached her hand in and tore his heart out. She held it aloft, still beating.

Neha found himself around the other side of the tree. What was he doing!?

He was shouting. Words of anger came from his mouth, but he did not know what he was saying.

The woman shrieked and pointed at him. The men below all turned and pointed their spears at him but they would not approach. The woman above moved her left arm out and pointed at the forest. A jaguar suddenly bounded from the jungle and stopped in front of the men gathered below. It turned and faced Neha. It showed him its fangs as it growled and walked towards him.

Neha was not moving, why was he not moving?

Something flew past his head…

The closest masked man to Neha collapsed, an arrow protruding from his mouth.

A line of warriors appeared to the left and right of Neha. They carried spears, clubs, bows and arrows.

They charged forward.

A sheet of lightning came from the sky. The jaguar, letting out a roar, sprinted towards Neha. It closed the ground fast. With jaws wide open it lunged for him.

Neha felt the hot breath of the jaguar on him, it was licking him. He was able to move now and he bolted upright and roared. He threw his fist at the creature. The yapping creature easily avoided his swipe and parried away. Neha was breathing heavily. Sweat poured down him. He was in his hut.

It was a dream… a dream. But a type of dream he had not had in a long time. His last one was about the men and the yellow creatures, just before they arrived, all those years earlier.

The yapping creature was whining. It scratched at the door frame and looked at Neha. Neha stood, opened the door and shooed it outside. A flash of lightning filled the hut. Karo was sleeping but his chest seemed to be moving up and down more normally.

Neha could hear the yapping creature barking now. He decided to go out and see what the problem was. As he stepped outside a rumble of thunder moved in the dawn air. The sky was red.

The yapping creature was near the edge of the river, still barking. Large grey storm clouds moved down the river. It was not the season for such weather. Neha told the yapping creature to stop making noise, but it ignored him. It went down on its haunches, pinned its ears back and began growling. Its hair was raised on its back.

Neha noticed that small tiny bumps appeared on his arms. He got a sudden headache. Along the river the water and trees started to move strangely. Suddenly, Neha smelt something terrible. It smelt like–

A howling, shrieking wind struck Neha and the yapping creature. They were pushed back instantly. Neha managed to reach out and grab the animal by a leg. He gathered it in his arms and moved back to his hut with great difficulty.

The storm clouds had reached them and the rain now swept through the wind. The rain stung like the darts of a blow pipe.

Neha reached the door of his hut. The door was banging wildly and he had to kick it back. With the yapping creature in his right arm, he placed his left hand in the door frame and pulled himself in. He then used his shoulder to wedge the door shut.

He placed the yapping creature on the floor. It was whining and giving the odd growl.

Another flash of lightning and Neha saw Karo sitting upright in his bed. Neha jumped backwards.

"She is here!" said Karo.

With that the sound of the wind roared around the hut. The door began to shake in its frame. As the shaking became more violent, the yapping creature began to snarl at the door. It stood straight and bared its teeth.

Neha felt a strong push on his arm as he found Karo between him and the door. Karo had his spear in his hands, with the spear tip aimed at the shaking door. Neha noticed some strange small pouches hanging from the tip of the spear.

Suddenly, the door sprang violently back and seemed to glue itself to the wall. There was no one there, though. Neha felt a strong wind push him back. He felt the yapping creature behind his legs.

But Karo, despite his emaciated form, stood steadfast. A roar came out of him and he stabbed the spear forwards… into nothing.

All of a sudden the wind died down. The door began to slowly swing closed on its hinges. Karo stepped forward and grasped the door with his left hand. He put his head out the doorframe and looked to his left and right. Neha could hear the wind outside, but it seemed to have cleared away from outside the hut. His headache receded.

Karo dropped his spear slowly and stood, cupping his hands to his mouth. He let out loud guttural noises in a slow rhythm for a few seconds. Neha guessed they were some kind of animal cry.

Neha tried to speak to Karo but Karo responded with a firm hand upwards. Suddenly two of Karo's tribe's people arrived at the door. It was the two boys. One looked like he would soon be a man but the other was much younger. The smaller boy carried a spear and the larger boy carried a hefty bow and arrow.

As Neha wondered how a boy his size could use such a thing, Karo gave the boys an order in a language that Neha did not understand. One boy moved to his left and the other to his right. The rain had eased and seemed to come down intermittently now, through a light wind.

Karo moved passed Neha to retrieve his spear. As he crouched down to pick it up, he looked at the yapping creature beside Neha. It panted gently as Karo began to rub its lower chin. Karo creased his brow for a second as he looked at the creature and then slowly looked up at Neha.

Karo stood, using the spear to assist him upwards as he rose. His gaze at Neha was piercing. "When was the last time you looked in the fire, Neha?"

Neha felt it was more an accusation than a question. But he was relieved that Karo seemed to remember much of their old tribal language – *Yine*.

"I have not been a Shaman… for so long. Not since our Chief turned us away from the old ways. Not since nearly all our elders died when we moved here. We had to take to this way of life and this way of life soon took us."

Karo turned his back to Neha and slowly began to move off.

Neha shooed the yapping creature into the hut and closed the door. He began to follow Karo and bellowed, "What happened, Karo? What is happening here?"

Neha passed Karo and stood in front of him. "Who is *she*?"

Karo looked at him dead on. Neha matched his stare. A stubborn silence ensued. It was like they never parted.

The sound of the wind seemed more pronounced to their side. They both looked in that direction. It was coming from the great fire pit at the centre of the village. Karo and Neha began to move towards it.

Arriving at the fire pit, Neha could see that last night's fire was slowly dying. The small flame at the centre was harassed and harried by the wind. Its dance suddenly died. Neha felt a rush of wind around him as the remaining embers and pieces of logs were sprayed out in various directions. Neha felt his heart beating.

The wind seemed to race past them both. They walked under a nearby shelter. Karo leant on his spear. Neha noticed his face seemed to hold a forlorn expression.

Neha touched the elaborate necklace on Karo's neck. "You are Chief of this tribe? How did that come to pass since you left us?"

Karo looked up. He frowned and his eyes bulged slightly. "You mean when you all," Karo's hand and arm moved about him from left to right, "left us!"

When the yellow creatures came, and their Chief decided that they would leave their home, Karo and some others decided to not go with them. It was a cold parting for all of them.

"And yet here you are, Karo. But has something followed you?" Neha looked up. Thick grey storm clouds seemed to churn overhead.

"I am Chief of the Hinti tribe. We came from deep in the forest. When we parted," Karo pointed at Neha and then back at himself, "I went on a long journey with the others. We passed through Venti territory and some of us were killed."

Neha grimaced at that. The Venti had killed their grandfather in a tribal war.

"We moved on quickly. We moved on and on and on. We came to a great waterfall and through its back, behind the water, we found a pass. Beyond it was the Hinti tribe. They had seen very few other people and had certainly never seen the white men and their yellow creatures. They welcomed us into their vibrant existence. They accepted us into their tribe.

"All was well for so long. Then the Venti came and I led a fight against them. We beat them back. I was bonded to the Chief's daughter. He passed on to the sky spirits and the elders made me Chief."

Karo paused a moment and seemed to gulp.

"Then this," Karo moved his hand in the air, "wind came. First, many hunts did not return. Then we all had strange occurrences happen to us. Strange and… frightening exchanges with spirits. We thought we had angered the spirits at first. We began to find members of the tribe in outlying places… dead… by person or animal… we could not tell.

"Our Shaman, Volo, did many rituals to contact the spirits. Finally, he had us do the Dance of the Dead. All the warriors put on their ceremonial garb and we did the dance for days in a circle around the village. Volo insisted we keep going. He seemed alarmed as he told me that he had seen the spirits of many of the tribe's ancestors sitting across the fire on a log. They were shouting at him. But he could not hear them properly because of… a strong wind. But Volo said he had learned enough and sent me and all the warriors on a quest. We had to find an ancient place, where *she* came from. We failed. We were chased back to the village, people started to die…"

Karo paused and looked in the distance.

"Tumudo, Vant, Breha, Shinhe, Vatu," Karo began.

Neha watched as Karo started to use the butt of his spear to scratch lines into the ground. Karo continued saying random words as he did so and Neha realised that they were names!

Neha put his hand to his head, as his headache started again. He thought he could hear a whimpering…. the sound of whimpering being carried on the wind. As a wind rushed around his head, he heard it again. It came from one direction, then another. It sounded like the yapping creature. The sounds became more desperate – it sounded in pain. It was crying.

"Can you hear that, Karo?"

But Karo was still obsessed with his strange task.

Neha left Karo and ran back to his hut. The door was wide open. He searched inside but it was not there. He called for the creature. He kept calling.

His headache subsided.

Neha found himself back at the fire pit. Karo stood still. Many, many lines now appeared in the ground in a series of rows. Neha stood beside him.

"This was my tribe," said Karo. "They are all dead. Only Volo remains, somewhere in there. We could not find him before we left."

A few moments passed as they both stared at the lines on the ground.

Neha heard rushing feet coming up behind him. As he turned, he saw it was one of the boys that Karo had sent off earlier. The boy stopped in front of Karo and began speaking.

Neha could not make out the words he was saying but he noted the boy kept his eyes on him. The boy's breathing seemed fast.

Karo looked down at the ground briefly and then at Neha. "Neha, Timku has found your four legged friend. He is dead. You must see."

Neha was stunned but began to follow Karo and Timku as they walked. Minutes later they approached a tree on the edge of the village. Neha could see something hanging from the tree, an animal… spirits no!

As Neha closed in, he could see the yapping creature hanging from a rope. It was cut open at its belly and its entrails hung out. Its feet had been cut off. As it spun slowly around on the rope, its head came into view. Blood spattered down from its gaping maw. The tongue had been cut out as well.

Its eyes bulged in its head. Neha's eyes locked with those terrified looking eyes.

"She has struck, Neha," said Karo. "This is just the beginning."

Neha stood stupefied. Karo and Timku lowered their heads and placed their left hands to their chests for a moment.

Karo turned to move off and looked up at the creature once more. "He shares the same colour eyes as you, Neha… like he was your kin."

Karo and Timku walked away.

Neha bowed his head as far as it would go into his chest. He clasped his hands in front of him, feeling vulnerable, as a child might, and snapped his eyes shut. "Yappy," he muttered.

As heavy rain began falling around Neha, tears poured down his face.

Chapter 6

Ed had the meeting with Deirdre O'Connor at the National Museum of Ireland tomorrow at 11 a.m. His friend, Google, told him it was on Kildare Street. Deirdre had said it was in a central location in Dublin city. So when browsing hotels, he found the Central Hotel and took a logical punt on that. He arrived, checked in, and dumped his bag in his room. He fancied a pint before dinner and decided to go for a wander.

His mate in London, who had been on a stag here lately said that Temple Bar was a stag and hen trap. Ridiculous drinking, ridiculous prices, so don't go there, he had advised Ed.

Ed heeded those wise words… for all of ten minutes. After some indecisive walking, he found himself in Temple Bar. He must have wandered into the area by accident – that, or his lust for beer had led him here.

As he ducked his head into the Dubliner pub, the place was heaving. A nice mixture of suits and casually dressed people. And an eclectic mix of Irish and tourist accents.

Ed used his height and managed to catch a bar person's attention. He had a 'when in Rome' moment and decided to order his first ever pint of Guinness. He nearly did the Macarena in order to get out of people's way but thankfully the pint came quickly. He got lucky then and found an empty stool near a large window.

Ed let the brown storm in the glass settle until a creamy white head sat at the top. He took a swig of his Guinness and leaned back in his stool. His eyes closed partially, and he tightened his lips inwards.

Jesus Christ, he thought. This was like gone off coffee! He forced a second large gulp. Same reaction as before.

He saw an older man beside him, in black jeans with a tight black leather jacket hugging his shoulders. His grey hair came down past his shoulders and competed with his equally long beard to see which would reach his beer belly first.

Ed watched as the man brought a full pint of Guinness to his mouth. He didn't so much as appear to drink it, more so he seemed to touch it with his lips. Nevertheless, when the man placed his pint back down, the black and white beverage had lowered in the glass, ever so slightly.

Ed decided to copy the man. He let the pint be and watched the mixture of people passing the window. Minutes passed, he sipped the pint and thought about nothing. He finished it and brought the glass back to the bar.

The barman caught his attention immediately. "Same again?" said the barman, as he stood at the Guinness tap pulling away. After a brief hesitation, Ed found himself saying, "Go on!"

Ed waited at the bar this time. He carried the next pint back to his stool and shook his head from side to side. He took a big gulp of this strange drink. The sensation of gone off coffee didn't seem as prominent this time. He got through the pint with ease now. Dare he ask himself, was he actually enjoying it?

He finished the pint and enough was enough. He got off the stool, grabbed his jacket and went outside. A cheeky cigarette and he would grab a burger somewhere. As his lit up his cigarette, he heard a whiny voice to his right. "All right, mate? Could I grab a light?"

Ed turned around to a woman, with long blonde hair and a backpack on her back.

"Sure, no problem," said Ed.

"Where you from, mate?" the girl asked in a clear Aussie accent.

Ed handed over the lighter. "Yorkshire, North England."

The girl lit up her cigarette and repeated what Ed had said, doing her best to imitate Ed's accent. Ed smirked and introduced himself using a makeshift Aussie accent. She replied that her name was Laura. The two of them then carried on a ridiculous exchange, while both trying to copy each other's accents. Sufficiently entertained, Ed said he had to leave. Laura nagged him to come in and meet her mates. They had just flown in and were itching for a pint.

Before Ed knew it, he was back in the Temple Bar pub and chatting away to three other Australians. The conversation was easy and free flowing, just like the pints. Ed fed himself on Irish crisps called 'Tayto'. They were instantly better than the Walkers crisps he was used to. Gary Lineker was clearly selling a lie.

They started into a pub crawl. This was a mission now… mission drink. No time for anything else. Three in the morning came, and Ed found himself outside a nightclub, feasting on some chips with goo on top, with the other Aussies.

Himself and Laura exchanged numbers and emails. Despite agreeing to keep in contact, Ed knew he never would.

Awaking in his bed the next day was not pleasant. He forced himself down to breakfast and wished the woman serving it could feed it to him. As he got back to his room, he desperately wanted nothing more than to collapse face down on the bed. But he had no time for a hangover. His meeting was in half an hour. He leapt in the shower and had his clothes on before he was properly dry.

Thankfully, he knew where he was going. The museum was less than a ten minute walk away. He stopped and grabbed some kind of sugary power nonsense drink. He downed it in one, some escaping down the side of his mouth and onto his jacket. It was moments like that where he could nearly sense his mother was disturbed, back in Yorkshire.

He carried on to Kildare Street and located the museum. Checking the time, he saw it was already 11 a.m. A huge queue greeted him upon going through two sets of double doors. Ed sighed as he shifted left and right to see to the top. There was some sort of reception desk up there with a man behind it, and he and a tourist of some sort were having a slow paced chin wag.

Ed walked down the left side of the queue. He had to stop where two poles with a red barrier rope blocked his way. He simply unhooked one end, walked through and quickly replaced it.

Ed darted forward now as he saw a security guard out of the corner of his eye moving at pace towards him.

"Excuse me, sir!" he heard the guard say in a terse tone.

Ed reached the reception desk. The man behind the desk was still engaged with an elderly tourist. A woman stood behind the receptionist, with her back turned, organising some files.

The rather large security man now stood a breath away from Ed. "Excuse me, sir, where do you think you are going?"

Ed slapped the palm of his hand down on the reception desk to get the reception man's attention. "Sorry, ehm, my name is Ed Marshall. I am slightly late for an appointment with Deirdre O'Connor." Ed made sure to make eye contact with the guard as he said the latter part.

The woman doing the paperwork stopped and half turned. Small reading glasses slid down her nose as she looked at Ed. "Ed? I'm Deirdre," she said in a soft Irish accent. Deirdre looked at the guard as she fully turned, holding a file. She shot out a hand with spindly fingers at him. "Don't worry, he's with me."

The guard looked flustered but turned away. "Sorry mate," Ed offered.

Deirdre moved over to the side of the reception desk and put her hand down to some kind of button. "Just move over through that door, Ed."

Ed saw a door to the left of the desk and pushed through it. Deirdre popped through an adjacent door and put out her hand to him with a smile. She was small and looked somewhere in her mid-fifties maybe. She had plum coloured hair just down to her neck and wore a green fleece with black jeans and something between runners or hiking boots on her feet.

Ed took her hand and they briefly shook.

"Sorry I'm late," said Ed

"Not a bother," she said.

She directed him towards some winding stairs ahead. They began walking in that direction.

"You had an okay journey?" she said.

"Yes, it was–"

"And did you hit Dublin town last night too?" said Deirdre, smiling at him, as they climbed the stairs.

"I had one or two. Nothing major –"

"And did you meet any nice Irish ladies?"

Ed's mouth fell open as he considered how to answer that.

"Sure there'll be plenty in Clare for you," Deirdre said, as she gave him a nice elbow.

They reached the top of the stairs through another set of double doors and down a dank musty corridor. It seemed devoid of light, colour or paintings.

Deirdre stopped at the fifth door down on the right side. She unzipped one of her fleece pockets and produced a set of jangling keys. When she found the required key, she held the doorknob firmly with one hand. Pulling it towards her, she jangled the key in the lock with the other hand.

She yanked and pulled at it. "Bloody thing!" she said.

Light suddenly hit Ed's face as Deirdre coaxed the door open. She marched straight in.

"Come on in, Ed, have a seat."

Ed walked in and saw the light was coming from a long and large old sash window at the other end of the room. A tree of some kind dominated much of the view, as it swayed gently in the wind.

As Ed moved into the cushioned seat in front of Deirdre's desk, he saw several pairs of hiking boots on newspaper. They were in front of a dusty electric heater with a solitary bar giving out heat.

Beside them was a coat rack filled with different coloured fleeces and rain jackets. Umbrellas were strewn around the base of the coat rack.

To his right Ed could see an old yellow stained couch, which blocked an old black marble fireplace. The mantel piece was full of mugs. The tips of spoons escaped the mug rims.

Random photos of flowers dotted the walls. A long hulking timber cabinet stood to the right of the desk. Otherwise, the office seemed rather bare.

Deirdre was fiddling with the mouse of her computer. The monitor was old, with its big back wobbling each time Deirdre touched the desk. The hard drive seemed to make lots of noise as it probably woke from 1992.

All in all, though, her office seemed much cleaner than Professor Barnes' – no towering files here.

Deirdre turned to the long brown cabinet behind her. She found a smaller key on her key set and opened the cabinet. As she opened it, Ed noticed that the cabinet was wedged with files from top to bottom. Random pages jutted out as if trying to escape. Deirdre, then, like Professor Barnes, was a hoarder, except she tried to hide the disease.

As Deirdre yanked one folder out of the middle of the file prison, another file made a break for it, falling down on the floor below. Pages sprayed across the floor. As Deirdre bent down to retrieve it, another file flopped out on her back.

"Oh, for feck sake!" she said.

Ed stood up and moved over to the prison break.

"It's okay, Ed, just leave it. I must clear it out at some stage."

Old dust filled the air now. Deirdre coughed.

"Shall I open the window?" asked Ed.

"That would be great, Ed! I am not here that much really."

Ed began fiddling with the window locks. "Yes, you strike me as an outdoors person," he said, as he nodded over to the hiking boots.

Ed was pulling his outstretched arms as hard as he could. He stopped and looked up. The seal at the top was covered in a light moss.

"Yes, I was up at Mayo recently at a dig; the bog water leads to a new type of saturation."

Ed pulled again, going red faced. The window snapped open and small pieces of moss fell onto Ed's face. The wind streamed in the window.

"Well done, Ed! Now sit down."

Ed sat, rubbing some moss off his left shoulder. Deirdre dumped the file she was holding on the desk and sat down.

"So, Ed, what's your plan? Will you grid it out? Will you go north or south first? How do you intend on getting permissions from the private owners for access? What sites are you considering for potential excavation?"

Ed knew he had a scared rabbit expression on his face, but he couldn't help it. He was stumped.

Deirdre's mouth fell open slightly and she slowly said, "Did you read the email, Ed?"

"No, I didn't get a chance. Intended on getting to it soon."

Deirdre paused before saying, "Right."

The wind was the only sound in the office for a moment.

"What do you know about flowers, Ed? The Burren is a wildlife sanctuary for 70% of Ireland's 900 species. It is a particular haven for some orchids that can only be found there… and in the Alps."

Ed simply nodded with interest.

"Have you ever seen a Spring Gentian, Ed?"

"Em… is that a red flower?"

Deirdre pointed over her left shoulder to a framed photo on the wall. Ed saw a blue flower staring back at him.

“It’s the signature plant of the Burren, Ed.”

Ed blushed. “Listen Deirdre, to be honest, I haven’t done as much research as I should have but I planned at throwing myself into it when I got there. Can you tell me a little about some of the archaeological sites that are there?”

“Sure, there are portal tombs, court tombs, wedge tombs, burial cairns, fulacht fiadhs, ring barrows, souterrains, stone forts, ring forts, holy wells, shrines, old churches. They are all spread over North Clare within the Burren National Park. It’s 360 square kilometres in size.”

Ed nodded away and waited until she finished. Then he started linking in his experience and knowledge with a lot of what she had just listed. He emphasised the outdoors experience he had more so. Ed went on for a few minutes and by the end Deirdre’s warm smile had returned.

“Well, I’m sure when you get a feel for the place, you’ll be flying in no time!” she said.

“I’m sure that file will help me,” said Ed, as he nodded at the file underneath Deirdre’s hand. “Was that compiled by the last person who did this?”

Deirdre began to rub the file with her hand. Her smile waned. She seemed to stare past Ed, before meekly saying, “She moved on.”

A wind harried into the office as the tree outside rustled noisily.

Deirdre made eye contact with Ed again. “But the file will help you.” She shoved the file towards Ed. He started to root through it.

“There’s a good bit of recent information gathered on the area included in that. There’s also the 1950s audit file at the bottom, although I doubt it will be of any use. The main aim, Ed, is we need to know the state of the sites down there. Which ones are decaying or in need of repair? Do some sites need to be cordoned off?

“Ironically, climate change may actually be revealing some yet undiscovered sites as well. We had a case recently in Mayo were some coastal erosion revealed an undiscovered Neolithic site. Keep your eyes peeled.

“And we will need a check-up of the flowers in the region. What is their density? Are any fading away on us? There’s more on that in the file and email I sent you.”

Ed looked and nodded as she finished speaking. He pointed at a picture of a wedge tomb.

“I assume these have all been excavated before?” Ed casually asked.

“No,” Deirdre responded sharply. “None of them have ever been excavated and nor should they be!”

Ed stopped perusing the file and leaned back in his chair. He grabbed both arm rests.

Deirdre sighed. “The project has a potential two year life span. We want a thorough job done but it shouldn’t technically take that long. The better the report, though, the better chance we have at getting funding from the Irish government.”

“Brilliant, okay,” said Ed. “Can you tell me more about the accommodation? Where that is?”

“Yes,” said Deirdre as she seemed more relaxed. “You’re staying in a lovely part of Clare, on the northern part of the Burren National Park. It is a small town called Ballyvaughan. Has most things you need and if you need more, you pop down the road to Kinvara. The accommodation is just off the edge of the town near a place called Lough Rask. An old woman lives there called Nuala. Herself and her deceased husband used to run a guesthouse there. Lots of hikers and explorers would use it.

“They have a small cottage beside the guesthouse. It was mainly used by the family or the odd writer or poet who found themselves there. I sent Nuala a message yesterday. She knows you’re coming.”

“Well, that all sounds great,” said Ed. “Thanks for the information. I will launch into it when I get down there.”

"There we have it, Ed. If you need anything else, drop me a line. Otherwise, I'll be checking in from time to time. But I will mainly be up in Mayo, and after that, the semester at the University starts again."

Deirdre held out her hand and stood. Ed grabbed her hand and thanked her. He picked up the file.

As Ed reached the door, Deirdre spoke. "Oh, Ed, one more thing. If you come across an American archaeologist called Flannery… stay away from him. He's bad news."

Ed shrugged, but nodded and walked out, closing the door behind him.

File in hand, he headed down the stairs and out the entrance. The security guard glared at him all the way out. 'Don't hate the player, hate the game,' was all Ed wanted to say to him.

He stood underneath the tree outside Deirdre's office and lit up a well-earned cigarette. Deirdre was hot and cold to say the least. He thought of the professor and how he had told Ed that Deirdre and this Irish operation were 'stuck'. Stuck maybe, but not as desperate as the professor had made out originally.

As Ed puffed away at his cigarette, he saw something hanging from the file in his arm. He left the cigarette in his mouth and looked closer. It seemed like a piece of brown leather string. He opened the file and moved the pages back until he got to its source. There he found that the leather string was attached to a white object of some kind. It was a necklace!

He examined the white object. It looked old. It was an artefact, he realised. As he examined it further, he could make out a faint inscription on it. It seemed cut off at the middle. Ed's interest was disturbed by the sound of the tree rustling violently beside him as a wind struck it. Ed dropped the file on the ground.

He looked up at the tree as he placed the two ends of the leather cord around his neck and tied them together.

"Fuck it, might bring some luck!"

Ed picked up the file, flicked his cigarette at the tree and walked off.

Chapter 7

Maria Estavez pivoted the long controlling arm of the engine to her right. The Caori river was quite choppy today. The wind seemed to streak upon the surface of the river at will. She had been in this small metal boat for over three hours.

Her employer, FUNAI (Brazil's agency for indigenous peoples), had been kept busy. In the past, it had been difficult enough for FUNAI with their limited manpower and vast swath of area to cover.

Maria was headed for the Javari valley. It was an area of more than eight million hectares (nearly 31,000 square miles) of rainforest that was home to native indigenous tribes, both discovered and undiscovered. FUNAI believed there were one hundred and thirteen uncontacted tribes living in the Brazilian Amazon – of which only twenty-seven groups had been confirmed.

But the protection of this tribal haven and incredible eco system was not guaranteed. In the past they had gotten into furious and sometimes dangerous exchanges with interlopers into the Javari valley and other parts of the rainforest. But intruders always had short stays when they caught them, simply because FUNAI had the law at their backs.

Now ranchers, loggers, miners, and even drug gangs indirectly; all had a full blown President at their back. Since the arrival of President Bolsonaro, they had all become more active in the rainforest. The laws were not enforced or constantly changing. The President had even accused non-governmental organisations of setting wildfires in the forest. He had, of course, no evidence to back this up.

The importance of the eco system of the rainforest, to both Brazil and the rest of the world, could not be emphasised enough. The forest itself was described by some as 'the lungs of the earth'. The World Wildlife Fund (WWF) estimated that the rainforest processed ninety to one hundred and forty billion tonnes of CO2. The Amazon River and its tributaries provided 20% of the Earth's unfrozen fresh water.

But many in Brazil did not understand, or simply did not care.

Between 2016 and 2017, the number of illegal mines discovered in the rainforest rose from 382 to 949. Loggers were now rampant in the forest as they harvested the valuable timber of the Brazilian walnut tree. Forest fires were now also far too common, as ranchers encroached more and more on the edges of the forest.

According to the WWF, almost 20% of the Amazon forest has disappeared in the last half-century, but this was accelerating. Between August 2017 and July 2018, 7,900 sq km – more than five times the area of London – was deforested in Brazil.

The protection of the indigenous tribes was in doubt. The long term effects on climate change could also be irreversible if the plundering of the rainforest continued.

The rest of the world understood this, thought Maria, so why couldn't the Brazilian Government?

Maria saw her destination, a small red flag stuck on a pole on the river bank to her right. She revved the engine and sped up, shunting forward as the boat wedged itself onto the river bank.

She clambered out the front with her backpack in one arm and a rope attached to the boat in the other. The river flies came at her instantly. No matter what spray or cream she tried, they never left her alone when she went out here. She wouldn't mind so much if the ranchers or loggers managed to take them out.

She tied the rope around the branch of a tree, tugging at it with both arms, making sure it was secure. The sun was at its height now, but grey clouds darted through the sky, blocking it from time to time. It was early in the New Year and this weather was unseasonal considering.

Around twenty feet away, her chariot awaited; the white jeep FUNAI left for its employees in this area. She went back to the boat and lifted the can of petrol out. As she reached the jeep, she put the petrol can down and began checking the vehicle. It was not uncommon to find FUNAI equipment vandalized. They weren't the most popular people when it came to 'progress'.

The hood of the jeep seemed undisturbed. The wheels seemed fine and all the windows were intact. Maria opened the petrol can and filled the jeep up. Placing the petrol can down, she remembered she needed to check underneath the vehicle too. As she crouched downwards, her phone rang in her pocket. *Strange*, she thought. She should have no reception here.

As she pulled the phone out of her pocket, she lowered herself onto her side. She answered, "Hello." Maria couldn't hear anyone, just something like the sound of… wind at the other end. Then she thought she heard breathing. "Hello," she repeated as she scanned underneath the vehicle. Still no response.

She carried on examining beneath the jeep, while still holding the phone to her ear. Nothing. Then she heard a hissing noise. Was this one of the tyres…?

Fear shot through Maria. She rolled back just in time as the snake lashed out. Its lunge and 'snap' just stopped short of her face. Maria rolled again quickly, managing to grab a loose branch, and swung it back towards the snake as it lunged again. The branch just made contact with the snake's head in time. Maria sprang upwards and away, still holding the branch. The snake hissed at her. Maria saw by its light green colouring that it was a forest pit viper. One bite, and she was dead.

She backed away slowly. The hissing snake turned and weaved its way through the grass towards the tree line. Maria didn't hesitate. She turned around, found the keys in her bag and opened the jeep. She yanked the boot open and threw in her backpack and the empty petrol can. Before she got in, she checked the back and the front seats.

Finally, she found her phone on the ground and got in the jeep. Instead of placing the phone back in her pocket, she threw it on the passenger seat and slammed the jeep door shut. She closed her eyes, leaned her head back, and ruffled her hands through the top of her long black hair, then puffed out a breath and opened her eyes. She put her right hand on the steering wheel and picked up her phone with her left hand. As she suspected, no reception, even as she moved the phone about. She checked for the call… but there was no call registered.

Maybe it would register, she thought, when she got back in a few days. Maria turned off her phone and placed it back on the passenger seat. She put the key in the ignition, brought the jeep to life and sped off.

She drove on what was more a rough path than a road. Loggers must have cut it long ago. There was no actual road per se, more that trees did not block the way. Long grass and bushes were now its main inhabitants. How the loggers had chosen or gotten their equipment this far down river was anyone's guess, but Maria noted the pleasant irony that the road they had cut could be used against them.

With each bump from the path, her trepidation went up and down too. She had not seen her father in some time. Truth be told, she avoided her father's tribe, the Laogo.

Her mother, like Maria, was an anthropologist. Before the loggers or miners had gone this far, the indigenous people were largely left alone. Maria's mother had gone on several expeditions into the Javari valley, an area the size of France. There, she had encountered the Laogo. She trod carefully at first as they had never seen anyone from the western world before, but the tribal elders eventually welcomed her in. She seemed to have a way with the younger children of the tribe. It enabled trust.

Over time she visited them more often and became more and more familiar with their tribal ways and rituals. She found herself there for a year, maybe two. In that time a much deeper relationship was forged with a man of the tribe who had already lost his Laogo wife to fever.

Maria's mother became pregnant. Her mother did not want Maria raised with the tribe and she also knew that if Maria's father found out too soon, he would have insisted that they both stay there. Maria's mother told her father about the pregnancy the day she was leaving. Her father was deeply angry that she would not stay. But Maria's mother did not want his tribal life, for her or her unborn child.

Instead, she travelled back to Sao Paulo, met a wealthy banker, and married him. That was the curt way of putting it. In fact, Maria's stepfather had done everything he could to be her normal dad. He had given her great support.

Maria was only introduced to her real father when she could be taken into the forest as a teenager. By then, tensions between her mother and her father were not the only issue. The tribe was considering moving out of their home and on down the Caori river. The loggers had used the stick and then the carrot. The move was not a major jump for the tribe, but neither was it their original home.

Maria checked in on them at least once a year. Relations with her father moved at a glacial rate but it was nothing in comparison to the non-existent relationship Maria's mother held with her father. Maria's mother had not been here for seventeen years and would probably not step foot in the place again.

Maria drove the jeep until the path ended. She got out and retrieved her backpack, quickly finding her water bottle. She drank deeply. The humidity was thick now and any movement led to streams of sweat. She took out her machete.

As she placed and tightened her backpack on her back, she attached her compass to her upper breast pocket. Machete gripped in her right hand, she got moving into the dense thicket in front of her, slashing the machete left and right as she went.

She was on the move for an hour when she heard what she was looking for, water. She came out of the foliage onto a small river bank. She had found the small tributary of the Caori river. She looked down river and could see her father's small village. The silt and mud of the bank came and went with the tide, but there seemed to be enough room on the bank to walk down.

She began walking carefully forward, as the river rushed by her on her left. She could see the wind streaking over the surface of the water here, too. As she moved forward, she could see cooking fires from the village emitting smoke in the distance. The river bank twisted to the right and as she took the corner she saw the bank jutted inwards briefly before carrying on in a straight line.

As Maria reached the middle of the small inlet, she noticed that the bank rose upwards and slanted left, down towards the water. Halfway across the high part of the bank she saw eyes looking at her below. As the heads of the black caimans rose upwards, she realised she must be close to some sort of nest. She breathed out slowly and kept her concentration.

A noise… her phone rang loudly in her pocket!

Maria's left foot slipped over the bank and she had to quickly lean to her right to balance herself. A particularly large caiman shot its head up and snapped at her, before splashing back to the water below.

That fucking phone, she thought. It stopped ringing.

She took her backpack off slowly. Better to carry it in one hand, she thought, as she could drop it quickly if she lost her footing or balance again.

She could feel her heart pounding in her chest. She planted her feet on the bank below and held onto a wet branch with both hands. She puffed out some air when her phone rang again. She took away one hand from the branch, snapping the phone out of her pocket. 'No Caller ID' it said, as she put it to her ear and answered.

"Motherfucker!" she shouted.

She heard the sound of wind again on the phone, together with a strange rasping laugh. The branch she held onto shook violently as a furious wind swept through the inlet. She lost her grip, wobbled, and both feet slid down the verge. As her chin slammed the edge of the bank, it slowed her fall, allowing her hands to get a grip on the bank in front of her. Through the searing pain, she maintained her grip but felt something touching her feet.

Maria turned her head. A caiman! It had climbed up.

She kicked at it and it slid back down. Now another caiman leapt up. She screamed and only avoided its snap by moving her legs to the left… just in time. The wind swirled around and her hair blocked her eyes. She could feel her hands losing their grip in the mud. Another caiman leapt up and its upper jaw connected with her calf before flopping down. She felt razor sharp teeth drawing blood. She screamed again.

As her hands slipped to the edge now, she kicked at the thrashing caiman as her legs went closer to the water. She couldn't hold on!

"NO, NO, NO," she shrieked.

One hand lost its grip. She couldn't hold on with the other…

As her other hand slipped off… a blue hand grabbed her wrist. She looked up as a head appeared and another arm swept downwards to grab her upper arm. She felt herself being pulled up. Another… blue man appeared and began to lift her too.

Maria was pulled up on the bank. As she sobbed into her chest, she felt herself being lifted up. One of her arms was stretched over the man's shoulder, while he put his other arm across her back. As the man moved forward she tried to match his steps through the trees and bushes. They broke through into a clearing. The village was not far off.

The man put her down. Maria went on all fours and retched until her breakfast came up. She sat on her bum and leaned backwards on her stretched out arms. She panted wildly.

She was drenched in sweat but could suddenly see her water bottle in her face. She grabbed the bottle from what looked like a boy in his late teens. He was covered all in blue too. She gulped the water down and looked at the other blue tribe's man, the one who had grabbed her initially.

Maria squinted at him. "Father?" she said, remembering to speak Yine.

He shook his head.

Maria got up off the ground and dusted herself down. As she moved her hair backwards, the teenage boy thrust her backpack towards her. She took it and managed a smile. As she placed the backpack on her back once more, the wiry man who resembled her father moved towards the village, as did the teenage boy. She followed along and as they reached the outskirts of the village. She realised that the smoke she had seen was not coming from cooking fires.

Random fires appeared to be dotted around the village. She crossed a threshold of smoke with the other two. They reached some of the dwellings; corrugated tin huts, many with a thatch roof of hay, leaves and straw intertwined. Outside one door, she saw a young woman. She was holding her young son in her arms.

Maria offered her a small smile. She got nothing in return except a cold glare. The woman turned on her heel and went through her doorway. Maria realised that even though she was known here, she was still a stranger. Their trust of her was on 'pause'.

Maria carried on walking with the other two and they reached the centre of the small village. Maria knew this was where they lit the village fire and did most of their communal cooking. The two men she was with stopped and began speaking. Maria did not understand the words. This was not Yine or even a dialect of it.

Maria interrupted them and asked them in basic Yine where her father was. The man stared at her and walked away. The boy followed him. Maria crossed over one of the outer logs and walked under a small shelter near the centre of the fire pit. She stopped, as she noticed strange lines carved into the ground at her feet. They were in rows and stretched out for a few metres. She looked around, still no sign of anyone else.

She decided to count the lines on the ground. When she finished, she reckoned there was just over three hundred of them. Her brow creased as she considered their meaning. Where they some kind of calendar? Days? Hours?

Her thoughts were broken when she saw her father walking towards her. The man who had saved her walked just behind him. As her father moved closer, Maria thought he looked older than he should have been, somehow.

Neha stopped in front of Maria. She managed a smile, but her short stocky father gave none in return. His large upper lip curved over his bottom one tightly. He said nothing.

"Hello Fath–" she said in Yine.

"You should not have come here, Maria."

Maria sighed. His welcome was worse than his normal lukewarm one.

"I had to, we had reports of heightened logger and mining activity. The ranchers are burning more and more of the forest and up in Yanti town, they said they brought some 'new' tribe's people here. We have also had reports of strange deaths in the area."

Maria pointed towards the man standing behind her father. "Who is this, Father? Is he one of the new tribe's people?"

"He is my brother, Karo."

Maria was confused as Neha pointed at the man who had rescued her. Did her father mean brother as in relation? Or tribal brother?

"Your brother rescued me. I was nearly eaten by caiman."

Maria saw Neha looking down towards her leg. Blood was still seeping from her calf. She had forgotten about it. Adrenaline probably.

"This way, Maria."

Neha led her by the arm and indicated she should sit on a log. She let her backpack slide through her arms and onto the ground and sat down. Neha walked away without explanation.

Maria caught Karo staring at her and noticed her leg was starting to ache a bit. She rooted through her bag and found her first aid pack. She took out some cotton wool, antiseptic, a roll of bandage and some tape and began dabbing the wound with the cotton wool. It stung.

As she reached for the antiseptic, she felt a hand on her shoulder. She turned.

"Wait, Maria. Not that," said Neha.

Maria saw he held a bowl in his hand. Neha crossed over the log and went down on one knee. He examined the wound.

She saw the bowl contained a mashed up plant of some sort. She watched as her father examined the materials in the first aid kit. He quickly flung the antiseptic over his shoulder. Neha placed a large amount of cotton wool on the ground and then a smaller amount beside it.

He grabbed the bowl and tilted it downwards towards the large piece of cotton wool. Some oily liquid started to drip down on the cotton wool. As the cotton wool now seemed damp, Neha placed the bowl down and picked up the smaller piece. He dipped it in the bowl and began to dab her wound. Each dab of the ointment covered wool stung. Maria grunted with pain and gritted her teeth.

Neha looked at Maria. "Your mother?"

"She did not come this time, Father." He always asked her.

Neha stopped dabbing the wound and grabbed the roll of bandage and scissors. He cut a long strip of bandage.

Finally, he grabbed the larger piece of cotton wool, placed it on her wound and wrapped the bandage around her calf. He reached for the tape with one hand and bit a piece of with his teeth. He stuck it on.

"Medicine man," Maria said to him, with a smile.

"Shaman," said Karo in Yine.

Maria slowly looked up at Karo. "Thank you for rescuing me today."

"We will all need rescuing soon," replied Karo. "If only Volo were here," he muttered.

"Is he part of your tribe?" said Maria. "Where did you come from, Karo? How many of you are there? Do more of your tribe need any help?"

Maria listened as Karo listed some names of people who had come with him. But then he went over and pointed at the lines in the ground and spoke in that other language she did not know. He walked away as other members of Neha's tribe placed logs around the centre of the fire pit.

Maria looked around at the fires she could see at the edge of the village. What was the problem here? Was it a predator?

"Is there a problem with a jaguar here, Father?"

Neha let out a small laugh and rubbed his black bowl haircut with one hand. Maria saw he was grimacing now as he looked to the ground.

"Much has changed here, Maria. We are being attacked by something. As to what it is, it has wiped out Karo's tribe." Maria saw him pointing at the lines on the ground.

"Plague? Feve–"

"Will you help me catch a frog, Maria?"

"Wha–"

"Will you help me catch a frog?" Neha stared at Maria.

"Why?" demanded Maria.

"I want to stare at the fire tonight," said Neha.

The frog! *Ridiculous hallucinogens*, thought Maria. She agreed anyway. She remembered it was the first thing that he had her do when she first met him as a young girl.

They moved through the village and made their way down the river bank. The waters here had receded, revealing a flat mud bank. No caiman in sight, thankfully.

Maria followed her father over the edge and dropped herself down to the silty bottom. Their heads were now level with the top of the river bank beside them. Maria watched as her father slowly moved forward, head down, watching the ground as he went.

Neha stopped. "Here," he said pointing at the ground.

Maria walked over and could see tiny tracks. Neha walked slowly forward again and pointed at more tracks as they came across them. They rounded a small bend and moved up a slight incline. The silt gave way to soil as they walked up. As they reached the brush above, Maria could hear frogs.

Neha crept slowly forward again. Maria could see something jumping ahead within the long grass. She saw a red frog to her right. She moved towards it.

"Not that one," said Neha. "Yellow," he whispered.

Maria moved slowly to her left. A sliver of yellow caught the corner of her right eye. She turned back to her right. There it was again. She crept over and saw a yellow frog jump. Big guy! The frog seemed to stay stationary on a rock now. She snuck over at its flank and moved slowly downwards, with her hands reaching out and her tongue stuck out between her lips.

The frog hopped forward again… and then again. It was bloody fast, and it was moving back towards the river bank. It would easily hide itself in the mud if it got that far.

Maria found herself nearly breaking into a slow jog as she pursued. It seemed to get faster and was a metre away from the bank.

It stopped. Maria reached it and it jumped. Maria jumped after it…

She caught it in the air…

But then landed face first in the mud!

As she raised her mud covered face, she unclasped her outstretched hands slightly in front of her. The frog didn't hesitate and jumped forward again.

"Shit!" shouted Maria.

The frog remained stationary a metre ahead.

Maria pushed herself up on her forearms. As she cleared mud from her face, two feet stepped in between her and the frog. Between the feet, two open hands now presented themselves in front of the creature. The frog obliged, and walked onto the hands.

"When you hunt any animal," said Neha, as he examined the frog, "be sure of your timing."

Maria slowly stood up, rubbing mud off herself.

"And be sure of your position," added Neha, as he looked Maria up and down.

With that her father turned on his heel and walked in the direction of the village.

Maria let out a long sigh, looked to the sky and placed her hands to her hips. What a day!

The sun went down quickly and before Maria knew it, a great fire was lit at the centre of the village. The whole tribe had gathered. People feasted on fish and wild birds that rotated on a spit, close to the fire.

Maria spent her time trying to talk with the blue tribe's people that had come from up the river. None would talk with her, though. She did not even try the one called Karo. His uninviting stare said it all. She instead tucked into some sort of wild roasted bird. As she took her last bite, she heard voices dying down around the fire.

To her left, her father stood. He wore a headdress of red feathers and had black and red paint across his face. He wore nothing else but a red tunic at his waist.

Her father was saying some strange words. His eyes seemed to roll in his head until he brought them down to his closed fist and revealed the yellow frog. He licked the back of it and released it. The frog jumped away from him, went around the fire and leapt up on the log beside Maria. It gave a heavy croak before moving off into the night.

Her father had stopped his strange chanting. Maria watched as he looked to his left and right. He suddenly walked over to an old woman and held out his hand. She raised herself up and gave a wondrous smile.

Neha was muttering to himself now as he led the woman to an empty log by the fire. She sat without asking. Then her father moved around the fire past several people but stopped… in front of her.

No…No…No, Maria thought.

Her father looked at her. Beads of sweat ran down his face and his pupils were dilated. He had clearly taken more than one lick of that frog!

"Take my hand, Maria," he said softly.

Maria didn't move. "Father, why don't you pic–"

"You must ground me to my right, Maria. Toco will ground me to my left. You both must hold my body here as I contact the spirits."

Maria saw everyone looking at her. Her father held out his hand. She took it and he led her to the log with the other woman.

Neha sat and took Toco's right hand in his left. As Maria sat, he took her left hand in his. He began to slowly rock back and forth. Then he started chanting as he closed his eyes.

Maria saw him stiffen and as he opened his eyes, she saw they rolled upwards. His hand went limp. Maria's brow creased as she tightened her grip on his hand.

Neha drifted. He felt the hands of the living below him… but he was drawn to the sky. He felt raised up, then floated upwards, until he could see the setting sun far in the distance, over the treeline.

He floated and floated, moving with the river, down the river. He heard an eagle close by. It soared to his right and he felt able to soar with it. Gliding in the air, minutes, hours, as long as it took... until he again heard the cry of the eagle and fell downwards.

Smoke, so much smoke… a cloak of feathers; blue paint in a bowl… being rubbed on skin and an eye…an eye...a green eye…with golden flecks around the iris.

Two eyes now… rimmed by painted yellow circles…

Two eyes…. of an old man…

Maria jumped as her father groaned and leant forward, nearly doubling over. As he raised himself slowly back up to a sitting position, he was breathing deeply. He looked around him.

"Father… Father!" was all Maria could say.

Somebody handed Toco a cup. She examined it and brought it to Neha's lips. He began to drink and then took the cup from her and guzzled it down. Maria saw water running down his chin.

He stopped, spluttered and coughed.

"Father, are you all right?"

He stood upright. "Karo!" he called.

Karo stepped in front of the fire, spear in hand.

"We must go to Volo. You must take me there."

Chapter 8

Billy Joe O'Brien weaved his car around the corner, slowing down as he reached the Pier Restaurant on the right hand side. A bus load of tourists were slowly making their way inside. Many wore t-shirts and sunglasses to match the fine weather they had been having.

The weather had played a huge part in the tourist season so far this year. He just hoped it would last. It would certainly aid his promise to local businesses to keep the tourists here an extra month this year.

Billy Joe dropped down a gear and opened his car window. He waved to two passing elderly constituents and they enthusiastically waved back. He smirked as he passed Mrs. Coombes' garden. It looked pristine. It should be, as he nearly broke his back doing it the last couple of weeks.

But it had finally paid off. Mowing a garden was largely irrelevant to the outside world but when you were on the cusp of running for an election, you needed people to churn these stories for you. First word got out in the local church, then the tidy towns group heard of it. He, of course, kept quiet about it. The more organic the story would seem, the better.

Billy Joe had been doing things like this for the past twelve months across his constituency; the Burren.

He was sure the election would come before the year ended; the government of the day were surviving motions of no confidence from week to week. The election convention to pick his party's candidate for this constituency was next week. And he was sure he had it sewn up.

His 'name' was what made the party hesitate for years, though.

His father had held the seat and his grandfather before him; his father being a successful minister for most of his time as a politician. That was until the economic crash hit Ireland in 2007/2008. His party were in power and held a comfortable majority.

Once the crash came things became difficult and did so fast. The pressure increased as emigration kicked in and jobs were lost. The volcano erupted when their leader of the day was photographed playing golf with some bankers who had largely caused the crash. His father was put out in front of the media to explain the unexplainable. In that sense he was loyal, but in another sense he made himself a patsy to fortune.

Billy Joe's soon to be political opponent, Liz O'Loughlin, had held the Burren seat for the past eight years. He would be damned if she held it any longer and he would do anything to get it back. The Burren was an O'Brien seat and that was that.

It had been hard going, though. Billy Joe had spent the earlier years absorbing the radioactivity of the crash from constituents. He would often have to stand there and simply listen to their anger; misguided or misconstrued, it did not matter. There was always a chance that people would at least remember that he took his beating and moved on; kept working for the constituency.

Thankfully, the radioactivity of his family name had largely assuaged over the last two years. He had put his head down and gone for actions, not for words. He had even gotten an 'in' at Doolin golf club, right in O'Loughlin's back yard.

This was his time… his year!

Billy Joe heard his phone buzzing on the passenger seat. Flipping it over, he checked the caller id and pulled over.

He had to take this, it was his main investor.

*****

Ed was well on the way now. He had been on the M4, or the 'Galway road' for some time. After the meeting with Deirdre, he was quick to get out of Dublin. He collected his bag at reception, got a few more directions and headed off.

He saw the turn off for the Burren, Co. Clare. He took it and kept going.

A half hour later and Ed could see some of the big grey hills of rock that were synonymous with the Burren National Park. They looked imposing, even from this distance.

As he drove on, his car crested a small hill before coming slowly down upon an unbelievable view. Grey mountains of rock dominated the scene to his left. Fields flowed down from the lower slopes of the mountains, creating an avalanche of green that stopped only at the bright blue waters of a large inlet.

Ed carried on driving, as his car kept in touching distance of the different sized inlets and coves, on his right. There was more than one old tower castle dotted around the landscape too.

He noticed a particular small tree in the hedgerows and fields as he drove. It looked to be a hawthorn tree but its limbs and branches were all doubled over and slanted in the extreme, stretching out in one direction. The gnarled looking branches of the trees clearly had to adapt to the windy conditions thrown at them.

As Ed turned onto another road, he saw the beginnings of life again, as sporadic B&Bs sprang up on the left and right. Ed caught sight of a lovely small harbour ahead. Various boats bobbed up and down on the water.

As Ed drove around another corner, a hulking mountain came into view. It seemed layered with a mixture of grey rock and green bushes. The mountain sloped downwards until it met the ocean in front of it. At its base, Ed could see life, a plethora of white houses and buildings. That must be Ballyvaughan, he reckoned, and it looked as if the town itself survived on the edges, wedged in between rock and water.

Ed drove on before a 'Welcome to Ballyvaughan' sign suddenly greeted him on his left. Remembering some of the directions, he was looking for a sign, 'Grey Hills Guesthouse'. Seeing buildings to his left and right, he realised he must have overshot his target. He slowed down. He saw a hotel to his left and a shop to his right with a red sign saying 'Spar'. It had a large parking lot. He pulled in, walked into the shop and asked where the turn off for Grey Hills Guesthouse was.

The shop assistant was helpful and confirmed he had overshot it. "Follow the signs for Lough Rask," he told Ed.

Ed went out and started his car. By the time he turned it round and had it facing the road, a funeral car appeared from the left, moving at a snail's pace. Ed turned off his radio.

Mourners walked slowly along behind. Many of the men wore black suits or suit jackets with black ties. An older man was out in front slightly, walking just behind the funeral car. He was tall and thin, maybe in his early eighties. He wore an old grey suit, with a tie half done, and a grey cap on his head. A small blue flower was clipped to the breast pocket of his jacket.

He made eye contact with Ed as he walked by and stared. Ed turned off his engine. The expression on the man's face was probably like many other relatives who had lost close people, a mixture of disbelief and shock.

The funeral car moved on down the street and took a left. The mourners carried on behind for another five minutes.

Ed started up his trusty steed and headed the way he came in. Two minutes down the road and he saw the sign for Lough Rask. He took the turn and remembered the last bit of the directions now. There were some houses to his left first and then a small housing estate featured on his right. Powerful looking grey stone hills surrounded the area here. They didn't look too far off, lying in front of him.

Down the road a bit and as it narrowed, he saw the left turn he needed to take. An old sign for the Grey Hills Guesthouse hung on a pole. It had a nice picture of a dolmen on it. He followed the sign and drove his car towards his final destination. The road, if you could call it that, only had room for one car. A long high tuft of grass stretched all the way down the middle of the road, which slanted downwards on either side. The stone walls at the sides, were being slowly suffocated by bushes and trees.

Ed reached the end of the road and drove through a gateway. He saw a large yellow house ahead. Ed pulled in, and stopped, just in front of it. He got out and began to peruse his surrounds. One hundred yards away, past a small garden, he saw what he guessed was the cottage he would be staying in.

It had white washed walls and three small green coloured windows. A green doorway jutted out at the front, placed just under the eave. Ed was happy with the old black slated roof. He had more time for that than a thatched one. Up behind the cottage the peaks of grey mountains revealed themselves through the gaps in the trees.

He could hear a few birds chirping around him but not much else. The sun was beating down on the tarmac. A small dog was sleeping on its side, under a tyre that hung from a rope attached to the branch of a tree. An air of calmness seemed to fill the area. He drank in some of the fresh air and exhaled slowly.

"Home, sweet home," he said.

A door opened to his right from the main house. Out of a dark hallway, an old woman on a cane appeared. She stopped at the doorway. "Are you Edward Marshall?" she asked in a pleasant voice.

"Oh, yes I am! Are you Nuala?"

"Yes." She smiled.

She walked out of her doorway, leaning on the cane. She was small with a short crop of grey hair. Despite the heat, she was wearing a cream woolly cardigan. She walked over to Ed slowly and Ed met her halfway, holding his hand out. She reached hers up and Ed felt something cold in his hand.

"Take it," she said. Ed took the object, a key.

"You can let yourself in… my favourite programme is on."

With that Nuala turned on her heel and slowly made her way back into her house.

"Thanks," Ed shouted as she closed the door.

Fuck it, thought Ed. When you reached that age, you were entitled to act as you please, really.

He made his way through a gap in the wall towards the entrance to the cottage. As he opened it, he realised it was one of those barn door jobs. As the half the door was now open, he battled to get the stiff bolt loose on the lower part of the door. It suddenly gave and shunted quickly to the side. The lower part of the door creaked open. Barn doors were a nice aesthetic in good weather, he thought, but a leaky bucket in winter conditions.

Ed stepped through the threshold and walked into a small hallway. One door faced him, and another two to his left and right. He chanced the one on his right and entered a good sized bedroom. Directly in front of him an old wardrobe stood with one door leaning open. To the right a double bed hugged the same wall as the wardrobe. Beside the bed, on the other side of the room, was a large window. A sink, basin and mirror stuck out of the other wall. The walls were white and appeared to have to some old, faded paintings on them. Ed went over and checked the window. Single paned. The freeze box window company had been here, he thought.

Ed moved to the next room, it was much smaller but somehow still held two small beds, a sink, mirror and smaller window. Several stuffed black refuse bags lay on the floor. The smell of dust and damp filled the air. Ed walked out and closed the door behind him.

He went towards door number three and hoped the holiday, car and cash prize were behind this one. He opened the door slowly for added effect.

No car, cash or holiday but he was still pleasantly surprised. An old black dresser was to his immediate left. It was covered in nice old plates and china. In front of that, two couches formed an L shape.

Another door lay ahead there, while to its right and in the centre of the far side of the room, a good sized black stove dominated the wall. A basket with a mixture of logs and turf sat beside it.

To Ed's immediate right there was a good sized kitchen table with four chairs. In front of that was a moderately sized flat screen television on a basic coffee table. Finally, in the far corner of the room there was two more timber doors at right angles to each other. Ed walked into the centre of the room with his hands in his pockets and examined the walls more closely. On the white painted walls, there was several pictures of stony grey hills, small lakes, flowers and the coastline. On some of the beams above his head, small pots, pans, tankards and other paraphernalia hung down. As Ed scanned the room around him, his bottom lip jutted out and he slowly nodded.

He moved to the far door to the right of the stove. Opening it, he found the kitchen. It was small and condensed. There was a classic four ring electric hob with a small oven underneath. A hip height white fridge hugged the left side of the oven. He opened the fridge and found old smelly things in it. Ed closed it quickly and sighed.

A small toaster and kettle were positioned to the right of a sink. He rooted through the cupboards underneath and found an old tin with tea inside. He would suffer a cup of it. He filled up the kettle, plugged it in and switched it on.

A small horizontal window was positioned above the sink. Ed leaned over the sink for a look. Long grass and some flowers lay at the base of the windowsill outside.

While the kettle boiled, Ed moved back to the main room to see what was in the door to the left of the stove. As he opened the door and entered, he had to duck his head as the roof seemed slightly lower here. It was a small bathroom with a standard sink and mirror, one glass paned window, and as he drew the shower curtain back, a standard early 1990s electric shower. The shower base was filled with all sorts of creepy crawlies.

He moved back to the kitchen and made a cup of black tea, exhaling slowly as he took the first sip. Not bad, he thought. He took another gulp of it and sucked at his teeth. He examined underneath the kitchen cupboard again and found an empty tea box; Barry's it was called. He could suffer this, he decided.

Ed suddenly had a sense of being watched. He turned back round to see the head of a large cow leaning down to the window and rubbing its chin against it.

Ed chuckled and raised his cup towards the window. "Cheers!"

Now he felt like a cigarette. He could see the final door that he hadn't walked through yet, from the kitchen. As he opened it, a tiny conservatory came into view. It still held the day's heat. A plethora of dead flies were strewn across the room and at least one dead mouse lay in a mouse trap. He saw the door to a tiny back garden and went straight for it.

Ed stood in the long grass outside. It was filled with the sound of bees and he watched as various coloured butterflies moved from wildflower to wildflower. He inhaled a large puff of smoke as he took in the nature around him. He heard an animal bellowing behind him. His friendly cow had its head over the wall. It looked at him and bellowed again.

"Sorry mate… I have nothing for you!"

Ed took one more swig of his tea and threw the rest on the grass. He placed the cup on a windowsill and put the embers of the cigarette inside.

Ed went out to his car and unloaded his bags and gear. He then wrote down a list of stuff he needed to get, in order to get the place up and running.

Hearing a knock on the door he went over and opened it.

Two people stood there, a man and a woman. They looked middle aged. Their faces were ashen. By the looks of their jackets, backpacks and hiking boots, they were out for a walk. They stood there silently, appearing to look through him… beyond him.

"Can I help you?" asked Ed.

"Yes," they replied in unison. Their response was deadpan and downbeat.

Ed heard a door bang behind him and he turned. A strong wind blew past him.

Ed turned back around… but the two hikers were gone. The tyre tied to the tree outside danced on the wind outside. He shrugged and closed the door.

He decided to walk back to the village to pick up some bits and grab a bite to eat. As he walked, the sun was starting to dip in the west and seemed to calm the whole place down, as the sounds of birds and bees dissipated somewhat.

The fifteen minute walk to the village was pleasant and it was nice to not be rushing by in a car. He went back to the store where he had asked for directions and picked up refuse sacks, cleaning products, milk, bread, butter and most importantly… coffee.

He looked directly across the road at the Wild Atlantic Lodge Hotel. He chanced it for a bite to eat. It was a modern but homely place. Had that type of nice, fresh, hotel smell. Ed passed the hotel reception and went into the small bar. No one else was around yet. The embers of a small fire were dwindling to his right. A barman walked by and gave him attention straightaway.

He sat Ed down in a larger part of the pub through an alcove. Ed got a menu and quickly targeted a T-bone steak with pepper sauce, with vegetables and chips on the side. He ordered a pint of Guinness. The steak never stood a chance when he got going. He soon demolished everything on the plate.

He handed over more than one note, but it was very reasonable for what he paid and sure fuck it, he thought… it was his first night here! Ed took his shopping bag and himself out of the hotel and went for a wander. The village was small, and its heart was placed at a T-junction with a signpost weighed down with local attraction signs.

Ballyvaughan looked like a place that sprouted up over time. The houses and buildings in the village were all different shapes and sizes. Some looked old and others modern.

Ed and his best mate, the shopping bag, wandered into another pub and chanced a pint of ale. Then Ed chanced another. Then a rock band started up. He began to find his high backed bar stool too comfortable. The blinds went down and time seemed meaningless…

He got home just before midnight. His shopping bag collapsed on the bedroom floor, while Ed collapsed face down on the bed, still dressed, and commenced snoring.

Ed, therefore, did not notice that his bed side lamp flickered on and off throughout the night.

Chapter 9

Neha moved his hand slowly down the long thin wooden tube. As he took his hand away, he saw his forefingers were dusty. He picked it up slowly and stood it up. It came up to his shoulder.

Next, Neha brought the tube to his lips and blew as hard as he could. He coughed as more dust and grime spat out the other end of the blow pipe. Neha could not remember the last time he had used it, but something told him… deep down, that he needed to bring this with him.

People told him that his trance, two days past, lasted some hours, yet his vision connecting him to Volo gave him the impression that they needed to make this journey quickly.

Karo had not argued and that was welcome. He would go, as would Timku. Paka, his son, was the only other person to volunteer. People had already started to leave their village.

As for his daughter, she proved to be as stubborn as an elderly sloth. He watched Maria messing with her 'sack' from his doorway. He told her much of the events that had taken place, but she countered with another explanation for nearly all of it. She had said the death of Yappy was probably the result of the altercation he had had with the fishermen two months ago.

Neha had become frustrated with her dismissive responses then and simply gave up. He didn't tell her about the dead bodies they had found since Yappy…

Two more had died recently. One found in a small pond nearby, his upper body trapped between two logs. His lower body… gone, eaten, probably by piranhas. They found the other woman at daybreak, or her head at least, just sitting there on a rock.

How Maria reminded him of her mother… and that's why he couldn't bring himself to tell her that she couldn't come.

*****

Maria knelt down and tightened the straps on her backpack. She glanced up and saw her father looking at her, disapproval etched on his weathered face.

She quickly looked away and stood up, examining the contents of her backpack spread out on the ground, before carefully repacking it. Her father had told her the apocalyptic tale that she and her colleagues all heard from cut off or uncontacted tribes. They all involved evil spirits, but the actual events always seemed caused by outsiders – other tribes, loggers, miners etc.

"She comes from the air," Karo had said.

She was sure that something had happened to Karo's tribe but the devastation they had described was probably exaggerated. Yet she was worried, because somebody had gotten to them, somewhere deep in the Javari valley. No one in FUNAI had gone in as deep as where Karo had described.

If, somehow, loggers, miners or worse, drug dealers, had found their way in there she had to find out. The war for this forest was moving in the wrong direction all too fast.

Maria examined the grid coordinates on her map of where she thought they may be going. She let out a puff of air. It could be weeks on foot, even after they took the boat ride down river to where her father had first encountered Karo.

She turned as she heard Karo and her father speaking. Karo seemed to be examining her father's blow pipe. He gave the pipe strange looks and gave Neha the same. Neha stood with his arms crossed and frowned as he peered at Karo.

Karo made some kind of comment or two and thrust the blowpipe back towards Neha. Neha snapped it from his hand and said something to Karo, prodding a finger against his chest. Karo retorted and moved forward to Neha's face. Their arguing didn't seem as if it was going to develop into a fist fight, it seemed… juvenile.

As Maria watched the continued bickering, she slowly realised that they must indeed be brothers and that would mean that Karo was her…

Maria's thoughts were interrupted by a rustling sound from her backpack behind her. She turned and saw that Paka had upended the contents of her backpack on the ground, rifling through them quickly.

As Maria stepped over to confront him, Paka was still crouched over the gear. "E-hem," said Maria.

Paka stood, revealing two piles of gear on the ground.

"These, but not those," said Paka as he pointed at the two piles.

He held no expression on his face as walked past her, placing a brief hand on her shoulder. Maria noted it as it was the first affection she had received from her estranged family.

She looked at the pile of discarded goods. She saw her logbook, satellite phone, small laptop, camera, tent, rain gear…

She shrugged, maybe she could do without the technology. Her phone had been no friend to her recently. She had refused largely to consider who had been at the other end of the phone. She decided to leave most of the gear Paka suggested except for the tent, rain gear and camera.

She watched as Paka moved back into view with a small pouch of his own on his back. He carried a machete. He stepped just short of the still bickering men and slapped them both on the chest with his right arm. "Time to go," he said.

As both men glared at Paka, Karo brought two fingers to his mouth and let out a whistle. Had he called full time?

Instead, Timku arrived. Yes, drill sergeant, thought Maria.

Paka moved past Maria and waved her behind him. As Maria put her backpack on, Karo walked over to her and started talking. Maria couldn't understand what he was saying but it sounded like the internationally understood language of 'whinging'.

As Karo tried to grab her backpack in the middle of his tirade, Maria slapped his hand away.

"Shut up, Uncle!" Maria said, doing her best to get the translation right in Yine.

Karo's eyes turned to lasers as his mouth opened wide. Maria walked away and left him for dead. She heard her father laughing and she turned to look at him. He was staring at Karo, still laughing, and was repeating her words to Karo. Karo simply stood, stony faced. Maria gave her father a small smile and he beamed back at her, his shoulders still vibrating as his laughter died down.

Maria saw Karo looking past them all, grabbing Timku's arm and pointing far off in the distance with his other arm. He had lost some pride so he would regain it elsewhere, she thought. She quietly queried with her father as to why Timku, an adolescent, maybe in his late teens, was going.

Neha responded by saying, "He is the guide!"

Maria did not bother asking any more.

At the jetty, Timku handed out strange looking pouches attached to cords. They each placed them around their heads. Neha glared at Maria until she put hers on.

They boarded Paka's thin boat. As Paka pushed away from the jetty and started the engine, none of them looked behind them as they got moving. They remained silent. Sometimes living from moment to moment was best, thought Maria, especially when the future seemed so uncertain.

A few more hours down river, and they reached the place where Karo had walked out of the jungle, months ago. This time Paka turned off the engine long before the sand spit so the boat drifted into the shallows. They all got out and carried the boat up onto solid ground.

They took on some water and Maria caught the other four men staring sombrely at the wall of green trees ahead of them. It seemed still, quiet. No sound. No movement. Maria ignored them and took a step to the edge of the beginning of the dense treeline. It suddenly shook uncontrollably as a wind shot through it. Maria felt herself being pushed back.

The wind died down but some of the trees still shook. As Maria turned to look at the four men, they all stood with gritted teeth and seemed to heave breaths in and out. Maria leaned to her left, looking past them, and pointed.

The men all turned. There on the prow of the boat sat a large golden eagle. It seemed to examine them as much as they examined it. It had light brown feathers around its head and neck. The rest of its body was dark brown, barring its large yellow talons, which looked fierce. Finally, it let out a cry, spread its wings, took to the air and swept over them all. It cried again as it passed over the tree line.

Maria stared at the sky, mouth agape. Neha strode pass her and moved into the jungle wall. The other men slowly walked in behind him. Maria took out her machete and followed.

*****

Maria hacked through vines and branches, back and forth. She moved her feet carefully amongst the large and tangled tree roots at her feet. Pausing for breath, she clutched a large vine. Sweat dripped down from her forehead. She told herself it was the humidity. The sound of macaw birds and the cawing of monkeys came from overhead. They seemed to make their noises in rotation, as if talking with each other.

It took her mind off the large maggots crawling beneath her skin. Her right leg had picked up a mosquito bite a few days ago. What she didn't know was that the mosquito carried a species of pium fly larvae, which the mosquito dispatched on Maria's wound. The larvae got into the wound and the invasion began.

Maria looked upwards. The thick canopy above gave little else away bar the noise. It was hard to know what the sky looked like above, for most of the days they had been out here.

They had been out here, four, maybe five weeks now. They continued to follow Timku, their 'guide'. Karo said Timku would lead them back to their territory.

Maria saw her father walk past her. He stopped, knelt, and began to examine her leg. She looked down briefly at the oozing wound. A maggot popped its head out. She closed her eyes and instead listened to the chanting of the monkeys overhead. What type were they? Tamarins?

Maria felt her father applying some sort of salve to her wound. She grimaced.

She saw some large yellow flower growing on the bark of the tree in front of her.

She had noticed types of flowers here that she did not recognise. All sorts of colours and sizes. She was sure they were probably some variant of others, but their distinct colours and strange shapes still caught her attention.

Maria felt her father finish his examination. The group moved on. The thicket of brush here looked like any other, but Timku led them on regardless. At any moment, he could veer sharply left or right, changing direction without warning, even though there was no visible sign, natural marker or obstacle to justify his decision. Karo strode close behind Timku, his purposeful steps giving Maria some confidence in Timku's navigation.

Then, an hour or two later and Timku stopped. Karo stopped just behind him and slowly nodded, placing a hand on Timku's shoulder. Trees rose up out of a heavy fog that shrouded the forest in front of them. The base of the tree trunks could not be seen but their height matched the canopy where the group stood. The ground dipped down slightly into the fog before them.

Timku began to lead them down a winding and jagged path. It took them a few minutes to clear the line of fog. As the fog dissipated, Maria realised that this was a small valley of some kind. They reached the valley floor after what Maria reckoned was close to a hundred foot descent.

The base of the wide trees here showed exactly how tall they actually were. Maria revelled in the wonder of the valley, as no helicopter, plane or drone could tell the difference from the air; the thick canopy above would look like any other part of the Brazilian rainforest.

She could hear rushing water now. It was not long before they came across its source. Water rushed out from a gap in a wall of stone in front of them. A waterfall. At least thirty feet high. The noisy, raging water formed a small frothy pool at its base before disappearing down another hole a few metres on.

Karo overtook Timku and waved them to follow him. They moved to the side of the waterfall and started up a small rocky path. Maria lost track of Karo and Timku. It looked like they had walked… into the waterfall. But as she reached the edge of the waterfall, the gap suddenly swerved left and she saw the rest of the group in front of a passage.

The passage must not have been very long as Maria could see light in the distance. The others started to walk in. Maria wobbled briefly, composed herself and walked in. Five to ten minutes later, she saw them all stopping at the other end.

As Maria joined them, she saw their shocked expressions and followed their gaze.

In front of them, smoke rose from many blackened tree stumps. The source of this destruction seemed concealed in a billowing smoke cloud ahead. Flames flickered from the black smoky centre of the cloud.

Maria stepped forward onto the seared soil. Walking towards the smoke cloud ahead, she saw shards of metal and debris scattered on the ground. As she reached the billowing smoke cloud, the wind pushed it sideways, revealing a small crater with the contorted hull of a metal vehicle at the centre.

Maria saw half a rotor blade sticking out of the ground. She coughed as she backed away slowly but nearly tripped. Looking down, she saw a small black duffle bag. Leaning down she picked it up, revealing the face of a woman.

Maria, gasping, put her hand to her mouth. Half the woman's face was burnt beyond recognition. Nearly the whole ball of her one remaining eye was exposed. Her lower jaw was missing. The rest of her body was missing too, sheared off by a clean cut just below the shoulders.

"Jesus!" said Maria.

As she backed away, she muttered what Karo had said, "She… comes… from… the… air."

Maria heard the shrill cry of a bird to her right and darted around to see two more rotor blades stuck in the ground. She let out a small cry as she saw pieces of the dead woman scattered on the ground ahead. She felt woozy…

Neha just got behind Maria as she collapsed. He caught her and Paka helped him steady her up. Neha could see… someone. They seemed to filter in and out of view, as waves of smoke distorted his vision.

The wind now pushed the billowing smoke in front of them. It seemed to thicken and totally block their view.

A man suddenly emerged from the wall of smoke and stood directly in front of Neha. He was shorter than Neha. He looked old. He wore a cape of feathers and had golden painted circles around his eyes. His small head revealed cropped white hair.

He looked at Karo and spoke in a language Neha could not understand. While still talking and looking at Karo, the old man grabbed Neha's wrist.

"*Chena.. vow.. ter…* does not matter you have come back, Karo. You have done well enough."

The old man looked at Neha. "You have brought him here."

The old man's voice seemed as cracked as his skin, but Neha could understand him. Neha looked into his eyes. The same eyes from his vision, the same eyes as Yappy… the same eyes as his.

"Who is this?" asked Paka.

"Volo, the man we came to meet," said Neha.

Volo reached his wrinkled hand out to Neha's blowpipe. Neha handed it over gently.

"Come, come, we have little time," said Volo.

Volo turned and began making steady strides forward, while leaning on the blowpipe. "Much better," said Volo as he led them on.

They cleared the smoke and moved on into some trees, which seemed as tall as the ones in the valley they had just left.

They soon came to another clearing. Neha saw that some huts came into view. The place seemed rather dim. Neha's mouth fell open as he looked to the ground. It was covered in mist but also with many dead and decaying bodies. Neha put his free hand to his nostrils. That acrid smell that carried on the wind weeks ago at his village was, Neha realised, the smell of the dead. That 'yenta' had struck here first, thought Neha… just as Karo had said.

He and Paka began to pick their footing carefully as they carried Maria.

As Neha looked at Karo, he saw a tear escape down his face. Neha placed his free hand on his shoulder as they made their way between and over dead bodies.

Neha began to hear slow chanting to his left. It was coming from a hut. The doorway was filled with inky blackness. The chanting droned out from many different voices, and was slightly incoherent, as it sounded further away at times.

"They sing their way to the spirit world," said Volo. "The song of the dead. I could not do it for them. Too many to bless; my song is not strong enough. They have no one left here… just like the bonshea. Nobody will sing for her… she will not move on." Volo gave a spiteful laugh. "We go over here," he said.

Volo led them to a moderately sized hut at the centre of the dead village. "Put her in here," said Volo.

Neha and Paka placed her onto a hammock, inside the hut.

Maria's bad leg was slung out at the side. Volo lifted the leg and smelt it. As he did, a maggot pushed out of the wound. The skin around the wound immediately changed colour, from ruby red to purple. As the maggot disappeared back inside, pus ran out of the wound.

Volo stood straight. "Aggressive. Have many animals… been attacking her, Neha?"

Neha shrugged. "I do not think so. I have been applying a salve we use for ant bites."

"Let me try," said Volo as he slowly moved off, shuffling away, still using Neha's blow pipe.

Volo returned minutes later with a palm leaf in his left hand, singeing slightly. In his right hand, he carried a wooden pipe which had four small holes at various intervals along it. It curved and narrowed at one end.

Volo moved the palm leaf to Maria's leg and blew some smoke over the wound. He muttered a few words, handing the leaf to Neha. He then raised the wooden pipe to his lips and paused. Neha and Paka exchanged a look.

As Volo closed his eyes and his cheeks puffed, the pipe began to make noise, almost like the pitch of a chirping bird. Volo moved his fingers over the holes and the pitch changed. He held it and moved it towards Maria's leg. As the pipe moved over her wound, Volo flickered his fingers and blew once more.

The tone, the high pitched noise, made Neha and Paka put their hands to their ears. As Volo carried on the awful tone the skin around Maria's wound began to writhe… then a maggot flopped out, followed by another and then another.

Soon, the maggots swarmed out, making quite a pile on the ground beneath them.

Red faced, Volo stopped. He seemed short of breath as he leaned on the hammock for support. Neha and Paka stomped on the maggot pile.

"Place some of your salve on the wound now, Neha," said Volo.

Neha did just that. He used one of Maria's 'band-aids' to close the wound.

A wind ran through the hut.

"Help me walk, Neha. Maybe Paka could mind Maria for a while."

The small man wrapped his arm inside Neha's and leaned towards him. Neha helped him out of the hut and Volo pointed at another hut across the clearing. As they reached it, a golden eagle landed on the stump of a tree just beside the hut. It gave a cry, locking eyes with Neha. Its eyes twinkled, revealing golden flecks around the iris.

Karo and Timku stood silently near the doorway. Volo turned at the entrance to his hut. Smoke billowed out at the top. Slivers of light escaped the walls, revealing a fire.

"Only Neha can cross through here with me… only Neha," said Volo.

Volo released himself from Neha's arm and walked to the entrance to his hut. Neha noticed several charms hanging from the doorway. Volo took down a handful and called Karo over. He handed them to Karo and spread his arm, left to right, across the clearing. Karo moved off. He then called over Timku and muttered several words to him. Timku strode off behind the hut and on into the forest, without question.

Volo crossed into his hut, taking a large step. Neha instinctively did the same, removing the remaining charms from his eye line. The hut seemed sparse from what Neha could see, veiled in a light smoke from a fire burning in the middle. A few solitary logs lay a metre back from the fire. A table stood at the far end of the hut.

Volo tried to reach down to a bowl at his feet but couldn't. Neha leant down and picked it up. Volo moved to his hammock nearby and picked up a bunch of large leaves. As he brought them back to Neha, he opened them outwards, revealing ants… blue ants. Most seemed dead. Neha had never seen their type before.

"Place as many as you can into the bowl, Neha."

Neha placed the dead ants into the bowl while Volo retrieved a plant from behind a log. It was almost a luminous green in colour, but not quite. It had elongated pointed leaves that curled upwards at their ends. Volo picked off several leaves, tearing them up and putting them into the bowl.

While Neha held the bowl with two hands, Volo crushed the mixture together. He began to sing, "*Yena yana ho…yena yana ho..nee yan..nee yan ho…*" Neha sang along, unsure as to how he knew the words.

Volo finished crushing the mixture and stopped the song. Neha held the bowl without moving.

"Bless the contents, Neha," said Volo.

Neha moved to the fire and waved smoke over the bowl. He sang a song of his ancestors. As Volo joined him, Neha looked at him, his brow creasing. It was a song he thought only his tribe knew.

Volo pointed at his cloak of red and yellow feathers. "The feathers connect us to the sky and help us soar to the sky spirits. What colour feather should you wear, Neha?"

Neha wasn't sure. He closed his eyes. He heard the cry of the eagle outside and opened his eyes. Volo smiled and walked over to the table, lifting off a blanket. There beneath it was a cloak of golden eagle feathers.

Volo lifted it and moved behind Neha. "As the eagle soars, so will you." He placed the cloak over Neha's shoulders and tied it at Neha's neck.

Volo moved to something akin to a small chest. Opening it, he retrieved two small lengths of wood, the length of a forearm. The wood went upwards at one end at a right angle, forming a small hollow. Volo went in front of Neha now and stuffed the hollows with the crushed ant/leaf mixture from the bowl.

As Volo moved the wooden ends to the fire, Neha realised that these were smoking pipes. Neha had seen his grandfather smoke regularly, but he had not practised it. As the pipe contents ignited, Volo smoked both pipes to ensure they were lit and handed one to Neha. Volo indicated he should sit on a small log by the fire. Volo sat beside him and started smoking deeply.

After a few small puffs of his pipe, Neha gave a bellowing cough. His throat became dry. But he carried on smoking, as did Volo.

The hut was soon enveloped in smoke. Volo looked at Neha.

"The smoke clouds our vision here so we may see the other place… the place in all of us… our shared being… our shared connection. Look," he said as his hand pointed at the far wall.

The image of a man appeared across the hut. He was sitting on a log at the other end of the hut, tending the same small fire that Neha and Volo sat beside. Neha could see he wore nothing but a red tunic around his waist, but the hut's smoky interior shrouded the rest of the man's features.

As a small breeze fluttered through the hut, the smoke slowly drifted away from the man who casually looked up at Neha and Volo. Neha could first see two painted yellow circles around his eyes. Then his full face became clearer. He nodded over to Neha and Volo.

Neha and Volo exchanged a look.

Neha's back straightened but he stayed composed. Neha and Volo nodded back to the man.

The man twisted around then and pointed behind him. Tribal warriors came into view. They stood around a larger fire, holding spears, bows and arrows. They stood on strange ground; grey flat rock, broken up with lines and gaps between them. The warriors looked across at something else.

The man sitting across the fire from Volo and Neha now turned to his other side, matching where the warriors were looking. A woman in a black cloak came into view. She was on her knees, her arms held by a tall warrior. She had red painted circles around her eyes. It was that woman, Neha realised. That horrible woman in his dream, the woman who hid in the wind…

Another woman came into view, just behind her. She wore the skin of a dead jaguar on her head and back. Her body was painted blue. She held a golden knife. Her long dark hair concealed her face.

The man in the red tunic sitting across from Neha and Volo began rocking back and forth, chanting loudly. His words echoed around the hut. He stood abruptly and walked over beside the woman holding the knife. As he continued to chant the woman in blue moved the blade to the other woman's throat. Her long hair parted, and Neha saw her painted face.

Neha's mouth opened.

The painted woman proceeded to slit the other woman's throat.

Neha was shocked by this….by all of this.

The woman in black writhed and screamed as blood poured out of her cut throat. The man holding her let her go, as the painted woman behind her kicked her back, grabbing her hair before she fell completely forward. She screamed again.

Neha now saw that she was being held over a hole between two large standing slabs of rock. As the woman's eyes rolled upwards into her skull, the painted woman pushed her forward with one foot. She fell into the hole, no, Neha realised – her grave.

The painted woman walked to the large fire where the warriors stood and grabbed a piece of ignited wood. She strode over and threw it into the grave. She placed her hand with the knife over the grave and let the bloody knife drop down. Flames leapt up now. She walked around the grave and took off a brown cord at her neck, with some pendant attached to it, and threw that in as well.

The man with the red tunic at his waist stopped singing and waved at someone. Four other men came into view carrying…

As Neha looked on and on, it was more than he could have guessed or imagined.

A small breeze blew through the hut and the smoke cleared. And with that light wind, the vision disappeared also. The embers of their fire were dying but the embers of a pre-dawn light crept in through the edges and seams of the hut.

They both agreed that it was not what they had expected. They began to debate what they had seen – debate what they should do. They went back and forth for some time until Volo stood up slowly, using the weight of Neha's blow pipe to help him. He began to shuffle towards the doorway.

Neha stood and took off his cloak of feathers. He followed Volo outside and. the orange haze of dawn greeted him. They must have been in the hut for hours.

Volo dipped a cup into a small bucket of water and raised it to his lips. He drank deeply.

"I should never have sent Karo and the others to her lair," said Volo in a rasping voice. "But I could not go myself," he said as Neha saw him moving his hand over his old body.

"Her prison has been disturbed by a new tribe, a strange one, Neha. They float in the air like a giant insect and drop their kin and servants to the ground. It was not long after they arrived when all this death was brought to us."

In the far distance, smoke billowed in the air above the treeline. Volo and Neha looked in that direction.

"They do not know what they do, but they must be saved from her, as well as us…"

Volo turned to Neha and with shaky hands undid the cord holding a strange pendant at his neck. "But she cannot see me, Neha, and she will not see you either." He moved it over Neha's head and tied it there.

"This was left outside my hut a few moons ago, the night you flew over to me. Another strange thing was left outside my hut too," he muttered. "You must finish this and soon. Lock her in, Neha. She will see me now."

Volo turned, looking at the far side of his hut. Neha looked on but no one was there.

Timku arrived around the corner carrying a bowl of small blue flowers. "These were the last, I can find no more," muttered Timku.

Volo said nothing to Timku, simply taking the bowl from his hands. "The wind, the water, the earth… fire. Our forest mother gave us and the animals these to live in but she also gave us these," he waved his hand over the bowl of flowers, "to balance all else. These small flowers make her retch, they perturb her vision… her senses. Mother forest put these near her prison to make her not wander too far. But there are not many left."

Volo gave a small whistle. It sounded exactly like a bird. Karo arrived from the other end of the village.

Volo looked at Neha. "Call Paka."

Neha shrugged and shouted to his son as Volo held his wrist once more. Neha noticed nothing strange about it.

Paka arrived as Volo was crushing the flowers in with sand, mud and water. He began to chant as he covered all their bodies in the ointment. Its smell was pungent, a sweet smell.

Volo nodded at them all. He held Karo's forearms with his hands. He stared at Karo, pursing his lips. "You must go on one more quest for me, Karo."

Volo turned after that pronouncement and moved back into the hut. He came out carrying Neha's blow pipe. One end held a piece of cloth blocking it. "The poison of our darts is more powerful than yours." Volo looked sternly at Neha. "Do not look for distractions, Neha… you will need none."

Neha sighed. He looked around at his blue hued party. Without words Karo moved off towards the treeline. Timku followed, as did Paka.

Neha began walking but Volo was nowhere to be seen.

*****

Maria got tired of hanging around. She wanted to examine the dead woman's bag she had picked up, away from prying eyes. She didn't like the sight of all these dead bodies, and she needed to find out what really happened here. That creepy old Shaman looked at her strangely when he was talking with her father. But even if he had told her father what was happening, she would still have to discern two levels of misconstrued 'shamanism' and differing tribal phrases, before she got to the truth.

She watched as they all covered themselves in blue mud. Then her father appeared to be shouting but instead he made strange bird noises and her half-brother came over to them. She was sure that coloured mud would not stop whatever they would find in there. She picked up the dead woman's bag and started walking through the dead village. At least her leg with the wound felt a lot better.

Moving into thicker trees, the strong sun still flickered through the high canopy overhead. She located her sunglasses and threw them on. She came to a small stream and made her way across. Just as she placed her foot onto the bank opposite, something glimmered in the sunlight in the corner of her right eye. She casually looked in that direction as she raised her other foot on the bank. Maria paused and then walked down the bank slowly. The glimmering intensified, spreading small flickers of golden light all around her.

Maria jumped back into the stream. A bit deeper here. She waded and stopped, placing both hands into the water and scooped up what the river bed would allow. As she took her hands slowly out of the water her mouth fell open.

Sparkles of gold shimmered amongst the sand in the strong sunlight. Looking around her she could see more and more under the water. Maria kept her hands enclosed as she carefully stepped back up on the bank. She placed the sand onto the ground and opened and up-ended the contents of the bag onto the river bank. Maria crouched down as two items caught her attention, a company identity card and a large hard back black folder.

Maria reached for the work pass first. 'Adriana Silva' read the name. The company symbol was at the bottom right, two capitalised 'M's. One blue, one red.

Maria picked up the folder and opened the first page. A letter was the first document and the title of the company revealed all of Maria's fears – 'Mendoza Mining Company'. Maria sighed as she flicked through the pages of the folder. Pictures of equipment, a schedule of dates and times. Coordinates and crucially – 'Lift Dates'. She bit her lip now as she came across a gridded map. Three locations were circled in red marker. They seemed to form a loose triangle. One of the coordinates had 'AU! AU! AU!' written around it. Maria remembered that was the periodic table symbol for gold.

She took out her own map to compare location and coordinates. From the comparison, she reckoned the dead village was at the centre of the triangle. The nearest red circled location was not the 'AU' one, but it was close by. She put all the crap back in the bag and headed straight for it.

Ten minutes on, and she stepped out into a small clearing. A few boxes and other equipment lay around. As Maria looked to her feet, she saw netting. There was lots of it strewn in the area. She picked up the netting at her feet and tried to gather it up. The open side was connected to long lines of additional rope and then strong looking hooks. Maria realised she was staring at long line equipment; netting that attached to helicopters.

She took out her camera and started snapping.

She walked over to stacked crates at the centre of the clearing, undid the clips of one and opened it. She hissed, putting her hands in and pulled out a gun… an AK- 47. She nodded in disbelief as she examined the weapon further. This was the preferred weapon of the terrorist, the extremist, and now the miner. She placed the gun back down and took a few snaps of the guns.

Maria heard the wind rustling the trees on the other side of the clearing. She could see some sort of track. She took out the miners' map again and examined the position – the track more than likely led to the next 'AU' site. And she more than likely would find her quarry, greedy miners, at that location. With her end goal in site, Maria strode down the narrow track.

But something followed Maria, attracted by the noise of the clicking camera. It moved soft footedly down the track behind her.

Chapter 10

Michael Murphy pulled up the handbrake on their moderately sized Honda Range Rover. "We are go for launch," he said in a mock Nasa voice. His five year old son Conor laughed from the back. "Here we goooo!" Michael added for comic value as he reversed out. He moved the car slowly towards the rental car park exit.

They had landed in Shannon airport one hour earlier. They were headed for the same place they had come to the last the few years – the Burren National Park. It was a hell of a trip from Chicago, but they all loved it. There was something in it for everyone.

Michael drove the car through the exit and joined a small roundabout. "Weeeeee!" Michael added as they went around. Conor thought it was hilarious. Niamh, his wife, grinned at him, letting her dagger green eyes be seen as her sunglasses sank down her nose. "This is going to be some trip, kids," she said.

Michael's smile was full of cheek as he looked in his rear view mirror. "How's Melissa? You're very quiet. You promised us an Irish song or two!"

Melissa, his eleven year old daughter, sat in the back. She had long strawberry blonde hair, just like her mother. Her arms were folded. "Oh, whatever!" was all Melissa could manage.

"I think the 'hanger' has taken over this car!" Michael replied, laughing.

Michael began to merge the car onto the motorway for Galway. As he did a black Audi raced up behind him. Michael was just getting up the gears but that wasn't good enough for the car hugging his ass behind. The Audi started beeping the horn and jerked to the right to overtake.

Michael decided to make a mockery of it. "These folks love the horn," he said using his silly voice for the benefit of his son. Michael began honking back and the Audi drew alongside. Shaven head youths with earrings appeared with the scowl of ignorance plastered across their faces. The driver leaned across the passenger seat; he tried to shout something.

Michael started up with his silly voice again. "I can't hear these folks! What are they saying!? Let's give them the horn… as that's how they seem to communicate!"

The Irish welcoming committee in the car beside them kept saying what Michael imagined was expletives but he methodically beeped the horn and said, "You're welcome anytime in Chicago!" The kids laughed at that. He even caught his wife vibrating beside him in the passenger seat. The Audi beside him soon had another fast car on its behind. They were forced to drive on. Michael was tempted to shout 'see you in hell' but thought better of it. Instead, he directed his family towards some nice looking sheep on the left hand side. Conor and Melissa tried to count them.

The journey moved smoothly onwards from there, and in no time at all they had made it to the turn off for Kinvara. Michael darted past one or two coaches at Ballyvauhan and onto the scenic road to Fanore. They were on the home straight and the kids were looking at the glimmering ocean to their right.

They would soon be at the holiday home. They were keen to try something new this year. They had been very happy at the local cottages in Ballyvaughan over the last few years, but this time the sea view on 'Hags Head' was simply too tempting.

As Michael pulled the car through the gates of the house, he nodded to the plaque on the wall – 'Journeys End'.

The car wound its way down a narrow drive sheltered by trees and emerged onto the large parking area beside a decent sized white holiday home. Michael stopped the car and got out without saying anything. He stepped in front of the car and took in the sea view in front of him, realising that the extra money this year was worth it.

Conor got out and raced past Michael. "Whoa there, Mr.," said Michael as he pulled Conor back towards him. "This is a lovely place, but I don't want you going near the edge without Mommy or Daddy. Okay?"

Conor shrugged and nodded, as his green and gold flecked eyes shimmered in the sunlight. Michael scooped him up on his shoulders and began bouncing him up and down.

As Niamh heard the two of them starting to sing some silly song together, she looked to Melissa. "Come on, Ms.! Let's check out our mansion!"

Niamh stopped as she got to the doorway.

"What's that?" asked Melissa.

Some strange parcels hung from the outer doorway.

"And that?" asked Melissa as she pointed at the ground. A line of white… stuff was on the ground. It stretched left and right, to the corners of the house.

"Eh… I'm not sure," responded Niamh.

Niamh stepped under the parcels and put the key in the door.

"Come on!" she said as she opened the door. "Let's go and see what other weird stuff the locals have left us!" she added, smiling at Melissa.

As Niamh located a broom under the stairs Melissa shouted, "Mom! There's more of those weird hanging things on the windows!"

"Okay honey," said Niamh as she walked with the broom to the doorway. "You start taking them down and I'll sweep away the white stuff outside."

Niamh stopped at the doorway and moved the stuff with her foot. It was grainy. She went down on her haunches and chanced tipping her finger into it. She looked at it and smelt it. "Salt!" she said out loud. "Maybe tomorrow we'll add the pepper!" she joked to herself. She stood up and started to broom the salt away from the house. She soon discovered it ringed the entire house.

As she walked back inside, Melissa handed her the 'hanging things'. She held them out to her as if they were dog poo. "They smell weird, Mom," she said.

Niamh took them, walked out and flung them onto a compost heap out the back.

"Who knows what tomorrow's Irish welcome will bring," she muttered to herself, and she went back inside.

*****

Ed fed the small black donkey a carrot as he rubbed it under its chin. As it chomped away, he appreciated the small pasture that it and its two companions called home. Their marshy retreat was directly beside the sea, protected by a small dock about 300 metres away. It meant the sea never rushed in but instead glided in and out at 'donkey' speed. There was always just enough grass on the higher edges for the donkeys to camp on when the tide was fully in. The waters never really looked like they would get very high anyway, maybe as far as the donkeys' midriffs, so the chances of drowning were low.

The sea water fed the long wild grass with various nutrients and minerals. The donkeys acted as a slow lawn mowing service, probably dining on the healthiest grass around. The symbiotic process carried on daily and the donkeys seemed to attract much attention.

Ed noticed that two parents with two small girls were waiting patiently to his right and realised he was hogging all the 'donkey' time for himself. He gave them a smile and quickly moved away from his daily donkey love affair.

In truth, there probably needed to be a sign up saying 'you need to be this small' to pet the donkey.

Ed glided on down the path heading towards the dock. Three small boats were tilted on their sides, touching the sandy seaweed floor beneath them. The boats were still enjoying their slumber as the waters made slow progress coming in beneath them. Their shift had not started. A heron patrolled the shallow water between them.

The waters themselves were glass like beyond the dock, shining in the white light of the morning. Galway was beyond, somewhere across the large bay. A small, cold wind swirled around Ed. He tightened the zipper at the top of his jacket so the collar closed around his neck and stuffed his hands in his jacket pockets as he walked along.

Ed had truly settled in here. It was the middle of August and the summer had been more than enjoyable.

Back in May he wasn't entirely sure about his surroundings in the Burren. Google would only offer so much information on the area. So he did his best to cheat. The tourist office offered up the best information. He bought one hill walking book on the area and a more general one on the Burren region itself.

Ed had instantly noticed the volume of tourists and buses moving in and around Ballyvaughan. An eclectic array of accents was heard each morning around the local shop. He had seen so many 'walkers' and 'hikers' around the place, and was delighted, as he saw an extra opportunity he had not envisaged before he came here.

From second year onwards of his Archaeology course, Ed offered tourists walking trips around the Lakelands district. It was a nice source of income and the well-off London types were easy to please. They were, after all, used to a world of skyscrapers, nasty commutes, traffic congestion, malfunctioning train systems and 'deadlines'. The Lakelands region of England offered the urban extremist a pause from all of that. They tipped well too!

So with good weather hitting this side of the Irish coast for the summer, Ed decided that the best way to find out about the area was to get out and walk it. He used his local walking tour guide book and tackled the Ballyvaughan Wood Loop, the Black Head Loop, the Caher Valley Loop, The Burren Way, and The Slievcarran Loop. He also went out on a sprinkling of guided walks too. Standing at the back of the walking groups, he would pose as a standard English tourist.

Ed had vaguely checked the licencing requirements for his side business but had shrugged it off. This, after all, wasn't the real reason why he was here.

Instead, he got a cheap Irish mobile phone and slapped up a few poster advertisements. Posing as 'Jack Royson', he accosted tourists outside the main shops and inside the pubs and cafes. He had his best hit rate with the American and Mediterranean girls that seemed to find their way here. They were all coming or going to or from Galway City.

He soon injected some banter into his walking trips, a few myths and legends from his local guide book, and he found himself being invited for pint after pint. One thing led to another and he realised that other opportunities may be available.

The American girls had travelled to the Emerald Isle and they were all searching for more than a holiday it seemed. Every man needs a story to single him out from the rest of the herd, don't you know. That was what was expected. Women seemed to keep trump cards of their lovers.

For them, his selling point was probably his height, his unique north English accent (he turned it up of course and added a dusting of Yorkshire phrases), his unique eye colouring (or so he was told) and his token line that he was there to do the audit, but also… find himself (he always made sure to look out in the distance at that part).

Then he would look into their eyes and move in for a kiss, and if he was lucky… a roll in the hay would follow, in his 'traditional Irish cottage' (the cottage being another selling point. He kept a bottle of 'traditional' Irish whiskey there too).

Ed gave a small smile, considering the last few months. He reached the Pier Restaurant on his left. The tables outside were made for the view, a seafood chowder and a pint. How he would love an afternoon of that, he could get a paper and…

Ed's phone began ringing. He didn't recognise the number.

He answered with a soft, "Hello." He was still distracted by the prospect of the Pier restaurant.

"Ed," a stern voice said. "It's Deirdre."

Ed's relaxation bubble burst. "Oh, hello Deirdre."

Silence.

"How are you?"

"I'm fine," she replied tersely.

Pause.

"How is the report going?" she asked.

"Oh, it's going well. I'm just out on some of the karst rock now… incredible landsc–"

"Where is the report?" snapped Deirdre.

"Well it's in progress Deirdre… I'm still finding my feet and it will probably take some time–"

"I mean the quarterly report, it's overdue!"

"Emmm."

Deirdre made a despondent noise down the phone. "THE QUARTERLY REPORT, ED. DID… YOU… READ… THE… FILE?"

"Yes, I've started going through it."

"Then you will have read that the quarterly report is needed, Ed. We need this report as we gear up before we go back to the Office of Public Works, the Government Department that looks after this. Where is the–"

"Deirdre, you never said anything about this." Ed had had enough of the haughty tone. "In fact, you said that I had one report to do with a potential two year life span. Yes, I haven't read the file fully but I'm not going to know about a report that is stuck in the middle of it."

Brief silence took over.

"Well, we need the report by next Wednesday."

"Right so. I'll get moving on it."

"Yes."

"Bye–"

Deirdre hung the phone up abruptly.

Ed leaned his head back, giving a small growl as he did.

Deirdre clearly (a) wasn't organised, (b) was a last minute Linda on deadlines, (c) had anxiety issues which manifested in her frustration with others or (d) had kick ass mood swings due to a long term coke habit.

He reckoned it was all of the above.

But to be fair, he had not examined any of the key structures, and despite the loop walks had missed many of the key sites. There were many sites and structures that were simply off the beaten track.

Ed turned on his heel and made for his cottage.

*****

Deirdre's phone call lit a fire under his ass. This job would be all the harder when the weather turned against him.

He grabbed the file from the kitchen table. He actually had to blow dust off the thing… it had sat there all summer, after all. He needed to get a better picture of what he had to do and although the walking tours had given him a good recce of where he might have to look, his predecessor's file might just point him in the right direction.

But he considered the paperwork element of this gig as nothing but homework. He would need to distract his malaise. So he yanked on his jacket, flung his laptop bag over his shoulder, propped the file under his arm and moved towards the door, pen in mouth.

Ed turned as his mobile, his 'Jack Royson' mobile, rang. He picked it up off the table. It was some foreign number. He would let it go to voicemail. 'Jack Royson's' business would need to go on ice for a while.

He scooted out the door and walked quickly down the thin road, the brush and trees at his sides appearing slightly scanter. It was an early autumn after all, he surmised as he took in the beautiful hues of brown and yellow leaves. The scantily clad trees also revealed more of the grey mountains and hills around Ballyvaughen. They were like castle walls, trying to keep Ballyvaughan in or the rest of the world out.

Ed carried on walking down the wider, yet still rural road. A spattering of houses to the left and right. The main road, if it could be called a main road, was just ahead. He said his customary hello to the brown horse in the field to his left. It shimmed its head in reply and Ed gave it a tap on the nose as he passed. Turning left onto the main road, he covered the five minute walk to the village at pace.

As he reached the village he hummed and hawed about where to go for a coffee. He wanted a coffee, but he needed space, too. He popped his head into the Wild Atlantic Lodge Hotel, but all the best spots were already taken. Once he went outside, he saw a bus load of tourists landing into the Hikers Hotel, so he went into O'Brien's pub.

Ed pushed through the door. Not a sinner in the place; ideal.

He parked himself in a secluded spot to the right. The barman seemed shocked to see him as he drank in Ed's order of a cappuccino.

Ed sat down at his chosen perch, took out his laptop and switched it on. He retrieved more a bowl than cup of coffee from the barman and got the wifi code too.

All set – no excuses. A healthy swig of coffee and Ed opened the file. A bundle of brochures and business cards wrapped in an elastic band greeted him first. He took off the elastic band and began with the brochures, identifying the significance of each one. Some seemed like historical or tourist sites that would be part of his audit. They related to structures, mainly. He placed the relevant brochures to his left, while taking a note of them on a word doc on his laptop. Satisfied with that he examined the business cards, sorting through them.

In the end, he was left with a handful of business cards and brochures that made little sense. Some of the business cards related to odd things, like cave diving and boat tours. Hard to know what relevance they brought to the audit party. Maybe they were… were…

Ed looked at the inside page of the file itself. Bingo!

Aine O'Sullivan was written in the top left corner. Her telephone number was there too.

"Aine O'Sullivan's hobbies?" said Ed out loud. He was slightly disappointed that no one answered him.

He saw the next elongated bundle he had to tackle, long white pages in another elastic band. He picked them up and something fell onto the bar floor. The back of another business card lay at his right foot. He picked it up and turned it around.

The picture of a dolmen occupied the left side of the business card. It read *Brian Flannery, Archaeological Consultant B.A., M.A. and PHD.* Small pen drawn hearts and smiley faces surrounded the name. Aine's pen pal?

Ed placed the business card down and unwrapped the bundle he was holding. These were maps and he could instantly see they were valuable to his cause. As he opened each one, he could see that Aine had kept busy. Each one seemed to be a roughly drawn grid of the Burren National Park and little coloured dots were drawn in between them, together with the closest town or village.

As he examined each map he saw what he thought were the initials for each of his targets at the top left: portal tombs, court tombs, burial cairns, fulacht fiadhs, ring barrows, souterrains, stone forts, ring forts, holy wells, shrines, old churches. They were all spread over North Clare within the Burren National Park.

Ed took notes on his word doc on the number of structures that appeared in each map, together with their rough location.

The last Map was marked 'WT'. He guessed that meant Wedge Tomb. He noticed the standard green dots Aine had used to mark the locations were joined by other red ones. She hadn't used red on any others.

As Ed reached the last bundle, he heard rain belting down on the Pyrex window on the roof above him. The barman appeared from the back and made a bee line for Ed's empty coffee cup. "Another?"

"No, thanks," Ed replied as he took in the soaked barman.

“No worries,” the barman said. “Bloody cats and dogs out there,” he added as he moved off with the coffee cup in hand.

Ed rattled down some more notes on his word doc before tackling the next bundle of paper. As he unwrapped it, he soon learnt that they were rough reports Aine must have drafted. They were all hand written and the writing was scrawled in parts; the readable bits were unfinished sentences. Aine must have suffered from the same academic curse as Professor Barnes – an allergy to technology.

Re-examining the maps, Ed could see a faint pencilled ‘tick’ or ‘x’ beside each dot. He did have some luck in linking some of the written reports back to the ‘ticks’ on the various maps – some luck, but not total. He would soon discover which sites they were linked too, he hoped, when he got out and about.

Finally, Ed picked up the last bundle. It was heaviest one. It seemed more chained than wrapped in old elastic bands. As he leafed through the first set of pages, many seemed old and yellow. He made out some of the faded writing and recognised some dates – 1954, 1955 etc.

This must be the 1950s file, he thought. He put the pages back in order and re-wrapped them in their elastic prison. This was for another day, he decided.

As Ed finished taking some more notes on his laptop, he felt a lot better. The information in the file was more than a good foundation to get the ball rolling. The next move was to do up an excel spreadsheet on what he had found and then build his own map. He could then decide where to tackle first. The reports Aine had drafted would all have to be re-done by the looks of it, but overall, this was a good start.

Ed was feeling peckish but certainly less anxious as he shut down his computer. He stood and carefully replaced all the documents into their respective bundles, placing the lot back into the folder then. He put his coat on, put the laptop bag strap over his shoulder and propped the heavy file under his left arm. He pushed the chair back in towards the table and made his way over to the old brown bar. The barman was nowhere in sight and that went for any other punters too. The empty coffee cup was the sole trader at the bar.

Ed coughed loudly and placed the file on the bar, making sure it landed with a thud. A few moments passed but there was still no sign of the barman. Ed let out a small sigh… and found himself locking eyes with a lady in a painting above the fireplace. It was an old painting but her distinct eyes seemed to be staring right at him. Ed imagined that if he started to move around the room, her eyes would follow him.

He suddenly heard a short sharp scrape and squeaking noise behind him. Ed darted round as his eyes flickered the area.

His chair… the chair he was sitting on… was out from the tab–

SMASH!

Ed jumped slightly as he turned back around to see the coffee cup and plate shattered all over the shale tiled floor. The barman walked out, leant over the bar and then looked at Ed's file. He shook his slowly from side to side, as his face went flushed.

He glared at Ed.

"That wasn't–"

"Right, that's €2.50," the barman responded gruffly.

Ed felt his heart beating faster than it should have. As he handed over the money and took the file, he offered, "It really wasn't my fault, don't know ho–"

"Don't worry, leave it," the barman said sternly looking at Ed with laser like eyes.

Ed's face went red. He turned on his heel as he decided to get away from the crime scene.

Out the front door and it was still bucketing down. He remained inside the inner door of the pub as he carefully let the folder and laptop bag drop down on the ground. He took out a cigarette, lit it, and was ever so happy to take that first drag.

As he watched the rain tumbling down, Ed noticed an old woman down the street to the right. She was standing out on the edge of the path looking upwards and downwards along the road. She was just in front of the shop. As Ed let out a puff of smoke, he watched as she strangely put her left foot out on the road and then took it back in quickly.

The rain died off suddenly and there she still stood, doing the same thing over and over. A group of teenagers walked past her. She looked at them, but they kept walking. Ed placed the laptop bag strap back over his head to the other shoulder, crouched down and slowly managed to get the folder back up under his left arm. Now Ed saw a middle-aged couple holding hands and passing near the old woman. Surely…

But no.

The old woman looked sullenly on as they passed, giving her no heed.

"Ridiculous," said Ed as took one more drag and threw the fag down on the ground. As Ed glanced back up while killing the fag with his foot, the old woman was looking straight at him.

Ed's head retreated into his shoulders and his throat tightened up. Busted!!

She gave Ed a large smile and a little wave. Ed responded immediately with a small smile and a little wave and started walking towards her. She looked even smaller the closer he got. She had plain brown shoes, followed by tights that met an equally light brown dress, just beyond her knee. A dark green jacket went down nearly as far as her dress. Her head was covered in a light pink shawl, grey hair escaping at the front. She had very light make up on.

Ed reached her.

"Sometimes you need someone to help you cross," she offered in a slow but chirpy Irish accent.

"Of course!" said Ed. "Not a problem! Shall I take your bag?"

"No, you're fine," she said. "I don't have far to go."

"Well, let me offer you my arm," said Ed as his gentleman mode kicked in.

"Thank you so much," she said as she wrapped her arm in his. Ed tightened his arm around hers.

"You have a very firm grip," she said.

Ed's brow creased as he saw that her jacket seemed perfectly dry.

He checked up and down the road. All clear. Ed took a step down onto the road. She moved slowly over with him. As they reached the path on the other side, she stopped him and looked back at the other side.

"Don't think you left anything there. Were you there long?" asked Ed.

"I think so… I can't really tell, but you're here now." She smiled at him.

As Ed walked down the path with her, two blokes walked by. One nearly knocked into her. They both gave Ed a strange look. Ed responded with his best 'go fuck yourself stare'.

"Are you sure I can't carry that bag for you?" Ed offered as he tried to distract the never ending stream of rude people they seemed to be encountering. All seemed to give them little room.

"No, it's all about balance you see… in the end."

She leaned to her right and Ed took the hint to turn right at the end of the road. A person was walking a dog on the other side of the street. It began whining and then barking at them.

The owner had to do what he could to restrain it. "Sorry man!" the bloke shouted at Ed.

Forget me, thought Ed. He was about ready to get the whole bloody village to apologise to the woman!

They carried on, soon reaching an old, impressive looking fountain. It was a tall grey granite square block with four small basins on each side. The basins seemed full of moss, weeds and putrid looking rainwater. Above each of them was an open mouthed brass lion. From the warn-out plaque, it was built in 17 something or other. Ed couldn't make out the date exactly.

"The water hides strange things," said the old woman.

A strange noise came from one of the brass lions before water started gushing out of its mouth, into the basin below.

Moving on a few more paces and the woman stopped in front of a blue door. Ed immediately noticed that the two ground floor windows on the front of this grey house were boarded up.

"Er..are you sure–"

"I'm back now…," she almost whispered.

"Do you have your keys?" asked Ed.

Ed noticed she was just staring blankly at the door. She had a deadpan expression on her face. Mouth slightly ajar.

Ed leaned across and banged the knocker on the door. Nothing.

He banged two more times. *Jesus,* thought Ed. *Don't tell me that her relations aren't home now!* Maybe she had no one?

As Ed leaned down to the letter box shutter to have a go at shouting in that, he heard a hushed distant voice, "*I… can… make… it…from… hereeee….*"

A large gust of wind rushed by Ed. A loud bang sounded from his left side. Ed turned and saw that a café sign must have come loose and was collapsed on the road.

Ed turned back to…

Where?

She was gone!

Ed looked around. No one. Not her or anyone. His face was flushed and he felt strangely embarrassed somehow.

Chapter 11

They had been on foot for an hour, maybe more. From the start every man made sure to place his feet carefully – there could be no sound.

Neha heard the cacophony of animals in the trees and forest die away. It was dead silent now as they crept slowly forward, moving vines with their hands and continuing to place their feet cautiously between the myriad of tree roots at their feet.

Karo stopped ahead. As Neha caught up, the dense foliage gave way to a strange plateau of cracked grey rock. Although it seemed flat on its surface, thick cracks permeated throughout the rock making ad hoc squares and rectangles. It was if a sky spirit had slapped its hand upon the ground in anger.

A slow eerie wind, whistling in their ears, was the only sound now.

They moved across the surface at pace but with care, keeping one eye on their footing. As they reached the other end, the rock moved downwards between two high banks of earth. A slight mist covered their feet as they slowly walked forward between the two banks.

Karo raised his spear forward and Timku kept an arrow slung on his bow. Neha and Paka got the idea, Paka raising up his machete and Neha holding his blow pipe in the same manner as Karo did his spear.

It seemed deathly quiet here, calm… dead calm. But the light had dwindled and it seemed far gloomier here.

Despite his soft footed moves forward, twigs cracked at Neha's feet, no matter how he distributed his weight. Whatever was gathered below felt fairly uneven too.

Karo raised his right arm upwards sharply and they all stopped. Something was ahead in the gloom…

Neha took a moment and looked downwards. A gaping hole greeted him, an eye socket from a skull looked at him from the mist below. Neha looked to his feet and the feet of the others. The mist moved away revealing the ground filled with bones and skulls.

Karo crouched down slightly, indicating with his hand that they should move forward. The banks on either side moved sharply, left and right, and seemed to increase in size into a wide circle, as another entrance appeared at the other side of this place.

Neha put a hand on Karo's shoulder, making him stop. The mist did not seem as prevalent here. The earth was rough and highly disturbed. Even in the gloom, Neha recognised the glimmering pieces of gold at his feet, spread out all over this deep depression.

The pendant Volo gave him began vibrating around his neck.

As Neha put his hand to the pendant, he saw the witch's lair ahead.

*****

Maria crossed a shaky wooden bridge, over a small river. Downstream, she could see large timber logs stretched out horizontally, piled on top of one another. The fuckers had dammed it, she realised. Resourceful shits.

Maria strode on into the clearing ahead.

She saw what looked like a large drilling machine in front of her. Its imposing size blocked her view of the rest of the clearing. But just to its left there was a large deep trench dug into the ground. The trench appeared to go on past the machine.

Maria took the camera hanging from her neck and opened the shutter. She began taking photos, the 'clicking' sound echoing off the machine in front of her. Walking slowly forward, she reached the edge of the trench and went down on one knee, aiming the camera down. There was that unmistakable shimmer… golden specks amongst the dirt. She took more photos.

She stood and moved the camera around her while she kept snapping. The whispering wind danced amongst her hair. At times it felt like fingers touching her head as Maria continuously propped her hair back into place.

As she was turning, she locked eyes with a man sitting at the side of the drilling machine. Dead eyes… they were dead eyes that stared at her. His throat had been slit. Stepping to her left she saw the rest of the clearing and the dead and mangled bodies that lay there.

She let out a scream as she dropped her camera and moved her hand to her mouth.

Maria heard a creaking noise behind her. She did a 180 degree turn. Her mouth fell open as she saw a huge black jaguar on the wooden bridge. It was staring right at her, with its head pointed but dipped just below its hunched shoulders. It had just taken another step forward as she saw it.

The creature straightened now – it was huge, much bigger than any other jaguar she had seen. It bared its teeth at her and started a low growl. Maria took a step back. But as she did, the jaguar broke into a fast walk towards her.

Maria scrambled backwards now.

The creature started running; she turned and did the same. Maria let out a scream as she busted a lung to keep ahead. The creature snarled behind her and the sounds of its paws thudded louder and louder.

Maria heard a shout, and something whistled past her head. She looked back and an arrow vibrated in the side of a crate, but the jaguar deftly dipped beneath it.

As Maria tired, she heard something else whistle in the air. It made a huge thud as it belted the ground behind her. She risked a look backwards as she heaved oxygen in an out.

It was a spear.

But the jaguar didn't go underneath this time. Instead, it sprang its front paws upwards onto the shaft and in an instant had carried its back paws up also, completing the cat like jump over the spear.

The creature skidded to a halt as a man stood in its way.

It was Karo, Maria realised.

He stood in front of the creature, a long knife in hand. The creature leapt at him but Karo tilted his body, absorbing the jaguar's blow as they both fell and rolled onto the ground. Karo lay on his back, one forearm up and barely holding the jaguar's neck upwards. Karo thrust the knife with his free arm into the creature's side… again and again. But although the jaguar winced in pain, its jaws made steady progress down to Karo.

Maria heard her heart beat in her ears. She ran to the spear and yanked it out of the ground. The sound of Karo's scream and the jaguar's came at once. As Maria looked up, she saw Karo had managed to roll away. But blood gushed out from a gaping wound in his neck. The creature had the knife sunk into its side, the hilt jutting out. It was getting back to its feet.

Maria reckoned they were twenty feet away from her now. She positioned herself, putting her left leg forward, and planted her feet. She raised the spear up with her right arm and brought the tip of the spear point to her outreached left hand. She lined the creature up as it was about to pounce at Karo once more. She let loose and the spear sang through the air…

It hit the jaguar in its midriff as it jumped, knocking it to the side. The creature made a painful sound as it fell. It lay still then.

Maria took a millisecond to recover.

She sprinted to Karo. He was coughing up blood. She leant down and took his extended hand.

He looked at her, before his gaze moved upwards. "You," he spat. His eyes bulged. "You!" he said again, as if surprised. "You now… Maria," he whispered, as he ripped the tribal necklace from his neck, thrusting it at her.

She took it.

A long breath escaped his mouth just as his chest stopped moving. He stared upwards.

Maria held his hand for a moment more before placing it gently to the ground. She looked at the necklace she held in her hands. She heard a scuffing noise on the ground behind her. She turned.

Maria's body was stunned as she did a sharp intake of breath. Another fucking jaguar stared at her, baring its teeth. Patches of blood surrounded its mouth and one of its paws seemed bloody also. It had three distinct scrapes across its head. It growled. She trembled, as she slowly moved towards the spear. It lunged and she fell backwards. Getting up, she realised she had fallen into the trench. Ignoring the pain, she ran forward.

The jaguar landed behind her and started sprinting.

Maria saw the end of the trench ahead. She quickly reached it and patted the wall, looking for a way up. No way out, she realised. She turned as the creature pounced forward, clamped her eyes shut and shrieked. She put her arms out in front of her as she heard a strange noise overhead.

Then nothing…

She opened her eyes.

The jaguar's head slid to a stop at her feet, twitching uncontrollably as foam and blood gushed out of its mouth.

Maria let out a small shout as she kicked its body. Only then did she see the strange black dart protruding from its head. She turned and looked upwards. And there, above… was her father standing on the bank, still holding the blow pipe close to his mouth.

*****

Neha, Maria and Timku exchanged no words on the way back to the dead village. Neha carried Paka on his shoulders. Timku carried Karo. As they walked back into the village, a dusk light embraced the clearing. Purple clouds hung in the sky with a glimmer of sunshine at their edges.

Neha knelt and gently placed his dead son on the ground. Timku did the same and placed Karo beside Paka. Neha and Timku stood a moment and simply stared at them both. Neha, Timku and Maria all turned as they heard the cry of an eagle close by. It came from Volo's hut.

They all shuffled in that direction, Maria reaching Volo's hut first. She looked through the doorway and her head moved left and right. She glanced at the other two, shaking her head. The cry of the eagle came again, from behind Volo's hut.

Neha and Timku moved behind. There was the eagle, its head shifting erratically as it stood on the ground beside a body. Its beak prodded at the body as it stopped and stared at Neha. Volo had been mauled by some creature. His entrails were spread out of his belly. Claw marks were spread across his face.

Maria joined the two other men as silent witnesses.

The eagle flew up to the top of Volo's hut and sang its cry again, the sound echoing around the village.

As their eyes followed the sound, they looked upon the ground. It was still covered with the dead and decaying bodies. Flies buzzed about them in the dusk air. Neha walked slowly to the middle of the clearing. He picked up a body and threw it upon another. Timku walked over, head down, and copied his action with another body close by. Maria followed suit.

They piled the dead in silence. Maria remained stony faced when adding a small baby to the pile. Night time came quickly. All three of them retched from time to time.

Timku lit some fires in the pits around the village. The sound of the night forest was a light distraction to their task, a normality returning to this forsaken place.

They began to move the last three bodies to the pile. Maria helped Neha with Paka. Timku and Neha lifted the disgorged remains of

Volo. Neha placed Karo gently down beside Paka. The two of them sat beside each other.

This morbid deed completed, they took on some water, rubbing blood and other human discard off them. Timku placed logs and branches around the edge of the dead pile. Neha lit three torches and handed one to Maria and then Timku. All three then moved to different ends of the pile.

Maria wasted no time in lighting the logs on her side. Timku soon followed. Neha then lit his side, in front of his son and his brother.

Maria silently walked over to her father, grabbed his hand and shoved Karo's tribal necklace into it. He grasped it in his hands and examined it for a time.

Timku arrived beside them. They stared at the lighting wood momentarily before Neha started to hum slowly. He then began to mutter words as he looked to the eyes of the sky spirits above. The fire gathered pace. He closed his eyes and sang.

Maria noted the pace and volume went back and forth, up and down with the dance of the flames themselves. Its mournful tone was notable. As the fire engulfed the top of the pile, Neha's song slowed and waned; then stopped.

They watched as smoke billowed upwards now, up and up into the night sky. There was no noise, except from the crackling and spitting fire.

The three then found a small hut, lay down and collapsed asleep.

But Neha's dream was not his own…

Two great eyes stared at Neha. Two great eyes with painted circles. They disappeared. He heard singing, yena yana ho…yena yana ho..nee yan..nee yan ho.

A wind blew and a great snake made a journey to a faraway land. Darkness again. Paka emerging, taking the knife from his chest and pointing, giving a war cry…

The place…the place…was far. Grey cracked rock strewn across the land…clouds moved at pace overhead. A clap of thunder…a cackle…

Paka pointing again…the vision of the landscape once more…

"A sacred structure disturbed," whispered the voice of Volo…

The image of a large stone falling…

Neha woke covered in sweat.

The bright sun beamed through the top of the hut. Neha stood as the other two woke also. They walked out to a forest full of noise around them. The fire for the dead was still alive but would probably burn out soon.

Timku announced he was staying. Maria tried to argue with him, but her father cut across her. He shook Timku's hand, exchanged a few words and strode off.

As Neha walked by Volo's hut a breeze shook the charms hanging from the doorway. Neha stopped, and then he walked through the entrance. As he peered around the gloomy hut a sack on a table caught his attention. Neha walked over and opened it. He first pulled out one smoking pipe, the end stuffed with Volo's mixture. Next, he pulled out a small pouch. As Neha looked inside, he saw it contained the remaining blue ants, and leaves of the near luminous green plant. Neha had still seen no evidence of either in the nearby forest. Neha pulled out a furry black garment from the sack that he had seen only recently. He closed his eyes as he pressed one hand across his mouth. He took a moment… to consider how wrong he and Volo had been.

Finally, Neha found his cloak of feathers inside. He wrapped all the items up in his cloak and slung them in the sack. He then picked up the sack and threw it over his shoulder, walking towards the doorway. Neha turned, before leaving, and took one more look at the empty hut. A sense of fear took him, worry that without Volo, all was lost – all at an end. An existence had lived but died with him. Neha's understanding of the Shaman world simply was not enough… for the journey he might make.

*****

Neha and Maria took a number of weeks to get back to the sand spit. Maria led the way, a bandana covering her head, with her hair tied up in a ponytail. She hacked mercilessly through vines and branches. Neha offered few words. Maria asked about Paka's death. He said little about it. He couldn't tell her, so he didn't tell her. In any case, Neha noted that Maria thought she had survived something entirely different. Maria kept talking about 'miners'. He worried for her. Especially after what he had experienced.

They finally arrived back in Neha's village in the morning. The village was peaceful… quiet. In some respects, it brought Neha a sense of calm, but he felt an underlying regret too. As he stood at the doorway to his hut, he could hear the gentle noise of a Cotinga bird from the trees nearby. The sound of the forest crickets was also soothing.

He could just stay, he realised… stay, live on his own. No people. He would like that.

But then the dream told him otherwise. Paka's war cry reverberated in his head… his soul. Neha's dream of Paka continued, his war cry whirring around his head as he woke each morning. He pushed his hands away from his doorway. What to do!?

Neha walked to the river. The tidal flow led its choppy waters at a small rush to his right. He soon found Maria at the riverside. She was on her knees, trying to get some of her contraptions to work. Neha stared down river.

An eagle appeared, soaring down from the sky, skimming the waters. It looked over to Neha and cried. Neha realised it was 'the eagle', Volo's eagle! It soared away up river. It carried on flying… against the tide.

"It flies against the tide, Maria!" said Neha exuberantly. "We cannot refuse this omen!"

Maria gave no response. She was still crouched down examining her gear.

“Maria, we must go–”

“Yes, Father, I know. This place is no longer for you.” Maria turned to look at a billowing smoke cloud just beyond the treeline.

“We must avenge Paka,” said Neha.

Maria stood, placing her hand on his shoulder. She spoke softly. “We will go after the miners, Father. When FUNAI see my report, we will seek justice.”

“No, Maria. What we fought was not the miners, it was something more. What killed Paka has escaped or been released in a faraway land.”

“Oh, Father–”

Neha turned slightly and stared at her.

Maria could hardly handle the glare. His eyes were stern but glistened as if on the edge of tears. He gently took her hand and put it to his heart. “Do this for me Maria.... or Paka will not rest.”

Maria hugged her father. It was the first hug she had tried for. He slowly put his hands around her. She closed her eyes, feeling something she never had.

“Okay, I will help you. Where is this place you want to go?”

“My dream showed me a grey, rocky, mountainous cracked landscape… far away.”

Maria released her father. *That could be anywhere,* she thought. “Come on, let’s go, Father.”

They gathered their belongings.

As they got to the edge of the village, Neha didn’t look back. He was invigorated, invigorated with a thought…

A cold thought.

Revenge.

*****

"Search Maria, Search!"

Maria switched on her large, outdated desktop computer. It had taken another three weeks to get back to civilisation. They had only arrived back in her apartment an hour ago.

"So where, Father, is the place you saw?"

"A grey, mountainous, rocky, cracked land."

"That could be anywhere in the worl–"

"I will know it when I see it," Neha replied.

Maria shrugged. Hopefully, if she at least found an image it might help him get it out of his system. She got into Google images and typed in the words her father had mentioned. Various images came up. Neha's head hung at her shoulder.

He pointed at each one, touching the screen, "No… No… No… No." She scrolled on.

She flicked onto the next page. The 'No's' and prodding of the screen carried on. Maria saw that the images on page three were starting to repeat themselves. Then at the bottom…

"Where is that?" asked Neha.

Maria clicked on the picture. It was grey cracked rock all right. A small hill in the picture showed different terraces of grey rocks. A blurb came up at the bottom – '*The Burren, one of the finest examples of a glacio-karst landscape in the world.*'

Maria typed the phrase 'the Burren', into Google images. A lot of images came up on the screen.

Neha slapped Maria on the shoulder. "That's it! We go there! Get us there, Maria."

Maria noted that the Burren was in Ireland. Hardly next door. She scrolled down the images slowly as she considered how to say no to her father. She had just passed one image, when she moved the mouse back to it sharply. The symbol behind two men shaking hands in the photo; no… it couldn't be…

She clicked on the image. '*Mendoza Mines makes significant investment in Clare, Ireland.*'

Maria stood up. "Yes, Father. We are going!"

Chapter 12

The light was dying fast. The sun was now just a thin red hue in the west, like the dying embers of a fire. Ed wasn't ready to go home. He needed to process this, clear his head. He found himself crossing the road once more. He saw a dim light on the wall to his left. It was a pub. 'Coughlin's' the green sign said, as Ed drew closer.

He walked through the outer doorway and was met by two timber doors with frosted pane glass. 'Push' the tiny metal signs on the door frame said. Ed did just that. A small room greeted him. The bar itself was at a right angle, hugging two halves of the room on the right. A slow Irish air played gently from a speaker in the far top corner.

The bar carried on down a slender passage on the left. A more private room looked to be down the back. Ed could see the flicker of flame dancing on the white brushed wall back there. Ed saw a number of free square cushioned black stools in order around the bar. He took one on the right side. It seemed close to the window and he could watch the bay as the twilight turned to night outside.

A few old farmer types seemed scattered around the pub. One was shuffling his way slowly down the left passage carrying a pint of stout. Two other farmy looking fellas occupied two stools around a barrel on the far side of the room.

An old woman appeared from a doorway behind the bar.

Ed went ashen as for a minute, thinking it was the woman who had disappeared near the door. As she asked him what he wanted, Ed took a few moments to register, confirming internally that this was not the woman he had helped cross the road.

But she looked bloody similar.

"Eh, pint of Guinness, please," said Ed as the barwoman seemed to sigh in relief.

As she started pouring his pint, the array of whiskey bottles stacked up on the two walls of the bar caught Ed's attention. 'Jameson'…'Powers'…'Paddy'…'Tullomore Dew'…'Middleton'.

"Can I have an 'Irish Mist' as well, please?"

The bar woman nodded without looking back at Ed.

As she delivered the whiskey, Ed took a gulp. The pint soon followed. Before the bar woman walked away, Ed said, "Impressive fountain you have outside. Seems to come to life of its own volition."

"Hasn't worked in years," she said as she shuffled off.

A wind suddenly tumbled down the empty chimney to Ed's right. An empty crisp packet floated off the bar in front of him. Ed thought he could hear the sound of hooves outside and the whinny of a horse, but on looking out the window he could see nothing but inky blackness.

One of the double doors to the bar made a loud noise as it shot open. A wind harried through the pub. Everyone looked at the doorway. Ed saw a man standing there. He wore a black top hat and long black cloak. He held a riding crop. His black boots were muddied as were his tight beige trousers. His cheeks were covered by thick, long, brown coloured locks. His cheeks were red. The sign of someone who spent most of his time outside.

As the man walked into the pub and strode up to the bar, Ed watched him but no one else seemed to. He had left the door open, Ed realised, as he saw other people in the bar still watching the doorway. They paid no heed to this strange looking man.

"Bar keep… bar keep!" the man shouted as he whacked his riding crop onto the bar. Ed noticed he seemed flustered as he looked around the place.

Ed saw that two patrons were standing by the doorway now. They seemed to be examining the door that was still open. They looked at the hinges. *The weirdo didn't shut the door,* thought Ed. *Just shut the thing and get over it.* This guy clearly would use that to fuel his mad performance. Be harder to get rid of him.

The two patrons shut the door and sat down.

"Bar keep!" the man shouted abruptly as Ed turned back to him.

The old woman who served Ed appeared from a doorway behind the bar. She casually shuffled in front of the man and started stacking some glasses under the bar.

"I need water and fodder for my horses!" he said with desperation in his voice.

The woman carried on with her task. Didn't even make eye contact.

"Woman… did you hear what I said?!"

The woman finished her task and walked back towards the doorway.

The man cursed under his breath and looped around. "The coach for Kinvara and Galway will be departing shortly," he announced to the bar. "One guinea to join now."

No takers, thought Ed, as no one said a thing. Ed shook his head briefly when the man looked to him, turning back towards the bar quickly.

"Young man!"

Ed didn't turn.

"Young man!"

Ed groaned internally as he turned towards him.

"Is there a blacksmith nearby?"

"No," said Ed. "You have no customers here… time you moved on," he added as he lightly slapped him on the back.

Ed was offering nothing more to this performance artist. He expected him to produce a pigeon from his top hat or a bouquet of flowers from his sleeve at any moment. The man instead gritted his teeth and went towards the door. Another wind rushed through the doorway as the man yanked the door open. He didn't shut it behind him. Ed soon heard the crack of a whip and the sound of horses clip clopping away. Must be some festival on or something, Ed reckoned.

One of the patrons stood and slowly shut the door, checking he could hear the click of the door as it shut. He waited a few seconds and watched it.

The old woman was back behind the bar.

"That door been giving you trouble, Teresa?" said the man by the door.

"The winds been blowing it open for weeks now," she responded lightly.

Ed chuckled at that dry wit. He caught her attention and mimed his order for the same again. The pint was nice, and the Irish Mist helped cloud his mind. Ed thought he noticed one or two people giving him a strange look, but he thought nothing of it.

A man sitting on the longer stretch of bar to his left looked straight at Ed. Ed hadn't noticed him previously.

"You drinking for one, or for many?" He smirked at Ed as the bar lady put his pint and whiskey down in front of him. The guy sounded American.

Ed chuckled. "Partially for me," Ed said as he downed the last of his older pint.

The man walked over and placed his pint down beside Ed, sitting down thereafter. He was taller than Ed, balding slightly, so he went with a shaven head. He was probably ten years older than him, give or take. Broad bloke. Looked after himself. Well dressed. He introduced himself as 'Brian'. Ed returned the courtesy.

They leaned back in their respective chairs and started to shoot the shit. It was the easy listening conversation, non- intrusive… at first. Then Brian asked him what he did. Ed flew into the story, handbrake off. As he did, he noticed that Brian said nothing back; his eyes examined Ed through small slits, his lips pursed. As Ed finished up with what started to feel like an interview, he lobbed the ball back over the net, asking Brian what he did.

Brian began talking and said a lot about nothing. He was into a lot of stuff. As Ed asked him what he was working at, three times, Brian answered – but then again, he didn't. Ed didn't ask the fourth time, fearing the man may actually have no job. He could be making him uncomfortable, Ed realised.

Brian got the attention of the bar lady. The pub seemed livelier now. He made a joke of not ordering a pint for the 'alco' in the corner. "You don't need any more!"

Ed laughed and nodded, his will power failing him once more. The bloke put out two fingers and the bar woman had two Guinness flowing.

Brian burped and made for the toilet. When he returned and saw his Guinness waiting for him, he slapped Ed on the back and sat back on his seat. As he took a swig of his pint, he kept his eyes on it, offering, "Yeah, I did that archaeology game for a while… you know."

Ed had never heard it referred to as 'a game' but nodded, letting him continue.

"Not much money in it."

"It's interesting though and–"

"To a point," said Brian forcefully as his face closed up into a grimace. "Eventually… you gotta look after you; you know what I mean?"

Ed drew a blank.

Brian gave a small laugh. "Make something for you…" He spread his hands to his sides. "Make some 'real' money for yourself!"

Ed gave a slow sigh. "Well, we could all use some more money. Were you doing some archaeological work around here?"

Brian got off his stool, downed his pint and moved around to Ed's chair. He slapped his right hand on Ed's right shoulder and grabbed his left arm with his left hand.

Ed couldn't wait for the touchy feely part of the evening to end.

"I am doing some private work around here, Ed," Brian said in a hushed voice as he glanced around the bar. "If you want to actually discover something and make some pocket money, you contact me."

With that Brian stuck a card into Ed's top jacket pocket. "Give me a call… I could use the help."

Ed was about to speak but Brian quickly followed with, "And you could use the money!" He chortled and smacked Ed on the back. "See ya later," he said as he turned on his heel.

Ed watched as Brian tried to exit the pub. Several people wanted to talk to him, though. He seemed like a minor celebrity to some as he shook their outreached hands, a politician to others as he listened intently, nodding away. He shared a lairy laugh with three old men at one table before finally exiting.

As Ed looked around, he realised how unpopular he seemed. No one looked in his direction. The bar woman didn't even look down his way. Ed stood up, grabbing his file, and stood out into the night air. It was fresh. His ears tingled with the cold as his head sank into his shoulders like a turtle head into its shell. He wished he had a hat!

The neon sign for 'Mr. Kebab's' shone in the dark street ahead, like a guiding star to a lost ship. How a Mr. Kebab had made it to this remote village was anyone's guess. Ed gravitated towards it without a second thought. He ordered a quarter pounder, curry cheese chips and a large can of coke. He slurred his words but the chipper man understood the order anyway, having clearly mastered the language of the 'drunk'.

As Ed gorged on his meal and pounded his coke, his sober mind told him he had just eaten the main causes for bowel cancer, heart disease and diabetes; nonetheless, his stomach seemed satisfied with his intake of fat.

Ed took off at a brisk walk back towards his cottage.

There seemed to be no one in the village now. As he walked the main road, a solitary car ghosted by.

Ed strode home, watching the stars blinking like eyes in the sky above. He reached the small road that would take him to his cottage. A wind rushed past his ears. He stopped… as he thought he heard voices. They whispered around him…

What were they saying?

That he was drunk, he quickly decided. He laughed.

Ed reached his front door and got inside. He dumped the file and his laptop on the table in the sitting room. Straight to the kitchen then and he boiled the kettle. Having made his cup of tea, he sat down at the sitting room table, swaying from left to right in his chair. He took a sip and placed it back down. Something white caught his attention.

Brian's business card was sticking out of his jacket pocket. He took it out and read it. '*Brian Flannery, Archaeological Consultant B.A., M.A. and PHD.*' Ed put it down and grabbed his work file from the across the table. He went through it and examined the different folders. He found the other business card he was looking for.

He held the business cards side to side. They were exactly the same. It seemed his predecessor, Aine, had known this exuberant man.

As Ed stopped swaying in his chair he straightened up, evening his keel, and felt like a ship set for a new course.

*****

Ed didn't take much time in getting to sleep. He awoke to a sound of tapping. As he sat up in bed, it stopped. He was surprised he could see.

He saw a stream of light coming in through the frame of his doorway. The light illuminated the ceiling around his doorway somewhat. He considered getting up and turning it off. *Fuck it*, he thought. He relaxed and was just closing his eyes when something moving blocked the light, like a person crossing the room?!

Ed stood up. He heard the wind rustling the trees outside. He felt cold.

He opened his bedroom door. The door to the main room was wide open and the main light was on. He walked into the hallway and on into the main room. He could see the other doors were all open and all the lights were on in the bathroom, the kitchen and conservatory. The windows were all open too, as the curtains danced and fluttered in the night wind.

Suddenly, all the lights flickered as a howling wind surged through the windows. The doors slammed one by one; the main door in front of him was the last to slam in his face. The lights all switched off at once. The wind stopped.

It was perfectly silent except for the sound of Ed's thumping heartbeat in his ears. He walked back into his room. Picking up his mobile, he checked the time – 3:00 a.m.

He threw his phone back on the bed.

Creeping back to the main door of the living room, he slowly grabbed the door knob, twisted it, and yanked the door open. Switching on the light revealed a calmer scene. The doors remained closed. No other lights appeared on. The curtains seemed static.

Ed quickly closed the windows he found open. He checked each room and switched the lights on and off in each room to make sure he wasn't going mad. He stood in the centre of the living room then with his arms at his sides, pointed outwards. He bit his bottom lip.

No answers tonight, he decided. He went back to bed.

Chapter 13

Maria was suspended without pay. FUNAI was closed pending a judicial review. The Government had a choke hold on them. Her part time journalist job would cover very little, although her editor was interested in her doing a weekly tourist article of her proposed Irish trip – '*Maria Estavez in the Emerald Isle*.'

Maria wasn't sure how they would get to Ireland. She could afford the flights, but from there, their accommodation and daily living expenses would last them a couple of days, at best. So she went back to her parents' house. She had rung to explain she needed some money from the off. "For a special mission," she had said.

Her mother sounded enthusiastic. Maria would not dare tell her over the phone.

As was customary in their household, Maria waited until they had finished dinner and were on their third glass of wine before raising the topic. She told the story as best she could, spending as little time on her father… as she could. Maria made sure to link in the journalistic work, too.

She watched as her mother's pleasant demeanour waned. Her face became stony. She stopped eye contact and stared at her wine as she swirled it in her glass. As Maria finished the story, she emphasised that it may bring some closure to her father. Her mother yawned and excused herself. Maria carefully looked at her step-father. He simply stared forward. Maria rubbed her hands softly together and stared downwards.

A minute passed.

She felt a hand being placed on hers.

"I'll do it," he said. "I'll cover the cost. Your father has been through a lot. He sounds like a decent man caught in an unforgiving world."

Maria thanked him profusely. He responded with a half joke. "It's your wedding fund anyway… and it doesn't look like you are letting anyone walk you down the aisle soon."

Maria blushed at that. Her stepfather suggested she leave. He would tell her mother. He wanted to do it now.

Maria gave him a hug and a kiss. As she left, she prayed they would still both be married by morning.

*****

This fishing village was the strangest and busiest that Neha had ever seen. It was enclosed in this giant hut. Everyone seemed to be rushing back and forth carrying their cargo on strange small metal wagons. There were types of people here from many different tribes that he had never seen before. Some had skin lighter than his, or darker. But he refused to be daunted by this. Maria had explained it would be different. This was all part of crossing this great lake called a 'sea'.

*****

Maria drew a breath. So far so good. They had arrived at Guarulhos International Airport, São Paulo, and thankfully no planes were evident in the sky. It was a miracle that her father had not seen the ones overhead over the last three days, but the cloud cover had helped. He had a grounded approach in any case, a greater connection to the land. Over the last couple of months he had not been overly daunted by life outside the forest. He had reacted to very little of what Maria feared a tribesperson may react to, although he had not left the apartment often.

Maria felt the sheer complexity of the journey ahead and explaining this to her father did not seem viable, especially the part about going in the air. So she had decided to lie, and lie well. This was to be a through the eye of the needle endeavour. It was get them on the plane and pray he would understand that it was the only way. She would tell him once he was buckled in and try to distract him with some magazines. She gripped her father's arm tightly as they reached the queue for security.

*****

Neha moved in line along with everyone else. He noticed that everyone had to walk through a doorway with no actual door. He then saw that some of them raised their arms horizontally to their sides. He saw his daughter place her bag onto the strange moving table beside them. It moved her bag and everyone else's into a small tunnel ahead.

Ahh… he realised that this was some kind of offering to the local tribes here. Gifts for the spirits. That was clearly what the empty doorway and small tunnel were for. When some of the people walked through, they would offer the blessing to the local Shamans beyond the doorway by stretching out their arms. Once they did this, the Shamans would then bless them with their hands and move strange grey wands about them. Well, he would make sure to respect their beliefs. He did not wish to offend anyone. Although, he would make sure to ask for his daughter's offering back. He would explain that her bag contained many sacred paints and powders with which she adorned her face daily.

Maria was getting nervous. Her father seemed in his own world as they reached the top of the security queue. She had made sure to check him for anything metal earlier. She walked through the security gate slowly and indicated that he should stay there.

Neha noted that his daughter failed to raise her arms in respect for the blessing. The Shamans in turn would not offer their blessing. How disrespectful of her. She may have been from the 'city', but he expected more from her. He raised his eyes to the sky spirits and swore he would not make the same mistake.

Maria picked up her bag and turned to see her father staring at her with a scowl on his face. He walked through the gate and stopped. She watched in horror as her father first puffed out his chest and then raised his arms slowly upwards, until they were horizontal at his sides. The security guards began nodding their heads and waving him through, but he refused to move.

Neha stood waiting. He could not believe that they had refused his blessing, but then again, his daughter had refused theirs. Even more disappointing, she had picked up her bag without asking the local Shamans first. He was livid with her.

Maria could not help but put her hand over her mouth. The security guards had become angry as her father had not moved. They then insisted on a full thorough check to the side of the queue.

Neha could see that the Shamans were angry, but they gave him a special blessing anyway. He placed his palms together and bowed gently as he left them. His daughter smiled at them and said something in Portuguese. She pulled him off by the arm. The shouting match they then had eventually brought other men to them. They wore yellow coats and flat peaked black hats.

Having remonstrated and apologised to the police, Maria found their boarding gate. Her father could not look at her and the feeling was mutual. He sat in a chair and folded his arms. Maria stormed off.

Maria browsed the shops to calm down. When she returned, she found her father standing at the window, staring at the plane outside. He seemed deep in thought.

*****

Neha stared at this vessel outside. It was huge, bigger than any other boat he had seen. It was raised up by three long stilts from the ground. This maybe was to assist it getting in and out of the water. He guessed they went inside the long enclosed part above the stilts, but how would they get in? He spotted the giant diesel engines on the strange long sides. He had seen smaller engines on the boats near his village. He was sure this vessel reminded him of some creature he had seen…

Neha suddenly noticed his daughter beside him. He began to converse with her in Yine. “This is the strangest boat I have ever seen.”

Maria bit her lower lip. "It is reliable, Father, and it's very fast. It will get us to our destination." She sighed. "It's time to board... the boat."

"Very well, Maria," Neha replied. "I trust you."

Maria pretended to fix her shoulder length jet black hair and averted her gaze. She choked back the guilt and looked at him. His gaze now seemed penetrating.

"Hold this," Maria said, as she shoved her handbag into her father's chest.

"Why?!"

"I am getting our documents... for the boat."

Maria opened her handbag and started to root through it.

"How can you find the official boat documents in there?" said Neha, gruffly.

"Just hold the bag," Maria responded forcefully. "Got them!"

Maria held their passports. The bureaucracy that she had to go through to get his was without comparison. It had also taken an inordinate amount of time to obtain. A man walks out of the deep forest and in today's world it was as if he had never existed. She did what she had to; she flirted and handed over an envelope stuffed with cash.

Maria opened his passport and smiled. She showed him his picture. His face remained expressionless.

Neha exhaled slowly. "It tells you nothing of the soul."

Maria instantly snapped the passport shut and gritted her teeth. She grabbed him by the arm and joined the queue to board the plane.

Neha hated the way she was grabbing his arm today. She would grab his arm just under the elbow and lift it up as if he were a dead curassow bird caught after a hunt. He noted that another Shaman was in front of them. Maria showed him the boat documents and they moved down a tunnel. They reached steps to take them to the outside. They descended and came out into the sunshine.

Neha saw that stairs had been moved into position beside this craft. He could see a door open on it, above. This was how they would get in! Maybe the reason for the boat having this roof was that this 'sea' was wild and they would need protection. Neha joined yet another long line of people. The line moved slowly forward towards the door above.

He saw Maria had taken out that strange flat black object again. He saw others in the queue with them. Neha nodded in despair. They made sounds like crickets or chirped like birds and made other soul disturbing noises he could not place. People talked with them or bent their heads and slavishly looked at them. They seemed obsessed.

Maria said that the messages came from other objects in the sky, high up. But surely not the sky spirits?

Neha noted that the queue began to move, and they reached the stairs. As they went slowly up the steps, he looked for signs of the sea. He could not see any. Strange. Was this boat on long stilts awaiting a tide to wash in? He knew something about fishing and tides. Clearly, they were all boarding this craft too early. As they reached the top of the plane, Neha tried not to be distracted by the strange interior.

Another Shaman stood inside the door. Neha observed that her face held far more of the sacred powders and paints than his daughter's. He grabbed Maria's arm and asked her to ask the Shaman where the sea was. How long the tide would be? Did they need a hand pulling the vessel to the water? Maria went pale. She seemed to freeze and said nothing.

Neha knew he had to take control. He looked directly at the Shaman and said loudly the words for 'water' and 'ropes' in Portuguese. He made pulling motions. The woman stared back at him, mouth agape. Neha realised that the sheer complexity of this was clearly lost on her as it must have been on all the others. They could be sitting on this contraption for a long time.

Maria closed her eyes and put a hand to her face. She opened her eyes through her fingers. The air hostess looked flabbergasted. A very tall, bulky bald man stood behind Neha. He wore a grey suit and tie, large sunglasses, and carried a laptop bag. He suddenly shoved past Neha. No excuse me, no manners. He was just all business. Other people in the queue began to shove past Neha too.

Neha felt a hand on his right upper arm. It was the Shaman. She smiled at him and pointed to her right. Maria grabbed him by the wrist and led him in that direction.

*****

This lie was slowly exploding before her eyes, Maria realised... before she had time to detonate the truth. As they moved down the aisle, her father's lips were pursed and he was squinting. She found their seats and of all the people sharing the row it was Mr. Business. Maria looked around but the plane was packed. Mr. Business' sunglasses failed to hide his annoyance as Maria moved Neha in to the seat beside him.

Neha was surprised as Maria put him into the seat beside the big man who had shoved past him. He stretched across the big man with his right arm and tapped the small glass window with his forefinger. Neha was further exasperated and tried to tell the man that these holes were pointless unless they could get their oars in the water.

Maria saw the immediate discomfort of Mr. Business as her father leaned across him, banging his forearm into the man's chest. Mr. Business went red, and he snapped at her father. He reached for the laptop bag at his feet and ripped the laptop from it. He turned it on and plugged his earphones into it. He smacked the armrest downwards between them. Maria knew this couldn't continue – it was time.

*****

Neha had not expected this oaf's response. Such a disappointment as well as this big man would be needed if they had to use the oars. He restrained himself though as he saw the man take out another type of flat black object. It was the biggest he had ever seen, a more advanced device to contact the sky spirits, he imagined. The man began by hitting strange glyphs on the black object with his fingers. He then started to speak to no one while holding white objects on strings in his ears. Neha realised that this man was probably more disconnected to the here and now than the rest of the poor souls he had seen earlier. He nodded slowly as he considered this tragedy unfolding before him. He felt Maria grab his left hand. He turned towards her.

"Father, I am sorry but I must tell you something–"

"Do not worry, Maria. I have noticed the problem with the holes here and I have alerted the Shaman to the issue with the sea. We can do no more. Who knows what magic will unfold here before the sun sleeps." Neha nodded over to Mr. Business who was typing furiously on his laptop.

Maria continued, "I have not told you everything about–"

"Wait, be quiet. The Shaman is performing some final tribal prayer."

Maria looked down the aisle and saw the air hostess was doing the safety instruction. She had gotten to the part where she placed the life jacket over her head and then placed the whistle attached between her lipstick covered lips. Maria turned to find her father was leaning past her, eyes wide and mouth slightly parted in a small smile. "Father!" she said sharply but he didn't respond. He seemed enthralled. Maria rolled her eyes. Her father… the indigenous tribesman, her father… the Shaman, was still… just like every other man.

Maria shook her head and pushed her father backwards.

"Father, this is not a boat, this is a plane. It flies in the air… like a bird. It will take us up in the sky. It is safe and is the only way to get us to our destination."

As she finished, the plane started moving and Neha looked out the window. He saw the 'wing' outside. Spirits above… these people were going up in the air!

Neha looked at Maria. "How could you do this? You liar!"

Neha began to shout at his daughter.

Maria could not calm him down. She tried to apologise but he instead stood up and grabbed the headrest on the seat in front of him. He began shouting expletives in Yine. Mr. Business turned around and launched a tirade of abuse. Maria fired her own salvo back. They both ceased fire as the loud voice of the captain interrupted on the intercom.

Mr. Business stood, took off his sunglasses and began chewing on one end. His brow was creased as he glanced back and forth from Maria to Neha. He suddenly hit the button above for the air hostess, but she was already moving towards them. Her face revealed her disapproval.

Maria feared they would be kicked off the plane.

The air hostess reached them but before she could speak, Mr. Business stretched his large arm across Neha and Maria and pointed at her. “If you want this plane to fly, get us two gin and tonics now! Make his a double!”

She hesitated, but Mr. Business simply glared at her and pointed towards where the drinks cart should be. Remarkably, she raced back to get them.

Mr Business turned to Neha and placed one hand on his back. He looked at Maria and nodded. He slowly moved Neha into his seat as the air hostess arrived back with the drinks. Mr. Business grabbed the two of them and handed the bigger one to Neha.

Mr. Business coughed and caught Maria’s eye. Maria turned and faced her father.

“This potion will make you feel much better. It will help you get accustomed with the air.”

Neha muttered, “A blessing to the sky spirits.”

Maria nodded her agreement.

Neha took a big drink of his gin and then another. The plane had now reached the runway and was paused for take-off. Mr. Business reached into his bag and produced four tablets. He knocked two back with a swig of his drink. “Sleeping tablets,” he said out loud so Maria could hear. He placed two of the tablets into Neha’s palm. Neha swallowed both with another gulp of gin.

Without warning, the plane accelerated on the runway. Neha let out a shout. Maria held his left hand and Mr. Business held his right one. Neha’s eyes remained shut as the plane jutted upwards off the runway. As the plane took off, it veered right. Maria saw her father now looking out the window. He was babbling something in panic, but she could not hear because of the noise of the engines. Cloud cover blocked the view as the plane climbed higher. But the plane soon broke through the clouds, and blue light beamed through the window. Sunshine lit up a carpet of white cloud below.

Neha let go of Mr. Business’ and Maria’s hands and with a sense of awe slowly said, “We are with the sky spirits… this is truly magic!”

Some time passed. Maria was exhausted and slightly inebriated. She took a drink from her own magical potion, a vodka and cranberry juice. She swore that she would tell her father about their connecting flight before they landed at Heathrow.

She looked at the slumbering couple beside her; her father and Mr. Business. Her father’s head was planted on the large man’s shoulder. They snored in rhythm, back and forth. Old world meets new, Maria thought. Maybe they could coalesce after all!

She closed her eyes and drifted off.

Chapter 14

Ed had gotten to Gortlecka and parked the car at around 8 a.m. It was around a forty-five minute drive south of Ballyvaughan. He was unsure of how to start this job… so he just got out the door and picked a location.

The morning rush hour out on these roads consisted largely of delivery vans storming through backroads… hither and dither. The tourist season wasn't over and like the vans, Ed wanted to be out early before the hikers and walkers got out here mid-morning.

Ed stood out on the limestone plateau, map in hand. He was smack bang in the middle of the Burren National Park. He had one knee leaning up on a rock, while he scanned the area.

The sky mirrored the grey vista around him. Today's existence lay between a grey floor and a grey ceiling. The terrain looked like cracked skin. The scattered cracks amongst the rock seemed woven onto the landscape itself.

The vista was daunting for both the conscious and subconscious parts of the mind. For Ed, the terrain best resembled a scattered thought frozen in time. Although he realised he could not make any real sense of this landscape, his subconscious refused to let it go. In that sense the limestone panorama was draining, but captivating and beautiful, nonetheless.

Still, some kind of conclusion or solution was needed. The curt explanation below from his guidebook, '*the terrain was formed by glacial erosion*', was too straightforward.

Maybe that was what drew visitors back here. They, too, wanted to solve this feeling of mystery evoked by the rock. The rock… this place had a tone of ancient about it. Maybe that's what connected with people. It resonated with something hidden within them.

Ed dusted his hands together. There, maybe he had made as much sense of the illogical as possible.

He took on some water before he carried on navigating his way over the clints and grikes of the limestone rock. The grikes were the fissures amongst the limestone pavement. They created the clints in between – the islands of rock amongst a limestone sea.

Ed had spent the morning doing the part of this audit that he had absolutely no clue about – flower hunting.

Within the grikes, one found the rare wildflowers of the Burren. And there were a remarkable number of wildflowers that Ed had to locate. Ed's final report needed to include an update on the status of at least fifty species of rare Burren wildflower. What was their location? What was their density, etc.?

He spotted an 'early purple orchid'. The Burren was a haven for the orchid species of Ireland; 22 out of 28 types of the orchids located in Ireland were found in the Burren.

Ed took a photo of the flower on his phone and logged the time, date and location in his small journal. Finally, he took a sample of it and placed it carefully in a plastic bag from his rucksack. He had already bagged some March Dandelion and Fen Violet nearby, on the edges of Lough Gealain.

He spotted a yellow flower peeking its head out of a grike ahead. He examined his small flower guidebook. He had no clue what it was. He took a sample and photo anyway. Logged it in his journal. Mr. Google would help him figure this out later.

Enough of the flower power for now. Time to move onto the main event at this location – Mullaghmore Mountain.

As Ed made his way towards the mountain ahead, he confirmed to his logical self that it was, in fact, a mountain. From a distance, it looked like a giant stony humpback whale trapped within the rock. A wind whipped at his face, knocking back his hood. Cold morning air swept around his head.

Something caught his attention at the corner of his eye. He carried on walking as he looked in that direction. There was another hiker out on the plateau… some distance away. They wore a distinctive pink jacket with the hood drawn up. A dark void filled the front of the hood, hiding the face. Too far away to make out any other features, he guessed it was a woman by her size. She was standing still, facing his direction. She must be taking in the morning air and Mullaghmore 'whale' mountain, Ed thought.

He turned back towards the mountain as he reached its base. It was a two hundred metre slow burn ascent, but it had a well-worn, safe path to the top. The journey could be broken up as each terrace was reached and Ed made sure to stop and examine the changing landscape around him.

As he reached the peak, the clouds above had broken up and parts of the Burren landscape were lit up around him, while other parts remained in shadow. The Burren liked to reveal itself in some ways and stay hidden in others, he thought.

Ed saw the Neolithic cairn in front of him and this, he realised, was why he had gotten into Archaeology. The mound of large stones was probably more than 4,000 years old. It had lain untouched, unmoved, for all that time. It had survived the elements, storms, and man, but most crucially it had truly survived the test of time.

Most modern tombstones lasted a generation before they lost their message – lost their point. No message lost here though. The message was much simpler – we were here!

Archaeological structures, like this, connected the past and future. Structures like this were special, Ed reckoned. Why? Because they transcended time itself… connecting the dead with the living. He looked forward to checking the rest of the twenty or so cairns he would have to examine and report on.

Underneath, it was suspected that the ancient dead lay there. It had not been excavated. At least the locals had the sense here to leave it that way. Ed took out his phone and started snapping the cairn, slowing moving around it. Looked good. He would measure it in a–

A flash of pink…

Ed looked over, and there was that woman again. Blond strands of hair escaped her dark hood, floating in the breeze. She pointed.

"Are you all right?" shouted Ed.

No response.

She turned and started moving around the cairn. As Ed walked towards her, she moved just out of sight.

"Hold on! Wait up!" he shouted.

Ed reached the other side and scanned the top of the mound. She wasn't there. He stood there, his mouth slightly parted, his lips dry. His heart beat a little bit faster. Something else caught his attention now. It was a stone, a loose stone. He picked it up. Must have fallen–

Wait, there were more…

Ed rushed around to the next part of the cairn. "Fuck saaaake!"

Stones were sprawled out on the ground everywhere…

As Ed scanned the mound and the rocks around him, he reckoned almost a third of the mound was damaged on this side. What to do!? Did he fix it? Should he take photos? Who would he tell? Was it vandalism? Had a storm done this? Or, worse, had someone been snooping around this ancient site who shouldn't have? An illegal excavation?

Ed took as many photos as he could. He had a bad feeling. As he descended, he noticed a figure below.

It was the woman again. He waved at her.

She stood still, motionless. *This is getting really old*, thought Ed.

As Ed got down halfway, he crossed behind a boulder, blocking his view briefly. When he emerged on the other side, the pink woman had disappeared. "Fucking Houdini!" Ed grumbled. She definitely had something to do with this.

He walked back down to his car and retrieved his supply of tape, thin metal poles and two of his plastic covered 'closed' signs. He trudged back up to the top of Mullaghmore and cordoned off the site, placing the two 'closed' signs at each end of the trail.

He decided to press on to Mullaghmore's sister hill – Knockanes. He would check the cairn there too.

*****

He checked the cairn on top of Knockanes, and thankfully, it appeared to be undisturbed. No apparent damage done.

An hour later, he made it back to his car.

Ed looked at his map as he chewed on a sandwich. There was a concentration of wedge tombs on Roughan Hill. Parknabinnia and Creevagh Wedge Tombs were the best known, probably because they were in the best condition. Roughan Hill didn't seem too far away, located between the villages of Killanboy and Carran. He could drive back towards Ballyvaughan afterwards and do some work on the file.

"Let's go kick the rock tyres on these," said Ed as he started the car.

The drive was easy and the location of the Roughan Hill was well sign posted. Ed parked his car and got out. He climbed over the roadside wall, stepping into long grass. Ahead he could see Parknabinnia wedge tomb.

Two long grey stones, a few metres apart, sat sideways on the earth. On top, a square capstone lay with a tuft of grass sticking out above it. Two smaller flat stones blocked the entrances on either side. The overall structure stretched up to Ed's torso. He moved his hand slowly down the top of the capstone as he walked down it. The wedge tomb had stood here for some time. Constructed between 2,500 – 2,000 BC, it was from the late Neolithic period.

Ed got out his measuring tape. The wedge tomb was a good ten metres long. He checked around the wedge tomb as he started taking photos. The stones seemed fine. All seemed in order. The large tuft of grass on the capstone, together with the thick moss that lay in the edges of the tomb itself, were a good sign. It meant the tomb hadn't been disturbed.

Ed noted the orientation of the wedge tomb, pointing southwest. It was as if the ancients were trying to call each other. Maybe someone way across the Atlantic, he surmised. He would compare all of this information with Aine's notes in the file later.

Ed moved on to Creevagh wedge tomb. He walked down a muddy track for ten minutes, before he thought he could see the wedge tomb to his right. As he got closer, he felt uneasy. The structure was damaged…

He examined the picture of the Creevagh wedge tomb from his guidebook. There should have been an outer stone facing him. But it was nowhere in sight. As to the tomb itself, only one of the side stones remained. The others lay in a heap at the ground.

Ed saw a sliver of grey at the top of a small mound in front of him. He walked up to the top. It was another stone; the missing outer stone, he guessed. He looked down from the mound. There in front of him was an archaeological bomb site. He recognised the square and rectangular cuts instantly and hurried down the mound, grasping his camera.

He walked around the small green area, snapping photos. He had read from his guidebook that many of the wedge tombs here weren't in the best condition to start with. Many now looked damaged and beyond repair. The signs of excavation were clear.

Ed stood in one dig site as he took notes. He spent an hour documenting what he could. He then dashed back to his car, retrieving his tape, poles and 'closed' signs and cordoned off what sites he could.

It started to rain so Ed decided to call it a day. He started walking back towards his car once more.

As he passed Creevagh wedge tomb, he heard a shuffling behind him. Ed turned.

There in front of the tomb was a man… a man dressed in some type of warrior garb. He wore a tunic, helmet, had a sword at his side, and held a shield. He was paunchy and had a thick ginger beard. He looked at Ed and waved him back over.

"No, thank you," said Ed with a slightly raised voice as he carried on walking.

The man looked the other way then and put a horn to his mouth. It was as if he was pretending to blow it. No sound.

Ed quickened his pace.

Fucking lunatic! It was amazing what seclusion and the lack of a sex life did to some men.

Ed reached his car and got back into it. He had a lot to figure out. What a strange start to this. He tried to look on the positive. If this kind of stuff was reported up the line, they were bound to get the funding to fix it. A local campaign could be started too.

The only concern now was to shut the sites down properly and get some reinforced fencing in place. That was the niggling issue to sort now. He really didn't want to tell Deirdre the news yet. She struck him as the 'shoot the messenger type'.

Ed made the quick drive back to Ballyvaughan. He parked his car outside his cottage and retrieved his file. He decided to do some work on it while treating himself to a slow pint. He made the walk down to the village and tried to clear his head as he did. He was more than a bit perturbed by what he had seen earlier. This audit could be a lot more work than he had anticipated.

Ed soon reached O'Brien's pub and walked in. A welcome heat hit his face and the room held the hum of many chattering voices. The place was heaving. A roaring fire spat on the left. Seats looked in demand. He navigated his way to the bar. There was an outer layer of people before the bar itself could be reached.

Ed walked to the edge of the queue at the left corner and as a small space opened up, he shunted forward. He dumped his file and forearm down across the wooden surface to anchor his position. He was relieved that there was a different bar person on from last time. The barman took his order and that of two others. He poured two pints at once, while also turning and putting money through the register and grabbing some change.

The barman soon plopped his pint down, the creamy top of his Guinness overflowing the rim of the glass. Ed had the exact amount ready and the barman snatched the note, quickly moving to the next punter.

Ed retreated from the bar with his file underarm and a Guinness in hand. He found a mantel piece where he could lean his pint and elbow. Five people suddenly sat down in front of him, picking up instruments. They began playing folk music and as they got going, Ed couldn't help but tap his foot. The music was quick, exuberant. He couldn't identify all the instruments, just the violins, whistle and the guitar. Ed asked the man beside him, and he explained that the others were a drum called a 'bodhran' and the pipes were called 'uilleann' pipes.

As the band took a brief break, Ed got lucky at the bar again and got back into position with another pint. The band looked to a middle aged lady at the edge of their table. She closed her eyes. Her song lilted slowly to life and the room soon quietened down. The song soon carried the room and the room carried the song. The words were unknown, but it was poetry in anyone's language. As her song went up in pitch it was as if she was telling a story of the ages… a story for the ages. Then her voice lowered and her song gently drifted away…

Silence.

Ed was left with a feeling that he and the rest of the pub had all gotten out at the wrong bus stop… that the song continued off on its journey, elsewhere. There was a collective intake of breath before a rapturous applause filled the room.

Ed recovered by consuming at least a third of his pint.

"Tis like a spell, isn't it," said the man beside him. "Like a bit of magic!"

Ed felt a tug on his jacket. He looked around, then down. It was Nuala. "Hello, Nuala!"

"Ed, I need a favour," she said, slurring. "Follow me."

Without waiting for a reply Nuala shuffled off to the right side of the bar. Ed followed her, weaving around people as he went. He emerged just behind Nuala into a larger room out the back. People seemed ordered at square tables and each had an A4 sheet. A man with a microphone stood at the top.

"Ah, Nuala, you found someone!"

"Yes," she announced. "This is Ed."

With that Ed resigned himself to the fact he was now doing a table quiz. He followed Nuala to her table and saw another lady sitting there.

"Hello, I'm Sheila." She held a hand out to Ed.

"Ed," he said shaking her hand and sitting down. "Nice to meet you."

"It's table quiz night and we lost one or two bodies," Sheila responded.

"Well I'm okay at these, not amazing though," said Ed with a light smirk.

"Oh, don't worry… sure it's only a bit of fun."

The first few rounds of the table quiz passed by. Nuala insisted on buying the table round after round of drinks. She placed a note into Sheila's or Ed's hand and crushed their hands shut with hers until they took it. Sheila and Ed obliged by getting the drinks, although Ed made sure on at least one occasion to secretly buy the round, giving Nuala back her cash in change instead.

Ed, Nuala and Sheila also had some nice chats in between the table quiz rounds. Ed discovered that Sheila was a local who lived up on Hags Head and cared for her aunt who had had a mild stroke. She looked after a holiday home too. When he revealed he was doing an audit of the park, she was incredibly supportive, interested and helpful.

When Ed discussed some of the difficulties he might face, especially with sites on private land, she started reaming off locations and surnames of owners. She said that he should pop up to her house with the file and they could go through it together. She knew some of the owners first hand.

Ed was delighted. As he was thanking her profusely, downing pint number… erh… unsure, a hush came around the room. The man with the mic began to give some of the answers of the first few rounds. Many hands were slapped to foreheads while others couldn't hide their glee. Exuberant chuckles came from some tables. As the current order of teams was spelled out, Ed couldn't help but slam the table. They were sixth.

Ed quickly got another round in, and the chatter died down. The next round was about to start. Each table began scrutinising the next. Ed and another lady from the team just ahead of them were now locking eyes more than once; this was on…

"Next round, everyone," came the mic man. "The Burren."

Ed scribbled down the answers as Nuala and Sheila spat out them out. They were a fountain of information. He found himself covering the page with one hand. He spotted a bloke coming back from the toilet… again. The man's eyes were on 'quick scan' of each table face. One lady even piped up that he shouldn't be allowed 'up and down' like this.

The mic man agreed and asked that he take a break from this round. Brief controversy ensued as his team were very vocal in their dissent. But the man with the mic was in charge, he knew the rules, and crucially… he was also sober.

The next round came, 'geography'. Sheila was incredible at this round. How she knew the name of that lake in Russia?

As the final leader board was called out, the man with the mic had trouble keeping the lunatics in the asylum calm. But Ed, Sheila and Nuala shared a smile. They were now 5th. Moving up in the world. The first three spots got prizes.

As the last round was commencing, Ed found himself locking eyes once more with the team just ahead of them.

The last round was announced, 'sport'.

Nuala and Sheila looked directly to him and smiled. The team just ahead of them wore aghast expressions on their faces – all women. Ed concentrated in the same manner as his Archaeology final exams. Half the questions were about English premiership football. As the questions rolled out, his inebriated brain did its best.

Relief and tiredness swept through the room. The final results would be in five minutes. Nearly the entire room took a toilet break.

As Ed was approaching the toilet door, the woman from the other team was coming out. She didn't hold the door open for him, staring past him.

"Stupid cow!" Ed said, while taking a piss. One or two others glanced at him.

As Ed got back, a hush had descended on the room. The results…

"In last place," the man with the mic started. He carried on going up the leader board and some punters were putting their hands over their mouths.

They had gotten past 5th place and weren't called out.

Fourth place was called out – it was the rival team. The woman gave Ed a sharp look.

"In third place, it's," the man with the mic paused, "team Nuala."

Ed, Sheila and Nuala let out a small jubilant cry.

The eventual winners were a team of hikers in the far corner. Ed, Sheila and Nuala gave a round of applause. The team with the bitter woman did not.

Ed clapped more enthusiastically, hoping it would annoy them.

I've got your box of chocolates and bottle of wine, he thought as he looked at his defeated rival.

Sheila excused herself as she went to the toilet.

Nuala peered across at Ed.

“Well that was lots of fun Nuala, than–”

“Be careful on your audit, Ed.”

Ed’s smile waned to a frown. “What do you mean, Nuala?”

“Well, you know…?”

Ed’s face was blank as he indicated he didn’t.

“That girl,” continued Nuala, “the one before you… eh, Anna?”

“Aine,” corrected Ed.

“She went missing, Ed. They didn’t find her.”

Ed couldn’t hide his concerned look.

Sheila arrived back at the table and told Ed that she would take Nuala home. She asked him to collect the prizes. She would get hers off him tomorrow and she suggested going through some of the locations Ed was having difficulty with. Ed happily agreed.

“I’m sure you’ll be fine, Ed,” said Nuala as she grasped his hand while walking out.

The prizes were handed out as the room emptied. He finished his pint and grabbed the bag of table quiz booty, together with his file. He made his way through the pub towards the entrance. It was much quieter now.

Ed stood out into the night air. It was fresh. He quickly reached the rural road outside the town and the only sound he could hear was of his steps scuffing the road.

As Ed turned onto the small solitary road towards his cottage, it became dead quiet. He felt as if he was floating down the road. He heard a loud snap in the shrubbery to his right. He jumped and dropped his file. “Shit!”

Some of the maps and the business cards had sprawled onto the road. Ed took out his phone, turned on the light and bent down, taking slow paces as he looked for the materials. He gathered the maps quickly but found himself chasing after one or two of the business cards as the wind danced and played with them.

As Ed picked up the last one, he saw a figure standing down the road. They seemed a shadowy reflection in the moonlight.

"Hello," bellowed Ed.

Another loud snap behind Ed. He swivelled round. As his breathing became heavier, Ed could see his exhales in the cold air, like big puffs of smoke. He turned back around and the figure seemed closer now. Ed still couldn't make them out. He or she turned abruptly then. The person moved slowly into the hedgerow and then… disappeared.

"Fuck this," Ed mumbled under his breath. He moved to the end of the laneway and right, through the front gates of Nuala's. No lights on in her house. But all the lights were on in his cottage…

None of the lights were on when he left!

As Ed got closer to the cottage, he noticed a mist floating around the base of the house. Not surprising, the cottage wasn't too far from Lough Rask. Reaching the doorway, Ed dropped his stuff on the ground and started fiddling in his pockets for the key.

"There we are," said Ed with a relieved sigh.

He put the key in, but the lock was stubborn. He tried turning it the other way. Wasn't budging. He tried pulling the door towards him this time as he tried to turn the key. Still wouldn't open!

"God's sake!" said Ed. He stood back a few feet, placing his arms at his sides.

His mouth fell open as each light turned off inside, one by one, in front of him. He could see the hall light coming through the keyhole. It was the last light still on. It suddenly flicked off.

Ed stepped forward slowly, raising the key towards the lock.

Just as it he was about to put it in, he heard a noise. It was the lock opening itself and the sound of a bolt on the half door. The top half door opened partially in front of him into the dark hallway. A small wind blew into his face and then died.

"Nuala?" said Ed sternly as he pushed the half door open a bit more. He got no response.

Ed's heartbeat was at a sprint. "If there's anyone in here, you'd better leg it," said Ed in his best deep man voice.

Ed reached in and undid the bottom bolt of the lower door. He moved in swiftly. Turning on lights as he went, Ed went into the living room, then the kitchen, then the conservatory, then the bathroom, the spare bedroom, and his room.

No one there.

He grimaced as he half jogged, checking the conservatory door lock and windows. All locked. Ed moved back towards the main doorway.

BANG!!

The door slammed shut in front of his face. Ed's heart was beating so fast that he thought it would burst out of his chest. Breathing fast, Ed slowly put his hand to the lock and opened it. He looked outside, no one there, but the mist was still on patrol. He picked up his gear and brought it inside.

Going into the kitchen he found a frozen pizza in the tiny fridge freezer. He switched on the power for the oven and switched the knob to 'nuclear', ripped the plastic off the pizza with his teeth and lashed it in.

As he wandered around the house, he tried to calm down. Must have been Nuala calling over and not telling him, he thought. The electrics must be dodgy. There must be a draft of some sort going from the conservatory door to the front door.

Ed turned on the radio and instantly felt better. It was like having someone in the room with him. He couldn't see them… but they were there. He lit a few logs and some local mossy turf in the stove. It wasn't long before he had heat for the body and soul.

He sliced up the pizza, got into his pyjamas and switched on the TV. Ireland's version of *Countryfile* was on. That would do. *This isn't so bad*, thought Ed. He sprawled on the couch and chilled out. The stove fire spat and crackled. The wind died down outside.

He tolerated the 'Brexit' news and watched the nice weather lady give her report.

A quick cup of tea and it was bed time. Bed before ten bells was a good idea. He would get up tomorrow and hit the tracks and trails. He brushed his teeth and switched off all the lights.

Into his bedroom and he lit his bedside lamp. He quickly got in under the covers and turned on his timed electric blanket. *What a great purchase*, he thought. As he heard rain shattering down outside, he turned off the lamp and drifted off.

*****

Ed could see a light… then it was gone.

He turned in his bed… back to sleep. There was the light again.

Gone again.

He saw light... in his dream… on and off.

Ed's eyes snapped open. His bedside lamp lightbulb was fluttering in intensity. He raised up in the bed slightly.

'Click!' The lamp switched on.

Ed took a moment. He sat up in the bed. He lifted his phone off the floor – 3:00 a.m. He put his phone down slowly and examined the lamp before switching it off.

Nothing. Darkness. Silence.

He lay down under the covers again and slowly relaxed – minutes passed. He shut his eyes. His breathing became deeper and longer.

The light… fluttering again. Ed shot up in the bed this time as the light in the bulb went up to an intensity he thought not possible.

A strong wind rumbled around the cottage. It was a shrieking loud wind. No, wait, it was a horrible sounding shriek!

Ed stood and put his hands to his ears. The wind – and the shriek – died down.

The intensity of the lamp light slowly died off to a small ember.

Ed kept his eyes on the lamp while turning on the main light. He then strode over and snapped the lamp plug out of the wall. He let out a sigh of relief that it had switched off and checked briefly out the side of the curtains. He could see mist still swirling around outside in the moonlight.

He needed to go to the loo now. Ed opened his door into the dank hallway. Walking through, he opened the door to the main room. Although the bathroom door was shut, he could easily see the light was on as it escaped around the doorframe. He walked across the room. As his hand reached the door handle a wind blew past him, the door handle went down and the door creaked open.

"Jesus!" shouted Ed.

He held his breath until he saw no one in there.

When he walked into the bathroom, he had never felt so afraid to take a piss. He even checked behind the shower curtain, yanking it back violently. He hurried out of the bathroom and ran to turn on the main light of the living room. He pulled out one of the chairs from the table and sat, beginning to rub his face with his hands.

What to do?

Ed saw tiny embers still alight in the stove. He walked over and threw in another fire lighter. He shoved the stove with more logs and turf. Shutting the stove door, the fire party got going quickly. He boiled the kettle next and poured himself some kind of herbal tea he found in the back of the kitchen cupboard. Checking out the small kitchen window, he could see no mist now. A bright full moon stared back at him from the sky.

Ed switched on the TV next and drank his herbal tea. Yawning, he grabbed a quilt from his room and lay himself on the couch. He finally fell asleep with the sounds of birds chirping in the pre-dawn air.

Chapter 15

Grainne O' Mahony sat in her rocking chair by the window. She was uneasy.

But it wasn't due to last month's mild stroke.

It was the small things she noticed, that others didn't. The wind had blown the hawthorn trees the opposite direction and looking out her window… the waves… the waves were being pushed onto the beach by the wind at strange angles. The birds no longer fed at her bird feeder. Her dog Misty would bark and growl at the wind outside. More importantly, her wrists and joints ached. Not too painful, mind, but noticeable. She felt a dull headache coming on.

Grainne managed to turn her head to the wall over the fireplace. Her favourite picture. Her and her nana a very long time ago. The picture was nearly as faded as the memory itself. But her granny's warming grin in the photo always seemed to transcend the years gone by.

Her nana talked about change a lot – the meaning of change around her. Good and bad. When her nana got the aches she told Grainne it meant there was danger. A storm perhaps… or worse, a death. Her nana insisted they stay inside. She would cuddle Grainne and they would–

"Well, Auntie, that's it from me," bellowed her niece Sheila as she opened the front door to her cottage.

Sheila walked in with her car keys in her hand. Grainne tried to respond but only managed a mumble.

"I've taken the washing in off the line and put out the bins," her niece said loudly, leaning in towards her. "I'll light the fire and head off!" Sheila bent down and struck match to a pre-prepared fire. She stood up and flicked on the TV, putting the remote control beside Grainne.

"I've to pop down the way to the holiday home. Check in on the Americans who have arrived. Have a lovely evening and I'll be down to you tomorrow, mid-morning." Sheila leant down and gave her a kiss on the forehead before shooting out the door.

Grainne turned off the TV. She had no interest in it now.

As the light faded, the wind began to pick up around the cottage, finding its way in any nook and cranny it could. Sometimes she thought she could hear… things… voices, in the wind.

SMASH!

The white net curtains fluttered out from the windowsill over the kitchen sink. A plant pot lay smashed on the floor. There was only a sliver of the window open at the bottom.

Grainne hoped the plant pot would be the only victim this night… but her aches were only getting worse.

*****

A strong cold wind buffeted Ed's back. He was crouched just behind a rock. His heart was thumping. He was breathing heavily. His eyes darted left and right. He moved himself into a sprinting position. "Just go!" he said out loud, but he could hardly bring himself to it. "Damn it, Ed, move!" he told himself. He couldn't hide here forever. No choice. He took a deep breath, gritted his teeth and ran.

Twenty metres on and his feet dashed into the cold water but he kept moving as the water reached his knees. Next was the killer part, the water reached his waist. He let out a cry like a schoolgirl. That was surely the end of him ever having children.

As Ed acclimatised to the cold water, he looked at Slieve Elva Mountain, positioned back over the beach. He thought he could see someone at the top moving erratically. What was he doing!? He was too close to the edge.

God!! He had slipped and was barely hanging on now!

Was there someone in front of him? They looked like a black figure. He couldn't be sure…

"Ohhh God! No!!" said Ed as the man fell. He quickly disappeared behind the sandy verge just before the road. Ed shut his eyes. Ed stood in the bracing sea water, but he no longer noticed the cold. Another type of chill ran through him now.

He rushed out of the water as quickly as he could and raced up the beach back to the rock. He did his best to yank his clothes on and ended up with wet patches and sand in all sorts of places. He gave up on trying to put on his socks and simply yanked his hiking boots on. He left the laces undone.

Getting to his car, he quickly got it started and turned onto the main road. He considered a left or right turn. He chanced left and drove for a minute or two. He saw a turn to the right, took it, and belted down the road. It cut off abruptly at a house and seemed too far from the incident.

Ed did a difficult three point turn, cursing a hedgerow as he completed it. Back on the main road and he hung a left. Five minutes later and he tried another left turn. There was a brown sign with the symbol of a hiker on it, a white stick man with some sort of bag on his back.

Feeling this was more promising, Ed raced along as far as the narrow bumpy road would allow. He scrambled out of the car and got his bearings. He looked far closer to the fall; the Slieve Elva mountain looked far more imposing here.

He set off on a trail in front of him and ten minutes later, he came across a tiny lake. Beyond it he could see a red bag on the rock face ahead. Various contents were splayed out on the ground. To the left of the small lake was a jut of earth that verged up sharply. He wouldn't get up that.

To the right of the lake was the sheer cliff face of the mountain. Ed sighed in annoyance and treading into the water took out his mobile phone. It got deep fast, going right up to his chest, as he raised his arms up over his shoulders, looking like he was surrendering to someone.

As he neared the other side it got shallower again. Just as he got out he slipped, slamming his knee onto the rocky shore.

"Argghh!"

Ed closed his eyes in pain but quickly recovered and limped on. He could see the bag just up on the flat rock face above. He reached the bag and the various contents spread around it. He carried on, over another small verge. Ten metres on and Ed was quickly horrified.

Blood and what looked like brains were splattered across the rock. A body lay at a strange angle. A huge hole was in the person's head. It resembled a cracked egg torn open; a piece of… skull hung from the empty hole, flapping in the wind.

Ed went pale, turned and had to stop himself from retching. He thought he heard a strange laugh carried on the wind as it rushed by him. He couldn't trace where it was from. As he looked up, he thought he saw something, a figure up on the mountain. Then it was gone…

Composing himself, he dialled 999 on his phone. He got through to someone, and through heaving breaths, stated what he had seen.

When she said an ambulance was coming, Ed responded that it probably wouldn't do any good. She said a Guard was on their way too. Ed did his best describe where he was, and the call ended. He sat down, still with his back to the tragic scene, and waited.

*****

Bean Garda Nicola Ahern got the call and quickly moved into her car, just outside her station at Kinvara. This was a strange one, she decided.

The job this year, in general, had been lot quieter than last year. She had only started here early last autumn when those people went missing. But her job hadn't been too serious of late. Her 9-5 over the last few months was tourist coaches clashing with cars around the periphery of the Burren. The odd holiday home burglary. But luckily, the burglars seemed as seasonal as the tourists in these parts. Warm weather creatures.

She had attended the odd drowning and helped with sea and search rescues. Thankfully, the drugs crisis still hadn't taken hold of this part of Clare. And god knows she could do with that, considering everything that had happened up in Limerick.

As Nicola weaved past another car on these narrow roads, she thanked heaven that police cars had sirens. She got down to Fanore and quickly spotted the flashing lights of a parked ambulance in the distance. She navigated her way there. The sun was going down in the west.

As she parked, she saw an ambulance medic attending to a man who was sitting at the back of the ambulance. As Nicola got out of the car and moved over to the ambulance, she saw the medic was examining the man's knee while dabbing some type of salve on an open wound.

"Are you Ed?" she said. "I'm Garda Ahern."

"Yeah… I made the call. I saw it happen. Made my way from the beach and crossed the lake there. Found the body."

She saw Ed grimace and close his eyes as the ambulance man continued to attend his wound.

"Right, well you stay here, and I'll be back," she said.

The medic quickly explained to her that she had to cross the small lake and he whispered that it was a mess.

She retrieved a small bag from her car with her note book, police cordoning off tape and a camera. She gave a deep breath as she started to cross the small lake. When she and her wet uniform made it to the other side, she quickly got up to the scene. Christ, it was a mess! Two ambulance men stood waiting.

She explained that she would investigate the scene, take photos and then they could remove the body. The body, removing it… 'better ye than me' she thought. Wouldn't be an open cask funeral.

From the devastation of the body and the blood stained rock, it looked like a fall. She began taking detailed notes of the scene before moving through the man's bag nearby. She found his wallet and his phone. She quickly opened his wallet.

Fuck! He was French. She would be dealing with the bereaved family from Shannon airport onwards.

After an hour's examination, she instructed the ambulance lads to get started. They asked if she would send their other colleague over to them when she managed to get back over. "Sure," she said.

She made the way back across the lake and it was no more enjoyable than the first time. Garda Ahern gave the disappointed ambulance man the lake news and moved around to Ed.

"Well, Ed, how are you?"

"A bit shook. I can't tell what's worse, seeing it happen or seeing the result."

"Yeah… doesn't look pleasant."

Garda Ahern took out her slightly damp logbook and held her pen at the ready. "So, can you tell me what happened then?"

"I had just gotten into the water down at Fanore beach when I turned and noticed some movement at the top of the mountain. I kept my eyes on the scene and started to see the person," Ed nodded in the direction of the lake, "moving erratically at the top. He looked in trouble. He soon reached the edge and seemed to be clinging on before fell. Horrifying. I knew I had to get out of the water as quickly as I could and find the area where he fell."

"You didn't think to ring the emergency services straight away?"

"No, I just thought, get there, as quickly as I could. I was thinking straight… to a degree."

"So you found the body and then called the emergency services?"

"Yeah, had to cross that lake to do it."

Garda Ahern looked down at where the beach should be and then back up at the mountain. "You must have some good eyesight to see that."

"Good timing, I guess. Or bad timing in another way," Ed said, babbling the last part.

Garda Ahern looked Ed up and down. "So you got wet crossing the small lake?"

"Yes… and oh! I thought there was someone else up there."

"Someone else?" asked Garda Ahern.

"Yes, up at the top," said Ed as he pointed up.

"Did you see them before or after the fall?"

"Both… I think. I saw them from the beach and when I got here."

Garda Ahern's pen stopped moving on her notebook but she kept looking down. "Right, and what did they look like?"

"Couldn't tell. Didn't get a great look. Think they were all in black."

"Man or woman?"

"Not sure."

"So you think there was another person? Dressed all in blac–"

"And I heard laughing then too."

"From the other person?" asked Ahern.

"Maybe. I heard it in the wind really."

Ahern looked up at Ed. "You saw a figure dressed in black, but you can't tell if they're a man or a woman, and you heard laughing in… the wind?"

"Yes, that's about it really." Ed sighed.

Garda Ahern looked towards the beach. She then casually looked down at Ed's knee and glanced back to her notebook. "How did you get that?"

"I fell down while getting out of the water on the other side of the lake."

Garda Ahern looked back up to the mountain and then back to the lake. Then flickered her eyes towards Ed's feet, down at his hiking boots. "You're into walking, Ed?"

"Yes," said Ed curtly.

Garda Ahern moved her eyes back to her notebook. "You a tourist, Ed?"

"No. I'm here working."

"At what?"

"Doing an audit."

Garda Ahern's face flushed red. She coughed. She looked directly at him, her eyes piercing. "What's your address, Ed?"

Ed rattled his address out to her. She asked for it again. He spoke slowly and loudly now.

Garda Ahern paused. "Right, okay. That's it," she said as she looked up and gave Ed a penetrating stare.

Ed said nothing in return, clambered out of the ambulance and started walking to his car.

"Oh, one more thing, Ed. Do you think the victim was pushed or fell?" Garda Ahern said in a matter of fact tone.

Ed turned slightly, but just half way. "Well, he fell. That's for sure. As for the other person… I'm unsure."

"So am I," she muttered.

"Well, we both are then," said Ed in a rude tone, turning his back to her.

Ed watched as Garda Ahern picked out a phone from her pocket. "Unlocked. Good. There seems to be a number here… Irish mobile. Rung two days ago. Let's give it a buzz."

Garda Ahern held the phone to her ear. She kept her eyes on Ed.

Half a minute later, she said, "Hi Jack, it's Garda Ahern here from the police. Could you give me a call back as soon as you get this? I need to talk with you. Thanks."

She took the phone down from her ear, pushed a button and placed the phone back in her pocket. She pursed her lips and stared at Ed.

Ed gritted his teeth and walked to his car. He didn't even try to turn it. He reversed his chariot away from this skirmish.

*****

Garda Ahern watched as Ed reversed down the road. She knew she had been testy with him. But there was something…

She would definitely find out who this Jack Royson was. He sounded English as well on his voicemail. She had jotted down Ed's make of car and its registration number.

Garda Ahern turned and looked at the lake. Well, she thought. Nothing for it. She would have to cross over again and tell the lads to stop what they were doing. She would call a forensics team on the other side.

*****

Ed got back down to the beach. His knee didn't feel as bad. It was stitched up and the paracetamol did the trick. He made himself walk a bit to calm down. Then he made himself smile. "Fuck it," he said as puffed out all the air he had. He looked at the setting sun to his left. "Out with the bad and in with the new."

Refreshed, Ed went back to his car. As he got into the driving seat he decided to leave today's incident up at the mountain. It happened. He did what he could. Tragic. Horrible. That's it! Draw a line; leave it. He would go back to Ballyvaughan for a pint and shoot the shit with an old timer!

He started the car and headed off, leaving Fanore and Slieve Elva behind him.

A few minutes into the drive and Ed's car wound around Gleninagh Mountain, which was to his right. To his left, a fifty metre drop down a sheer cliff gave way to an angry looking sea. The road looked in danger of being pushed over the edge by the mountain. In truth, it had probably been trying since the road had arrived.

The churning sea to his left was cast in a purple hue, the red setting sun becoming a sliver in the distance. Between the mountain and the sea, Ed couldn't help but feel like he was trapped between two worlds.

As Ed rounded another bend he saw a thick fog bank ahead. He dropped down a gear and carried on. As the fog got thicker, he turned on his fog lights. Around another bend, and there was a person, a hitch hiker of all people. Ed shook his head in disbelief and indicated to his left. He slowly pulled in just past the man, making sure to turn on his hazard lights as he did.

Ed sat and waited, looking to his passenger door for the individual. Nothing. He couldn't make out much in the rear view mirror. Ed considered driving on, but his conscience let him down. He got out of the car and looked towards where he thought the hitch hiker should be standing. "Hello," he shouted.

The guy was nowhere.

Oh for God's sake, Ed thought - *where is the bastard?*

As thick fog rolled around his car, Ed could hear the low tone of a buoy bell out on the sea. It clanged back and forth. He shook his head and sat back into the car.

"JESUS CHRIST!" Ed shouted, as he slapped his left hand to his chest, leaning back.

A man was sitting in the passenger seat. Ed looked him up and down, mouth slightly open.

The guy was maybe in his twenties. He had some kind of funky black hair style. Kind of like Elvis but cropped and shorter. He wore a black open leather jacket with a white shirt underneath. Top button undone at the neck. Blue jeans and what looked like a pair of black dockers on his feet. His face seemed ashen.

"What are you, a fucking Ninja or something?" asked Ed.

The man seemed to pause at that and grimaced slightly. "I...don't...think...so," the man said.

"I'm off to the gig… in Ennis," said the bloke. "Been waitin' for it all month. Thin Lizzy. Nice car," he said looking about.

Ed shook his head. He indicated to his right and moved off slowly. He could just about make out the road markings as he stayed in second gear.

"What's your name?" asked the man.

"Ed."

Ed's mouth felt dry. There was a smell of salt in the air… the sea, he thought. Must be carrying on the fog, although he had the windows closed.

"What's yours?" said Ed with a slow indifference.

"My name… my name is…"

Ed looked at the guy as he looked at Ed. He seemed pale, his dark eyes giving nothing away. The guy's lips were blue. Ed gestured to him with his hand, looking for a response.

"Tah… Tah…" the man responded.

"Fuck sake," Ed said under his breath. He would drop this guy like a hot potato at Ballyvaughan. Just his luck he picked up the fucking hipster with the fucking drug problem. He was fairly sure that Ennis was the other way, anyhow.

"Tah… Tah… Tommy," the man finally spat out.

"Well, Tommy, I'm heading as far as Ballyvaughan so you'll HAVE TO MAKE YOUR OWN WAY FROM THERE." Ed said the last part a bit louder than intended, just to make sure that Ground Control had succeeded in getting through to Major Tom.

"You're not going to the gig yourself?" asked Tommy. "All me mates are going!"

Ed caught Tommy smiling at that but gave him no reply.

"Fancy radio you have," said Tommy.

Ed gave an inward sigh and blinked slowly, offering no reply back. This fancy radio was as fancy as his 1996 Honda allowed.

Tommy reached his hand towards the radio. Ed pushed it away. "Not while I'm driving in this fog!" he snapped.

The fog carried on and Ed stayed in second gear.

Music suddenly came from the radio, but neither Ed nor Tommy had switched it on. Tommy simply stared at it.

"That's a weird one," Tommy said.

Ed moved his hand to turn it off but paused momentarily as his radio started to flick through the channels itself. Ed hit the knob. The channels still flicked on, regardless.

"Strange music… I liked mine better," said Tommy.

Ed ignored Tommy as he kept one hand on the wheel and now held the button of the radio down. Still wouldn't stop! If anything, it sped up its channel flicking and was getting really loud! Ed was sweating now, his heart beating quickly. He looked at Tommy.

Tommy looked back at him. He seemed to be slouched slightly against the passenger door.

"I should have waited," said Tommy.

"Waited for what!?" said Ed with sternness in his voice.

Tommy looked forward now. "Until the fog cleared," said Tommy as he raised his hand up and pointed forwards.

Ed turned his head back to the road.

"FUUUCCCCK!!!" said Ed as he slammed the brakes. A random cow stood in the road. The car reared forward and Ed banged his head off the wheel slightly. He leaned back, breathing deeply, eyes shut, holding his hands to his head.

"Are you all right?" said Ed as he turned towards Tommy… but Tommy wasn't there. Ed quickly stretched back and looked to the back seat. Where was he!?

He breathed deeply as the fog began to dissipate around the car. The cow casually moved off the road, swaying its tail back and forth. Ed got out of the car and looked up and down the road. The fog seemed to be retreating up the mountain side.

"Tommy," shouted Ed.

He leaned forward, rubbed his hands on his knees and sighed deeply. As he straightened back up, his eyes followed the beam of the fog lights. He squinted… and his mouth fell open.

As Ed walked forward, he shook his head. He had found… Tommy.

His picture was in the middle of a brown cross stuck on the side of the road. Underneath, the caption read, '*RIP Tommy Beirne, Our Lovely Boy, 1967- 1985.*"

Chapter 16

Ed walked into his house, leaving a howling wind and stinging rain behind him. Despite his raingear he was saturated; the rain and wind found weaknesses in his defences throughout the day. It had been like this over the last three weeks. He knew now his 'Jack Royson' business had taken up too much of his time.

He stripped at the door. Even the leather cord of his pendant seemed wet, so he took that off as well. He grabbed a towel from his room and headed straight for the shower. But he found little comfort in the warming water. His brain still couldn't comprehend his meeting with Tommy.

He also found the news about Aine made him very uncomfortable indeed. Professor Barnes and Deirdre seemed quite uncontactable since he had sent them messages on the topic. Although, his drunken rant down the phone the other night on Professor Barnes' mobile voicemail probably did him no favours.

To take his mind off Tommy and Aine, he decided to get to work. He was fearful, but the fear of returning to the UK with nothing tangible on his CV was worse. The sooner he completed his job here, the sooner he could leave.

He had criss-crossed the Burren over the last few days. He had gotten down to Doolin, Killanboy, Kilfernora, Carran and Corofin. He had tackled many backroads in his endeavours to find the portal tombs, court tombs, burial cairns, fulacht fiadhs, ring barrows, souterrains, stone forts, ring forts, holy wells, shrines and old churches.

He had gathered a lot of information for the audit. But he had also come across more and more sites that were damaged. He had cordoned off what he could. He had rung Deirdre the previous week and explained about the numerous damaged sites he was encountering but she gave him short shrift. "Just finish the audit, Ed! That's why we need the funding!" she had said.

Even worse, his meetings with the strange characters around the place continued. His heart leapt again today as he saw that woman… the woman in the pink jacket. Every time he approached her, she moved behind a tree, rock or wall. There was no sign of her when he checked further. It was as if she had the ability to disappear!

Who was she? Why was she stalking him?

Ed tried and tried to not think about any of this. His brief conclusion was that he was in a modern day version of the story from the *Wicker Man*. However, he planned to be long gone before they put him in a giant man made of straw and burnt him alive. Archaeologists, both authorised and un-authorised, were given mixed greetings. Maybe this Burren audit was a threat to someone. They didn't like the work Aine had completed or the work he was currently doing.

Ed finished his shower and heard the storm picking up outside. He quickly lit a fire and turned the TV on and the volume right up to drown out the noise of the weather.

He checked the stew he had left in his slow cooker that morning. "Fuck sake!" roared Ed. The bloody thing hadn't cooked! He was sure he had switched it on; he remembered seeing the green light on the device shining from the kitchen when he was leaving. How he wished he had confronted Nuala about this stuff at the table quiz. Ed boiled the kettle and made a knock off pot noodle. Spaghetti hoops on toast completed his makeshift dinner.

He did some brief work on his laptop, collating the information he had gathered that day. He could add it all to the formal report soon. As Ed alternated between his large audit file and examined his excel worksheet called 'Plan', he registered that the one piece he hadn't finished was the audit of the wedge tombs. He had checked all the ones on Aine's map that were marked by green dots. But he hadn't checked the ones marked by the red dots. Many seemed on private land.

He decided his first thing to do tomorrow morning was see if he could get hold of Sheila. If she knew the private owners, or even better, had a rapport with those owners, it would save him having to skulk around on some else's land. 'Option B' they called it in the Archaeological world.

As Ed was shutting down his laptop, the light above him flickered. He started hearing a banging noise at the back of the cottage. He walked to the edge of the kitchen and heard the source – the conservatory room. He opened the door and could feel the wind and rain hitting his face. He turned on the light. The outer conservatory door was wide open. Inky blackness lay beyond.

As Ed approached the door, it banged closed. He stopped.

Then the glass door slowly creaked open. He went to grab the door handle but the door slammed in his face. Then it rushed open again, closing violently once more. Opening again, it slammed just as quick. Ed took a step backwards as the door opened and shut at a rate that no draft or person could probably manage. Ed's heart was beating nearly as wildly as the door.

The door suddenly stopped having a fit and remained closed. A rush of wind and rain seemed to slam the conservatory roof. Ed rushed forward and pressed his shoulder up against the door, turning the key and locking it. He slowly stepped away, looked around the room and drew a breath. An empty press was stationed on the wall to his right. He tested it. Seemed heavy enough. He shunted the press over by the door, with little regard to the scrapes the press made to the tiled flooring below.

Satisfied, Ed was just walking out of the room when the main sitting room light flickered again. Three slow thumps came at his front door. At least two or three seconds between the noises. The main light switched off. Ed stood like a statue in the dark as he was left with the sound of heavy rain and gusting wind outside.

Everything in this place seemed to be attacking his sanity, he thought. And he was so bloody tired of it!

As his eyes adjusted to the dark, he darted to his room. He turned on the light on his phone and found an old golf stick beside the wardrobe, a rusted 4 iron. Golf stick in hand, he crept to the main door. He undid the bolts as quickly as he could, ripping open the top half door.

No one there.

"Come on, you bastard!" he shouted. That was more for his shattered confidence than to scare any assailant, he realised.

He opened the bottom door. The evening was dark, but he could see the grass in front of him moving erratically in the wind. Ed noticed something at his feet. He looked down, pointing the light of his phone at it. There on his doorstep was… was a dead animal, with its guts splayed out over it. Blood all over the place. Its jaw was wide open. One eye stared forward. It looked like a cat.

Ed let out a shout as he quickly kicked it away, before slamming the doors and re-bolting them. The lights flickered back to life. He ran and checked the conservatory door straight away. All good there. He then checked every room for open windows. He kept moving, his body reacting where his stunned mind could not.

He had his bags packed in ten minutes, having shoved his gear in, any which way it would fit. Tomorrow morning, he was out of here. Gone! He would go to a local hotel and decide from there what his next move would be.

Ed got his torch and put on a pot of coffee.

A few hours passed. He checked the time. It was 1:00 a.m.

He sat in the main sitting room holding an empty coffee cup. He kept all the lights on in the cottage, the fire topped up and the TV off. The wind and rain still howled around him.

He let out a yawn. Then another. He looked across at the wall at a nice picture of a wave hitting some cliffs and closed his eyes for second.

Then opened them. He shifted his position from the warm part of the couch to the colder part he hadn't sat on.

He closed his eyes for just another second…

'Tap'… 'Tap', 'Tap', 'Tap', 'Tap', 'Tap', 'Tap'…

Ed shuddered awake. "Fuck!" he said quietly. He sat in darkness.

He got up and checked the lights. They weren't working. He checked the time on his phone – 3:00 a.m. The weather sounded as if it had eased off outside. As Ed's eyes adjusted to the dark, he saw some light coming through the edge of the curtains. He parted some of the curtain behind him and a full bright moon stared back at him.

Ed stopped moving as the 'tapping' noise started again. It sounded like it was coming from his bedroom. He slowly reached for his torch and his trusty 4 iron again.

Switching on the torch, he crept towards the hallway and did his best to slow his breathing. The tapping noise got louder as he reached his room. Pushing the door open, it creaked on its hinges. He felt a mixture of anger and fear as he silently wished he could rip the door off its hinges. He shone the light around the room, raising the golf club up to a swinging position.

Ed realised the tapping noise was coming from the window on the far side of the room. He turned the torch off. The tapping continued as his eyes adjusted to darkness again. The moonlight must have gotten brighter outside as he could see the silhouette of a person behind the curtains.

"Who's there?!" roared Ed.

The tapping grew louder.

Ed moved at pace, gripped the curtain and thrust it to his left. No one there. No tapping now. He gritted his teeth, closed his eyes and bent his head downwards. A few more hours he told himself.

Ed heard another sound… a whisper at first.

It seemed mingled in with a light breeze outside. The noise intensified as the wind picked up. The sound was now unmistakable – "*HHeellllpppp.*"

It began to repeat itself over and over again, surrounding the cottage as the wind swirled about. The latter part of the word drifted with the dying wind each time.

Ed had had enough. He turned on his torch and upended one of his packed bags. He put on another jumper, hiking boots, wet gear, and found his jacket. Torch in hand he marched through to the conservatory. Whoever or whatever it was would see him in the moonlight, but so be it. Ed pushed the dresser back quickly, creating yet more scrapes on the floor. He flung open the door and stood outside. The wind instantaneously smacked him with cold air and the 'help' sound.

Ed began to follow the noise, with his torch switched off at first. As he reached the small road outside Nuala's, he had to switch it on. Just too dark. He would trip or fall. At the end of the road, the 'help' wind struck again, coming from his left. He turned sharply and kept up a quick pace, following the sound. As clouds crossed over the moon, he moved the setting on his torch to its strongest.

There just at the end of the beam, he saw her… the woman in the pink jacket. Her back was turned to him as she walked off into the dark.

Ed carried on, following the noise, following her; through hedges, fields, old tracks…

He kept his senses at bay. There would be plenty of time to react to this tomorrow. This needed to be concluded.

He followed on for what seemed an hour, walking up and over Moneen Mountain. His mouth was dry and he found it hard to keep pace with the pink lady. He nearly lost his footing twice in some grikes underfoot. If it wasn't for his torch, a twisted ankle or bad fall were guaranteed.

Ed trudged on through the night, the wind and *help* sound picking up as he went. He spotted her ahead several times. Finally, after another hour, he reached the base of what he guessed was Turlough Hill, popular with both hikers and locals. Even in the darkness it loomed large. It was probably difficult enough to climb during daylight.

As Ed reached the base of a large boulder, the pink woman suddenly stood out from behind it. She faced him, not ten metres away. She stood, illuminated by the moonlight. Strands of blonde hair escaped the hood and seemed to float around. But as before, no face could be seen behind the hood, just darkness.

'*Hhhelllppppp*,' the voice came again, so clear and it seemed all round him at once.

With that her left arm extended up behind her and she pointed at the summit of the hill. At that moment, Ed's torch flickered and died. She disappeared.

Ed tried to listen to the logical voice in his brain now. It told him through exhaustion and fear that he should turn back. Going up a hill in pitch black over karst rock seemed beyond stupid. Hikers and climbers could easily get into trouble in daylight hours on this terrain. But his gut told him to go up and investigate. He didn't want to leave the Burren forever wondering what had lured him out this night.

As the moon came back out from the clouds, Ed's eyes had re-adjusted to the darkness. He took it slow, real slow. His eyes navigated the limestone rock at his feet, where it was getting harder and harder to distinguish between a grike or a large piece of soil or moss.

Around thirty minutes later, he reached the top. The surface here was uneven. The summit had plenty of broken rocks bumping up in the moonlight. The ground, even up here, still seemed covered in the karst limestone rock of clints and grikes. The moonlight revealed shadowed depressions at various places. As Ed moved forward, he accidently kicked some stones at his feet, hearing a plopping noise as they fell into some water in a hidden crevice or grike. He realised he needed to slow down again.

As Ed climbed a steep small verge, almost on his hands and knees, he saw a structure ahead in the darkness. He straightened himself up and looked at it, squinting his eyes to see what it was. Closing in on the structure, he realised it was a dolmen. Quickly scanning the area, he couldn't see any grikes ahead. He took a leap forward to close the ground and fell straight down, smacking his chin on the edge of a rocky edge as he did.

SPLASH!

Ed was stunned as he was submerged in cold, dark water. Raw, sharp pain ripped through his head as his feet landed on something. He managed to reach out a hand to the side… there was a side. His head broke free and he coughed up peaty tasting water. Steadying himself, the floor of what he was in didn't seem stable. It moved at his feet. Ed used both hands to orientate himself, spreading them left and right to connect with the wall on either side. Thankfully, this grike, or whatever this was, wasn't that wide.

His jaw and head still humming, he noticed his torch tethered and hanging from his right wrist. His feet still shuffling on the slippery bottom below, he chanced his torch. It worked – full beam!

Ed drew a breath as he took in where he was, using the torchlight. He must have fallen at least ten metres into the cold dark boggy water here. The opening at the top was neither big nor small, but thankfully he could see some stars above. Barring one end of the grike, the rock seemed un-climbable. His thought process was interrupted by a sound in front of him and he turned the torch light down on it.

Bubbles were bursting up in front of him as his feet slipped on something below. He nearly lost his balance as something surged up out of the water, splashing him in the face. Ed let out a cry, shielding his face briefly.

His sudden fear that some kind of evil bog fish or monster had come for him disappeared quickly as a long yellow backpack floated in front of him. He touched it. It was heavy, even allowing for the trapped air that was puffing the bag outwards.

Ed scrambled forward over the uneven ground, heading towards the end where he thought he had a chance of climbing out. He pushed the yellow backpack in front of him. Getting as best a foothold as possible, Ed began throwing the bag upwards with the little energy he had left. His teeth were chattering now as the cold water made its presence felt.

Four, maybe five times, the bag splashed back down, once falling on Ed's head. It became harder and harder for Ed to try to propel the bag up through the gap at the top. He took a quick break and with a small roar launched the bag upwards again.

The bag flopped over the top and wobbled, before balancing itself on the edge.

Ed leant against the side, breathing hard. He took a minute or two. Closing his eyes, he opened them sharply. The last thing he needed was to lose consciousness. He primed himself for the climb upwards. As Ed shifted his feet to the side, he could feel something else bumpy below, moving…

More bubbles now.

Something else rocketed high up out of the water, up into the air, before landing on top of Ed. Ed slipped backwards as he lost his footing, his head dipping below the cold water briefly. He gripped whatever it was with his free hand. It was heavy and right on top of him. The smell was disgusting, putrid. Ed shone the torch on it and immediately gagged.

A face… nearly on top of his. It was shrunken, contorted and brown. Pieces of skin were hanging off. It had no nose. Clenched teeth smiled at him through a lipless mouth. The eyeballs were fully exposed and rolled upwards in their sockets. Ed squirmed and whimpered as he pushed the rotting face away from him. The body flopped backwards and floated face down in the water. Ed kept his distance as he kept the torch on it. The body was in a coat.

The pink jacket…

Strands of thin looking blonde hair floated out and around the hood. A single hand, near skeletal, floated out the end of one jacket arm. Pale, scattered flesh hung off it, barely connected to the bone. Ed coughed and struggled to breathe, hyperventilating. The body floated to the other side. Ed regathered himself through chattering teeth. He mustn't go into shock, he told himself.

His breathing returned to a semblance of normal as his heart continued to sprint.

He pointed the torch upwards, grabbed an old looking tree root with his left hand and shunted his right boot upwards. Slowly he pivoted his way up, his left foot scrambling for a hold. He found it and chose his next move cautiously.

He turned his body so his back faced one wall and his feet the other. He shunted his way upwards and as the space narrowed, it got easier. He moved quicker now, losing his last bit of energy to get his torso over the edge. He took a good minute to get his left leg over, rolled out… and away.

Flopped on his back, he stared at the sky. Twinkling stars. He heard a crunching noise in front of him. There she was – the woman in pink. He reckoned he knew who this was.

"What do you want, Aine?!" Ed shouted in panic.

Silhouetted by the moonlight behind her, her right arm stretched out towards the backpack.

As a breeze washed over him, Ed heard two distinct words, "*baaaagg… kniffffe*."

When the words stopped, Ed leaned up on his forearms. A heavier gust hit him and Aine evaporated before his eyes.

"*Thhannkkk yoouuuu*."

Ed lay there for some minutes. He closed his eyes again before hearing the all too familiar noise of his chattering teeth. He must get up… and go, or the hyperthermia would finish him off.

As Ed stood, he saw a man near the dolmen. He shone the torch light at him. He was bald with a long bushy red beard. He wore a black cloak. His head was covered in blue paint. There were yellow circles around his eyes. The man put a horn to his mouth and blew. It made no sound even though the man's cheeks puffed outwards. He seemed to blow several times.

As he did, Ed saw something rolling up the hill behind the man. It was a fog bank and it sped up the hill towards the dolmen. The man was soon engulfed in it. As the fog moved towards Ed, his torch failed again. Ed's heart dropped with the fading light.

He took a few steps back and picked up the yellow backpack just as the fog engulfed him too.

*****

Ed somehow composed himself once more, flinging the yellow backpack over his shoulders and tightening it close to his back. He hoped it would keep him straight and give him an incentive to stay standing. He checked his phone – it was 5:10 a.m. The fog was thick, and he could hardly see his nose in front of his face. He decided to carry on past the dolmen and got moving.

He watched the ground as he moved, making doubly sure that he wouldn't fall down another grike or crevice. Ed thought he was descending, when out of the fog he came across another structure. A dolmen. Strange, it looked like the one he had just passed. As Ed moved along again, he started to wonder when he would reach one of the stony terraces that would lead him down. He watched the ground intensely for any kind of ledge, a tell-tale sign of a terrace, but he also looked intensely so he wouldn't fall off.

Out of the fog, Ed saw another dolmen. His breathing got heavier – it looked exactly the same as the one he had just seen. The same white patch appeared on the left side of the capstone. The same tuft of moss sat on the top. Ed turned his back to it, putting his arms under his armpits. His eyelids starting to feel like weights. His body cried out to take a break, sit down. He knew if he did… it was over.

He checked the time again. What the fuck!? The time still registered as 5:10 a.m.

His phone must have been wonky since he went into the grike. As Ed put his phone back in his pocket, he felt something else in there. It was circular. He took it out with a shaky hand. Eureka! It was his compass.

He straightened. He went to the other side of the dolmen and waited until the compass pointed south. He started walking, feeling an amazing sense of relief. Minutes past and Ed was sure the terrain looked slightly different. He heard a sound to his right, like a rock falling. He jumped slightly. The fog in that direction dissipated briefly. He thought he saw a figure in black.

As Ed walked on, he heard a 'splash' to his left. Something heavy going into water. Then he heard rocks falling to his right again. Ed kept his compass pointed, quickening his pace.

Out of the fog, he saw…

The dolmen, the same fucking dolmen again! As he reached it, he heard the sound of a twig snapping to his left.

"Who's there?" he managed in a crackled voice. He didn't realise how dry his mouth was.

A slow laugh started to his left. It sounded like a woman. It intensified as it seemed to come from all around him. It sounded like a cackle now as it grew and grew in pace and volume, until…

Until it sounded utterly insane. It was everywhere at once… echoing all around Ed now. The crazy noise closed in on Ed. His bottom lip quivered and he felt a tear drop down his face.

He had no moves left to make. He had a feeling of complete helplessness. This crazy woman or thing sounded all too close now. His tired brain rebooted once more. If he ran, there was no guarantee he would not just end up back here. Also, there was a good chance he would fall, injuring himself badly. But the terrible noise was approaching fast.

The hairs raised up on the back of his neck, together with goose bumps on his arms. The noise – that crazy cackle – stopped. Ed could only hear his heavy breaths.

Through the fog, something black approached. It cackled again as it was just metres from Ed. It floated above the ground. It looked like a person… a woman maybe. She wore a long black hooded cloak. She, or it, had a sunken face with hollows where the eyes should be. Her dark skin seemed cracked. She beamed a mouthful of blackened teeth at him. Grey scraggly hair flowed out of her hood. She pointed a skeletal finger at him and let out a shriek that filled his mind, body and soul.

Ed took off, sprinting to his left. He ran and ran. Falling once, his right hip connected with a jagged rock. He let out a grunt, the only acknowledgement he would dare give the pain. He heard insane laughter not too far behind him. As he stood, he was pushed by a howling wind backwards. He didn't want to turn around; he knew what was waiting for him.

Ed began shouting with fear. "NO… NO… NO!"

His feet were losing their grip just as he heard a different noise overhead.

Chapter 17

Dominik Zielinski walked out of the Village Café with a cappuccino in one hand and a bacon butty in the other. He got into his car. Taking a quick swig of coffee, he got moving, taking bites out of the butty as he drove.

Like many people in Ballyvaughan, he was a blow in. From Wroclaw in Poland, he had wanted a change of scenery. And although he only intended to work at the Ailbh Caves Bird Sanctuary for one summer, he had stayed on for two. He liked the area; there was a calmness about it. He was a solitary type of guy too. So his experience of falconry had finally served him well.

Dominik arrived at the caves, parked his car and got out. He grabbed his cappuccino and found his key for the main cage door into the bird enclosure. The dawn air was bracing. But he didn't mind the early starts any more. They had gotten so lucky with an incredible creature that had arrived at the sanctuary. It was an eagle they called 'Sparkles' due to its unique eye colouring.

It had come all the way from the Amazon forest. How the sanctuary had obtained the licencing and money to get this bird, was anyone's guess. His boss had joked that it was as if the eagle had picked the place himself!

Sparkles was the star of the show all summer. They say dogs and dolphins are clever. Well, this eagle needed little training and seemed to know what you wanted before you even asked. It was incredible with the tricks and great with people, particularly kids. Dominik found himself talking with Sparkles nearly all the time. He loved doing training with him. And those eyes… it was as if they stared into the soul itself.

Dominik whistled as he walked down the small tunnel before coming out to the animal cages.

An intake of breath and he dropped his coffee. He jogged up and down along the cages. They were all open. He scanned quickly again. None of the birds were there.

He fumbled for the whistles. He found the one he used for Sparkles first and ran out on the grass where they did the demonstrations. He blew and waited a few seconds. He blew again and waited another minute, but there was still no sign.

He blew and blew the whistle over intervals for the next half hour. No bird, no Sparkles.

Dominik stood there, lowering his head.

The cage doors banged in the wind behind him.

*****

Neha stared at the small fire. It was the best he could do with the twigs and leaves he had gathered.

All was still; it was just before dawn. He hadn't slept since they arrived at their 'hotel'. He knew he had to get a sense of the place, get a connection with this land – with this tribe, with their spirits.

His dream had told him to come here. Now he needed more.

He had left Maria in her bed. He told her he was going for a walk. He didn't want to disturb her sleep any further, and he also didn't want any disturbance. He grabbed his small duffle bag and set off into the night air. He turned off his thoughts and trusted his feet, and impulses, to take him where he needed to go.

In the moonlight he saw the silhouette of a large arched mound that they called a 'mountain'. He had walked towards it – drawn almost. He ascended it, slowly, methodically, taking pieces of foliage, leaves and loose branches as he went.

At the top he found a spot – the spot – and built his fire, rubbing the twigs together to give birth to a small flame that was now dwindling in the pre-dawn air. Neha sat on a stone, his face painted and his eagle feather cloak on, drawn close in the cold air.

The darkness turned to a morning twilight. He realised he was at the edge…

The fire died out in front of him.

The wind swirled around and gusted past.

The flame suddenly shot up from the wood in front of him, spreading to the branches, engulfing all it touched. Neha stood and let go of his cloak, letting it flutter in this wind around him.

A shimmer of light on the horizon, the birth of the day.

The flame crackled beside him. Neha looked into it as more sunlight spread over the valley beneath him. He began to walk around the fire with… slow, steady, considered foot falls. He turned and twisted as he started his dance, the sun dance.

The sun grew beyond and as it did Neha saw a circle. It was the same size as the sun rising beside it. It was the outline of… a golden circle.

Neha sped up his dance and the centre of the sun disappeared, matching the outline of the golden semi-circle beside it.

Two eyes appeared.

Neha twisted once more as he swiftly sat on his rock – the two eyes stared at him.

Neha closed his eyes and the two eyes remained. He began his chant. The song surged through him as he rocked back and forth. As he sang, he heard an answering voice that echoed around the valley and in the crevices beneath him. These were eyes he had seen and known – the eyes of Volo.

The eyes blinked and Neha instantly stopped singing. He heard Volo's chant echoing around him… it was the incantation for the witch, except he stopped at a certain part and then sang the same amount each time.

The song… the song was incomplete!

Volo's eyes closed and disappeared.

Neha looked at the fire before him as smoke plumed through the air. In the smoke an image formed, an old woman in a chair…singing. She looked of this land. She sang of her tribe but the words, he could not hear them; he did not know them!!

The image disappeared and another formed in the now great plume of smoke, rising into the air, that of a man, out on a rocky surface. He held something in front of him, a large sheet of what Maria had called paper. The man pointed forward.

He was the guide.

A sound came – Paka's war cry!

The fire sparked at his feet. It shone brightly momentarily, and he saw something take form. It was the image of a knife.

The fire snuffed out before Neha's eyes. Neha heard the loud cry of a bird overhead and looked up. It was an eagle.

It was Volo's eagle, he realised.

No, he thought. It was his eagle now…

*****

Maria sat drinking a coffee in the Ailbh Caves café. They had gotten into Shannon airport late at night. She had planned forward enough to book accommodation but had to rent a car. The fresh breeze that flew in their faces at Shannon airport told them both that they were not adequately dressed for this location.

Maria had assaulted the information desk lady at the airport for as much information as she could get on the Burren – accommodation, local activities, history, transport, locations etc. She was surprised at how quickly her English came back to her. The lady had tried to shut the conversation down several times, but Maria just wouldn't stop. She didn't exactly share her father's motivation for this trip, but she shared his drive and sense of urgency.

Maria was a bit more impressed with Ballyvaughan in daylight. Arriving at any location in the dead of night makes it all look a bit gloomy. The scenery here was impressive. Their hotel – The Wild Atlantic Lodge Hotel – was clean, fresh, warm and comfortable.

Maria wondered whether the local tour buses where as deadly as the pit viper she had encountered back in the forest. They would snap across the white line on the thin roads here at will, forcing you into the ditch. She had nearly gone in twice while travelling to the Ailbh Caves so she was doubly thankful that her father had not gone with her in the car. He was not used to being a passenger in a car yet. He argued about the seatbelt every time.

He had woken her in the early hours to tell her he was going for a walk. She tried to disagree at first, but he ignored her. He said he would not go far. She gave up on her worry; he was probably jet lagged.

After breakfast, she decided it was the perfect time to get out and about and do some work for her news article. She asked at reception and they recommended several places. She fancied a drive to stick her nose around the place, so she tried here. The bird sanctuary had attracted her, but it was closed.

She had then walked further up the hill compound, to the main visitor centre, and discovered that the caves themselves were closed for two weeks. The tone of the woman who sat behind the visitor desk told Maria that the lady didn't seem very impressed. So Maria had settled for a coffee, cake and some article writing instead. She chose a table away from other visitors, close to the cave entrance.

As she tapped away on her laptop she heard echoing footsteps. Men started to appear from the cave entrance. They dipped under the 'Do Not Pass' sign. They were dressed in red overalls and had yellow hard hats, protective ear muffs and eye goggles on their heads and faces. They carried what looked like drills and jackhammers.

Two other men walked out of the cave entrance. They both had the helmets, ear protectors and eye goggles, but otherwise they were dressed differently. One took his goggles off and flicked a pair of shades on. He wore a long black coat with a black suit underneath.

Maria thought he looked Hispanic. The other guy was tall, bald, western looking. He wore jeans and a checked shirt, and hard boots. They stopped beside her and to her surprise, they started speaking Portuguese.

"Brian, that could not be going any better," the suited man said. "You have a real nose for this," he said laughing.

"Yeah, well, I can't believe how good it is in there," the other man responded.

Maria detected the North American accent.

"To think these people have no clue what is really in there," said the suited man, smirking. "Did you secure the cut?" he added in a serious tone.

"We blocked it off, they'll never know we were there!" the North American man responded.

"Excellent, my friend, we will move this precious cargo out soon," the suited man responded.

"Let's grab a bite of lunch," the North American man replied.

They both walked towards the exit. As they moved towards it, Maria got a better look at their faces. She was sure she recognised one of them.

Her laptop bleeped at her. It was an email from her editor. She began typing again. A few minutes later she had the bones of an article put together. She whipped it over to her boss. He would probably tear it apart anyway. She shut her laptop down and put it into its bag, stood, and put the laptop bag strap over her shoulder. As she did, she knocked the menu off the table.

As she bent down and picked it up her eyes scanned the menu, still in writing mode. She saw the word 'yellow'. It was in the blurb 'About the Ailbh Caves'. She read the full sentence: *The name Ailbh is derived from the Irish name, Aill Bhui, which means 'yellow cliff'.*

Maria took out her phone and took a picture. There had been too many 'cave coincidences' here for her liking…

*****

Maria located her father in their room back at their hotel. She suggested some lunch and he agreed. They left the hotel and started walking down the street.

She saw a pub of some kind on the left – The Hikers Hotel.

She nodded and led her father through the open double doors in the front. The interior was rustic but homely. The wide windows at the front allowed plenty of light in. There seemed to be a good mixture of tourists, hikers and cyclists inside. The bar staff were busy as they leapt from table to table.

It was a wide bar with plenty of tables spanned out left and right. Each had their own menus. Maria sat them near a crackling fire with their backs to the wall. This would allow them to 'drink' the place in and her father to acclimatise to the place better.

Maria ordered them some food. Neha enjoyed the simplest bowl of soup. He said it was 'warming'. Maria couldn't help but agree as she ate hers. Although he then scrutinised his sandwich, only nibbling at the bread, he was still doing well for a fish out of water. She skipped off to the loo, leaving him examining the bustling surroundings.

Neha wondered how he would tell her – when he could tell Maria… the full truth. He shut his eyes for a moment. His dream… his vision, told him that the sacred structure he was searching for had been damaged.

He opened his eyes and looked around this strange place with its strange tribe. The sky spirits had not been kind with the sun to the people who inhabited this land.

Neha stared at the fire to his left. He was at least happy that the people here knew enough to do this, to ward off the evil spirit that would soon plague this place. He found it confusing that they did not cook near it, though.

Maria returned and stood beside him, putting her hands out, open palmed towards the fire. She gave a soothing sigh.

Neha started to speak to Maria in Yine. “We need to find the sacred sites. We have work to do if we are to stop her ravaging this place.”

“Yes, Father… I know,” Maria replied softly. “I will gather information today on where we should go next.”

Maria saw droplets of water hitting one of the bar windows. “But we’d best get some proper rain gear or we could be saturated as we look.”

Neha nodded in agreement.

Maria hoped he would get this all out of his system once they had seen a good number of tourist sites here. Hell, there were worse places to go to, she thought. In any case, she needed the ammunition for her newspaper articles. “Let’s have a look down the street, Father.”

They walked out of the pub and down the street to their right. As a cold gust of wind blew past them, they both shuddered. Maria grabbed her father’s hand and pulled him into a tourist shop. She located enough gear for them, both warm clothes and rain gear. She had him carry the items as she expertly weaved her way through the aisles of the shop.

As she located a thick looking ‘Aran jumper’ and framed it up against her father, his laser like eyes indicated that he was quite finished in here. She paid a pretty penny for the gear, but it seemed worth it. They left the tourist shop and headed back towards their hotel.

Suddenly, a great gust of wind swept down the road, stopping them in their tracks. Maria had to briefly put a hand in front of her face. A woman across the street lost all her shopping as bits and bobs scattered down the street.

CRASH!

Maria and Neha turned to see a splayed bunch of cyclists on the road, a dozen or so collapsed on each other. The wind died out, without warning, just as it had started. Maria saw some of the cyclists hobbling over to the other side of the road.

Her father was already assisting the woman gather her items strewn out on the path. *What a gentleman,* thought Maria. Maybe this trip would be good for him, before she sat him down for a serious conversation of what he would do next in Brazil.

Something white caught her eye ahead. It was a piece of paper fluttering off a lamp post. It ripped off and the wind carried and danced it down the street. It sailed up towards Maria's chest. She caught it, just as her father rejoined her. As Maria straightened the piece of paper, and read it, she smiled – '*Jack Royson, Guided Burren Walks, Scenic Views, Historic Sites. All abilities catered for!*' There was a telephone number at the bottom.

"This is what we are looking for, Father! This man takes people out in the Burren. We'll call him."

As Neha nodded his approval, Maria folded up the piece of paper into her pocket.

*****

"Go left, Maria," said Neha. "No, not that way!" Neha's elbows and forearms fluttered around the place like a flapping angry bird.

Maria put the car into reverse again. Her eyes rolled up. She sighed and wondered if her eyes could actually roll all the way back in her skull. Probably not possible, until tonight's events that was…

It was pitch black, around 4:30 a.m. Her father had insisted that she take him out in the car. His snoring had kept her awake for most of the night. She had just drifted off when he shook her awake. He said that they had to find someone, their guide. He wouldn't say who that was exactly, but he said it was someone important. She had snapped back that they had him… that Jack Royson. But he ripped the quilt off her.

She was in the car now, only because she was now sure that her father was suffering from Post-Traumatic Stress Disorder. She would give this nonsense ten more minutes and that was it!

Chapter 18

Neha rolled to his left as Maria drove the car quickly around another bend.

Neha had heard the sound of the horn in his dream first.

Then he saw… a man, the image of a man. It was the man he had seen in his vision on the mountain. It was their guide… running from the witch.

As Neha's eyes snapped open, the sound of the horn came again.

He had woken Maria and she had reacted like an angry snake. He knew he wasn't helping the situation by not telling her the full story. But they had little time…

As he told Maria to take a right, Neha heard a different sound now… the sound of an eagle.

*****

Two arms reached forth from the fog in front of Ed, grabbing him and pulling him forward. Ed stopped hearing the wind as he was nearly nose to nose with… another apparition.

He was shorter than Ed, but broad. He had a bowl shaped haircut. Black hair. His skin was tanned. His lips were pressed together. His eyes, they seemed to glitter, a bright green with golden flecks around the iris. Those eyes were just like…

Ed heard the cry of a bird overhead. The man nodded directly behind him, dragging Ed by one arm. Ed didn't resist.

The man stopped from time to time. When the bird cried above, they moved. But they seemed to move in a very strange direction. At one point, Ed, delirious or not, was sure the man took him in a circle. Ed heard him muttering to himself now as well. Then with another cry of the bird above, the man turned Ed in the complete opposite direction they had been walking.

And suddenly they emerged from the fog.

Ed raised his forearm and half closed his eyes as an early morning sun beamed down on them. As Ed's eyes adjusted, he saw a car parked down at the road in front of them. Ed followed the man without question.

A young woman got out of the car. As they reached the road, Ed stopped, sitting down and nearly collapsing heavily in the process. The yellow backpack felt like a ton weight now. Ed's chest heaved in and out.

A water bottle was thrust in his face. Ed snatched at it and emptied the bottle into his mouth as much of the water spilled out onto his clothes.

Ed heard the cry of the bird above once more. He looked up. It was big. A hunting bird of some kind. Down it spiralled from the sky, landing on a stone wall just behind him. It fluttered its wings and screeched at the man. He simply nodded to it. The woman wore a surprised expression, mouth hung open. She said something quickly to the man in a language Ed didn't understand before continuing to scrutinise the bird.

The eagle, Ed guessed, tilted its head and squawked at the man again before leaping up and taking off into the morning air. Ed lost sight of it as it flew into the morning sunlight.

*****

Ed lay in his bath in his hotel room. The two tourists had taken him back to their hotel. As luck would have it, Pat the owner knew Ed from his hiking business during the summer. He saw the state Ed was in. He assisted him up to one of his free rooms straight away and then called Dr. Flynn, the local G.P. The doctor arrived and checked Ed out. Ed insisted on not going to hospital. He said he wanted heat and rest.

"Nothing broken," said the doctor. He had to stitch up Ed's chin though and clean out a nasty cut on his elbow. But otherwise, he concurred with Ed, said he'd be waiting in the hospital forever before he got seen to. Dr. Flynn left him with an abundance of paracetamol and other stronger pain killers.

Ed followed the doctor's instructions, had a hot shower and collapsed into bed. He slept like a dead person, waking in the late afternoon. He had many bangs and bruises, and not least, a very sore jaw. He got up and ran a hot bath to regulate his temperature as the doctor had said. He now lay in the hot water and ruminated on the events of last night. There was no escaping the issues. He had to face up the facts:

1. There was some kind of supernatural event taking place around here.

2. He had witnessed and nearly been killed by something paranormal.

3. This evil paranormal entity may have killed Aine, probably the poor man near Fanore beach … and possibly many others; and

4. He was seeing dead people.

Ed sighed as he tried to accept… all of this.

Leaving was, of course, the only realistic course of action.

But could he leave this here? Could he park this trauma and carry on with life elsewhere, knowing that this had actually happened? If he told anyone, they would think him psychotic. What if he saw dead people in the future? Was there any solution or conclusion he could cling to before he left? That's what addled him, he realised, placing his hand over his mouth.

The only conclusion that Ed could draw, if any, was there was no port for this storm.

His troubled mind was interrupted by knocking on the door. He had ordered a full meal to his room. Starter, main course, dessert. The full trimmings. Ed got out of the bath and put on his robe, the pendant around his neck the only other thing he was wearing. He opened the door, but it wasn't to a nice staff member with a tray. It was the kind woman who had driven him back to the hotel.

"Oh, hello," Ed managed.

"Hello, how are you feeling?" the woman asked.

"Pretty tired," Ed offered.

The woman paused before saying anything, as if expecting something. "My name is Maria," she continued. "My father and I are tourists here and we need to see the Burren and some of the sites." Maria took out a piece of paper and unwrapped it, handing it to Ed.

Ed gave a long sigh, not hiding his annoyance. It was one of the Jack Royson adds he stuck up months ago. He was sure he had picked them all up but clearly not.

"Pat downstairs said you provide this service," Maria added.

"Look," said Ed. "I am not sure that you–"

"We have travelled a very long way, Mr. Royson, and as far as I remember, we rescued you last night!" Maria said sternly. "We need you to take us to whatever 'sacred sites' are around here."

Ed nodded, noting that her eyes bulged now. He found it hard to make eye contact. "Well, I'm not sure how long I can give you. There are lots of sacred sites–"

"Could you not try? Give us a day, even?" Maria shot out.

He pursed his lips. "Okay, I will take you out. But just for one day. You have gear?"

"Yes."

"Meet me downstairs then, ready to go at 8 a.m."

"Fine," said Maria.

Maria turned and started to walk away. "And I don't expect us to be charged!"

"Yeah, that's fair," Ed offered with a very small smile. "Maria!" he shouted.

She half turned, glaring at him.

"Thank you, thank you very much, and your dad for helping me," Ed offered with a small smile.

Maria gave Ed a nod.

Ed shut the door.

He had lost his appetite. She was a bloody stunner!

*****

Sergeant Ahern sat at her desk, placing the completed report into Aine O'Sullivan's file. She closed the file and shoved it to her left. She would offer some sense of closure to Aine's parents tomorrow. The anonymous tip had come via voicemail. Strange accent, muffled voice. She listened to it several times after they found the body up on Turlough Hill.

Aine didn't resemble herself at all. But how could she, trapped in that crevice for the past year. She had gotten forensics down for this. She hadn't contacted Billy Joe about it either. She knew what the answer would be. His point of view on these incidents was becoming too tired and too forceful.

She was Sergeant here. She had to remind herself of that daily. But Billy Joe, her uncle, had dug her out of a hole in Limerick. She tried to never think about it. It made her skin crawl. Finding Aine, but more to the point, finding out what happened to her was all Ahern cared about now.

She had met the family of the French hiker at Shannon Airport and assisted in the repatriation of the body to France. She offered that he had slipped and fell. But she did no final report for that. Billy Joe had made her pull the forensics team. His never ending fear of damaging the tourist season here seemed to motivate his every decision.

"Forensics could leak it. Bring the media down unnecessarily," Billy Joe had said. "The answer is tragic but obvious, he fell," he concluded.

Ahern squeezed the thin top of her nose between her forefinger and thumb. She shut her eyes. Two other hikers had gone missing in the last few months. Hardly anyone knew. She had accepted Billy Joe's answers for calling off the searches. Had she accepted or… had she been bullied? Somewhere in between perhaps.

She had protested at first but then he would look away and talk about what a bind she had been in before. How he had to do a lot to fix it. She of course 'could make the final call' he had said.

Ahern pushed a few buttons on her desk phone. She twisted in her chair and stared at her reflection in the window. It was clear on the window pane as the lamplight struck it. She continued staring at her reflection, as she listened to the anonymous voicemail tip.

She would sit there and listen to it many more times before leaving.

Chapter 19

Maria watched as her father patted his highlighter pink 'Great Outdoors' jacket with his hands, as he took slow methodical steps towards the car. She reminded herself that he wasn't used to wearing clothes or footwear like this. She had neglected to tell him that the jacket was, in fact, a lady's jacket. But it fit him perfectly and the shop had no others.

She had to admit that the hiking boots took some getting used to. So for her father, hiking boots were probably an uncomfortable and strange experience. He got as close as sandals for his feet in the forest, if at all.

Maria noted the curious expression on Ed's face. Yes, 'Ed', she thought. He had clarified that his name was Ed, not Jack. She didn't ask why.

Neha shuffled into the car in his own particular manner. He sat in the passenger seat beside Ed.

As Ed continued to stare at her father, she saw him simply turn to Ed and point his finger forwards. Ed shrugged, started the car, and moved towards the exit of the small hotel cark park. Maria supposed that Ed had gotten more of a reaction from her father this time, unlike this morning when Ed had thanked them profusely for the rescue at the hotel reception. Her father gave Ed the simplest nod in acknowledgement before repeating the phrase he had plagued her with, 'sacred sites'.

She thought Ed had been ungrateful at first, after she called up to his room, but it was probably equally rude for her to not ask how he had ended up in that desperate situation, out on the rock. But she had the whole day to broach the subject. And this day was certainly needed as her editor had been on to her about getting the next part of her 'Irish Adventure' in.

Ed turned the car to the right and sped off out of Ballyvaughan. He explained that they were heading to a 'sacred site' close by called the Poulnabrone Portal Dolmen. They would then make the short drive to Poulawack Cairn. If they had time, Ed explained, they would finish at Corcomroe Abbey, close to Ballyvaughan. He clarified he was doing some sort of audit and he needed to check it.

As Ed drove on, Maria looked out the window.

The sun darted in and out between a patchwork of white cloud and blue sky. The sea filtered in and out of view between trees and other obstacles on her left side. But the picture up in the two front seats seemed rather different to the pleasant scenery outside. They seemed quiet, both of them. They stared forwards.

It was like something was weighing them down.

*****

Ed was making the short drive from Poulnabrone Dolmen to Poulawack Cairn.

He watched Neha as he bounced up and down in the seat beside him. He sat in the seat like a person trapped in a straightjacket, his arms hugged around his body. To say the least, it was distracting when they came to bumps in the road. Neha's body would bob up and down, back and forth, side to side. Tight lipped, he would say nothing.

When Neha got into the car, he dealt with the situation as if he was getting up on a horse. Standing to the side of the car, he would first raise his right leg sideways and in. Sitting then, he would loop in his left leg. When he got out, he would hang from the doorway as if he was about to do a parachute jump from a plane.

Just five minutes ago Neha had argued with Maria about the seatbelt… again. Ed didn't understand their language, but he could tell they weren't holding back in their heated exchange.

Their trip to Poulnabrone Dolmen had been interesting. Poulnabrone Dolmen was probably the biggest tourist hotspot around. Ed had watched as Neha skipped the queue, hopped over the rope and went in under the dolmen, examining it as if he were a car mechanic looking at the base of a raised car. Then he slowly walked around the structure and started chanting.

When Ed asked Maria what he was doing, she responded but kept her head tilted into her right hand, eyes shut. She said that he must put the 'ancients' to rest.

As Ed parked the car in a lay by near Poulawack Cairn, he decided he would have to keep a close eye on Neha.

*****

Maria looked across the grey cracked landscape in front of her. It looked like nothing she had seen before. She watched her father navigate his feet slowly over the fissures between the rocky slabs. Slow and steady steps and accentuated high knee movements up and down.

Maria realised that his walk matched the rocky terrain in front of her as it resembled pictures of the moon. It certainly seemed other worldly. Only the sound of a whistling wind reminded her she was still on earth.

She looked to her left and saw Ed. He seemed distracted, looking to his left, his right, then behind him. His teeth were clenched. He noticed her looking over.

"All right then, let's move towards the hill over there."

In the distance Maria could see the hill sitting there. As a grey cloud darted over it, the hill seemed hidden in shadow.

"What's he doing?" Ed asked, pointing past Maria.

Turning, she saw her father's hiking boots to his side. He was just finishing taking off his socks, exposing his feet. He stood up.

"Father, what are you–"

But her father was already off, darting quickly over the limestone blocks towards the mountain.

"He'll cut himself or he'll do an ankle," said Ed sternly.

Ed was just cupping his hands around his mouth to bellow when Maria touched his elbow. "Leave him," Maria said. "He is full of surprises."

Maria set off after him. Ed quickly followed.

*****

Neha skirted amongst the rocky ground and fissures with ease now. As the wind slowly moved around him, he wondered if he could tell the others about the voices he was hearing. It was in a language he couldn't understand but the voices seemed longing or… desperate. He sensed that they were linked to something on top of that hill, which Ed had taken them to see.

As Neha reached the base of the hill he stopped, looking for the safest way up. A hand grabbed his arm, yanking him round.

Ed was puffing hard through red cheeks. Maria was just behind him.

"Slow down," said Ed. Maria began translating for her father. "You can't go that fast when we are going up there," Ed continued. "Also, I'm not sure you should climb up in bare feet–"

Neha placed his left hand onto Ed's wrist and left it there for a few seconds as they both locked eyes. "*Yane bens hut di* calling for us… they need our help," said Neha as he broke free of Ed's grip and started moving forwards.

Had Ed heard him correctly… had Neha spoken English?

Ed scrambled ahead of Neha. "Follow me!" he said, pointing the forefinger of his right hand at Neha's face. "And let's take it slow," he added as he turned and moved up.

Ed soon found the trail that would take them up to the first terrace. Neha seemed to have no issue and followed directly behind Ed on his left.

Maria was a bit slower.

As they reached the top of the first terrace, Ed stopped and turned. Neha passed him and stopped too. Maria reached them both. As she did, she slipped forward, Ed catching her by her elbows. She regained her footing and Ed pulled her up. They were chest to chest, nearly face to face.

As Maria retracted her neck backwards, Ed asked, "Do have your footing?"

"Yes, fine," she replied sharply. She moved her arms out of his hands, as if untangling them from something.

"Oh right… sorry!" said Ed with a wobble in his voice as he released Maria.

Maria could see the trail and moved on swiftly.

Neha followed her.

As they reached the ledge of the second terrace, Maria and Neha didn't wait for instructions. They climbed up easily. Ed followed. The trail veered up and sharply left.

"We are nearly there," said Ed. "Another ten minutes and it will flatten out a bit."

He looked down at the limestone terrace below. He could see figures moving in the morning light, hikers in twos and threes making their way over the clints and grikes. Some were already at the base of the hill. The tourist trail would lead them up here.

As Ed was about to move off, he found Neha beside him. Ed jumped, slightly startled. The man seemed to have a gift for appearing out of nowhere. Ed saw he was just staring out at the sky. Maria arrived at his left.

"Do you see the cloud bank ahead, Ed?" Maria began translating for Ed as her father spoke.

Ed could see a large cloud bank clinging to the horizon. He nodded his affirmation.

"It reaches towards us in one sense but stretches back a long way into the distance. It seems white at our end but dark and grey… and distant beyond."

"Well, the distance is the horizon–"

"And beyond that you see the line of light at its base?"

"Yes, sure," said Ed, as he swallowed a yawn.

"That is the edge, Ed, the edge of two worlds. It represents the connection with us and the sky spirits. They are there, Ed… beyond."

Yeah... and so are the fucking Care Bears, mate, thought Ed. He put on a straight face and nodded to Neha as he looked at the sky.

Ed waited a further moment before directing them back towards the trail. A short time later, they arrived at the summit and the stony cairn came into view. Ed started to give Neha and Maria some information on the cairn as they moved closer.

He said that construction of the 21 metre sized rocky structure had taken place over 1,800 years, starting in approximately 3350 BC. That its purpose was probably to act as a prehistoric burial site, likely for someone very important. Ed took out his camera and a small clipboard from his backpack and started taking some notes.

Maria stretched her hand out and rubbed it on one of the ancient stones. She walked on.

Neha stretched his hand forth but much slower. His hand seemed to glance on the side of one rock. Keeping it at that level, he began slowly walking the length of it. Ed saw his lips moving and could hear some words being repeated over and over.

Ed put away his clipboard and started to walk around the cairn, taking pictures with his camera as he did so. He reached the far side…

"NO!" he shouted.

Nearly a third of the cairn was badly damaged. Rocks were strewn across the ground, some clearly having tumbled down the slanted side of the mountain.

Ed cursed internally. Not here as well! His brain scrambled for an answer, but he realised all logical explanations had left his brain long ago. There might be specialists somewhere who could put this back together, but it would never be the same.

"Who could have done this!?" Ed snarled the words out loudly.

Neha arrived alongside Ed, touching his wrist briefly. "You know who, Ed… she did."

Ed gave Neha a confused look before closing his eyes briefly and shivering. He grasped his coat collar tightly. He took off his backpack again. He still had some tape and poles in the car, but it would be a bloody forty minute walk down and back up.

Neha walked past Ed, and Ed did a double take.

Neha had one of the stones in his hands. He walked over to the cairn and delicately placed it down. Then he marched past Ed again and began scanning the ground.

Ed looked at Maria, who had arrived at his side. "Tell him to stop what he is doing, immediately!" said Ed in an exasperated tone.

Maria stepped forward and began speaking with her father. He simply stepped around her with another stone in his hand. As he carefully placed the stone down, two hikers walked by them. They stopped, with open mouths and aghast expressions. They looked at the sprawling rocks and then at Neha placing another stone on the pile.

Ed rubbed his right hand over his face, clamping his eyes shut. His face flushed red. As he opened his eyes, he saw a much larger group of hikers arrive on the scene, at least twenty of them. They all had similar green jackets on. They stood with stunned expressions.

Ed stormed over to Neha, quickly followed by Maria. "STOP THIS NOW!" Ed bellowed.

Maria did not bother translating that.

Neha placed another stone on the cairn, twisting and turning the stone in place, until satisfied.

"YOU ARE DAMAGING AN ANCIENT ARCHEOLIGICAL SITE THAT HAS STOOD HERE FOR THOUSANDS OF YEARS!"

Maria translated.

With a calmness in his voice Neha responded, "The dead have no power to rebuild their home. They have been disconnected from their place beyond and are confused and unsure of… here. We must help them," he added as he reached past Ed and took a stone from out reached hands. Ed turned to see a middle aged female hiker.

"Please stop!" said Ed.

She responded in something like Italian. The tone was very matter of fact. The rebuttal clear.

Ed watched as Maria now started to help them. She began indicating to her father with stone in hand as to where she thought the stones should go. Neha and Maria began bickering on the point until she was waved away by him with an exaggerated movement of his right arm, as if casting away an evil spirit.

Suddenly, two hikers split from the large group of green jacketed hikers and began passing stones up. Then three more, then four more…then the whole group joined.

Ed turned back and a systematic line had formed with random hikers joining all the time. They passed the stones up. As Neha received each stone carefully, he seemed more assured of the placing of each as he carried on.

Ed placed his hands behind his head. Shrugging, he trudged down the hill, joining the bottom of the line. Soon more hikers arrived. Some joined while others took pictures or videos on their phones. Within an hour, the line of hikers had formed a well organised supply line.

By midday, a camera crew had arrived. Ed did his best to hide his face. He noticed that a strange looking small, chubby bald man had broken into the line and was handing Ed stones. As the journalist stood in front of the camera, mic in hand, the small man dropped the stone just before handing it to Ed and raced over to the camera crew. The stone just missed Ed's foot as it landed with a thud. The journalist seemed delighted to accommodate the man who spread and flapped his hands around the place. Ed saw the journalist lean a microphone towards the man.

As Ed passed a stone to the next person, he turned for the next one, but a green jacketed hiker said, "That's it. That's the lot."

Ed instead concentrated his attention on the camera crew and the interview being conducted with the small chubby man. The wind carried such statements as:

"There is great community spirit in this region and you see that around you here…"

"We respect our ancient sites…."

"This is a hands on constituency. I'm happy to help being a hands on person and politician."

But the interview soon stopped as the camera man moved the camera, pointing over the interviewer's head to something upwards.

As Ed heard the song being sung, he knew who it was before he turned.

Ed and everyone else watched as Neha stood in front of the re-built cairn. He sang a song, low and humming. Ed could make out words but could not say what they were. Neha carried on for at least five minutes. The song got stronger and louder as he went on.

Then he suddenly stopped and bowed his head and a brief silence took hold of the hill side. The fast moving clouds overhead changed the scene between dark and light quickly.

Somebody began a slow clap. Then others started until there was a full applause. Ed watched as the camera man peeled his camera across the scene.

As the applause died down, the journalist stood back in front of the camera, placing the mic up to her lips. The small bald man darted over to Ed and started shaking his hand, thanking him. He carried on with others, his radius just behind the journalist noticeable.

As Ed went to walk away, the man who had been handing him the stones stopped him. "This has been remarkable," said the man in an American accent. "What your friend did...." he puffed out air, "exceptional!"

Ed tried a reply, "Well yes, I suppose–"

"Hey, do you and your buddies want to come with us? We are a group of archaeologists from Harvard. We are about to go for lunch in Carran."

"I'm not sure we have the tim–"

"For a free lunch… surely you do?" said the man quickly. "I'm Professor Jackson," he said as he led Ed up towards Neha.

The professor explained that the group were over on a field trip to commemorate the Harvard archaeologists who had travelled over in the '50s and originally excavated Poulawack. They were staying nearby at Galway University's Archaeological Research Centre.

As the professor, Maria, Ed and Neha converged on the hill, Ed ran the lunch idea past Maria and Neha. Maria and Neha seemed happy with that and Neha was keen to get information on the area. Soon, the whole thing was agreed. What harm, Ed reckoned as his stomach rumbled.

As Ed reached the base of the hill, he turned back. In the distance, three people stood at the top, in front of the cairn. He placed his hand over his brow and peered up at them.

They weren't hikers.

Two women and one man dressed in… animal garments. His best guess. When Professor Jackson called to Ed, all three raised their right hands to their chests.

Ed turned away and joined the group.

*****

Ed pulled his car into Costigan's pub car park.

On entering the homely looking pub, the green jacketed group were spanned out across the spacious room. The pub seemed made for mingling, Ed realised. Who knows, he thought, he might get lucky here and get himself over to Harvard. That would be a just reward for the ordeal he had gone through here. This lunch stop was now a networking opportunity!

As they walked into the centre of the room, Neha and Maria were soon swarmed by green jackets. Maria, to be fair, smiled at them all and explained who they were, translating their questions to her father and giving them his responses.

Ed wasted no time and warmly introduced himself to the people standing closest to him, as he rummaged in his pockets, searching for his business cards.

Soon platters of warm sandwiches and soup arrived. Most people stayed on their feet as they delved into the sandwich platters. A few of the American team had gotten half pints of Guinness. Excellent, thought Ed, as this would mellow them all out even further.

Ed wandered around the room, sandwich in hand, chatting as he went. He saw Neha and Maria sitting in one corner, their soup bowls empty. Neha elbowed Maria, pointing at her watch. She held up the watch towards Ed, tapping the face with one finger so Ed got the point.

But he was doing well.

He had met two other professors and they seemed more than interested in the work he was doing. He handed them his card. As he offered a fake laugh to a boring joke, he saw a man sitting just to his right, on his own. He wore the same jacket as the rest of the group. He guessed he was either African or African American by his complexion. The man was bald on top but had longs tufts of black to grey hair stuck out at the sides of his head. Small circular glasses hung at his nose. Ed hoped he was another professor.

“Hello there, you enjoying your stay?” Ed noted that the group he was talking with seemed to turn away.

"I would do, but no one attended my lecture this morning," said the man in a slightly whiney voice as he stared forward.

"Oh, timing issue?" responded Ed.

"Who knows, they all went out on a hike anyhow."

Ed stopped that line of questioning as the man let out a long and sensitive sounding sigh.

"What was the lecture on?" asked Ed.

The man immediately looked at Ed. "The ancients, energies and time portals," he said enthusiastically.

Ed didn't know what to say.

"Hey Ed, come on over here. There is someone I would like you to meet," Professor Jackson said, appearing out of nowhere.

"Nice to talk with you," said Ed to the man.

"Likewise," he replied almost sullenly as Professor Jackson pulled Ed by the arm, leading him away.

"That's Professor Whaley," whispered Professor Jackson. "He's on our trip," he said through a scrunched up face, "but he's here for very different reasons to the rest of the group. He was a last minute addition," he concluded.

Ed nodded. "Well his lecture sounds… unique."

Professor Jackson nodded slowly, looking over Ed's shoulder at Professor Whaley. "Oh… I would say it's entertaining." The professor chuckled lightly. "He had some of my students searching the Burren earlier this week," he made eye contact with Ed, "for ghosts!"

The man driving the group's coach came in and bellowed it was time to get going.

"Well, that's us, Ed!" said the professor. "We are heading up to Ballyvaughan for the night. Staying in the Hikers Hotel. Might catch you there later." He prodded Ed as he turned to leave. "Could tell you all about Harvard. There's a few positions popping up next year."

Ed couldn't hide his enthusiasm in his, "Oh great, I'll see you later," reply. It was far louder than intended.

With that the professor filtered out of the pub door with the rest of the group.

Ed found Neha to his left, glaring at him. He prodded Ed with a finger on his shoulder and said something stern to him. He began tapping the face of Ed's watch.

Maria was just coming back from the toilet when the view out of a large window to her left caught her attention. The sun lit up a large lake out the back – a few grey Burren hills could also be seen in the distance. She saw a picture of the lake on a wall nearby. She scanned it quickly: *Carran Turlough, the largest 'disappearing lake' in the Burren.*

As Maria turned back around, she saw a waitress standing near the window. She stared out but directed her comment at Maria. "I don't know what they are doing out there. They've been at it for weeks!" The lady shuffled off with an armful of plates and soup bowls.

Maria looked out the window and squinted. Four small dinghies held two divers a piece. A larger boat had some kind of tube or pipe going from its deck into the water. The divers, nearly in unison, splashed into the water, falling in backwards.

"Come on, Maria," shouted Ed. "Your father's keen to get going."

Chapter 20

Ed parked his car on the side of the road. Corcomroe Abbey stood a hundred feet away. Even from this distance it seemed tall and proud, hugging the side of a grassy hill behind it.

As they got out of the car, Ed began to feed Neha and Maria with the history and facts. “It was built in the late 12th century, 1194 being the best estimate, by a ruling family in the region called the O’Brien’s.”

As Ed carried on, Neha was already through a gap in the wall, but Maria stayed and nodded slowly as Ed imparted what knowledge he had. By the time Maria and Ed reached the small graveyard beside the abbey itself, Neha had disappeared out of view.

Ed considered the structure in good nick considering it had no roof. Many of the high walls were still in place.

Ed and Maria walked through the main entrance. He began explaining to Maria about the significance of the length of the building, which in turn differentiated it from a standard church. From the air, he opined, it would probably look like the sign of the cross. They slowly walked down the old aisle, hands clasped behind their backs.

“The Abbey has a nave with an aisle on the south side. Just take note of some of the archways and their height here. Now if we can imagine how this looked if the roof was still on, how the chancel and east windows were designed to bring light in. So well planned out,” concluded Ed.

He saw Maria was staring out a small empty arched doorway to their right. Ed looked through, seeing Neha walking in the old graveyard. He seemed to be examining each grave, placing a hand to the ground at each and then shaking his head.

Maria looked down and slowly sighed. A brief silence ensued as Ed took his camera out and took a few snaps of the walls, some cracks catching his attention. He took a few pictures of the grave slabs dotted on the ground. They stretched forward across the Abbey floor.

As the silence continued, Ed glanced to Maria and saw her still staring down. He turned around and went to take another shot. "Your dad… is he okay? A lot going on back in Brazil?"

Maria rubbed her hand on her face and keeping her eyes closed said, "Yes, a lot has happened to us both." She held her hand in position over her eyes.

"Here take one end of this," said Ed as Maria opened her eyes to the end of a measuring tape.

As she stretched across one end of the building and Ed the other, Maria began telling her abridged version of the facts. They carried on walking towards the head of the church. At intervals, Ed would stop and take photos or notes. The measuring tape would come out again and she would assist. He asked her to pose in a picture or two so he could get perspective on the size of the Abbey. All the while she spilled her guts on what had happened in Brazil. How she and her father had come here. How she didn't know why they were really here.

Ed made sure not to make eye contact. This was like blind therapy and he knew that could ruin it. They stopped just before the middle 'cross' part of the Abbey where the sides extended left or right.

Maria finished her story.

Ed couldn't think of much to say except, "It sounds like that's a lot, all right. Maybe we should sit down and talk more about it later. Have a few pints – forget our woes."

Maria slowly nodded, a light smile showing on her face.

As they turned around the left corner, Ed carried on, "If truth be told, I have a hell of a story to–"

Ed stopped talking as he saw something dripping on Maria's face. They both stopped walking as she tapped her face. It was red…

They looked up.

Some type of animal was twisting on a rope, a few metres up, its entrails hanging from its belly. A pool of blood lay beneath them on the ground. As the creature twisted on the rope, its front revealed a head with no jaw. Its eyes shimmered in the late afternoon light. It was a fox, Ed realised.

Ed slowly moved forward, seeing something else. A stone slab had been removed on the floor. The earth beneath was dug up and disturbed. After years of archaeological digs, Ed could tell that no spade or other tool was responsible for the erratic looking nature of the soil. There was nothing careful or ordered about this.

“Look!” said Maria, nearly shouting.

Bones lay scattered across the floor. Human bones.

Ed saw an old stone plaque near the wall, lying partially cracked on the wall. There was blood on this too. He tried to rub it out with his hands. “Conor O’Brien… King of Thomond…. Died 1268.”

Ed turned around. Maria’s eyes were locked on the fox.

“He said this happened to his dog,” Maria muttered.

Ed thought by the tone that she would have said that whether he was there or not.

A strong wind blew by them. The fox began to swing back and forth.

“Come on, Maria! Let’s find your father and get out of here!”

“Shouldn’t we?” Maria said staring at the fox.

“No, we leave that,” replied Ed. “I don’t think that thing is for touching,” he said softly as he started moving. Maria quickly followed him.

As they got outside, quite a gale was drumming up. Trees nearby swayed around. The clouds streaked by overhead as the late September light began to dwindle.

Ed stopped, mouth hanging open.

Neha stood in what looked like a bomb site, the earth dug up all over the place.

A low keening wind moved around Maria and Ed. Maria's jacket hood flopped back and forward strangely, as if being examined. The strange breeze went beneath Ed's jacket and puffed its way around, before belting out near his hood.

Maria and Ed looked at each other with ashen faces. This was unexplainable, so neither of them tried.

Then Ed thought he could see something, people, on top of the hill. A long line of men. Some were dressed in mail, pieces of armour. Some even wore kilts. At either end of the line, a man held a pole with a flag that fluttered in the wind. He could see one man holding a large drum and another – bagpipes he thought.

A man stepped forward and unsheathed a sword, swinging it over his head. The other men raised swords, axes and spears above them. They appeared to be roaring but Ed couldn't hear anything.

The wind raced past Maria and Ed, as horses with warriors on their backs charged from behind the trees to their right. Men with axes, swords, shields and armour ran from the Abbey behind them. They seemed to run around them as they sprinted forward.

"DON'T MOVE, MARIA!!" Ed said as he wrapped his arms around her.

She gave him nothing but a perplexed look in response.

Ed saw the line of men on the hill charging down now. He looked on in horror as the warriors seemed to be converging on Neha's position. They had taken no notice of Maria or Ed.

Ed bungled through his pockets, grabbing his car keys and shoving them into Maria's hands. "Quickly, back to the car. Don't go back in there. Go around. Lock yourself in!"

Maria leaned her head back in surprise but turned and did as Ed wanted anyway.

*****

Neha stood in the middle of this burial site. It wasn't here! There were bones everywhere. It wasn't in the burial mound from earlier, either, but she was disturbing the sleeping spirits everywhere it seemed…

Neha stopped and looked up on the hill. A noise carried on the wind, the sound of drums and a strange instrumental sound he could not place. He heard the enormous cry of… men, no, warriors, coming down the hill. He knew what a battle cry sounded like!

He looked in the other direction as the sound of more warriors seemed to be running from the holy building. Some large animals made the ground shake.

She had woken the dead here… woken them to before their death. Woken them to their last battle.

Neha stood as stiff as a large Imbuia tree as the battle converged around him. He couldn't make out all of the sounds, but he recognised the sounds of men, the screams and the shouts, the clashing of their weapons. He saw Ed in the distance.

He seemed to be doing some strange elaborate dance as he made his way towards his position.

*****

Ed couldn't believe this! He pivoted past another fighting pair as they exchanged violent sword and axe blows on each other's shields, then ducked as a huge warrior swung a sword directly at him. It connected with a man behind him, cleaving off his head.

Despite this, Ed was nearly through the melee and wondered why Neha was just standing there. Ed rolled to his left as a horse charged past him, the man on top pointing his spear at a warrior ahead.

The warrior on the ground swung his sword. He succeeded in slowing the horse as it half turned. But he didn't succeed in raising his shield up in time as the man on top of the horse cut through him with the spear. The spear stuck in the ground, impaling the man, leaving him in a half standing position.

As the horseman reeled his horse around, he stopped and stared at Ed, as if he had just appeared to him. He drew a sword from his belt, just as a small arrow went through the side of his head. The horse moved in a panicked circle as the sword fell from the man's hand, the man sliding off the horse thereafter.

Ed raced on.

As Ed reached Neha, he collided with the back of another warrior. The warrior slipped and Ed nearly did too, before regaining his feet.

*****

Neha could hear the battle getting ever more intense. As Ed reached him, he shouted, "We must leave, Ed. We are in the midst of a great battle."

Ed spoke back but he could not understand him.

"Where is Maria?" demanded Neha.

"*Yoko uim aka* Maria?" was all Ed heard Neha say.

Neha grabbed Ed's wrists and stared at him. "Where is Maria?"

"Back at the car," shouted Ed confusedly.

Ed turned to see a band of warriors moving towards them at a slow run, weapons raised. He grabbed Neha and shouted, "Come on!"

They both ran for the right side of the Abbey.

Other men raced past, swords and spears at the ready. As Ed turned, he saw they had each engaged with the men who had been running at them.

Neha and Ed reached the side of the Abbey. A tall, broad man with a thick red beard, mail coat and axe, nearly as high as him, stood by the entrance. He wore a silver band around his head. Two other large warriors stood behind him.

He looked at Ed and pointed to the other side of the Abbey. He said something that Ed couldn't make out.

'*Hurry*!' Neha heard a voice say in the wind.

*****

Maria stood on the far side of the Abbey. Ed's car wasn't too far off. She stared at the ground near one of the high walls, taking small steps. She could have sworn that a wind knocked the car keys out of her hand. She wanted to find them quickly and get out of here. Her father was acting strangely and now Ed too.

But what disturbed her most was the sight of that fox.

Her rational brain could barely comprehend it. The similarity with the death of her father's dog, thousands of miles away…

A cloud made a shadow over the grass as Maria's phone buzzed in her pocket. She stood straight and stopped looking for the keys, taking out her phone. 'Unknown number' it said.

She hit 'answer' and placed it to her ear. She heard… a wind, then heavy breathing. She knew this, she thought as a cold streak went through her. The hairs on her neck stood up.

"Who is this!?" she half screamed, half begged.

She heard a horrible crackling laugh down the phone… a woman's voice she guessed.

A huge wind pushed her back towards the Abbey. The crackling laughter turned hysterical on the phone. The wall started to collapse in front of her.

She dropped the phone and screamed.

*****

Ed and Neha rounded the corner as a huge wind surged past them. Ed saw the wall vibrating and Maria all too close. Lungs already red raw inside, he sprinted towards her as the first rocks fell, one catching him on the shoulder. He smashed into her with something akin to a flying rugby tackle. Both of them lost their footing and slid along the ground.

The huge wall made a crunching sound and fell forward, thudding to the ground, bits of rubble and dust bobbling at their feet. Out of the dust cloud walked Neha. He grabbed a hand each and pulled them up. As they dusted themselves down, all three took in the scene. One whole wall of the Abbey had collapsed. They ran their fingers through their hair.

Maria said, “I was looking for the car keys when–”

Neha held them up. Ed snatched at them. “Let’s just get out of here and discuss everything back in Ballyvaughan.”

All three did a fast walk back to the car.

Maria examined her missed calls with an ashen looking face.

Just before the car, a hand ripped the phone from her. Her father had taken it and he subsequently threw it away as far as he could. He cursed. As he strode past her, she opened her mouth to say something, but the words never came.

Saying nothing, Ed jogged over and found the phone. He put it in his pocket.

They silently got into the car.

Ed drove off at speed.

*****

They sat in the Hikers Hotel. Three Irish stews were devoured. Little eye contact was made at the table. A small fire flickered to their left. It seemed livelier than the ‘matter of fact’ exchanges that passed for conversation at the table.

Ed and Maria excused themselves and went to the toilet.

Neha said nothing. He was coming to terms with how exposed this place was to the spirit world. He had never come across anything like it. But he noted that everyone here was not aware of this connection. If anything, they suffered the same plague he had seen in the ‘city’ in Brazil. As he scanned the pub, he saw they all had ‘mobile phones’ as well, even the children. Other distractions were these televisions. A small crowd seemed fixated on something on one, over in the far corner.

Neha needed to find the local Shaman… and soon. He could not navigate this ancient place without them. He needed someone who could speak to the ancestors of this place. Without that 'connection', he would never find the knife or the witch's lair.

Ed had the connection to the spirit world, but he didn't have the connection to this place. He also didn't seem to understand the gift he had. He had much to discuss with Ed and Maria. His daughter's life was in danger, but she was critical to the whole reason they had come here. He decided it was time to tell them both everything… before it was too late.

Neha's attention was drawn to a collection of people who sat near what Maria called 'the bar'. He understood enough to know the man behind it was serving 'alcohol'. Something was very wrong, though. Some of it looked golden and bubbly. Yellow water wasn't good, but some other drinks looked very bad… gone off… sick. The glass he stared at was full of black mud with a white slick on top of it. He had seen such white froths on the rivers at home. They only meant infection or disease. These people must have been in a stupor; they could not tell what they were drinking. Too much 'hallucinogens'. This 'man of the bar' was trying to poison them.

As one man raised his glass to his lips, Neha reached him just in time.

*****

As Ed walked back from the toilet, he decided he had to come clean. He hardly knew Maria or Neha, but he knew he had to tell them everything. If he got it off his chest he could leave this place with some semblance of sanity - maybe.

He stopped off at the bar and ordered a pint. As he leaned on the bar he noticed a small crowd, including Maria, watching a television. Ed's face went pale as he saw Aine's picture on the TV screen with the caption at the bottom reading 'Body of Missing Archaeologist Found'. Garda Ahern did an interview next with a forensics team in the background of the picture.

Ed turned away and saw something else at the far end of the pub. He watched as Neha grabbed a pint of Guinness out of the patron's hand and poured it down the sink behind the bar. "What the fuck!?" the bar fly said. He was a big unit too. The guy yanked the glass from Neha's hand and stood up.

Red Alert, thought Ed as he moved quickly from across the bar with his full pint of Guinness. He stood in front of the hulking man. "One pint of Guinness, son, just poured!"

The swaying giant examined the still settling Guinness in front of him.

"No harm done… he's just not used to this!" Ed smiled and rolled his eyes.

The large man slowly settled back into his seat. "Ah yeah… sure the lunatics always find their way outa the asylum." The man gave a guttural laugh.

Ed laughed back and nodded in agreement. "I'll just go find his minder," he said as he broke off and grabbed Neha by the arm.

Neha looked angry as he snapped his arm out of Ed's grasp.

Ed and Maria briefly looked at each other as they made their way back through the busy bar. The wide glass windows at the front of the pub showed a dusk light outside.

As Maria, Neha and Ed sat down, there was silence. The pub was slowly filling up, a blind man and his dog taking a table near them.

Ed clasped his hands, looking down, letting out a puff of air. Neha's hands moved forward on the table as he leant in. Maria and Ed followed suit.

They all interrupted each other at once, holding their hands upwards.

"Listen–"

"I must tell you–"

"We have to discuss–"

Each was insistent that they had to go first. Then they began talking over each other.

Maria noted that people were looking at them, but she carried on. This was all too important.

They all stopped as a tray clanked down on the table. Four glasses were on top of the tray. They were full up with ice and something brown. The three looked up.

"Hey there!" said Professor Whaley. "I was hoping I could join you?"

"We are in the middle–"

"All the other places are taken," the professor said as he took a seat. He passed out the glasses to each of them.

"Oh yes," said Ed. "Of… course," he added with a slow reluctance.

The professor took a swig of his drink. Ed shrugged and took a large gulp himself. Maria took a sip of hers and smiled at the professor. Neha examined the glass in front of his face first. He then smelled the drink and with a furrowed brow allowed the drink to touch his lips. He nodded in approval as he took a large sip.

"I have had quite a day and didn't fancy drinking alone," said the professor in an exasperated tone.

"We know the feeling," muttered Maria.

"Are Professor Jackson and the rest of the Harvard crowd not around?" said Ed as he scanned the packed pub.

"Nope, they went for a meal," said the professor, slurring his words slightly. "Neglected to tell me until the last minute. Fully booked, apparently. No one was willing to listen to my lecture earlier either. If they had, they would have learned about this…"

The professor rummaged through his bag and produced a strange looking object from his bag. It was small and white. Some green lights flickered on a tiny arched light panel.

“It looks like a wifi modem?” guessed Ed.

“That, my sir, is a graviton,” answered the professor.

“What does it do?” asked Maria.

“It measures energy, particularly the energy of ancient places. If you had gone to my lecture, you would all understand,” he added as he pointed at each of them individually. “Ancient places give off an energy, but it is sometimes not detectable as it is on the edge of our reasoning.”

Neha looked at Maria for an explanation. She quickly translated what the professor had said.

Neha downed the contents of his glass and placed it on the table. He leant forward, urging the professor to talk on with a flick of his hand, thrusting his empty glass towards Ed and dismissing him with his other hand towards the bar behind him.

“Right, then,” said Ed. “Point taken!”

Ed took a brief drinks order and headed to the bar. Maria, meanwhile, filled in the professor on who she was and more pointedly, who her father was and where he came from. She explained he was a Shaman… following her father’s insistence.

As Ed returned to the table, with the drinks, he heard the professor say, “Well, your dad is in some ways a walking graviton.”

The professor placed a hand on the small device as the green lights continued to flicker. “I came up with this device with a friend. I was checking out the Americas whilst he was transiting Europe. Recently I got word that he died here, had a horrible fall. But Adrien said that this place was ‘active’ in his last email to me.”

The professor took a swig of his pint. The other three did the same with their drinks but all kept their eyes on him.

“He had other gifts that enabled him to reach this conclusion. Rare gifts,” the professor said as he glanced to Neha and Ed.

Ed felt himself going pale. He started to feel like the poker player who had to ‘call’ but was simply too afraid.

"Well, Professor," Ed sighed. "I think I saw your friend fall. I called it in into the local police."

Ed told the table the story, making eye contact with no one.

"You think Adrien fell or was pushed by a person in black?" asked the professor.

"It was far away–"

"The witch!" said Neha, grabbing Maria's hand. "It has to be!"

Maria translated Neha's words with an apologetic face to the professor. Ed noted that he needed no translation…

Ed paused. "I think she was there the other night, too. The night you found me out in the Burren," he said as he looked at Neha.

Neha nodded enthusiastically, looking at Maria. "She has come here!" he said but Maria was looking away and didn't translate.

"This must sound rather illogical, Professor," said Ed.

"Not in the slightest. In fact, it is very on point."

Maria got up, indicating she was getting another round.

Ed's back straightened as realisation swept through him. "Professor Jackson told me you were looking for ghosts?"

Professor Whaley finished his pint and gave Ed a small smile. "In a manner of speaking," he replied through nearly clenched teeth. "Ancient places can carry or hold ancient energy, of many types. But I strongly believe it can hold that of people too."

There was a pause as Maria handed out the drinks and sat down.

"So ghosts… then?" prodded Ed as he turned his hand in a circular motion.

The professor's face contorted in what looked like pain. "The Burren is a place full of rock," he said, as Neha elbowed Maria until she started translating again.

The professor leaned in now, whispering, "Certain types of landscapes can hold minerals or gas. This place is instead a conductor for energy.

If I'm right, this energy is now being released somehow and it is causing some strange events to occur."

"But what does that have to do with the rock here, and ghosts?" Ed pushed.

The professor seemed to become slightly frustrated with Ed. "Where have you heard ghosts being associated with?"

Ed shrugged. The professor glared at him.

"I don't know," said Ed. "Stories… places… myths."

"Houses!" said Maria.

"Yes, and?" urged the professor as he pointed across at her.

"Eh. Buildings?" guessed Maria.

"Right on!" said the professor enthusiastically. "Most ghosts," he said, as he paused to use the inverted commas sign with his hands for 'ghosts', "are in fact an energy. They are an energy often associated with where they lived, and those places were commonly houses or buildings."

Ed shifted in his chair. "There's hardly many of them in the Burren, or at least not enough to explain what's going on."

"I'm getting there, Ed. Hold on. You should have come to my lecture and you wouldn't be so far behind!" the professor said, smiling.

Maria and Ed chuckled at that. Neha did too once the translation went through.

"Most ghosts are associated with people. Those people lived in those houses or buildings. As they did, their very essence interacted with the surroundings they were in… I believe right down to the granular or quantum level.

"As they moved around their surroundings something inside them, this energy, left its traces there every day. The house itself, the structure, the materials, stored that energy in various ways, but only as a memory in some cases."

A small silence gripped the table as each took a good swig of their drinks.

"This energy is the spirit," said Neha, as Maria translated.

"Or the soul," Ed muttered, his mouth covered over with one finger.

"Maybe so, guys. This energy, the spirit, the soul, quantum mechanics – it could all be interlinked in the end."

The professor paused as if considering his own statement, then continued, "You may or may not have heard of the ghost that is always sighted, that repeats the same action. The energy or memory of it can manifest itself in the most basic fashion; walking through the same wall, for example. I believe that if you knock down the building or house, the energy goes away with it because it can no longer manifest from the materials within that house."

"So it goes into… the air?" said Maria.

"Yes, it could do, or into other elements. But some places, we are now discovering; some types of rocks, in abundance, can store, resonate and enhance this energy into something greater. The Burren, for example, is full of a huge abundance of limestone rock. And it's full of these grikes and clints?" said the professor, directing the question to Ed.

The professor caught the attention of a passing bar employee and waved his hand like a magician over the four glasses.

"Caused by glacial erosion," offered Ed.

"Maybe, Ed, but those grikes could also act like a grid, keeping the energy apart or joining it up at other moments or… maybe monuments."

"Like joining it at the tombs?" said Ed, with hesitancy in his voice.

"Yes, Ed! They're called portal tombs or portal dolmens for a reason, but not the reason we archaeologists got used to!"

"It sounds like you're onto an interesting theory there–"

"But I didn't discover it, Ed! The ancients did first. You said it yourself. The 'Portal' Dolmens! I am saying that the ancients knew all about the afterlife but also about this energy, spirit or soul," he said, waving his hand to Neha and Ed, "long before we did. They were in tune–"

"Connected," said Maria, translating for Neha.

"With their surroundings," the professor continued. "The Neolithic, the Mesolithic, the Bronze Age peoples and most notably, the Egyptians… all built structures not only to honour the dead but to hold their energy, too."

Neha nodded, saying, "So they are together in life and in death." Maria translated.

"They built an afterlife for themselves?" said Ed.

"Quite possibly, Ed. That is what the Egyptians were very direct about," the professor added.

As a staff member added some logs to the fire at their left, the conversation broke down.

After a minute or two, Neha said something to Maria. She paused before translating, rolling her eyes slightly.

"The witch… the witch escaped here, how?"

The professor paused before shifting in his chair. "I assume you mean this witch is an energy," he mumbled. "Ed, you remember your early archaeological studies. Energy grids of the earth?"

Ed looked bamboozled.

"Something along those linnessss," the professor goaded, emphasising the last word. "Some of the 'filler' they taught you in your first year."

Ed moved his hand to his pint, but the professor moved Ed's glass back.

"Come on, I know you can connect this," he said as Ed sighed.

An expression of realisation dawned across Ed's face as he scrambled in his pocket. He produced his phone. "One minute," he mumbled. "Here!" he said, as he moved the phone to the centre of the table. "Ley lines, Professor?"

"Correct, Ed!"

All four looked at the screen. A world map appeared with diagonal lines strewn across it.

As Maria explained to her father what the image was, the professor picked up the phone and seemed to be zooming in with his fingers on something. After he placed it back down, an image of South America and the edge of Europe was zoned in. The professor looked at Maria and she in turn began explaining the image to her father. He nodded quickly back to the professor.

"Ley lines in their most basic form are believed to be energy lines. Remarkably, the ancient cultures not only built their structures on these lines, but corresponding structures over large distances seem to link the lines into these diagonal formations. This would suggest that the ancients recognised these energy lines but also knew their path.

"If we were to really reach with this theory, it would seem that one ancient culture knew another had built a structure and they in turn built one to correspond, or balance or channel the energy that the ley or energy line had."

"A possible form of communication?" said Ed, as he stared at the phone.

"Maybe and maybe not. Certainly, if it was also for communication, it might not have been for the type of communication we use today. Maybe the structure in some respect was an acknowledgement of a connection elsewhere on earth."

"So they couldn't communicate with each other?" asked Maria.

"Not necessarily, I can't tell that for sure, but your father as a Shaman may understand more than we ever will about that. I could only go as far as saying that they felt a need to build the structures; to channel, respect or even restrict the energy associated with such lines. My final conclusion is that some vast burial sites were constructed with a mind to build a real afterlife for themselves. Two things back up my theory, first this Graviton device and secondly, your father."

Maria looked confused.

"I would bet that there is certainly more than meets the eye about him. He reminds me of Adrien… he has a twinkle about his eyes."

The professor smiled across at Neha.

As Maria translated, Neha's face went stony and he leaned back in his chair.

Ed pointed at the professor's phone. "Looking at this ley line, Professor, it seems to transverse across Peru or Brazil and carry on across the Atlantic to–"

"Here," the professor said, smiling like a Cheshire cat.

He looked at Maria. "Although these maps aren't accurate, if a 'witch' or in my belief, a type of energy, has escaped where your father came from, this might mean that a structure, holding the energy there, has also been damaged or disturbed."

Maria carried on translating for her father.

"But that would mean there would have to be a structure damaged here as well, if she was to travel on the ley line and be… released here," said Ed.

"I would not say 'released' as such but more an 'un-balancing' of the energy in the region," said the professor. "You might say that there has been an energy spike here. That is what I have concluded and that is what Adrien detected. The movement of an energy to this location may have led to the build-up of energy we are now seeing in this region. This build-up, in turn, has led to the activity, or in layman's terms, the hauntings you may have encountered. This witch could be the reason for that. Or another ancient and powerful energy, soul or spirit."

"A structure disturbed," mumbled Neha, as he stared at his drink. Maria translated.

"Was there a structure disturbed in your forest, Neha?" the professor asked.

As Maria translated, Neha glared at him and folded his arms.

The professor shifted in his chair uncomfortably.

"And Ed," he stuttered, "have you come across any disturbed structures in the Burren whilst conducting your audit?"

Ed glanced at all three of them as he replied, "One too many."

"Well, there we have it. This place could soon be a powder keg," the professor finished.

A few moments of silence passed. The table seemed to be drawn to the crackling fire beside them.

Ed clasped his hands together. "I have something to tell the table but before I do that, I'll get one more round in."

Ed went to the bar without waiting for an answer to his plan. Neha got up and told Maria he was going to the toilet.

Maria checked the time – 11:45 pm. Where had the time gone, she wondered. As she raised the glass to her mouth, something flickered in front of her. She put her glass down and saw the light bars on the professor's device shoot from green to amber. Then down again, then back up to the middle section.

"Eh… Professor," Maria said.

The blind man's dog raised its head up off the ground, its ears standing to attention.

As the professor turned and Maria pointed to the graviton, the lights spiked up higher, into the amber range.

The lights of the pub flickered, went back to normal and then flickered again.

The dog stood, and baring its teeth, began a low growl. People began to stare at it.

Maria and the professor watched open mouthed as the lights on the graviton spiked again and again until they finally pitched all the way up to end of the red spectrum.

The double doors of the pub blasted open. The windows shook in their frames. A roaring gale went through the pub as the lights went out. The wind hurried down the chimney and the fire was lashed until the logs sprayed out on the floor.

Screams. Shouts. The dog was barking wildly now, and people began constant screaming as glasses were knocked from tables, breaking on the ground. Bottles behind the bar could be heard smashing down on the floor.

The wind seemed to die down momentarily. But it picked up again.

Then a low pitched, reverberating noise started outside. As it went up in intensity, Maria thought it sounded like the screech of a woman. It increased in volume, seeming to be everywhere at once. It was terrifying. The wind surged through the pub again, but the screech didn't stop. It went so high the dog beside her began to whimper.

Maria put her hands to her ears and as her eyes adjusted to the darkness, she could see the professor and others doing the same. Maria started screaming, the pain was terrible. Bottles behind the bar shattered and exploded.

Then the shriek died down somewhat, as did the wind.

She took her hands from her ears… she heard another noise now.

It was the sound of singing.

She could hear the song moving up and down in pitch. It seemed to have words at one point and was a groan at other times. She suddenly saw her father walking through the pub towards the double doors, his silhouette lit up by the small flame of a lit candle he was holding. As his singing became more intense, the shriek died off and the wind calmed down.

Maria and the professor watched as the light bars on the Graviton went down one by one…

Her father had reached the open double doors, placing his back to them. He stopped singing and shut his eyes. The double doors behind him slowly closed, creaking as they did.

Neha blew out the candle.

The fire sparked back to life beside Maria as flames quickly stormed up the chimney. She jumped in fright. The lights came back on. Everyone in the pub was staring at her father but a dead silence filled the air.

Neha opened his eyes and looked around the pub. His eyes stopped at Maria. She stood and hurried towards him.

Ed watched them embrace.

He stood with his back to the bar, his arms outstretched and clinging to the wood frame as if he were a man holding the side of a boat in a squall. Even his hair matched the picture, dishevelled by that… haunted wind.

Chapter 21

Maria swirled her coffee and without looking down, took another sip. She stared out the window of the Wildflower Café. Beyond the rain pelted terrace, a charcoal sea churned beyond the dock. An old style sailing boat dipped and rose in the waves. Its bow looked as if it was being punched as opposed to pushed upwards by the oncoming waves.

Maria's view was blocked by a man who had lost control of his umbrella and she decided that there certainly was a wind of change about this place…

Ed had called to their room earlier that morning. He said they should all talk. They grimly walked down to the reception and out the door, hurrying past the Hikers Hotel – none of them looked at it. Ed told them that Professor Whaley had sent him a message. He had to leave on urgent business, but he wished them all luck. They were aiming for the Pier Restaurant, but the weather was miserable so they had gone into this café instead.

Maria looked around again at the people sitting at the other round timber tables. None had taken off their jackets or hats. They were hunched forward, arms crossed, speaking in hushed voices. But they locked eyes with Maria on more than one occasion and stared at her father when he wasn't looking.

As a wind whipped at the main door, it shook violently in its frame for a few seconds. Everyone looked at it until it stopped.

Maria turned her head as Ed quickly sat down in his chair, having returned from the toilet.

He raised his coffee cup high and tilted his head back, the bottom of the large coffee cup blocking his face as he chugged down the contents. Slamming the cup onto the saucer, it was as if he had pounded a shot of tequila.

"Right, so I have had a number of paranormal events here. Especially round the cottage. I was nearly killed, and I can see dead people," offered Ed.

Silence. Deadpan faces.

Ed went red faced and spewed out the whole story, hammering his forefinger down on the timber frame as he did. "I have been through more than your imagination could conjure," he said forcefully, spreading his hands wide.

Neha chuckled at Ed. Shaking his head, he said, "You have no idea, Ed."

"I still can't believe you can speak English all of sudden. That I can understand you!" replied Ed sharply.

"But, Ed," whispered Maria, "he spoke to you in Yine!"

Ed's mouth fell open.

Neha placed a hand on Ed's arm, giving him a sympathetic look. "I understand, Ed. We have been through much also. It is the witch. She has escaped here. I was not sure how. My dreams and the sky spirits told me. That man last night confirmed it and then she attacked last night."

"Well… I'm just not sure… I'm just not sure about any of this, anymore," said Ed, as he rubbed his hands through his hair. "You came all the way here to hunt her down?" he asked.

"Yes, and avenge my son's death, Paka."

Neha's head sunk in his chest then. "There is much I must tell you both," said Neha as he raised he eyes back up.

Ed and Maria leaned in.

"If we are to defeat her, we must find–"

"Excuse me," said a soft female voice.

All three looked up. Two elderly women stood there.

Ed raised his eyes to heaven. "Now is an awful tim–"

"We'd like to thank you," the woman carried on as she looked at Neha, "for helping in the pub last night."

"We were there!" chimed in the other lady.

Maria put her hands up. "Thank you, but we really need some priva–"

But it was too late. The women carried on nattering at a rate that Ed couldn't believe, the general gist being how amazing they thought Neha had been.

Another man came over and asked if he was the one who re-built the cairn. Soon, Neha had a small crowd around him as his hands were continuously shaken. Maria sighed, falling into her role as 'translator'.

Others came over and asked whether he could do anything about the voices in the wind or the strange noises around their houses.

Suddenly, the main door banged open and a wind rushed through the doorway, knocking over some coffee cups and a cake platter on a nearby cupboard. A cat that had been sleeping nearby stood near the door and hissed at nothing. There was more than one intake of breath as the conflab around their table died down.

Ed, Maria and Neha were already out of their chairs when the door slammed shut.

The people around their table dispersed hurriedly, many making their way to the till. A large queue soon formed as one of the staff desperately tried to clean the mess close to the door.

The door slammed open again…

A lady gave a small cry. But this time, a lad walked through. He didn't bother closing the door behind him. The guy was tall but slim. He wore a grey tracksuit, with the ends tucked into his white socks. He had some flashy red runners on. His hair was bladed right up the sides of his head. His black hair was short on top but gelled and matted so his fringe pointed sharply down. Ed could see he had some kind of a gold chain on too.

Ed and the rest of the café customers peered at him as he walked past the queue and up to the till. As a very old lady hunched forward on a walking stick moved up to the till the guy stepped in front of her. She had to catch the side of a table nearby and the person behind had to steady her.

"Three coffees to go!" he said to the woman in a whiney Irish accent that Ed wasn't familiar with.

Someone in the queue challenged him but he didn't even turn around while telling them to 'relax', he was only 'getting coffee'.

The young girl behind the till glared at him but did nothing.

Ed was furious, but Neha was a pace or two ahead of him and out of his chair like a bullet. He walked over to the bloke, faced him, and pushed him hard. The lad fell back towards a fridge.

Ed was over like a shot as the guy got up, starting into some tirade with his arms spread outwards, going nose to nose with Neha. Ed walked behind the guy and gave him a decent shoulder in the back. He was knocked off kilter momentarily. As he turned to Ed, his facial expression dropped as Ed's bulging eyes stared down at him.

"Sorry mate," said Ed as he emphasised the 'te' in mate. "Were you trying to queue?" he asked as he raised his right arm outwards to the on-looking queue.

The guy looked ashen, realising the whole café was staring at him.

The door opened again. A fella in a white tracksuit this time. "Cam on, Shades! We gotta get goin!"

The guy named Shades began backing away from Ed, raising his arms outwards once more. "Whattevvver!" he said as he nearly tripped over someone's foot. He walked out the door and the café people looked at Ed and Neha.

Shouts came of "fair play", "thank you", "well done" and "too right!"

"Well done Ed!"

Ed turned around. It was Sheila, from the table quiz.

"It was nothing, really." Ed half smiled.

He noticed the old woman who had nearly been knocked over was clinging slightly to Sheila's side. "Oh, is this your auntie?" said Ed as he noticed Maria at his side now too.

Maria smiled at him, giving him an elbow as congratulations.

The woman was slow to raise her head up. Her face seemed slightly crestfallen, wrinkled, but through a mop of grey hair her eyes twinkled. Golden flecks around an emerald iris. Neha stormed in front of Ed. He grabbed the lady's hand and they stared at each other.

"This is Grainne," said Sheila. Sheila began looking back and forth between Neha and her auntie.

"He has the same unique eye colouring as my auntie!" said Sheila. "I haven't come across anyone else really." Sheila did a double take at Ed. "So do you, Ed!" she said, while pointing at him. "Sure, that's uncanny. Unbelievable!"

"There's a lot more that's unbelievable," said Ed, despondently. "Believe… you… me!" He heaved a sigh.

Neha let go of Grainne's hand.

Grainne mumbled something at Sheila through the side of a crooked mouth. Sheila leant down to listen.

"My aunt wants to go, she doesn't like being out for long. But she wants you all to come up to her cottage."

Neha turned to Maria. "This is the person we need to talk to… she is the local Shaman. She has the connection to this place," he finished in Yine.

"We would be delighted to come up," said Maria to Sheila.

"Oh, great!" said Sheila. "There's enough room in the car."

As they went outside, rain and wind swept around them. Sheila held an umbrella over Grainne's head. When they reached Sheila's car Ed opened the passenger seat to help Grainne in. Neha took the umbrella from Sheila's hand with a smile and held it over Grainne. Neha stood in front of Ed, smacking his forearm into Ed's chest and pushing him back. Ed took the obvious hint and got into the back seat with Maria.

Neha took great care helping Grainne in before getting in himself.

"He's quite the gentleman," said Sheila, catching her breath, as she matted down her sodden hair. Sheila started the car and took off.

Ed helped with the introductions of Maria and Neha. He explained they were on a type of hiking trip.

"Well, it's some weather for it... it's gotten terrible of late."

A few minutes later, they drove onto what looked like a small peninsula. At points along the drive the road revealed a cliff face with waves crashing upwards. The bad weather went on 'pause' for now, although grey clouds continued to streak overhead, pushed along by a prevailing wind.

Sheila took a turn into a small driveway and pulled in alongside a small but sturdy looking cottage. It had a high thatched roof and whitewashed, pebble dashed walls. Small windows were sunk into the thick walls, painted blue at the edges. A matching blue door finished the postcard picture.

Neha was first out of the car and was straight around to Grainne on the other side. He had the passenger door open and was offering Grainne his hand before the rest of them had even opened their doors.

"He's a great helper!". Sheila exclaimed.

As Neha got Grainne out of the car, Sheila retrieved her walking stick from the boot.

Grainne took the stick and began to shuffle forward with the aid of Neha holding her at her side. She stopped at the threshold to the house, catching Neha's attention and waving her hand to the ground below.

Ed could see Neha nod enthusiastically at a line of white on the ground. His eyes followed it around the periphery of the house.

“What is that?” he asked Sheila.

“It’s salt,” she responded glumly. “She started placing it around the house after she had her mini stroke.”

They watched Grainne slowly lead Neha forward to the door.

Ed could see strange, small parcels or poultices hanging from twine around the doorframe. Grainne raised her hand up tentatively and touched one of them, making eye contact with Neha again. Neha grabbed one and smelled it, nodding approvingly once more. He spoke exuberantly in Yine.

“She’s been hanging those bloody things all over the door, the windows, the house,” said Sheila as she put the key into the door. “She even put them down at the guest house. God knows what the Americans think of it!”

As the door opened, Neha and Grainne walked through, and Sheila beckoned Ed and Maria in.

Ed stopped at one of the hanging parcels and smelt it.

“What does it smell like?” asked Maria.

Ed wasn’t sure, but something in there reminded him of Sunday roasts. “I think some of it could be sage,” he said, his tone going higher as he queried his own guess.

They walked through a small hallway to their right and into another larger room. Neha was just helping Grainne into a rocking chair by a window. The rest of the large rectangular room held a comforting heat. Ed recognised the large cooking range to their left. His uncle had a similar one on his farm in Cumbria. The other half of the room held a moderately sized kitchen table and small cooker and fridge. There was a Grandfather clock in the corner.

The sound of a spark brought Ed’s attention back to the centre of the room as a red ember flickered up from a blackened log that sat in the centre of a large fireplace. A very old black bar stretched across the back wall of the hearth. Made for old school cooking, Ed reckoned.

Grainne muttered to Neha as she pointed to the dying fire. Neha had grabbed a chair and was sitting beside her.

Neha looked at the fire and snapped his fingers at Ed. "Ed, the fire," he managed loudly in English. Ed strode forward to a log and turf basket close by, adhering to the command. He threw a mixture of logs and turf on.

As Sheila produced a china tea pot, cups and saucers from a side room, Maria moved over to the kitchen table with her and began helping her. "How long has your auntie been in that way?" asked Maria.

"She was caught out in a storm earlier this year. When I found her, she had fallen, barely breathing. Your father seems greatly interested in her, but it might be best to give her a little space."

Maria took the hint and walked over to him. "Father," she whispered, placing a hand on his shoulder.

He did not turn around.

"Grainne has had a mild stroke and–"

"This is no 'stroke'," replied Neha. "She has been cursed."

Neha stood straight abruptly. He stared past Maria and into space as he placed a finger to his chin. He began looking around the kitchen and living room as if it was the first time he had seen it. He stopped as he saw Sheila pouring boiling water into the tea pot.

Neha snapped his fingers and began searching around the room now. He asked Maria to ask Sheila where Grainne kept the materials for which she made the charms outside. As Maria asked, Sheila didn't register with the question at first.

"Charms," she muttered with confusion. "Oh, those hanging yokes! Yes, she keeps that stuff in the top cupboard there," said Sheila, pointing.

Neha didn't need to wait for the translation as he yanked the white cupboard door open. His mouth dropped first before it turned into a large smile. Jar after jar of varied coloured plants, flowers and herbs were packed into the cabinet.

“She’s always foraged the area for wildflowers and the likes,” added Sheila as she poured tea into four waiting cups. “Her nana always had her out with her looking for stuff, or so she told me.”

Neha began taking out each one and placed them on the kitchen table. He opened each lid and took a sample out, smelling it and shutting the jar abruptly or placing the flower or herb gently onto the table.

“Will he not leave that stuff alone. I mean… it’s not his!” said Sheila, the annoyance clear.

Neha detected the tone and began speaking with Maria in Yine.

Maria explained that Neha was considered a type of healer where he came from. He only wanted to make her a type of special herbal tea. Maria deliberately left out the word ‘potion’ as her father had used.

Grainne gently caught Sheila’s attention and Sheila walked over and bent down. After a few whispered words from Grainne, Sheila said, “Okay, Auntie, I will leave him at it!”

Neha walked towards the fire and looked at the black bar stretched across it. He began looking around the room once more and pointed above them to one of the rafters.

“Ed,” he simply said whilst continuing to point.

Ed used his long arms and stretched, retrieving what looked like a very old black kettle. Take away the tiny spout and it was more like a pot, Ed thought. Neha took it from his hands and walked towards the sink, turning on the tap. As he began washing it, more than one big spider dashed out of the hole at the top.

“I see what he is doing,” said Sheila. “I’ll boil some water for him,” she added, starting to laugh. “But that thing hasn’t been used in years. Sure, even Auntie Grainne doesn’t use it. She calls it her ‘nana’s cauldron’. And so did we, as kids.”

Neha stuffed a fine collection of various herbs and multi-coloured flowers into the large pot. Maria told Neha that Sheila was just boiling some water for him. “No need,” responded Neha as he filled up the large pot from the tap.

Grainne waved at Neha and he walked over to her. She spoke in a hushed tone and pointed at the mantel piece over the fireplace. Neha retrieved a small, half full, plastic bottle. He walked over and poured the contents into the pot.

"Sure, that's Holy water from St. Coleman's Well!" said Sheila as she took a drink of tea. "The two witchdoctors are at it!"

Neha walked over to the fireplace, pot in hand, and attached the handle of the pot to a small hook hanging from the black bar within the hearth. The pot swung briefly before steadying.

Grainne smiled at Neha and Neha smiled back.

Neha turned and faced the fire. He began to mutter something. He cast the palm of his left hand from right to left slowly over the fire beneath. Then did the same with right. As it passed over, the fire kicked into life. The logs crackled and the flames lit up the back of the hearth. Neha sat down on the small chair beside Grainne. She held out his hand to him. He gently took it.

Sheila, Ed and Maria sat down at the kitchen table with their teacups.

"Is he some kind of magician or something?" asked Sheila as she looked at both Maria and Ed.

Both opened their mouths to answer… but the words never came.

"Wait!!" said Sheila, tongue in her cheek. "He's the fella I heard about from last night in the Hikers Hotel!?" Sheila looked at Ed and Maria as their heads dropped to their teacups. "I never knew the hotel was haunted. The strangest thing… but the story ended with a foreign man standing at the doorway."

Sheila paused. "Neha, he's some kind of… spirit healer," she said, smiling this time.

The pot jumped lightly on the bar over the fire. They all looked as a heavy amount of steam came out of the small kettle spout.

"Here… he'll need this," said Sheila with excitement. She stood and leant up, taking down a black bar from above a cupboard. It had a small hook at the end.

She handed it to Neha. He deftly slotted the hook under the kettle handle and lifted it free. In one continuous motion, he cleared the fire and looped around to land the pot onto the old black cooking range behind him.

Minutes past while Sheila, Ed and Maria watched, drinking their tea.

Neha stood and stared at the pot, while his hands leaned on the edge of the range. He selected two large mugs from a collection nearby and poured the contents into both cups. He brought one cup to the fire and began chanting a slow song and brushing the smoke from the fire outwards with his free hand, so it touched the cup. He handed it to Grainne. Her hands trembled as they received the mug.

Neha quickly repeated the same process with his own cup and sat beside Grainne. He took a drink from his mug immediately and urged Grainne to do the same by pointing at her mug. She took a sip, her expression unsure. Then she took another and smiled. She leaned over and began muttering to Neha.

"Well, at least she's happy," said Sheila.

Ed gulped the last of his tea. Making eye contact with no one in particular, he said, "Well I'm glad someone is. The story you heard last night isn't far from the truth, Sheila. You and your aunt should be careful. As for me, it's time I left here and went home. I was doing the audit but I've had enough… Going to pack my bags and be gone this evening. Maria, when you are ready and your dad has finished his tea, we should make tracks."

With that Ed stood from the table and avoiding eye contact said he was just popping to the loo.

Maria paused for a minute before crossing the room to her father. She whispered into his ear.

Chapter 22

Conor sat in the small living room watching some cartoon on the TV. The early morning light streamed through the windows.

Where were his mom, dad and sister? What a pack of lazy bones! Daddy had promised him loads of fun adventures today. He was determined to win the running race on the beach this time! Daddy also promised him he would play all the board games with him and play hide and seek. But most of all, Daddy had promised him they would go leprechaun hunting!

Conor walked to the bottom of the stairs and listened. He could still hear his dad snoring. His daddy was probably tired as those leprechauns had been playing tricks he had said. Although his mommy didn't agree!

Daddy couldn't light a fire in the fireplace as a wind kept shooting down the chimney and blowing it out. Then each night, Daddy found all the windows and doors open downstairs, with the cold wind streaming through the house. He caught Mommy saying that she heard wailing outside, but Daddy made a funny joke about the leprechauns again. His sister, Melissa, kept waking up with nightmares.

These leprechauns were really silly, thought Conor.

A wind buffeted up against the glass in the living room behind him. Conor walked back over and climbed up on the couch. He propped himself on a pillow and looked out over the top of the couch and into the garden.

It looked so nice outside! The wind made the leaves in the large square hedge rattle. A tree on the far side of the garden swayed back and forth. Conor saw a small red ball roll out from beneath the right hedgerow. It sat there momentarily … before a long bony hand stretched out and prodded it forward.

Oh my gosh That must be the leprechaun! And it wanted to play with him!

Conor raced upstairs and told his dad that a leprechaun was out in the back garden and that it wanted to play with him. His dad reacted by turning over and telling him to go back downstairs. His mum was still sleeping. So he went downstairs, with his head on his chest and his bottom lip bulging outwards.

He went back to the couch. The red ball seemed to move around the garden of its own accord now. Conor laughed. It must be the leprechauns or the wind. It looked like such fun, but the back door was locked and he couldn't get outside.

As Conor watched the red ball dance on the grass and leap around in the air, he heard the noise of something metal and a creak. He turned around and saw the back door open as a wind blew into his face. *The leprechaun must have opened it,* he thought.

His little feet nearly danced across the floor as he reached the door. He ran out onto the grass. The ball was still dancing outside as he chased it. He was always just too late to grab it. His laughing and shouting was drowned out by the wind. Conor stopped as he was out of breath.

The wind died down a bit. The red ball stopped just a metre away from him. Conor smiled as he began to creep forward to get it. Conor slowly reached his hands forward to pick it up.

As a wind moved through the garden, the ball rushed forward into the hedge. Conor shouted in annoyance as he ran to the hedge and peered underneath. He couldn't see where it went but he saw that he could get through the hedgerow if he wanted. There was no wire here.

As Conor rubbed his small hands together, he looked down the garden back at the living room window. Still no sign of Mom or Dad. Well, he would only be just a minute, he reckoned. The ball couldn't have gone in that far. And he wanted to tell Daddy that he could get the ball and that he didn't need help. Dad told him that the leprechauns were fast and that he had to be ready!

Conor bent down and moved into the hedge. It was dark but he could see a chink of light ahead. Maybe the ball went that way. He moved slowly forward on his hands and knees and emerged on the side of the cliff. He could see the sea. Wow! And his red ball was just there, ahead.

Conor stood and scrambled to grab his ball. The wind suddenly blew and the ball moved away with it. Silly ball! Those pesky leprechauns! As Conor caught up, the ball was slowly bouncing down some steep steps towards the sea. *Safety Check!* his mommy and daddy would say to him, he thought.

Conor was about to walk away when he saw the ball roll to a stop on a small jetty below. He looked back for his dad again and wrung his hands briefly. The ball wasn't that close to the edge and he was a brave boy.

He started to make his way down the steps. He went down on his bum as his mommy had shown him to do when dealing with steps. She would be happy with that.

He reached the bottom and the red ball sat in the same position.

He stood and slowly crept towards the ball…

He snatched at it.

Got it!

This was where the game must have ended, he realised. But as Conor turned the wind howled at him, pushing him backwards.

His little legs couldn't keep their place.

He started to scream as his feet lost their grip.

He fell forwards as he also slid towards the edge, letting go of the ball. It rolled past him towards the water.

"Daddy! Daddy!" he screamed as he went over the edge, grasping on with his little hands to the wall.

The wind stopped pushing him.

But then something snatched at his little hands and he fell into the water. Cold. Darkness. Before he bounced back up to the surface. His little heart was beating hard and he thrashed his legs and arms. In between mouthfuls of water, he screamed for his dad and looked to the top of the cliff face for him.

Then he started to sink. "Daddddyyyy!" he cried once more.

No one heard his terrified, high pitched shriek as he sank into the cold dark waters. Alone. Afraid. Not able to breathe…

*****

Ed felt more of a release in the toilet than intended. His decision to leave wasn't right. It wasn't wrong, but it was his decision. He let out a puff of air as he opened the toilet door. Neha immediately grabbed him by the arm and forced him into a nearby room.

Closing the door, Neha closed the space with Ed until they were nearly chest to chest. "Ed, you must stay!"

"No," Ed said as he looked out the window, turning away from Neha. "I feel like my life is in danger. I can't come to terms with the exposure in this place. I feel targeted."

"We need you, Ed, if we are to find the knife," said Neha.

"What are you talking about?" demanded Ed.

"You have come here for your work but also because of your gifts. The spirits have willed it. You are our guide. Hidden somewhere in the sacred sites of this land is the knife. A knife linked to the ancient tribe of this area. The knife can kill her, Ed."

"A knife can kill a ghost?" replied Ed in a sarcastic tone.

"I had a dream, Ed, a dream before I came, of Paka taking a knife out of his chest and pointing. It was not fully clear, but it showed me this land. But then I had a vision when I arrived here, and that vision showed me the knife. It showed me you… I wasn't sure why the witch came here but that professor told us how she got here. She must have plagued these people here too, long ago."

"You're on a doomsday mission," said Ed staring at Neha.

"That woman outside, Grainne, told me she is having a dream. The same dream over and over again. It involves a knife, she says. She, or her ancestors, are the connection to this land. But you are our guide, Ed. I will need your help in deciphering this dream. We must find the knife, Ed." Neha stepped forward and grabbed Ed's arms. "We must find her lair!"

Ed sighed. "There are plenty of people around here with more local knowledge than me."

"I am sure there are, Ed. But how many of them can see the dead?"

Ed's back tensed and his lips clamped shut.

"You share the same eyes as Grainne, the same as me. You are linked to the spirit world. You can see the dead of this place. That is your connection…"

"I can't stay," Ed spat out, still looking away.

"If you leave, others will die."

"Well," said Ed making for the door, "I suggest you leave too!"

As Ed touched the door handle, Neha quickly shouted, "If you leave, Maria dies!"

Ed paused, then turned around. "What?" he demanded. "Why would she die?"

"The animal attacks, what happened at the Abbey." Neha stepped towards Ed. "The witch is targeting her too, Ed, and she will die without your help."

"Then leave!" roared Ed. "Get the hell out of here!"

"We cannot do that!" Neha roared back. "Maria is important," he said, calming slightly.

He stared at Ed and Ed stared back.

“What aren’t you telling me?” demanded Ed.

“I will tell you, but you must give me your sacred oath,” Neha raised one arm upwards and extended his hand, “to not tell her.”

Neha waited.

“For Fuck Sake!” said Ed. “Fine, I promise!” he said as he clasped Neha’s hand.

*****

Maria had a bad feeling. She watched as her father stormed into the hallway, closing the door after him. The next few minutes passed and neither her father, nor Ed appeared. Sheila was talking away but Maria was hardly listening. She heard raised voices from the other end of the cottage, excused herself and stood up. Going into the small main hallway she moved past the open door to her right and towards the closed one ahead. She stopped. She heard her father and Ed speaking inside.

“You can’t hide this from her… you can’t!” said Ed sternly.

“This is the only way, Ed!”

Maria knocked on the door.

Ed opened the door sharply. He stopped in the doorway and both his arms seemed to go limp at his sides. The stunned expression on his face was evident.

“Maria… eh,” said Ed, then his mouth hung open.

“What is going on in here?” she responded in a hushed but harsh voice. She directed the question at Ed and her father, who was standing just behind Ed.

“Er… well,” stumbled Ed.

Neha placed a hand on Ed’s left shoulder and squeezed.

“I’m going,” stuttered Ed.

“Well?” demanded Maria with her hands pressed to her hips, elbows out.

"I'm going," said Ed as he moved past Maria at pace, "for a cigarette."

*****

As Ed went out the door, Grainne's dog, Misty, skittered out at his feet. Ed walked along a small path as Misty sniffed frantically along a hedgerow to his right. Misty then stopped, barked at something and sprinted underneath the hedgerow.

Ed carried on, walking past a nice looking white washed farm house. Must be the holiday home Sheila looked after, he reckoned. The path wound past the holiday home and a gap in the wall seemed to give Ed the option of getting closer to the sea. He took it, reaching the edge of a cliff face within a small inlet. The frothy emerald coloured sea was below.

Ed lit up a cigarette. He happily took in the first drag as he watched a seagull sway over the waves below. There were a number of lobster pot buoys floating about. He saw Misty break out of hedgerow to his right. The dog began barking at the sea below. The dog saw Ed and sprinted over. It began biting and pulling at Ed's right leg.

"Get off me, you stupid mutt!"

Misty did just that as Ed launched a kick that missed. The dog had already turned and was making its way down some steep steps to a small jetty below. Misty stopped at the edge and barked furiously at a buoy close to the edge.

Ed took another long drag of his cigarette while shaking his head, but he did a double take as he saw something white pop out of the sea. He stopped in his tracks and saw it again – a tiny hand – reaching above a wave.

Ed's cigarette fell out of his mouth. What to do!?

The hand didn't re-emerge. No time!

He looked at the drop into the sea below… around twenty or thirty feet. No rocks he could see. Looked deep. Ed took a step back and bounded two steps over the edge. He thought he heard Maria shout his name just as he leapt off.

He plunged feet first into the water. The shock of the cold gripped him immediately. The waters were dark and murky. He fought as quickly as he could to break to the surface. He began to more flop his arms in the water than swim. Getting his bearings, he followed the barks of Misty and reached the lobster buoy near the jetty. He looked to grab onto the attached rope underneath but quickly realised there was none. It was just a red ball…

Ed took a deep breath and dove head first. He kicked down and could see something grey below in the green hued water. He snatched at it. Some piece of clothing. There was something heavy attached. Ed kicked above as hard as he could. He coughed as he reached the surface, looking at the small child he held fast at his chest. No coughing from the child though. Eyes shut.

He heard Maria and Misty close by. He turned his back, placed the child on top of him and kicked his legs. Reaching the edge of the jetty, he felt the small boy being pulled up. Ed thrashed his legs once more, turned and gripped the edge of the jetty, pulling himself up. Maria was already performing CPR on the child.

The boy was pale, his lips blue.

Ed sat there watching this surreal experience unfold further. He was shivering. He couldn't think. Two other people arrived. The woman was screaming, the man shouting.

As Maria near punched the boy's chest, he spluttered up water. Maria turned him on his side. The boy coughed up more water as he drew a breath.

"The car. The car!" the man shouted to the woman as he picked the small toddler up. She ran up the steps.

"I will call the emergency services and let them know!" said Maria.

"Ennis hospital, Ennis hospital," was all Ed could manage.

"Thank you both… thank you!" he said, as he scrambled up the steps.

Ed tried to get up. He faltered, Maria caught him, and Ed felt another strong arm under him. He looked to his right and saw it was Neha.

"He needs heat," said Neha.

"Il get Sheila to run him a bath," said Maria.

*****

Ed sat near the fire, covered in a blanket. He clutched a whiskey, his second, but he needed it. They had run a warm bath for him. Then he had been handed a blanket and put by the fire. Grainne was asleep and Neha sat close by her. It was getting dark outside. A twilight sky streamed through the window.

Sheila had left for Ennis hospital to check on the tourists and their son. She had texted that the boy was fine now. She asked that they stay in the cottage until she got back.

The room was silent but for the crackling of the fire. Neha, Ed, and Maria made little eye contact. They instead stared down or off into the distance.

"THE KNIFE, THE KNIFE, THE KNIFE!"

Ed dropped his glass and it shattered on the floor.

The shouts came from Grainne. She leaned forward in her chair, gripping Neha's hand. She stared at each of them. "The knife, my dream, the knife. You must find it… before she does; the banshee!" She continued to talk but then her language changed. She began speaking something completely different.

Neha responded to her. She smiled at him and calmed down. They continued speaking in that strange language.

"What are they saying?" asked Maria as she moved beside Ed.

"I think it's Gaelic, or Irish as they call it here," replied Ed.

As Neha and Grainne carried on talking, Ed looked sullenly at Maria. "Maria, there is a lot we need to disc–"

"You were very brave today," said Maria as she gave him a warm smile. She placed a hand on his.

Ed couldn't help but feel like an awkward teenage boy. "I did my best." He smiled back. "Shame about the temperature of the water here though. They must get that looked at!"

They shared a small laugh.

"That boy…" said Maria. "He shared the same eye colouring as my father." She looked down and back up. "And you."

"I know, Maria. I am starting to accept it." Ed paused.

"Will you stay?" asked Maria.

Ed blushed. "Yes, I'll stay. We need to discuss a lo–"

"She has seen the knife in her dreams," said Neha loudly. "But much more this time. It is gold, and slithers like a snake. She keeps mentioning a half moon surrounded by water. Ed, will you help?" Neha threw the question out without looking at him.

"Yes. Not much to go on, though," said Ed, as he rubbed his chin.

He looked over but Grainne had settled back down. Her eyes shut.

"The water is a clue?" guessed Ed.

"Could the snake be a stream?" added Maria.

"Possibly, but I can't think of any site or structure I have seen that resembles a half-moon."

"What about the woman, Ed? The body you found the night we found you? The bag you found with her?" queried Maria.

"You're right!" said Ed. He slapped his hand to his forehead. "How could I have forgotten? She even pointed to the bloody thing before she… she…"

"Disappeared," finished Maria.

"The words… she said the words… 'bag'… 'knife'," said Ed. "We need that bag and the file! But the bag is still in the hotel and my file is in my cottage."

Maria suggested that they all rest tonight and start fresh tomorrow.

Ed and Neha agreed.

"The hunt starts tomorrow," concluded Neha.

Chapter 23

Ed slept well. The hotel experience was refreshing, but he decided he'd better check the bill soon.

He met Maria and Neha early for breakfast. They muttered at their table as to what was in the bag. Could the knife be there? If it wasn't, what sites or structures had Ed not looked at yet? He shook his head as he still couldn't think of any half-moon structures. He looked in the guidebooks again too; nothing there.

Ed's phone rang. He took the call away from the table and came back smiling.

He said it was Sheila. She said Grainne was in great form, walking around and far more confident with her speech. Sheila asked them to come up as she wanted Neha to make more of his tea. Neha insisted they do this as he might garner more information from Grainne on not just the knife, but the location of the witch's lair, too. Ed and Maria agreed they could do the research up there. It would also be a better option to open the bag in a secluded location.

"Base camp Grainne then!" said Ed as they left the breakfast table.

Ed went back to his room to retrieve Aine's bag. Pat had kept it at reception the morning Ed had arrived before dropping it up to Ed's room that same evening. Ed had put it in the wardrobe. It helped hide the bag and helped hide the problem. Out of sight, out of mind, Ed had decided.

Ed hugged it as he rushed it down the hotel stairs, feeling as if he were handling illicit goods or dangerous material. He handed it to Maria outside and she put it in the boot of her rented car. She would take her father up to Sheila's. Ed would follow once he got the file from his cottage.

Maria and Neha got going in the car.

Ed made the walk to his cottage quickly.

He reached the door and found his key. He was just placing it in… when his forehead was banged harshly against the door. He was twisted around and his face connected quickly with a fist to his nose. He was thrust up against the door and another fist flew at him.

His groggy mind made his body slip to the left sharply. The fist slammed the door and the man in front of him shouted in pain. Ed pushed him back to buy a few seconds before falling backwards on his arse, the pain of the first punch just taking hold.

Ed got up and saw the big frame of Flannery staring at him.

Flannery came at him again, but Ed closed the space quicker. They both connected with punches, but Ed reckoned his was better, getting Flannery with a heavy blow to his right temple.

Ed felt his left eye closing but he charged forward, rugby tackling Flannery to the ground. He pressed his knee to his chest and gave him two thundering blows on his nose. Blood spurted down Flannery's face but his long left arm just managed to push Ed's face back so Ed could not connect anymore.

Ed fell backwards. Flannery got to his feet. As Ed got upright, he realised he had little time. Flannery wasn't exactly heaving the breaths in and out. He could go a few more rounds.

Ed roared as he closed again, catching Flannery with a swift punch just under his chest. Flannery stopped Ed, grabbing him by the collar with one hand, but Ed's connection was enough to wind Flannery. That was when Ed swiftly grabbed Flannery's extended arm with his left hand and swung from below as hard as he could with his right. Ed's uppercut connected with Flannery's jaw and Flannery toppled over.

The manner in which he collapsed backwards and hardly moved told Ed that he was either unconscious or semi.

Ed stopped, bent down, and placed his hands on his knees. He could taste the blood in his mouth and spat it out. He could hardly catch his breath. His lungs were burning.

But Flannery seemed in worse condition, bent over on his knees, his head touching the ground. It was as far as he could move from the flat of his back. He was coughing and heaving furiously.

The age gap had paid off, Ed thought. "Right, you had enough, you fucking bollocks!?"

As Flannery managed to get to one knee, he stared at Ed. Again, it was that same type of stare that he had given him in Coughlin's. That assessing stare.

Flannery slowly raised his arm upwards with the palm out.

"Fine," said Ed, "but you'll fucking come in and give me an explanation about all of this. About Aine," finished Ed as he pointed a forefinger at Flannery.

"Yeah, sure… no problem," said Flannery. He reached a hand upwards towards Ed. Ed took it reluctantly and pulled him up.

He kept an eye on Flannery and opened the door, indicating that Flannery should go ahead of him. Flannery walked through to the living room and sat himself down at the main table… as if he had done it before.

Ed rooted through his freezer and found a pack of frozen peas for his eye. He wrapped up some ice in a tea towel and gave that to Flannery who held it to a nasty looking bulge on his cheek.

Ed retrieved two glasses from the kitchen and a bottle of whiskey from a cabinet. He slammed the glasses on the table and poured heavy portions in both, then sat down. They both took a long gulp of their drinks.

"Well?" said Ed. "You've been here before, clearly," he added in a matter of fact tone.

"I knew Aine, sure!" replied Flannery. He swirled the whiskey around in his glass and stared at the table. "Met her out on the karst rock. She was lost and so was I. We got a coffee and it turned out we were after the same thing."

"Which was?" said Ed.

Flannery took another drink. "She was doing your audit. The job no–one else would do?" he said looking at Ed. Ed gave no response.

"I told her I was doing a project, an audit for a private company. But we both shared a passion for Archaeology. I showed her a few artefacts that I found, and she soon became more interested in coming out with me than doing her audit. She was interested in what I had to offer her, Ed. And it wasn't just the money before you ask."

Flannery poured himself another drink and topped up Ed's.

"What did you find? Where did you find it?" asked Ed.

"I've always found I've had a sixth sense for this kind of thing, Ed… ya know?" said Flannery, as he smiled at Ed. He took another drink.

Ed responded with a heavy frown.

"You good at getting the 'finds' out on digs? You seem to make the big discoveries where no one else does?" asked Flannery. He paused with the glass close to his mouth. "You see things others don't?"

Ed folded his arms and shrugged.

"Oh, come on, Ed. You must know what I mean!? That night in Coughlin's! That guy… that weirdo!"

Ed leant back in his chair now, tight lipped.

"What's wrong, Ed? Do you think you're the only one who can see ghosts!?"

Flannery laughed. His eyes glittered as he did. Ed's mouth parted slightly when he took a proper look at Flannery's eyes.

"This god damn place is full of em!" said Flannery. "But it's also full of ancient stuff. Ancient stuff that people on private markets like to buy. That's why I offered you a job, Ed. I saw what you had!" Flannery finished his drink and stared back at Ed.

"All right, fine, I've been seeing things," admitted Ed. "You ever talk with Professor Whaley?" he asked.

"Professor who?" asked Flannery.

"Never mind," said Ed as he polished off his drink. "So you and Aine went out and found these artefacts on the side, with the help of your… gift?"

"And hers!" said Flannery.

Ed shifted position in his chair. "You've cut up a lot of the area, Flannery. The wedge tombs! The cairns!"

"The wedge tombs, yeah fine. Good finds there," responded Flannery. "But the cairns… I didn't go near them. Neither did Aine. Too exposed. We coulda got caught!"

"Right well, to cut to the fucking chase," said Ed leaning forward, "why the fuck did you just try to kick the living shit out of me?"

Flannery bit his busted lip briefly. "I loved her, Ed," muttered Flannery. "I loved her," he said again as he played with the glass in his hands for a minute.

"I heard on the grapevine that they found her body and I also heard that the police got an anonymous tip from an English sounding fella, with maybe a Northern English accent. I got to reckoning that that fella knew her whereabouts for a lot longer than a couple of days ago – more so, he probably knew her location since she went missing last year."

Flannery looked at Ed with clenched teeth. "I got to reckoning that that person may well just have put her there too!"

"Well, you've heard and assumed an awful lot," said Ed. "I'd say you know an awful lot and I'd say you're not telling me everything, too."

Flannery straightened himself in his chair and leant forward to Ed. "Is…that…so?" he said. The threat in his voice was evident.

"Probably," replied Ed sharply.

Ed noticed that both had re-clenched their fists on the table. Maybe the whiskey wasn't a good idea.

"I don't have a clue what happened to Aine," said Ed. "I wasn't even in the country last year. "But yes… I stumbled upon her body, out on a hike. Up on Turlough Hill. She looked like she was out there for some time. That's it."

Ed looked away. Flannery stared off into the distance.

"She rang me before she went missing," said Flannery. "She said she found something… something big. Did you find anything with her?" he asked.

Ed shook his head. "No," he said with as much conviction as he could manage.

The conversation stopped dead then.

"Well, good luck with the rest of your audit," said Flannery.

"I've finished. Heading back to the UK."

"Righto, chap!" smiled Flannery as he did his best to put on a posh English accent.

Ed couldn't bring himself to smile, but stood up instead.

Flannery stood up too. "I'll see myself out. Safe journey home," said Flannery. "And sorry for the Punch and Judy!" he shouted as he walked to the door.

As Ed heard the door closing outside, he considered whether to believe if Flannery was a vengeful forlorn lover, or a dangerous devious bastard.

Ed pondered this.

He decided on the latter because he was confident that if Flannery instead had Ed doubled over coughing and heaving for breath, that he wouldn't have given Ed the option of a truce.

No… he would have smashed Ed's head in.

*****

Flannery got into his car. That hadn't gone as he expected. He knew Ed was lying. He was sure though, that Ed had found that bitch's bag…

He drove off. He had a big day's work ahead of him with the mining company.

*****

Sheila shook, no clasped Neha's hands for five minutes, continuously thanking him.

Neha put his free hand to his breast and bowed softly to her. "Holy woman," he kept repeating to Sheila while pointing at Grainne.

They watched as Grainne was able to move by herself now, without a cane.

As Ed arrived, he quickly told them about his engagement with Flannery, concluding with, "Who knows what he has taken."

"Who knows what he has disturbed," mumbled Neha.

Ed lifted Aine's bag onto Sheila's kitchen table. He handed the file to Maria. She sat down, opened it, and immediately started to go through it.

Ed carefully undid the clasps of Aine's bag and untied the cord that tightened the top cover. The outer layer was damp but the inner layer appeared to be dry – this waterproof bag had done its job! He moved his head left and right as he slowly reached his hand in and began forensically taking what he found out, one by one. As his bag autopsy ended, Neha and Ed stared at the contents on the table. T-shirts, water bottles, maps, a phone, a torch, an old bar and a separate cloth bag.

Neha pulled the cloth bag towards him. He took out the first item.

Ed had a sharp intake of breath.

Gold…

A golden cup shimmered in the firelight, followed by a plate, necklace, brooch and mask. All pure gold as well. The last item was oval, thin. An individual with a circle mouth sat in the middle, lines representing their hair stretched out over the object. The hair seemed to turn into swirls… like wind. A distinctive, uneven line crossed through the middle of the ornament. It seemed to split the image into yin and yang type symbols.

"These are incredible," said Ed with a sense of awe.

"These are hers," said Neha. "She used these… in her sacrifices."

As Ed examined the oval ornament, Neha planted his finger on it, moving his finger down the dividing line.

"The divide. The edge." He pointed his finger at one side. "This world." Then he pointed to the other side. "And the spirit world."

"I think these swirls are the wind," offered Ed.

"Yes, Ed, and they cross over between the two worlds. But we have no knife," concluded Neha.

Both Neha and Ed stood with creased brows, staring at the objects on the table.

"Look at this," interrupted Maria. "What are these, Ed?"

Ed took the piece of paper from Maria.

"Oh, yes, these are the Wedge Tombs. This is one of Aine's Maps. The wedge tombs marked in green I have looked at, but the ones marked in red I haven't. I totally forgot about them. They're on private land.

"I can't imagine a wedge tomb being half-moon shaped though," he muttered.

"Maybe our target is inside something half-moon shaped, like a valley or the side of a cliff?" suggested Maria. She quickly followed on with, "Or maybe it's a wedge tomb near or inside a half-moon shaped area?"

"Maybe," Ed agreed.

"Er, Sheila, could you take a look at this?" called Ed.

Ed handed her Aine's map and she examined it.

"We are interested in the red dots," said Ed.

"Yes," said Sheila as she traced her index finger on the map. "Well, out of these seven, three are on the Riordan's, Mulcahy's and the O'Connell's farms. I'm not familiar with the rest."

"Could you take us out on the ones you know?"

"Yes, sure, Ed," said Sheila looking at a slumbering Grainne. "My auntie tells me this is a very serious situation."

Sheila's phone rang and she took the call in another room.

"But what if the knife and her… lair, are in one and the same place?" pondered Maria.

"I doubt it," said Neha and Ed at the same time.

"She searches for it, as we do," said Neha. "Grainne's dreams confirm it."

"Flannery must have been chopping up a lot of the sites around here. But if we choose to believe him, he didn't dig up the cairns," said Ed.

"Meaning she did," concluded Maria.

Ed nodded.

"Okay but if we find her lair, what then?" Maria asked looking at her father.

"Nothing can be done without that knife!" Neha declared, as he strode away to Grainne.

Sheila came back into the room. She looked pale.

"Are you okay?" asked Maria.

"That was one of my friends," she slowly responded. "She said that her husband is in intensive care. He had a very strange accident. But she broke down on the phone then." Sheila stopped.

"What else, Sheila?" asked Maria softly.

"She was so upset because… she says they are being haunted."

"Neha and I will deal with that!"

It was Grainne, standing just behind Sheila. She turned and said something to Neha in Irish. Neha nodded and left the room.

"Take us there now, Sheila," said Grainne. "This can't wait."

Chapter 24

Maria pulled her hood tighter around her head as another flurry of rain fell.

The weather was changeable today. It was like the sunshine and rain were two boxers exchanging rapid blow for blow. Neither would give, and the flora and fauna of the area had to put up with it. Maybe that was why they hid amongst the grikes and clints of the area.

She stood on the Mulcahy farm. She had decided to come down and help Ed, but she also wanted to see what some of the sights here held beyond… artefacts. Since Ed had told her the story about Flannery and then the bag had produced those gold artefacts, her 'spidy senses' began tingling. Sheila said she didn't know the Mulcahy's that well but Mrs. Mulcahy was keen to hear all about Grainne.

Sheila had suggested they not launch up to the farms announcing they were looking for artefacts or gold. She instead produced two very old looking Kodak cameras, complete with boxes with leather handles. Ed and Maria were to be 'keen bird watchers'. The ruse has worked perfectly and now Maria walked about a small field, pretending to take photos from time to time.

Mr. Mulcahy even stopped in his tractor and before they had offered a full explanation of what they were doing, he was pointing them in the direction off to her right, suggesting birds of all hues and sizes were camped there.

Ed and Maria thanked him and moved off in that direction. Once the tractor turned a corner though, Ed turned, lightly grabbing Maria's elbow.

"But he said…" hushed Maria.

"Go that way. Exactly."

They started walking into a side field in the opposite direction.

"What makes you think there is anything this way?" whispered Maria, looking over her shoulder.

Ed grinned at her. "A little bird told me!"

She gave him a joke elbow and let out a small laugh.

They got to the end of the field. Scanning their horizon, there was not much beyond except karst rock and bent over hawthorn trees. Maria turned as she saw Ed walk along an old stone wall. The land went up a small verge and at the top, Ed stopped. Maria stopped with him and looked around. All she could see was more long grass dancing in the wind.

"What?" she said. "What is it?"

"There," said Ed as he pointed forward and slightly to the right.

Maria squinted in that direction. She could see it now… some piece of plastic or cord fluttering above the grass in the wind.

They both began walking towards it. They reached a kind of hollow in front of them. A grey structure lay in the middle. Red and white tape surrounded the space, tied onto thin metal rods. A 'do not disturb' sign was tied to a post nearby. Maria walked over and began reading the small print. The distinctive MM symbol was labelled at the bottom, although the Mendoza Mining words were not written down.

"The ground seems really cut up down there," said Ed.

"I'm not surprised," said Maria. "Just as I feared, those mother fuckers have been here!"

"Who?"

"Mendoza Mining. Remember them, I mentioned them in the Abbey."

"Oh yeah," replied Ed. "As if things weren't strange enough. Would Flannery use a mining company for his illicit archaeology finds?"

"I think we need to do some web research later on," said Maria.

"I agree," said Ed. "Let's take a look down there."

Maria and Ed both slid down a slope on their bums. There didn't seem to be any other way down there. They landed on the muddy bottom. Before Ed even reached what looked like a large wedge tomb in the middle, he saw the tell-tale signs of archaeological digging. He saw intermittent squares dug around the space and the work of small archaeological trowels.

As Ed picked up a small pin marker, he saw it attached to a piece of twine. It was commonly used to make out the corner of a square or rectangular hole in the ground so no one walked in, or inadvertently fell in.

"They dug this up pretty good," said Ed as he threw the muddy pin marker over his shoulder.

"There must have been something here," said Maria as she moved towards the wedge tomb.

Ed followed her over, scanning the ground as he did.

The wedge tomb was long, at least fifteen feet. The heavy looking capstone had been moved halfway to the side. One of the narrow horizontal standing stones holding it up was tilted.

"This may not stand for much longer," said Ed as he aimed a flashlight into the tomb.

Bones lay scattered across it. "I doubt very much the ancient people here left a body like this inside."

Ed looked around him. He bent down and picked up a twig. "Apologies, old friend," he said as he moved the bones around.

Maria walked past the wedge tomb. She stopped, barely catching herself from falling into a trench in front of her. It was cut perfectly across a line. It looked four foot deep. She found herself looking for a jaguar before she got in…

Maria lowered herself in, walked down the 'cut' and moved her hand down the side of the wall. She stopped as her boot splashed into some water beneath. She let the water steady until she could see her reflection. Clouds raced over her head. A flash of sunlight filled the trench momentarily. Maria twisted her head as she saw the glimmer in the water.

She went down on her haunches and scooped her hands into the water and soil underneath, taking out as much as her hands would carry. She managed to step out at the one end of the trench and back over to Ed.

"Well, no knife in here," he said as she came over.

He did a double take, walked over and stared at the contents of her hands.

"Is that…?"

"Gold, Ed," responded Maria. "Small but unmistakable."

"I doubt they'll stop for anyone."

They heard the sound of a tractor nearby.

Ed found a plastic bag in his hiking bag and Maria scooped the contents inside. They quickly scanned the ground once more before sneaking back to the farm house.

Sheila took them to the next two farms and the ruse was repeated successfully again. They found no knife, but the same disturbed ground, disturbed wedge tomb and more tiny samples of gold.

They made their way back to Sheila's. Ed and Maria made a plan to head back to Ballyvaughan. They agreed they needed to get on a laptop and start searching.

Neha and Grainne were already outside the cottage. Both had some kind of poultice around their necks. Neha was following Grainne around with a small wicker basket. She was pointing in the long grass as Neha pulled up one flower or another. Earlier that morning, Sheila had dropped them to yet another house that had complained of… hauntings. They left with a fine array of those hanging parcels and a tub of salt.

"Thick as thieves, the two of them," said Sheila as she parked the car.

Ed and Maria got into Ed's car and drove back to the Wild Atlantic Lodge Hotel. Ed and Maria quickly checked their respective bills. They both agreed that staying another night wasn't a great option.

"Come to think of it, we probably need to check out of the hotel," said Maria.

"You and your dad can stay at mine," said Ed.

He explained there was a guestroom and that the cottage wasn't far from Ballyvaughan.

Maria shrugged. "I guess it's time to see how the other half lives, then," she quipped. "Keep the rent low, please," she added, smirking.

That sorted, Maria got her laptop and Ed got the coffees.

They sat close to the fire. They Google searched for Brian Flannery first. Nothing came up. They tried several different variants of the name but still got no hits. Then they tried his name with several variants of 'archaeology' and 'consultant' followed by combinations of the two words. Still nothing relevant.

"Let's move onto Mendoza," suggested Ed. "Where did you first get a hit?"

Maria explained it was when she first searched for the Burren, for her father. After a few searches she remembered what she keyed into Google images. The image loaded on the screen. There were the two blokes standing in front of the MM symbol.

"Fuck!" said Ed a little louder than intended. "That's Flannery!"

"I saw him in the Ailbh caves!" said Maria. She quickly told Ed the story.

"Let's go check out the main Mendoza company page," suggested Ed.

They moved onto the Mendoza Mining main web site. The main company webpage had various options, but they located the subsidiaries link in the 'About' section. Low and behold, 'Ireland' was an option. As the page rolled up, there was scant information. The company was established as an 'exploration hub' in 2018.

Then Maria scrolled down the page and they both took a sharp intake of breath.

Another photo of Flannery. Maria read the small writing beneath his photo, "*Mendoza Mining Ireland, Company Director: Brian Flannery.*"

"Looks like we have more problems… than the witch," muttered Ed as he looked around the pub. "Aine got in over her head, I reckon."

"Or she was in cahoots," replied Maria as she typed Aine's full name into Google.

The article headline shot up, 'Archaeologist Still Missing'.

Ed and Maria read in silence.

"Aine pointed to her bag for the knife, Ed… but maybe it was for a different reason too."

Maria picked up her phone and rang Sheila. She asked her to do them a favour and search the side pockets of Aine's bag for any receipts or documentation.

Sheila hummed and hawed on the phone. "Nothing so far," she said.

Then they heard the sound of a zipper.

"There's something here, it's a ticket… Green Island ferries," said Sheila.

"Is there any date on it?" asked Maria.

"18th November 2018."

"In the article we are staring at, she went missing on the 20th."

Maria thanked Sheila and the call ended.

Maria brought up the website for Green Island Ferries. Ed's head seemed to move into the screen as the website loaded up. They clicked on each destination until one image stood out.

A half stone fort stood on the edge of a cliff on one of the Aran Islands. "Our half-moon!" said Maria.

Maria and Ed both tried and failed to pronounce their destination, 'Dún Aonghasa'.

Maria wasted little time in booking three tickets for tomorrow's ferry to Inis Mhor island.

They packed up their belongings and checked out of the hotel, quickly got into Maria's car and collected Neha. They made the short drive back to Ed's cottage. Maria and Neha got out of the car. Ed was the last one to slowly do so. The cottage and surrounding trees and bushes were covered in the hue of twilight.

"Seems nice and peaceful," offered Maria.

Ed looked over at her. "Don't be so sure!"

Neha nodded enthusiastically. "Good, Good! This area seems secluded… hidden."

Ed opened the cottage and showed them the guest bedroom. He started to help Maria make the beds. When they were finished, they looked for Neha but instead found the same hanging parcels up on all the windows. Going outside, they saw a salt line starting at the door and moving left. Neha appeared from the right corner of the house, salt shaker in hand.

Ed looked at Maria. "He's going to be a great tenant!"

Chapter 25

There's always one, thought Jim. "Always one," he muttered, as he got out of the driver's seat.

The woman stared at him as he went down the steps of the bus.

Jim had parked the bus at a popular scenic layby along the Ballyryan strip, where the karst rock met the sea. He stood outside and inhaled some of his vape, looking at the other tourists. They were taking photos, examining the big grey boulders or walking near the edge of the bluff to look at the sea. Aka, they were enjoying themselves!

Jim laughed lightly as four young American girls ran back from the edge, away from some sea spray. They screamed and then laughed together. As for yer one on the bus…

He put his forefinger and thumb to the crook of his nose. She had paid for this tour, paid for her flights, paid for accommodation, chosen to come here.

And yet there she was, insisting she stay on the bus. She was Scandinavian he guessed by her accent. She had already quizzed him about the time, asking when they were going. How long more it would take?

He kept being as polite as he could but her latest response was that there was something strange about the wind. If there was something strange here, Jim reckoned, it wasn't with the wind. A chilly breeze blew down his shirt. Jim scrunched his shoulders, taking one last puff of his vape.

As he got back on, she glared at him immediately, making a show of checking her watch. He sat back into the driver's seat and quickly picked up his phone. Wait until he told the lads later. The tourists starting making their way back on board. Next stop, the Cliffs of Cahir.

*****

The crests of the waves sparkled in the morning sunlight. The smell of salt air filled Neha's nostrils. He stood at the back of the 'Emerald Green'. The sun was kind to them today. It seemed the perfect day for it.

They had departed only recently but none of them stood together. He, Ed and Maria had separated on the boat. Each needed their space, their time to think.

Their morning had been relaxed, even jovial. Maria had driven. Herself and Ed seemed to get on very well now. They shared many jokes he did not follow. They had even stopped for something called 'ice- cream' which he had to admit, he enjoyed. For the morning then, they had forgotten the quest they were on. Stepping back on this vessel made it all the more close though.

They had to march down this path together, this path of hot coals. Neha knew part of its end… and he was prepared for it. But he needed to prepare Maria and Ed. He swore he would tell them everything, once they had the knife.

He watched as large waves crashed up against the cliffs in the distance. Two worlds met, but only on the frontiers and edges of their existence. The crashing waves continued pounding the rocks, demanding an answer. The rock stood steadfast in its rejection, giving nothing away. But maybe the waves sought answers the rock could never give.

Neha realised he was the wave, probing the spirit world, the rocks. He had gleaned some answers but not enough. He needed more. He had never done what his gut was telling him to do… it was full of risk. But if they went into the vipers' pit without answers, they were all sure to die.

Neha turned as the sound of another boat engine disturbed his thoughts, a blue vessel. It looked similar to theirs. Must be another tourist boat, he decided. A large hand slapped down on Neha's shoulder.

"All right sailor!?" said Ed.

"Yes, Ed, I was drifting, looking at the view."

"I know what ya mean. It's calming… helps the mind wander."

"This place reminds me of home, different but a natural beauty nonetheless."

"Certainly in the sun, anyway," Ed quipped.

Ed looked behind him and then back to Neha.

"Listen, Maria, she has shared a lot about Mendoza and it turns out they are closer to the issue than we would have thought. She's bought in so maybe we should share–"

"I intend to tell her, and you, everything once we have the knife. Everything that I know."

Ed was about to respond until Neha turned and looked him directly in the eye.

"I love my daughter, Ed. She is all I really have left."

Ed held fire on a response and slowly nodded. Suddenly they both heard the cry of an eagle.

"Your friend has found us," said Ed.

There, hovering above the ship, was Neha's eagle.

"He is your friend too," replied Neha, as the eagle soared upwards and away.

They both carried on looking at the sea view around them.

*****

Maria had spent her voyage sitting up the front of the craft. She had spoken with an elderly German couple for most of the voyage and gotten so lost in their pleasant conversation that she hardly noticed the boat docking. As she got ready to disembark, she saw her father and Ed standing on the pier waiting for her.

She was distracted by the sound of a small black helicopter overhead. She swore she saw the symbol of an 'M' on the side. She quickly dismissed it as Ed called her over. She needed to put a cap on the paranoia and focus on the mission at hand. Ed informed them that they had landed in Kilronan on the east of the island. Dún Aonghasa fort was on the western part.

The small village had a standard pub and tourist shops. Ed went to find out how they could get to Dún Aonghasa. He soon returned, smiling, pushing two bikes. He said it was the quickest way across the island. Maria voiced her objection. She seemed quite annoyed. Neha's face was a picture of that sentiment.

But Ed soon convinced them by getting on one bike and doing a circle. He pointed to other tourists as they also struggled to keep their bikes in a straight line. "It's everyone's problem," he said. "But if we need to be quick, this is the best answer."

He bit his lip as much as possible as he tried not to laugh at their attempts to cycle initially. He had to 'launch' Neha on his bike. Eventually he couldn't hold the laughter in. Maria shot him daggers with her eyes, more than once.

Neha soon looked like he could handle at least staying upright on his bike. So Ed retrieved his bike, and they got going. Neha settled into his saddle and quickly became competent. Then, to Ed's surprise, Neha started to get competitive! Around corners, he would try to overtake Ed. Then he hollered at Ed as he overtook him. Ed allowed this for a short time until Neha began to revel in his lead, turning and taunting Ed.

Maria laughed.

Well, Ed had had enough and the two soon starting racing for real. Maria struggled to keep up until they both took a corner too quickly and flew off the road.

She stood there, arms folded, as they dusted themselves off. “Men!” she said as she rolled her eyes upwards.

The three took off again. Over the next ten minutes they lowered their gears… in all ways.

They entered a small village called Cill Mhuirbhigh and followed the signs for Dún Aonghasa fort. They soon found the fort and as they approached, they could see a visitors’ centre of some kind. They parked their bikes against the wall outside as a metal bar blocked the gateway to a small gravel car park.

Ed looked around briefly before getting over the small wall. Neha and Maria followed suit. At the entrance an ominous red ‘Closed’ sign greeted them, followed by a written note that said ‘Fort Closed For Maintenance’. Ed looked at the other two and they all gave a silent nod. They went to the corner of the building and opened a small, knee high timber gate. They could see the outskirts of the fort ahead of them. But some construction railing was blocking them. They walked up and down for a minute until Maria found a weak point.

Through the gap they went.

The ground sloped upwards slightly as they came to a cluster of jagged blocks of rock. The blocks were up to their waists and this field of stone carried on for around thirty metres.

“What do you know about this fort, Ed?” asked Neha.

“It’s a bronze age structure, constructed around 1100 BC. It has an outer ring wall that we are walking up to now and then an inner ring, followed by the actual fort itself.”

“Not too many places to hide a knife, then?” said Maria.

“No, I would think not,” replied Ed.

Next was the inner ring, the first wall of the fort. It was up to Ed’s shoulder and erosion had not been kind to it. It only looped around a third of the space. Crossing through a small space in between, they quickly came to the next wall. It stretched just over their heads and appeared to ring more of the area than the last. Lastly, they came to the final wall of the ring fort. It was the most robust and well maintained, a good fifteen metres high.

Walking through the gap, the sound of the sea hit their ears instantly. They could hear waves crashing against rock. This main part of the fort was shaped like a horseshoe, where two ends of the wall eventually met the cliff.

They walked forward.

Ed explained that the other half of the fort wall had fallen away into the sea, as the cliff side they were standing on was being slowly eroded over time. They reached the cliff edge and looked over. A wave thundered into the cliff below as they looked down the eighty metre drop.

"No wonder this place collapsed!" said Ed.

"Assaulted by the elements," added Neha.

"I guess we should spread out and search," said Ed. "Remember, watch out for disturbances in the ground or in the rocks themselves."

Ed walked away to the left and Maria to her right.

Neha stood still. His bottom lip protruded as he thought about the knife. Hard to know, barring the walls around them, where Aine may have hidden it. She was like Ed it seemed, skilled in understanding ancient sites. But from what Ed had said, she must have had other gifts. Abilities that no one else in her tribe had. In that sense, she was probably like him… a Shaman.

So where would he expect a Shaman to hide something? A person caught between two worlds…

Neha pondered this momentarily as he paced slowly around. He stopped suddenly and strode back towards the edge of the cliff. He looked over the edge as the waves continued to thunder into the cliff face below. The knife, he realised, could only be an arm's reach away…

Neha heard the loud cry of a bird. Looking up he saw it was the eagle. He saw it standing on the very edge of the right wall of the fort, exactly at the point where the corner of the wall met the cliff face. The eagle looked at Neha, spread its wings and let out a large cry before springing off the wall. It disappeared down over the cliff side.

Neha walked towards the right wall of the fort. He glanced and saw Ed and Maria had reached the far point of the fort near the entrance. They shrugged at each other. Neha reached the wall, placed his hands on it and looked around carefully.

There he saw two stones jutting out of the wall that faced the sea. Neha knelt and stretched his hand out to the lower stone. He pulled but it wouldn't budge. He stopped momentarily before trying once more. It was stuck fast.

The other stone was further out but at chest height. As he stared at it, a wind rolled up the cliff and the stone wobbled. Neha nodded briefly. Aine had done well.

Neha placed his right hand on the upper wall. Making sure of his grip, he stretched his left foot outwards and tested the lower stone, applying various pressure until he was satisfied that the stone would hold, and that his foot would fit on it. He went for it, placing the full pressure of his left foot on the stone while stretching out with his left arm to the higher stone.

A bead of sweat ran down Neha's head as his left hand toggled at the rock. It came part out, but then his foot slipped. He barely caught some hold with his left hand before the pressure on his right hand gave.

Regaining his footing, he made the mistake of looking down. His body shivered, his heartbeat pounded in his ears and he closed his eyes. An image of his son, Paka, flashed in his mind. He heard a whispering word on the wind, "*Fathhherrrrr.*"

Neha opened his eyes and reached without hesitation to the top stone. With a slight pull, it gave and fell out. Neha could see a piece of cloth flutter out of a small hole. He reached his hand into the hole and retrieved something heavy. A quick glance and it was wrapped in–

Neha's foot slipped again.

His right hand slid off… before a firm hand caught his wrist.

Ed's grimacing face appeared over the edge as he latched his other hand onto Neha's wrist, and pulled. Neha used his feet to help himself up. As Neha got over the edge safely, they both collapsed in a heap.

Maria rushed over.

"You need to quit the Big Macs, mate!" said Ed smirking.

"What are 'Big Macs'?"

"Never mind!" chuckled Ed.

Ed helped him up.

"Is that it?" asked Maria.

"Yes, this is it," said Neha as he handed her the knife.

She took it. It was wrapped in a very old dark green cloth with a pink ribbon keeping it together. Maria raised it to her nose. "It smells floral… and sweet."

She went to untie the pink ribbon. Neha's hand flashed over hers.

"Not here. Not now. But you hold onto it," he said as he moved his hand away.

Ed checked the time. "Come on, there's a ferry in an hour."

They started walking towards the entrance. A slow wind whispered around the fort in the midday sun.

A man walked out of the shadows. "Ed!" he said. "Fancy meeting you here!"

Ed stood out in front of the other two.

"We'll be on our way," Ed responded pointedly.

"No, I think you have time to chat!" muttered Flannery indifferently as he examined his fingernails.

The sound of two clicks came from behind them. As they turned around two heavy looking men stood in long black jackets. They wore shades. Most notably, they were pointing guns at them.

"I think your lady friend needs to hand over what's mine."

"It's not yours," said Ed. "And it won't be."

Flannery chuckled. "Funny, Aine said the same thing."

"You killed her, Flannery, didn't you?"

Flannery smirked. "I didn't do that, never got the chance. She rang me. Told me she was hearing voices. Told me she was having dreams. She went to my house when I wasn't there. She disappeared with the knife and then she disappeared herself!"

"My two colleagues here," Flannery waved his hand at the two men behind them, "chased her in the fog on Turlough Hill. Couldn't find the bitch! But I was so disappointed. We were such a great team!"

"Aine knew it had a purpose," said Neha.

"This guy's a real rarity, Ed. I should have offered him a job. Far more talented than you or I."

"Why are you, Mendoza, here? In the Burren?" said Maria sharply.

"Ah FUNAI! You're like Ed, playing on the boring, dead end team. You should always go where the wind is blowing, young lady, and for FUNAI, their time is up. I told Ed I had a sixth sense for these things, finds… for Mendoza, like minerals, and even…gold!

"We were deep in the Brazilian forest finding very little, and I started to hear whispers. I had a powerful draw to a certain location. You know where that is, Maria?"

"You were there!?" said Maria.

"You released her!?" said Neha as he marched up to Flannery.

"Sure did, short stuff!"

"She showed me this place, then," Flannery said deadpan, looking past them, "this place had gold. Another knife."

"And she followed you here?" suggested Ed.

"No idea, Ed. Don't really care. She's not my problem. I just want to sell that knife, then retire."

Ed walked up beside Neha who was still glaring up at Flannery. He placed a hand in front of Neha's chest.

"It can't leave here, Flannery," Ed said in his most reasoned voice, "or else that witch will be on the loose."

"Sorry 'mate'," Flannery said in a mock English accent, "but there has to be winners and losers in every game."

Flannery produced a gun from his pocket. "Now back off, Ed," he said as he quickly yanked Neha around and held by him the neck. Neha's arms grabbed Flannery's forearm as he clenched his teeth, through the squeeze.

The two other men grabbed Maria and Ed.

"Stop what you are doing everyone!" said a strong voice from the top of the fort wall.

They all looked up and saw a guard holding a gun.

"Ah, Garda Ahern, we were just apprehending this bunch–"

"With guns, I see Flannery! Put them down immediately, release that man and everyone move to the centre."

Garda Ahern kept the gun and her eyes pointed down on the group while she reached for her radio.

"DOWN I SAID!! GUNS DOWN NOW!!"

"Foxtrot to Tango 1." The radio gave her back white noise. "Foxtrot to Alpha 1." She got back white noise again.

"Watch out!" cried Ed.

Garda Ahern turned too late before being hit with the butt of a rifle. She went straight down.

"Bring her over here and be quick about it," said Flannery.

The man picked her up on his shoulder and made his way down.

Ed and Maria felt two guns being pointed at their backs. The lackies had their other hands holding onto an arm.

"You've gone too far, Flannery," roared Ed. "What next, are you going to shoot us! Just take the bloody knife and piss off!"

Flannery laughed at that. "Oh, I'll take the knife all right, Ed. But I'm not going to shoot you… you are all going to have an accident!"

He began moving Neha forward. Ed and Maria were shoved by the other men towards the cliff edge. The man carrying Garda Ahern followed them.

They were all shoved closer to the edge.

"You'll go to hell for this!" said Ed.

"Oh, Ed, I'll be a rich man in this life… and rich in the next, wherever I end up!" replied Flannery. "Throw them–"

Something made a noise overhead. A quick flutter of wings…

The eagle landed on the guy holding Maria. Its claws clung into his head as it pecked at his eye. He screamed.

The man holding Ed let go as he pointed the gun towards the eagle. "Stay still!" he roared to the other man being attacked.

The guy's gun went off, just as the eagle let go. The other guy's head was blown off.

Ed hacked at the guy's arm, bringing his gun arm down while planting a light punch on the side of his head.

Neha bit Flannery's forearm. Flannery shouted and tried to point the gun at Neha, but the eagle was back, and it attacked and pulled at his arm.

Maria went straight over to the other guy who had now dropped Ahern, but she was quick and planted her foot in his privates. He tumbled down.

Gunshot. The eagle avoided Flannery's attempt, but Flannery had dropped the gun in the process.

Neha quickly grabbed him by the upper part of his front coat collar with his left hand and punched Flannery with blow after blow with his right fist. Flannery couldn't get a swing in but instead put his left hand in Neha's face, trying to push him away. But Neha's left fist was anchored in position on Flannery's jacket as he still connected with his right fist. Their dance moved closer and closer to the edge.

Ed was wrestling with the guy on the ground now. The guy was big, and he managed to get Ed on the flat of his back. Ed had one hand on the guy's wrist that held the gun. He tried to wrestle it out of his hand as much as keep it away. Ed had the other hand clinging to the guy's collar beneath his neck, trying to push him off.

The guy managed to pin Ed properly to the ground with his free hand.

Ed gritted his teeth as he was just holding him off. But the fucker was making progress, as he slowly moved the gun over Ed's face. The guy was red faced with the effort and spittle flew out of his mouth, onto Ed's face. Ed gave one last try, his legs flopped beneath the guy, he tried to twist his body to keep the gun away. But this big bastard kept going, redoubling his effort. The gun went over Ed's face!

BANG!

Blood spurted on Ed's face as half the guy's face blew off. He slid forward onto Ed. Ed pushed him off and turned. Garda Ahern still had the gun raised upwards, as she lay on her front.

Maria screamed as her hair was pulled from behind, but Garda Ahern was up, grabbing that guy from behind.

Ed saw Flannery's face was pummelled but he had gotten Neha to the ground. Ed was straight over, launching a full force kick but slipped in the process. As Ed tried to get up, he saw Flannery up quicker, running for the gun he had dropped on the ground. But the eagle came out of nowhere, swooping low and snapping it off the ground.

Ed was up, as Flannery continued to fumble on the ground. As Ed was poised to leap on him, Flannery looped around with something grey in his hand. It whacked Ed in the head.

Ed went straight down.

Neha was up now and saw Flannery hit Ed with a stone. Neha caught Flannery hard to the side of the head with a good punch. Flannery stumbled, but he recovered and punched Neha dead on.

Ed was groggy, pain seared through his head. He barely managed to get in a sitting position. He saw Maria down on the ground, her long black hair drawn over her face.

The last of Flannery's lackeys had Garda Ahern by the neck and the arm that held her gun pointing in the air. He shook it until she dropped the gun. He moved her back towards the cliff. As he pushed her onto the cliff edge, Garda Ahern managed to twist sideways at the last moment, just as the eagle soared full on straight into the guy's face. He fell backwards over the edge, his scream drowned out by the crashing waves below.

Ed was up on his feet and running.

Garda Ahern shrieked as she went over… Ed scrambled just in time, grabbing her by the arm. She hung, as Ed grimaced, his arms outstretched, holding her by the wrist and forearm.

"Focus," shouted Ed. "Use your feet!"

Ed looked to his left as he struggled to hold onto Ahern.

Flannery was throwing wild punches now. Neha was ducking and diving, but he was also being pushed towards the cliff edge. Now Flannery connected with a punch, then another. Neha faltered sideways, far too close to the edge.

Ed could see Maria in a sitting position. He began roaring at her as he desperately tried to haul Ahern up.

Maria was halfway to standing. She touched something hot on her head. Blood filled her hand. She heard Ed shouting and saw Flannery beating her father. She reached her other hand out on the ground to help push her upwards but instead felt something else. She looked slowly at it. It was the cloth parcel with the knife inside. She began to untie the pink ribbon…

"Neha!" shouted Ed, as Neha nearly went over the edge. He had to wave his arms to his side to re-balance himself.

As he did, Flannery swung wildly again. Neha ducked and smacked him with a left, then a right, then another left/right combo.

Ed actually found himself shouting, “Go on, my son!”

Neha’s last punch twisted Flannery around.

But Ed missed it. He had just managed to get Ahern back over the cliff edge.

Ed heard a slight whistle in his ears. Turning, he saw Maria’s right arm out stretched. Something golden spun through the air.

Ed heard a thud.

Flannery spread his arms wide as he looked at his chest, the hilt of a knife protruding from it. His arms fell to his sides and he stumbled backwards. His face held an expression of disbelief that then turned to terror. He tried to grab the knife out of his chest as he limped further back towards the edge. As Flannery fell to his knees, Maria reached him. Blood began seeping from his mouth as he reached out his right arm to her.

“Help me,” he begged.

She slowly closed her hand around his wrist. Flannery looked down as her other hand went to the hilt of the knife. Maria yanked out the knife while simultaneously kicking Flannery’s chest with her right foot. He toppled over the edge. His scream seemed to echo in the air, the wind carrying it up the cliff face as he fell.

Neha watched him fall. Flannery landed on some rocks below. A wave crashed over him and as it retreated Flannery’s shattered body had disappeared.

“His soul needed to be cleansed,” said Neha.

They all turned their attention to Maria. Her long black hair streamed out behind her in the wind. She stared out at the ocean, bloody knife in hand.

A thunder cloud seemed to form from nowhere on the sea. Streaks of lightning scattered throughout the sky. Rolls of thunder followed.

Neha picked up the cloth that held the knife and saw an array of… flowers. He briefly smelt the inside.

"Maria," he said.

Maria still stood in the same position, staring at the storm.

"Maria, give me the knife."

Neha held out his hand close to hers.

"Maria," Neha said softly once more.

Without looking at him, she handed him the knife with a trembling hand. Neha quickly wrapped the knife inside the cloth.

Another flash of lightning. Thunder rolled around them.

Neha turned to Ed. "We need to get out of here – now!"

Chapter 26

The boat sailed just as they got on board. There weren't many spaces left. Neha sat with Maria at one end of the boat while Ed and Ahern sat down the other end. They all received strange looks from the other passengers. Ed didn't even want to look at his reflection. He, Neha, Ahern and Maria all looked pretty banged up.

As the ticket lady asked Ahern for her ticket she was doubled over with her head in her hands. She didn't respond. Ed fumbled in his pocket, retrieving his wallet, and paid her ticket.

"Seems I'm doing you all the favours of late," said Ed, nonchalantly.

She looked up at him. "How could I have been so stupid!?" She ruffled her hands in her hair before sitting up straight.

"You clearly thought I was up to something. Why?" demanded Ed.

"I'm sorry. I am. But I thought you had something to do with that hiker who fell, and I'm certain that you were the anonymous tipster regarding Aine O'Sullivan?"

Ed nodded. "I didn't think the exchange we had down at Fanore went too well. I did find Aine, but it was no accident how I did," he continued. "You wouldn't believe my story."

"Try me," said Ahern.

Ed shrugged and told her the story. An abridged version of the hauntings, the mysterious encounters and how he came across Aine's body. He told her there was a hell of a lot more going on and Mendoza seemed to be in the bloody thick of it. He told her the biggest problem was – a dead witch. He felt too drained to tell her anything else.

A minute or two of silence passed between them.

"It doesn't sound as far-fetched… not after that encounter," said Ahern. "Plus," she hesitated rubbing her hand through her hair, "we have been getting reports. Hauntings. Strange animal attacks around the place. The Hikers Hotel incident. You were there?"

"Yip," said Ed. "Front and centre."

"And that eagle," said Ahern. "Incredible. We had had a report of escaped birds up at the Ailbh Cave bird sanctuary, but for an eagle to do what it did today…"

"Well, I couldn't have been everywhere at once," quipped Ed with a light smirk.

"No, you couldn't. I didn't really engage with all the strange reports we got," she said. "I just thought you or whoever you were dealing with could have been the focus of a lot of it. There was something strange about you. You seemed in all the wrong places at the right time."

"You could be right," muttered Ed, as he looked out to sea.

Ahern stared out in the same direction as him for a minute. "Other hikers went missing, Ed. Before. Two of them. I thought if I undid one seam of your activities, the rest would unfold. I was trying to solve it all and I thought you were…" she hesitated.

"A magic bullet?" suggested Ed.

She nodded. "Oh! And I got a call off Flannery, too. He told me you attacked him," she said.

Ed hissed as he shook his head. "What about Mendoza? They seem well entrenched here," he said.

"There's only one man with connections to get them up and running here. They certainly had no licences for those guns, let alone their exploration activities," replied Ahern.

"In terms of the hikers and the strange goings on, it can only be Mendoza or… the witch," said Ed glumly.

Ahern gave Ed a hard look before turning and looking over at Neha and Maria. "What about those two? They seem in the thick of it."

"They are on a journey," replied Ed. He turned to look at them. "One of revenge and one of, I guess… destiny."

*****

Neha stared at Maria. He had tried to talk with her, but she simply stared down at her feet. "Maria," he tried as he moved his hand to her shoulder.

She slapped it away and glared at him, her eyes ablaze. "The spear, the knife, the animal encounters, the near death experiences… you knew this would happen! You have lured me to this place, using your loneliness to do it!"

"Maria, I couldn't tell you everyth–"

"Why!?" she half shouted. People looked over. "Because I wouldn't have come if you told me?" she spat. "What sane person would!?"

Neha paused before responding. "I tried, Maria… to stop her in the jungle. I didn't want you to come with us, remember? But you came anyway. I wasn't going to put two of my children in jeopardy."

Maria looked away.

"But the knife… we got it all wrong," said Neha.

Neha leaned his face into one hand.

"What do you mean?" asked Maria.

"Do you remember that Volo would let only me into his hut?"

Maria nodded.

"The vision in Volo's hut was the clearest I have ever seen, but Volo and I made so many mistakes. The vision appeared to show a past time, Maria… a time when the witch was caught and killed. They sacrificed her. Slit her throat.

"A tribal leader and a Shaman were key to the ritual. I saw a man, the Shaman… who looked just like me… saying the words. But then we saw the tribal leader, she wore the skin of a jaguar and had a painted face." Neha stopped and looked at Maria. "She took the knife and slit the witch's throat."

Neha paused. Maria's brow was creased. Then her hand went over her mouth.

"She looked like–"

"Me!" Maria said, as her eyes opened wide. Her mouth fell open. "Me – I'm the one to wield the knife," she said with a stunned realisation.

"That was the mistake we made. The leader, the tribal leader, the person who is responsible for the tribe as it lives and as it dies. They hold the responsibility. The great responsibility of who lives… and who dies. But Volo and I interpreted the vision so very wrong, even though the answer was in front of our faces. We decided that you appeared in the vision only because you had made the journey to Volo, with me. That you could not be the one… someone so disconnected to the forest."

"But how could you have gotten it so wrong?" demanded Maria.

"We were not sure, but we had so little time! We thought the spirits had given them, the tribe of the past, our faces, to help us understand the vision's message better. Volo had already sent Karo, the leader, to kill her. He failed."

Maria reached a hand to her father and he took it.

"But Father, are you absolutely sure? You are sure this time… that it has to be me?"

"You remember what Karo told you before he passed. He handed you his tribal band of Chief. Karo was stubborn, but a mighty warrior. He was no fool. He saw it before he crossed. Somehow, these places are connected, but we are connected to what passed before as well. This time I must say the incantation, you are the leader, Maria. You must wield the knife!"

"And you, Ed, are the guide," Neha concluded, as he saw Ed and Ahern walking over.

"Yes, I'm the guide," repeated Ed, deadpan. "Care to fill me in?"

"Not right now," replied Maria.

"Ladies and gentlemen, you're very welcome on the second half of our tour today. We hope you enjoyed Inis Mhor. We are closing in on the Cliffs of Cahir now, the most impressive cliffs in Ireland. The cliffs run along this coastline here for nine miles."

The voice on the monitor carried on as people made their way to the front of the boat. The four of them followed. Maria and Neha drifted away from Ed and Ahern. They found a spot at the side rail. Ed and Ahern found another spot and looked up at the cliffs for a few minutes. Ed thought he could make out people at the top.

"Are you still going to report all of this?" said Ed out of the side of his mouth.

"Yes," she said, pausing. "I'll report that you did nothing untoward. That you're a dead end."

"What about Mendoza?" said Ed. "And the two dead bodies still at the fort?" Ed looked around him.

"Mendoza strike me as the type of people who don't want to be seen or heard," she replied, as she looked up at the cliffs. "I don't expect a call from them. As for the bodies, I didn't see them there today," she muttered. "I'm sure they'll pop up in time. Someone will find them. Random drug deal gone wrong… I imagine." Ahern looked at Ed with a light smirk. "Although maybe I'll receive another anonymous tip shortly. The source will never be traced."

Ed nodded but continued looking in another direction.

"One fucker I will be ringing, though, is Billy Joe," she said.

"You should consider searching Flannery's house. Who knows what you'd find there?" said Ed as he looked at Ahern.

"Maybe I'll do that," said Ahern.

The sea became far choppier the closer they got to the cliffs. Ed and Ahern grabbed the side rail tightly. But Ed saw that Neha lost his footing momentarily and the knife dropped out of the cloth pouch. It began sliding on the deck. Neha scrambled to pick it up, getting it back in the cloth as quickly as he could.

They heard the rumble in the distance. Ed turned as the wind picked up. He saw the storm cloud over Inis Mhor was gathering pace, moving towards them.

Ed raced to the boat's cabin as they passed some kind of large sea stack.

"If you look at the cliff, just there on the right, you'll see a host of gannets. The cliffs are home to several species of–"

Ed grabbed the man by his sleeve and yanked him around.

"How long is this tour?" said Ed loudly.

The man looked slowly at Ed's hand on his jacket. "Take your hand off me… and take a seat," he said with unreserved anger.

"How long?" Ed demanded.

"An hour, sir," the man growled as he yanked his arm out of Ed's grip. "Now, get out of this cabin and sit down or I'll call the guards and they will arrest you on the pier."

"But look at the storm clouds there." Ed pointed behind him. "They can't be good news. Believe me… they aren't good news!"

"Now, sir," the man said more calmly putting his two hands up by his shoulders. "Just relax… nothing is going to happen. Just take a seat there," he said, pointing at a lone seat just outside the cabin. He quickly turned round to continue as the boat rocked side to side more and more. The grey clouds rumbled and twisted above them now.

"If you look up on the left hand side of the cliff, you'll see O'Brien's Tower. The cliffs reach their highest point there, approximately 214 metres in height. The Cliffs of Cahir Visitor Centre is just there also. Another great tourist spot. I highly recommend you see the cliffs from down here and up there."

The man's voice seemed to drone off. "What's that?" he said over the mic, almost hushed.

A large 'splash' was heard to the left of the boat. Then another splash and another.

"My God…," the man said as the mic dropped from his hand. Screams and shouts came from the deck now, as people saw what was falling.

*****

Jim had continued the tour, taking the coast road. The sun and conditions were kind to them. It made the driving easier and meant he didn't have to go into greater detail on his tour monologues. He spiced things up with some jokes, good and bad. He pulled the bus in at the large car park adjacent to the Cliffs of Cahir. Many other buses were already parked there. It looked busy as people streamed back and forth in both directions.

"Well, folks, go across to the visitors' centre there and your tour guide, Cathy, is waiting for you. We have a good hour here so enjoy the view!"

The bus began to empty but low and behold, that lady stayed on. Jim looked down for a second as his face flushed. She had short cropped blonde hair. She wasn't young, but she wasn't ancient either. Maybe somewhere in her mid-sixties. He hadn't detected or seen any walking stick either. He had to avoid the 'I want my money back discussion' at the end or 'I want to make a complaint and then have my money back'. Even if she got out at just one stop that would be the argument to save the hassle he now thought inevitable.

Jim walked down the bus towards her once more. He made sure to smile as she seemed to make sure to frown. Her glimmering green eyes locked onto his.

"Would you not get out here?" he said as pleasantly as possible. "The Cliffs are one of the main attractions on the island."

"No. Could we leave soon? There is a storm over there," she quickly replied, looking out the window.

Jim looked across at some thick grey clouds. They weren't far but they were hardly close either. "I don't think they'll come towards us, sure.

Tis a lovely day anyway. Blue skies! It's rare on this island, believe you me," said Jim, as he broke into a mock chuckle.

She glared back at him as she sank further into her seat. "I shouldn't have come here… I have made a mistake," she said. "It's the wind. There is something wrong… something in the wind."

Jim couldn't help but roll his eyes. Then he realised, maybe she was just afraid of heights. He felt sympathy overcoming his sarcastic impression of the lady. "There's a lovely gift shop and the café isn't half bad either. Good wholesome bowl of soup? The lasagne is very good," he said as he patted his stomach.

A flash of lightning went off around them, quickly followed by a clap of thunder. Jim ducked slightly as he looked out the window. Hailstones battered the ground. "I'd say that will clear off quickly. It's out of kilter with the good weather we've had today."

She said nothing and stared forward.

"Well, I'm going in for a bite to eat but I have to lock the bus."

She said nothing as Jim walked away. As he grabbed his jacket and opened the bus door the wind swept into his face. The bus shook with the power of it.

Jim went down one step…

"If you go out there," she said standing, "you'll die!"

Jim stopped, looking down at her again. She glared at him with her strange coloured eyes. Jim openly laughed as he stepped off the bus. He turned and locked it as he walked off.

The weather, as he had predicted, improved. The grey clouds remained but the hailstones had stopped. The thunder and lightning had stopped too. Jim was just opening the visitor centre door when a gust raced past him, forcing it shut. He was about to open it again when he heard a cry.

He looked to his left towards the cliff…

The four American girls he had seen earlier were close to the cliff side. They walked forward, leaning into the wind, making slow progress as they took one step after the other. He shrugged and turned away.

But then another cry… they were all screaming. Three had gotten away but the last girl was behind them, clinging to a metal lamp post. She looked as if she was being buffeted violently by the wind. Jim saw other people on the cliff now being pushed towards the edge by the wind. He ran as quickly as he could towards the girl. She was barely keeping her grip on the metal pole. The wind raced him forward the last few paces. He had to hold his hands out to his front to soften the collision as he thudded against the pole.

"Right, come on, I'll–"

She lost her grip just as Jim stretched forward to grab her hand. Jim let go of the pole, reaching out to her outstretched hand. The tips of their fingers brushed together as their feet rushed beneath them, their deadly dance bringing them far too close to the edge.

Then, Jim got a grip of her out-reached hand with his right one. He quickly slapped his left hand onto her hand too, digging his heels into the ground. She slowed and they both stopped. The gusting wind died down.

"Thank Go–"

Then Jim and the girl looked down the cliff side and saw them…

Others, reaching their arms out, their faces locked in horror before they went over! As both Jim and the girl tried to run, a howling wind blasted into them. They were thrown over the edge. They still gripped each other as terror gripped them both.

They shrieked and shrieked as they tumbled, soon colliding with their watery graves below.

*****

Ed watched with the others in sheer terror as body after body flew off the cliffs above. Some hit the walls as they fell before hitting the churning water beneath.

"BANG!"

A high pitched scream.

A contorted body lay on the deck.

Another body crashed on the deck. Then another. People shouted and screamed. Ed and everyone else ducked for cover. They scrambled about. The boat listed right as a howling gale filled their ears. Ed saw the captain leave the cabin; then a body struck him. The captain fell over the side as Ed tripped on another body at his feet. He felt himself being dragged up.

It was Ahern. "What the fuck is going on!?" she roared at him over the noise.

A wave smacked the side of the vessel. Three or four people screamed as they toppled over the side… the rest hung on for their dear lives.

"The cabin… the cabin!" Ed pointed. "Quickly!"

Ed and Ahern made it inside. Neha and Maria were already there.

Ahern stepped up to the controls.

"Can you drive this thing?" demanded Ed.

"Maybe," she shouted.

Neha pointed at something in the distance.

"Now what!?" shouted Ed.

In the distance, the sea seemed taller somehow. Something was rolling towards them on the sea.

"Christ! That's a fucking wave!"

The massive wave churned over the sea as it closed in on them. The sound of it eclipsed the howling gale around them. The few survivors on board shouted as they tried to hold onto something.

"There!" Maria shouted as she pressed in between Ed and Ahern. "Go there, behind that sea stack!"

Ahern shouted, "But–"

"Quickly!" snapped Maria. "There's no time!"

Ahern manoeuvred the boat towards it and put the throttle up.

Ed looked at the chaos behind them on deck. He ran out. "Get away from the sides! As many as you can – into the cabin!"

As Ahern positioned the boat behind the large sea stack, Ed wondered whether the stack would hold. Whether it would break up. And even if it managed to slow the wave somewhat, that they still wouldn't be smashed up against the cliffs.

But cold logic told him it was the only card they had left to play. The huge wave was only twenty meters away.

"I'm going to try something when the wave hits," said Ahern frantically. "Hold on!" she shouted as the wave crashed into the stack.

The tip of the wave was nearly as big as the stack itself. The wave surged around the sea stack, pushing the boat's bow up sharply. Two people tumbled out of the cabin door, screaming… as they plunged into the sea.

As their vessel was carried on by the wave, the boat was twisted around so the bow now faced the cliffs. Ahern immediately put the throttle into reverse and turned the wheel as far as it would go to the left.

Another tourist boat raced past to the port side. It was already capsized. The wave smashed it into the cliff. It split in two before disappearing beneath the surf.

Their boat still surged along with the strong wave.

Then it slowed slightly but not enough… Screams, shouts as they closed in on the cliff.

"COME ON! COME ON!" shouted Ahern desperately, as she tried to twist the wheel even more.

But the cliffs were only metres away now…

Then the boat began slowing. It slowed some more. The boat's bow suddenly turned left and then began turning in a full circle.

The surge of the wave created a back wash off the cliff. Ahern let the boat turn once more before straightening up the wheel. She reversed the throttle as the backwash hit them. They moved forward and away from the cliff, getting in behind the sea stack again as a second, smaller wave crashed by.

*****

Ed tried relaxing as he soaked in the warm water of the shower. His body heated up but he still felt numb. It was already too late, he realised. There was no way out. He had a chance to get off this crazy motorway before, but now… now he was trapped. Trapped on a bullet train and the final destination seemed assured.

Their boat had gotten back to port with a skeleton crew. A RNLI rescue vessel had towed them as their engines gave out a mile on from the cliff. Thankfully, the storm clouds and wind had dissipated after the second wave.

The four of them disembarked together with the seven others who had survived. As they stepped off, there was no avoiding the bloody seawater that swirled around on the deck. The RNLI crew offered basic medical assistance where necessary. Ahern gave them a lift back to the cottage in her police car. No one spoke.

However, as Ed was getting out Ahern slipped him a card with her contact details on it. She asked him to keep an eye out for those two missing hikers. He agreed. She wished him luck and told him to call her if he needed anything.

When they got back into the cottage, all three were exhausted and traumatised in equal measure. No dinner was suggested. Maria went straight to bed, Neha started a fire and Ed went for a shower.

Ed stood in the warm water a minute longer, before turning off the shower. He dried himself and wrapped the towel around him. Opening the bathroom door, he walked by Neha. Neha was staring into a blazing fire in the stove.

Neha gave him the briefest glance. Then he sharply turned in his chair and stared at Ed. "What," said Neha as he leaned forward with a shocked expression on his face, "is that?" Neha pointed at Ed's chest.

It took Ed a moment to register. “Oh this,” said Ed. “It’s a pendant of some sort. An artefact of some kind, I’d say bronze age–”

“Where did you find it?” Neha asked as he stood, moving over and examining it with his hand. “Did you find it anywhere here?”

“It was in Aine’s file. Why?” replied Ed, as he reached his hands up and started to take the pendant off.

“Do not do that!” Neha said sternly.

Neha produced something from under his t- shirt. Ed saw it looked very similar to the pendant on his chest. Neha examined the two ornaments side by side. They formed a full circle.

“A connection – a connection to this place,” said Neha as his words drifted off.

Neha looked past Ed, while chewing on his lip. He let go of Ed’s pendant.

“Good night,” Ed said, walking away.

“Good night,” Neha responded meekly. “Oh, and Ed,” he said.

Ed turned around.

“Don’t take that off!”

With that Neha sat down and continued to stare at the flames in front of him.

Chapter 27

Maria woke up. She had no idea who she was, where she was.

She took in the room around her and as she did her brain re-booted and the flood of trauma and events came rushing back. Maria felt as if she part of a disaster movie, but she couldn't leave. She saw her father's bed was still made across the room. Untouched. His bag lay on top.

She got up and found her jumper, wondering what dangerous or supernatural event would occur to them today. She opened the door and felt heat from the living room. She walked in and saw her father sitting in a chair beside a dwindling fire. He had a blanket wrapped around him.

He woke as she pulled a chair over and sat across from him. "Maria," he said, half shocked.

Ed walked into the room, yawning. The two stared at him. He stared back momentarily, before pulling another chair over. He sat.

All three stared into the fire now. 'Good mornings' did not seem the order of the day.

"How can we kill a witch?" Ed asked sullenly, still staring into the flames.

"I already tried… and failed," responded Neha.

"What!?" said Ed.

"Yes, me, Karo, Timku… and Paka," he said as he looked to the floor. "I let him down."

Ed and Maria exchanged a look.

"What happened to Paka, Father?"

Neha stared at the fire in front of him. "When we left Volo at the village, we were on foot for maybe an hour. We found her lair. It looked as if it was inside a hollow. I recognised the two large standing stones from the vision I had shared with Volo, in his hut. The stones stood a few metres apart. There was a hole in the middle and he ground looked torn up inside. I searched it for the knife.

"I located the large flat rock that was to be placed on the stone across the small clearing. It appeared to be sitting at some kind of wide entrance. When we walked over to the flat rock, I realised that the entrance was actually a river bed and that we were standing in a small empty lake. But it made sense, as the end of the vision showed us water pouring over her grave. The water would stop her getting back to the air.

"Karo and I followed the river bed and we found a wall of logs. We climbed up the sides of the river and onto the bank. We could see the small river beyond the dam. We saw dead men up there alongside strange contraptions they used to disturb the earth."

"The miners?" said Maria.

"I guess so," replied Neha as he continued to stare at the fire. "I shared a look with Karo and he nodded. We both knew that the dam had to come down. We found two axes near a tree stump. Then we walked back to the standing stones, to Paka and Timku. The time for silence was over. Karo and I gave them the plan. We lifted the capstone and we were surprised to see a dead man beneath. He clung to a golden knife. I yanked it from his closed fist.

"Next, we all lifted the capstone into position until one side was balanced at the top. Paka held it so it neither slid off nor fully fell into place. Karo and Timku hurried off to break the dam with the axes. I stood the opposite side of the standing stones to Paka. I went down on one knee and touched the soil, closing my eyes as a gust of wind passed by. I heard a voice…Volo's voice on the wind. *Say the words, Neha... say the words.* I started chanting the incantation. I held the pendant up and stood. Thunder rattled in the air as a wind began to swirl around me. It got stronger and stronger…

“The pendant shook in my hand as I felt water at my feet. I quickened my chant and said it louder and louder. The water soon reached our calves as a huge streak of lightning went through the air. Thunder rolled around the tree tops. A wail, a wail of a cracked and old voice echoed around me. It seemed to the fill the air. Then a horrible shriek came. In the raging wind above me, a few feet up, she appeared.

“She was a decrepit specimen. She was blackened as if burnt and her cheeks were hollowed, her eye sockets empty. She was like a skeleton barely holding its skin on. Streaks of white hair flowed behind her. She was covered in a torn and ramshackle black cloak. She reached forward to me and wailed.

“I continued singing the words as best I could. An incredible wind surged around me. The witch drifted down in the air and reached for the golden knife in my hand. Paka shouted that he could not hold the stone in place much longer. I stood still and kept the incantation flowing as she reached me. She wailed again, a long moan… ending in a soft growl.

“Her scrawny, bony hands reached towards my throat and the knife. I stepped back between the two standing stones. She followed almost face to face with me. At the last second, I yanked the pendant free from my neck and put it around her monstrous head. She screamed and screamed as she straightened in the air and moved towards the ground.

“I could see Paka struggling. He gritted his teeth as he held the stone upwards. I felt a tornado of wind at my back. The witch clutched at the pendant cord around her neck as she tried to grab the knife in my hand. I stopped her other hand reaching my throat as I saw a torrent of water race down the river bank behind Paka. As it surged forward, I lost my concentration… breaking the incantation. The witch grabbed the knife from my hand. I shouted at Paka to ‘hold on’ as the water clattered into us. I was thrown a few feet backwards by the rushing water. Paka somehow stayed in position. The witch cackled above the noise of the wind and water, as she raised the knife towards Paka. She held it aloft as a streak of lightning filled the sky.

"'WORRRSHIP!' she cried. "The word filled the air. I got up and rushed back through the water. I started to bellow out the incantation again. I reached the middle of the standing stones and snatched the knife from the witch's hand. As she turned towards me, I thrust the knife as hard as I could at her chest. She stood motionless. I saw my whole arm had gone through her body… but I had felt a connection."

Neha looked to the floor. "Her contorted face let out a slow laugh. It got louder and louder. I withdrew my arm, but I could only see the hilt of the knife, no blade. I heard Paka mutter my name with a weak voice. I looked past the witch, over the rising water. Paka was spitting blood. The blade was stuck deep in his chest. I reached the crescendo of my incantation. Paka's arms heaved upwards… somehow. The witch screamed as the capstone above slid down into place… and she disappeared.

"The pendant floated towards me. I grabbed it and swam around to Paka. He was face down in the water. The rising water lifted us both up beside the top of the capstone. I dragged Paka up in my arms. Our eyes met….

"Then his body twitched and he stared off… into nothing. I screamed his name over and over, but the… spark of his spirit had left his body.

"My boy… My boy."

Ed was on the very edge of his chair.

Maria was agape.

Tears rolled down Neha's cheeks.

"Oh, Father," said Maria as she took one of his hands in hers.

"I killed him… I killed him," he said, sobbing now.

"Father, you did not kill him. You were killing the witch! Anyone else in your position would have done the same," she added.

"If you ask me, Paka sounded like a brave warrior. He held the stone, then got it up," said Ed as he placed a hand on Neha's shoulder. "He did his job," he added with conviction. "And if he did his job, let's do ours!"

Neha stopped weeping, his face going stony. "I'll kill her!" he said, as his eyes shimmered in the morning light that crept through the curtains. "I'll kill her!" he rasped.

Maria stood abruptly and walked out of the room. Ed heard the conservatory door banging. He sat with Neha for a moment more before saying, "I'll be back in a minute. I'll boil the kettle and we can plan our next move."

Neha said nothing as Ed got up. He stared at the dying flame in front of him.

Ed walked through the conservatory and out the back door. Maria stood in the grass outside, with her back to him. Her arms were folded in front of her. Ed took a step forward just behind her. She placed one hand to her forehead and dipped her head.

"Oh, Ed!" she said, as she suddenly looped around and stepped into his chest. Ed was stunned momentarily. She kept her head down. He kept his head pointed upwards to hide his flushed face. He slowly wrapped his arms around her. She squeezed into him.

"It'll be–"

"If I hadn't gone into the forest after the miners, that time, Karo and Timku wouldn't have had to rescue me. They could have helped my father and Paka."

Ed closed his eyes and waited. "Sounds to me like your father would have plunged the knife into the witch no matter what. Even if Timku and Karo were there, would they have stopped him? Would anyone? And if they had come back, they would probably only have helped Paka with the stone. Sounds like he was stuck in position anyway." Ed found himself rubbing her back.

She leaned out from him, wiping a tear from her eye. "Thanks, Ed," she said as she stepped away, quickly folding her arms again.

They both found themselves staring at a cow that was staring at them, from over a wall.

Ed didn't know what to do but he didn't want to start fidgeting. He rummaged in his pockets until he found his cigarettes. "Besides, your dad said he'll kill her," he said as he put a cigarette into his mouth. "But he's wrong," he added as he raised the lighter up to his mouth. "We'll kill her!"

"And they'll kill you," said Maria, as she yanked the cigarette out of his mouth and threw it away.

She walked off. The cow bellowed at Ed.

Ed went back inside and made three cups of tea. He brought them in to Neha and Maria. A few moments passed as they quietly sipped their brew.

"From the description in your story, logic would dictate that her lair is a dolmen," said Ed to Neha. "You saw one at Poulnabrone. Do you remember? When I took you out? Was it like that?"

"Yes," said Neha. "It was similar. But the visions I have had since the confrontation with the witch have only shown me a falling flat rock."

"What about the wedge tomb sites?" Maria said. "There's something about those ones we did search, something I can't put my finger on. And what about the ones we have not searched, from Aine's map?"

"It's likely we'll just find disturbed wedge tombs, I imagine," replied Ed. "I think we've got to just focus on the dolmen. If that was the structure Neha encountered in the rainforest, it's the best lead we have. Not sure at this point where that dolmen could be though," he mused. "I've had a very good look around the place because of the audit."

Neha shifted to the front of his seat. He held his pendant in his hand. "Somehow the forest and the Burren are connected. And we are connected to what passed before," said Neha. "Ed, do you remember the oval artefact we found in Aine's bag? Can you get it?"

Ed got up and rummaged in his room. He returned, handing the artefact to Neha. Neha held it in his hands and showed them both. He took his pendant and leaned it towards Ed. Ed leaned his towards Neha's. They connected.

"The connection between two worlds… between two places… between two tribes," said Neha.

Maria squinted at the linked pendants. Neha's was black, Ed's was white. "They seem to match the image on the artefact," she said with surprise.

"Can this help us with the location of her lair?" Ed said.

"There is more we must know than the location of her lair," replied Neha.

Neha disconnected the pendants carefully, stood, and went into his room. He brought back a long piece of wood and something wrapped in brown cloth. The piece of wood went upwards at one end, at a right angle, forming a small hollow.

"Is that a pipe?" asked Ed.

"Yes," said Neha as he sat back down. "Grainne is the last connection to the spirits of this place, the tribe that went before."

"So you plan… a vision, Father, to connect with the spirits…with Grainne, using those?"

"Not with Grainne," he said. "Through Grainne, to speak with her grandmother. Grainne has the gift, but she told me much about her grandmother. Crucially, she told me that her grandmother used to look into the fire… and contact the souls of the dead. This," he held up the small cloth parcel, "will help me do that."

"What is it?" asked Maria.

"This represents the most powerful connection to the spirit world I have ever encountered."

Neha opened the cloth parcel and showed it to Maria. She examined the inside before raising her eyebrows and leaning back in her chair. Neha next showed Ed the contents. Inside, he could see blue coloured insects and a luminous green leaf of some sort.

"You are sure you can contact her there, in the spirit world, and have a full blown conversation?" asked Ed.

"No, I am not," replied Neha. "But I am sure that we are running out of time and as of yesterday, the witch's power will soon grow beyond a point where we can stop her."

Ed nodded. "And will Grainne–"

"Grainne and I have already discussed it," said Neha, pre-empting Ed's question.

Maria's phone rang from her room. She got up, went in and answered it.

She raced back out. "It's Sheila!" Maria put her on speaker and placed the phone down.

Sheila quickly told them that Grainne had a fall. She wasn't well… a doctor had looked at her. Her heart was failing. Sheila said that all Grainne could talk about was Neha. That she wanted to see Neha straight away. Tell Neha, 'It was time'.

The three quickly made a plan, or at least two of them did. Neha insisted that Maria stay within the confines of the cottage, within the charms and salt barrier.

She was outraged. "I'm going!" she insisted.

Neha refused this.

They went nose to nose with each other. "I'm the tribal leader now!" Maria said.

"I'm your father!" Neha shouted back.

Ed calmed things by suggesting that Maria do this "for now."

Ed produced the file and said he would go out and look at the dolmens again and check his guidebooks as well for any he may have missed. As he opened the file, Maria shoved him out of the way. She meticulously deconstructed the file into ordered bundles on the table. Ed decided not to argue. She quickly found Aine's map of the dolmens and took note of them on a separate piece of paper. Ed folded the dolmen map into his pocket.

"Have you looked at all of this?" she asked.

"Most," said Ed. "Not so much this bundle," he added holding the old 1950s report up.

"The largest one?" said Maria glaring at him.

"Well I had a quick look at–"

"Just get going!" said Maria. "I'll call you if I find anything. I want to have good look through everything anyway. There's something gnawing at me."

Neha was ready, changed and waiting at the cottage door.

Ed quickly got changed too. As he went to open the door, he asked Neha, "How will I know if it's the right dolmen?"

"The capstone will be off!" shouted Maria from the other room.

"Your pendant, Ed," said Neha. "It will shake."

*****

Ed dropped Neha up to Grainne's cottage. Then he quickly darted around the Burren for the morning. But at each dolmen location he found all the capstones were in place, on top.

His phone buzzed and he answered at the wheel, "Maria, nothing so–"

"There's one you haven't looked at. It's referenced in the 1950s bundle."

"Where?"

"Eagle Rock, on top of Slieve Elva."

Ed pulled over. Maria gave him the exact coordinates. "I'm pretty sure that's where the French man, Adrien, fell off," said Ed softly.

"Be careful, Ed."

Ed guided his car towards the base of Slieve Elva, just opposite Fanore beach. The sound of crunching stone under foot annoyed him as he made the forty minute ascent. Finally, he got up and could see the dolmen in the distance. The capstone had fallen, standing diagonally between the two standing stones.

The sound of a low breeze chimed in his ears. He instinctively stopped, going down on one knee. He then, as quietly as he could, placed a hand into his hiking bag and retrieved a pair of binoculars. Raising them up and adjusting the focus, he could see blue and white tape around the dolmen. He quickly registered that must have been Ahern. She must have checked it and cordoned it off.

Ed took the binoculars away from his face, looked around and then put them back up to his eyes. He could see nothing else. He couldn't decide whether he actually wanted to 'see' anything else. He placed the binoculars down beside him and stood, placing one hand to the pendant.

He took one slow step forward and then another. He held his free hand up slightly in front of him as he walked. Ed's slow steps continued for five minutes. He couldn't help but feel like a fly going into a spider's web.

He was closing in now; it didn't seem too far. He did a massive exhale as he bent down, going in under the police tape. A large bead of sweat ran down his face, falling onto the grey stone below.

His mission impossible continued. He was two, maybe three metres away. The pendant still wasn't shaking or vibrating.

In reaching distance now, he reached a hand out. He clenched his teeth as his hand touched the nearest standing stone.

Ed's phone went off – full blast! A howling wind rolled past.

"FUCK SAKE!"

Ed placed his hands on the stone. He clamped his eyes shut and scrunched his head into his shoulders, as if a bomb was about to go off.

The wind died down. He opened one eye and then the other. His pendant did nothing. Nothing happened at all. Ed took his hand away and sighed, bent down and rubbed his knees. He stood straight, taking out his phone.

Missed call – Maria.

He rang.

She answered. "How are you–"

"It's not it," said Ed breathing heavily. "It's not it."

"Okay. Well, Sheila rang. Grainne is slipping away but she and Neha want to do the... the…"

"Vision?" Ed tried to help.

"Yes. He wants you down there now. He needs help. I want to get back to the file. Chat later." She hung up.

Ed trudged back down the mountain wondering who he could 'bill' when this was all over.

*****

Swirls of smoke gathered at the ceiling of the cottage. There had been steady puffs coming from Neha's pipe. Ed had never attended a séance or trance, or whatever this was supposed to be, before. Ed's role was to 'keep watch'. Watch Neha and Grainne while also watching for anything else...

When he arrived, Grainne and Neha were speaking in hushed tones. Grainne was propped in an old high back wooden chair in front of the fire. She was tilted slightly to her left. She was pale and her breathing was laboured.

Grainne called Sheila over and asked her to go out for the night. "Come back tomorrow," she said. "The night is closing in fast, but the dawn will soon follow," she concluded.

Sheila argued vehemently but Grainne told her there was a storm coming. As she took Sheila's hand in hers, she said, "My time is up. I will not survive this storm, but you can."

Sheila broke down as she accepted. "Thank you, child," Grainne said, as they embraced. They exchanged a few words in Irish and Sheila left.

Neha sat in another high back wooden chair to the left of Grainne He had given Grainne the luminous plant/blue ant mixture via her tea. He had ground down the last of the mixture in a bowl nearby. But Neha also said he needed something connected to this place, this land. Grainne had gotten a sense of what Neha might be looking for.

She waved her good hand at the press to her right. Ed opened it, locating a bottle of clear liquid at the back. He opened it and smelled it. Pure moonshine. Or Poitin as they called it around here. Ed poured two glasses. Grainne knocked hers back, while Neha sipped his. Neha finished and placed his glass on the kitchen table to his left and nodded to Ed.

Ed had already lit the candles around the room. He turned off the main light.

Neha held Grainne's left hand and waved his hand over his face, indicating that they should shut their eyes. It was time. He slowly and softly chanted a song for a few minutes. He stopped or the song simply drifted from him…

He could hear the snap of wood in the fire in front of him. He let out a long breath and felt the heat. He tightened Grainne's hand slowly. His head bowed and his breathing slowed. The fire suddenly felt more intense and louder…

Ed noticed how Grainne's and Neha's heads leaned back in their chairs at the same time, their eyes remaining shut.

Neha opened his eyes and saw before him a great bonfire. His left hand felt a large wooden log beneath him. Barring the bonfire, there was nothing else around them except the murk of night… or simply darkness. He noticed Grainne beside him. Her eyes were open also.

Suddenly, to their right, the light of the bonfire stretched out, revealing a man. He sat a short distance away on a similar wooden log. He was bald with a long bushy red beard. His head was covered in blue paint with painted yellow circles around the eyes. He wore a black cloak, which was pinned at the neck by a metal object. It was golden and circular in appearance and had a metal rod running through it.

A green garment covered his chest underneath, stretching down to his knees. The green material had strange square red patterns interwoven into the garb. A wide belt covered his middle. Long grey hair boots covered the rest of his calves and feet. The man held a type of small wooden pipe to his mouth and slowly smoked. He held a horn in his other hand. The man's eyes glimmered in the fire light. Neha noticed they were a vibrant green, like his, with specks of yellow or gold, prominent around the iris.

The Shaman nodded to them and looked directly at Neha.

Ed watched them both. A minute ago, they both jolted in their chairs. It made him jump. He watched as they both began muttering. After this escapade, he decided, he would need a daily source of Valium...

The Shaman spoke to Neha in Yine, "Welcome." The sound seemed to echo around them everywhere at once. "You have travelled far. You chase the banshee."

"Why is she here?" asked Grainne.

"She travelled the ancient tracks, escaping her tomb from there," he said, as he nodded at Neha. "She found the gate open here," he added as he waved his hands around him, "as she did before."

"How do we defeat her?" asked Neha. "I must know the song. And what of the pendants and her lair?"

A strange wind began to roll in from behind them. It carried a noise that became louder and louder. It was a woman's scream, now a shriek… now a wail. It became so loud that Grainne and Neha each had to block their ears.

Ed could hear a screaming wind around the cottage, he was fearful it was her...

He briefly considered waking them up as he watched them put their hands to their ears and writhe in their chairs.

The wail and wind died off.

The Shaman stood and threw back his cloak. A small bronze sword revealed itself. It was slender and looked sharp at the edges. He stepped forward towards the bonfire. He drew his sword and used it to stoke the flames.

A pair of red eyes appeared behind him. Out of the murk, a large paw with long razor like claws banged its way upon the log. Then another. Suddenly an enormous wolf leapt over the log the Shaman had been sitting on. It was only shorter in height than Neha by a foot. Its broad shoulders were in front of a good two metre torso. It was covered with black and grey ruffled hair. Its long snout revealed fangs from a nightmare. It drooled as it slowly moved towards the Shaman.

Grainne gripped Neha's hand tightly now. Neha tried to move but could not. "Behind you!"' Grainne roared. The Shaman still did not move but looked at them both.

Ed was paralysed where he stood as Grainne let out a high pitched scream. He saw that they both gripped each other's hands in a vice like manner. The pressure wasn't easing. Their other hands clung, white knuckled, to the wooden sides of their armrests. Then Ed thought heard the sound of a fog horn or boat horn out on the sea...

As the wolf seemed to pounce, the Shaman picked a piece of burning wood from the fire and spun round, quick enough to smack the wolf in the face. It let out a whimper as it moved back. As it backed towards Neha and Grainne, the Shaman threw a burning log which landed at Grainne's feet. Then the Shaman threw another to its right side. The wolf ran to its left to escape but the Shaman threw a burning log there too. A ring of fire formed which surrounded and trapped the wolf from escaping.

The Shaman stared at Neha and then stared beyond into the ether. He brought the horn to his lips and blew. Nothing happened for a moment. Then they could hear singing…

Another man appeared. It was Volo.

He had black paint on his face, with yellow circles around his eyes. He wore a crown of red feathers with a matching red tunic at his waist. Otherwise he was bare. He held a wooden stick.

Volo looked directly at Neha as he sang. He stamped his feet and banged his chest. Neha stood, instinctively beginning to sing with him even though he did not know the words. Volo raised his right hand open ended up above his head. It began to rain heavily now but the bonfire and ring of fire around the wolf were still ablaze. Soon Neha and Volo were singing in harmony and water began to slowly flow from behind Volo's feet towards them.

Ed watched as a fire log suddenly fell from the fireplace and landed not too far from Grainne's feet. It had started raining heavily outside. The rain was finding its way through a gap in the roof above and was rapidly falling into an old paint bucket on top of the stove behind them. Neha was standing, chest puffed out, and singing. Ed had no idea what the song or dance meant but it reminded him of the passionate singing and dance that the New Zealand rugby team performed when doing the 'haka'. Neha was just belting out his song...

The Irish Shaman turned and beckoned someone from behind and beyond the great fire. Out of the darkness, an old woman in a black shawl appeared. She carried a cane. She was slightly hunched over with long grey hair escaping the top of her shawl. Underneath she seemed to have a plain beige dress that reached to her calves. She was barefoot.

Grainne stood and let go of Neha's hand. The look on her face was one of wonder. The old woman smiled at Grainne and then looked at Neha. She sang a low song that lilted to life and gathered pace. Grainne began to sing along as Neha listened intently…

Volo and the old woman walked up to the circle of fire. The wolf snarled and whined.

The Irish Shaman moved his foot to the edge of the fire circle. The ground inside the circle began to dip. It formed a deep hole. The water began gushing into the hole.

Volo and the old woman took something from their necks and held them aloft. Neha recognised the two pendants. They carried on singing and as the song became one, they linked the pendants. A full moon appeared above the bonfire as they did.

The song ended and the old woman retreated into the darkness behind the Irish Shaman. Grainne reached a longing hand out to her. The Irish

Shaman stepped through the fire circle and stabbed the creature with his bronze sword.

The paint bucket had toppled from the stove and water spilled across the floor towards the feet of Grainne and Neha. Ed scrambled to sort it just as he heard the terrible howl of an animal outside...

Volo, the Irish Shaman and the wolf... all disappeared. Neha and Grainne were left with the great bonfire crackling ahead of them.

A moment passed.

Then, the light of the bonfire suddenly stretched to its left side this time. Neha saw the Irish Shaman was now sitting on a log to the left of the bonfire. He gave a small smile to Grainne and pointed across to the far right side of the bonfire. The old woman with the shawl was standing there now.

Grainne stood and let go of Neha's hand. She moved past the Irish Shaman. He put his right hand to his heart as she passed. She mutually responded.

Neha saw she now moved out of sight behind the bonfire. A moment passed and then another.

A small girl suddenly stepped out to the right of the bonfire, on the far side. She wore a plaited yellow dress and had strawberry blonde hair in pig tails. She could not have been more than five or six. She darted to the old woman. The old woman held her arms wide and smiled. The child and old woman shared a warm embrace.

The old woman and child exchanged some kind words. The old woman carried on speaking and the little girl nodded intently. Then the old woman looked directly at Neha and took something small from her pocket. She handed it to the child and squeezed her cheek. The child turned and skipped back to the right side of the bonfire but did not cross over to Neha's side completely.

Neha instinctively walked halfway to meet the little girl. She held up a blue flower for him. Neha noticed her strong green eyes with the sparkle of gold around the iris. He realised... who this was. He took the flower and bent down. They shared a hug. The little girl gave him a kiss on the cheek.

"Goodbye, Neha," she said. "I'm going to pick flowers in the meadow with Nana." She scampered back to the old woman then. The old woman held her right hand to her heart and gave Neha a warm smile. With that she opened her shawl and the little girl moved underneath. They turned and disappeared into the darkness.

A strong wind struck Neha.

Christ! Ed thought. It had all kicked off here. He had just mopped up the water. Then a strong howling wind roared outside. It seemed to blow in through a crack in the window, the gap in the roof and down the chimney. The candles all blew out and barring the fire, Ed had no light.

Three slow knocks came at the front door. He shivered but he knew he was responsible for the two behind him. He moved to the door and drew a breath, yanking it open with gritted teeth.

No one there – he stepped out slowly and took a good look left and right. All that was visible was a full moon overhead. The rain had cleared off. "Hello," said Ed.

No answer.

He let out a long sigh. He was about to shut the door when he noticed something on the doorstep. He picked it up. It was a blue flower.

*****

Ed scrambled to turn on the main light. It flickered on. He saw Neha listing in his chair. Ed rushed over. Neha groaned as he opened his eyes. He still held Grainne's hand. He jolted forward suddenly and started to shake Grainne's hand. But he soon stopped, put his head momentarily down and cupped her limp hand with both of his.

Ed moved towards Grainne. Her eyes were open but dilated. He slowly checked her pulse with his right hand. "My God… she's… she's," said Ed.

"Gone," finished Neha. "She went with that woman," he added pointing up over Ed's shoulder.

Ed turned and stepped closer to the wall above the fireplace. The picture was a faded black and white. An old lady with a shawl smiled. A little girl stood beside her. The sound of the Grandfather clock behind them suddenly stopped dead. Neha and Ed both looked over at it.

"What is that in your hand?" demanded Neha.

Ed handed him the small blue flower.

Neha twisted it in his hand as he examined it. "Tomorrow, Ed, you get out there and find this flower. It is the key to everything."

Chapter 28

Neha sat in Ed's cottage, twisting the blue flower in his hand. He never thought he would see it again. He thought about Grainne and her grandmother. Grainne the old woman, Grainne the little girl.

Maybe that was how the spirits interacted with each other in the afterlife… at a time and place when they were most happy. For them then, time had no meaning. Maybe that was the grace the afterlife offered, in that human lives here were finite but the bonds shared in this life could continue into the afterlife. The bonds we share here… could be eternal.

Neha stood. He had probably come as close to anyone in experiencing the world at the edges, the world beyond.

He would tell no one.

*****

"Stairway to Heaven" played on Ed's car radio as he pulled into a small petrol station. He walked in and ordered a breakfast sandwich and a coffee.

They had stayed at Sheila's. He had rung Sheila last night, to let her know the news about Grainne. She had cried instantly. Sheila said she wasn't surprised. She said it didn't matter. Grainne had told her all about the plan for the trance before she left last night.

"Stubborn as a mule!" she had said then, laughing. "She went the way she wanted, on her terms. Not many can say that!"

When she arrived back at the cottage, Ed offered her a big bear hug. He got her a large glass of whiskey. Neha sat beside her and comforted her. He told her how special Grainne really was. He couldn't seem to stop. As he carried on, Sheila had her hand on her heart and a smile fixed on her face. She was adamant all three of them attend the funeral. Ed did not agree or disagree. She then insisted that Neha and Ed sleep in the guest room as it was so late.

Ed got a few hours' sleep before Neha shook him awake. Neha was urging him out the front door, as Sheila was just finishing laying out a handsome breakfast on the kitchen table. "Search for that flower, Ed!" said Neha as Ed reluctantly left the cottage.

Ed had taken a few photos of the flower on his phone. It looked exactly like a Spring Gentian, but it couldn't be. Grainne's grandmother would hardly steer them towards the signature plant of the Burren. The bloody thing was everywhere, when in season. But it was September. And the Gentian, as the name suggested, was a spring flower.

He had no idea where to go.

As he got back into the car, he moved his sandwich up for a bite and his phone rang. Maria.

"Hello," he said in an aggravated tone. He explained what had happened. He got to the part about the flower quickly; how her father reckoned if they found that, they would find the witch's lair.

"Hold on," Maria said as Ed heard paper and documents being shuffled in the background. "I've been all over the main file, Ed. I'm still going through the 1950s section. It's full of information. Ah, here we are," she said. "I found a leaflet here for the Burren Perfumery, they make perfumes, cosmetics."

"How does that help?"

"They use local flora in their products and 'have a wide array of Burren wildflowers in their gardens'."

Ed replied, "Okay, so they might know the flower."

"Or know where to find it," said Maria.

"I'll go straight there," said Ed as he hung up.

Ed drove to the perfumery, taking bites of his sandwich as he did. He reached the car park as the perfumery was just opening. He could see a fine array of multi-coloured flowers, even at this time of year, in the gardens surrounding the main building.

As Ed got out of the car, he could see a café and gift shop on the right. But to the left, open double doors revealed a specialist lab of some sort. He went straight for the lab and saw a woman just putting on a white coat and goggles. Ed ran up to her and showed her the pictures of the flower on his phone.

"I think that's just a Spring Gentian," she said, shrugging.

Ed's face went red. He politely but forcefully disagreed.

She suggested that he watch the Burren Perfumery informative video in the next room.

Ed did just that. He intensely watched and looked at every image of a flower as if he were watching a thriller movie. But in the end, the movie didn't solve his mystery. He went outside and saw some gardening staff walking by. He held up the images of the flower on his phone, but they too didn't know and shrugged. Ed went and looked around the gardens themselves.

He searched in between the flowers and even bushes. He was meticulous. But he found nothing.

Ed couldn't think of anything else to do… so he decided a cigarette might spark his senses. Lighting it up, he strolled behind the main building on a narrow path. A few drags later and he saw a building ahead, a greenhouse. He walked up and saw another vast array of flowers inside, all different shapes and sizes. A 'private' sign hung on the plastic transparent door.

As Ed finished his cigarette, he saw a man inside. He looked elderly. He wore a brown gardening apron, green wellies and had orange gloves on. Ed decided to ignore the private sign. There was no time left for p's and q's.

As Ed walked in, the man looked down to him. "Are you lost?" he asked in a thick Irish accent.

"Probably," said Ed as he gave the man a light smile.

"How can I help you?" the man said.

The man reached up with a pair of small clippers in his hand. He clipped underneath the head of one flower, but Ed saw that the flower head didn't fall over. The man did it with two other flower stems, but the clippers made no cuts…

Ed's smile waned.

"I was looking for this," Ed said as he produced the pictures of the flower on his phone.

The man leaned over and looked.

"Can…you…see....it?" said Ed slowly.

"Of course I can see it!" the man said sternly. "Hold these," he said, as he handed Ed his clippers.

Ed took them as he flicked between the photos of the flower with his free hand.

"Everyone says it's a Spring Gentian," said Ed calmly.

The man held his hand out for the clippers and Ed handed them to him. The man turned and carried on with his clipping. Then he stopped. "There now… miles better!" he said staring at the flowers.

Ed quickly agreed.

"That's no Spring Gentian," said the man turning to Ed. "It's a close relative so the mistake is easily made. The first indicator is that it has six petals – the Spring Gentian has only five. Underneath one of the petals in your photos, there are red dots. That's the sign of a water plant. They are very rare and hard to find. If I were you, I would take a look at some T–"

"Excuse me!!" came a shrill voice behind Ed.

Ed turned round to a middle aged lady with her arms leaning on her sides.

"What are you doing in here? This is private!"

Ed turned back around but the man had disappeared. Ed's shoulders sank. He quickly had a look down the back for him as the woman now shouted at him to "Get out!"

Ed apologised as he left.

As Ed got back into the car, his phone rang. It was Maria again.

"Oh, Maria… I was so close–"

"Ed," she interrupted. "I think I found something in the 1950's file."

"Go on," he said.

"There was an old gridded map of lakes, or 'Turloughs' as the map was entitled. I put that map over Aine's wedge tomb map."

"Yes, yes, carry on!" willed Ed.

"The hidden wedge tombs we examined, Ed, they were Turloughs… drained Turloughs! Her lair could be in a drained Turlough or lake we haven't examined!"

"Great!" said Ed. "That seems to match in with something I just heard."

Ed sped back to the cottage, ignoring all speed limits.

*****

Ed got back to the cottage where Neha and Maria were already in the middle of a conversation.

"We're discussing last night's vision, Ed," said Maria. "Once you find the witch's lair, we will need to act fast," she added.

"I understand that, I want this over with as much as you do, but first we need to find the lion's den and then we need a bloody good plan before we walk into it!" said Ed. "Recognisance!"

"It's about the moon, Ed." Neha handed him the oval ornament that they found in Aine's bag. Ed remembered the yin and yang type symbols as he brushed them with his thumb.

"This represents our two pendants," said Neha. "You see the outer edge?"

Ed started at the circular shapes and crescents around the disc like ornament. “These are moons!” he realised.

“Yes.” Neha pointed at each, giving them names. He explained the names were the ones his tribe used. “At the very top is ‘wolfmoon’.” Neha explained more about his vision, together with the pendants, wolf, water and moon.

Ed took a moment as his face scrunched up. “We must drown the moon?” he asked.

Maria burst out laughing.

“I am still interpreting the vision,” said Neha. “But I believe that we have until the wolfmoon to strike at the witch.”

“When is–”

“Two days,” answered Maria.

“We have a lot to do before then,” said Ed, still red faced from Maria’s jibe. He told them what had happened at the Burren Perfumery.

Maria moved to the table. The contents of the file were sprawled out on top. She showed Ed the map and they tried to draw some comparisons. They circled the Turloughs on the 1950s map that appeared on or close to the Wedge Tombs in Aine’s map.

Ed quickly examined one of his Burren guidebooks and found a chapter on Turloughs, or ‘Disappearing Lakes’, as they were also known. The map in the guidebook didn’t seem to have the same number of Turloughs listed as the 1950s map did. The 1950s map showed far more… big and small.

Ed and Maria next discounted the larger Turloughs together with the Wedge Tomb sites they had already searched. It left them with ten small Turlough sites and three of those seemed closely linked to Wedge Tomb sites that were marked by red dots on Aine’s map. But all ten locations were spread out all over the Burren.

Ed reached into his pocket and took out his phone. He located his wallet and found Ahern’s card. He rang.

"Ed," she said, picking up. It sounded like she was in a car. "I'm getting more and more strange reports–"

"We are working on the source of that problem, but we need your help. We don't have much time left."

"Go on," she responded.

Ed told her about the ten Turlough locations and that he couldn't cover them all. She agreed to help straight away. Ed grabbed the Turlough map that he and Maria worked on. He said he would take the three wedge tomb locations. Ahern said she would do the rest. As she pulled her car over, he told her where to look and what to look for.

"And don't get too close… if you find something, call me first!"

The call ended.

As Ed hurried out the door with the map in his hand, Maria shouted, "That goes for you too!"

Ed turned as he was getting into his car.

"If you find anything… call me!" she added.

Ed got going. He found the first two just fine, one at Killanboy and the other at Boston. The third was close to the village of Turlough itself. This was harder to find but he did it.

He asked no one for permission to go on any land and he also made sure to creep up. He kept his distance, at first, and used his binoculars. This would marry into the bird watching theme if some angry local found him.

All three Turloughs had been drained. There were also large mobile looking pipes going in and out of them. This was a sure sign Mendoza Mining had visited, he thought. But none of the Turloughs had any blue flower nearby. They each had a wedge tomb inside, but Ed's pendant didn't shake when he slowly moved forward at each one.

He drove back to the cottage, chewing his lip as did, hoping Ahern had found something.

He walked into the cottage and told Maria and Neha he had found nothing. They all turned at the sound of knocking on their door.

Ed rushed to open it. "This could be Ahern!"

But instead, it was Nuala.

"I need a lift to the church tomorrow," she said.

"Oh, Nuala, I can't–"

"It's Grainne's funeral," she said glaring at him. "You knew her, didn't you?" she added, stony eyed.

Ed's phone buzzed. It was Ahern! He shot the phone up to his ear.

"No luck, Ed. Searched them all. No flower, wedge tomb, portal dolmen…."

"Right… okay," said Ed in a dismal tone. "Thanks," he managed before hung up.

"What is a 'funeral'?" asked Neha. Maria explained to her father.

"Sheila called earlier, Ed," said Maria. "She needs two more people to carry Grainne's coffin tomorrow morning." She gave Ed an equally stony eyed glare.

Neha placed a hand on Ed's shoulder. "In honouring the dead, especially that of the local Shaman, the spirits may give us the answers we seek."

"Yes," said Ed as his eyes shifted left and right. He realised they could also canvass the funeral goers about the flower…

Chapter 29

The morning was fine, not too cold. A small breeze gusted around now and again. It appeared to make the remaining September flowers wave at passers-by.

Ed had arrived in the church early with Nuala, as per his instructions. They sat a few aisles from the front. Nuala greeted and chatted to many others as they arrived. Ed had forgotten what these funerals probably meant to smaller communities – a chance to see someone off but also a chance to socialise.

The church was filling up as the priest greeted everyone at the door. Grainne's coffin was front and centre. Ed had no suit or tie. But he dug out a clean shirt, navy jeans and a brown corduroy jacket, complete with elbow pads. He had brought this 1970s wonder with him to Ireland in case he ended up at anything 'academicee' where schmoozing might be required. However, that chance had never arisen.

He did manage black shoes, though. Maria said "they screamed funeral." He hoped she was right. The church looked full now. Ed checked the time. Neha was supposed to be here. For some reason he didn't want to go with Ed. He insisted that he needed to "get ready on his own."

The chatter died down as the priest made his way to the alter. Ed felt his phone buzz. It was a text from Maria. It was about Neha. Ed went pale.

"You're all very welcome today…," the priest said.

The door sprang open again.

Hushed voices and small chatter erupted around the church. The priest stopped speaking and tilted his head forward until his glasses hung at the end of his nose.

Neha walked, no, strutted into the church and stood facing the congregation with his back to Grainne's coffin. He wore a red tunic at his waist and a hat of feathers. His face was painted black. Aside from a cloak of feathers, he wore nothing else. He was barefoot.

"It's him!" someone shouted. "That's the fella from the pub!" cried another.

"And the cairn!" cried another person.

The chatter died down as Neha brought his arms outstretched horizontally in front of him. He waved them downwards. The congregation's chatter ceased at once.

Neha turned to the priest and made a respectful 'carry on' motion with his hand.

The priest's face still held a stunned expression. He held it, as if on pause. Then he fixed his glasses and smirked slightly. "Well, good morning everyone who came… from… near… and far."

He got a light laugh from the crowd.

"But you are all very welcome here to celebrate the passing of Grainne O'Mahony."

The mass carried on and Neha held his stoic position in front of Grainne's coffin until the end.

The priest was nearly finished the mass. "Go in peace, Grainne, we'll miss you. Let us pray."

There was a brief silence.

Then a slow drone came from the front of the church. Ed saw it was Neha. His humming drone grew to a chant and got louder. His eyes closed. His song reverberated around the church and the audience seemed captured by it. Some bowed their heads and others stared forward with calm pondering expressions.

A shard of sunlight suddenly came down from the stained glass window behind the priest. It landed on Grainne's coffin. A butterfly appeared, fluttering above the alter. It followed the stream of light before landing on the brass cross at the head of Grainne's coffin.

Neha's song reached a crescendo and then slowly died down. He bowed his head. There was a brief pause before the church erupted in applause. It went on for a good minute.

The priest asked for those who were to lift the coffin to come forward. Ed moved out of the aisle. Neha and Ed were positioned at the back of the coffin. Despite their different sizes, Neha seemed more than able to carry his load.

Out to the graveyard they went, and a strong gust was starting to blow. Ed noticed that some people looked around in alarm.

The priest did not spend much time saying the graveside oration, and the coffin was speedily lowered down. The butterfly stayed on Grainne's coffin until the first pieces of earth fell. Then it floated upwards and was carried away in the wind…

Nuala walked over to Ed. He was about to say something, but she walked straight past him. She looped her arm around Neha's arm and led him slowly off, smiling around her.

Ed followed Neha and Nuala towards the Hikers Hotel. There would be soup and sandwiches. The hotel was soon thronged, and Ed couldn't get near Neha. He stood with Nuala as people came over to shake Neha's hand.

Nuala announced to many well-wishers that "Neha is staying at my cottage."

Where's my bloody handshake, thought Ed. *I've only nearly died around fifty times trying to sort this witch shit out!* Ed snapped out of it. He looked around. People were huddled together into groups, speaking in hushed tones, if at all. Many had bags under their eyes.

Ed yanked out his phone and pulled up the pictures of the flower. He started moving from group to group, from table to table. By the end he sounded like a man from a local market shouting his wares. "Any lakes? Turloughs? Have you seen this flower?"

But he got a pile of negative nods or Spring Gentian answers.

An hour later and the place started to empty. Having no luck, Ed walked back over to Neha and Nuala. He sat down beside them. He put his phone down and grabbed a sandwich. He started munching.

"I know that flower," said Nuala casually as she looked at Ed's phone, taking a drink of her tea.

Ed nearly choked on his sandwich. He began coughing.

Neha gripped the table with one hand and quickly placed his other hand onto Nuala's wrist. "Where have you seen that!?"

"You're sure you don't think that's a Spring Gentian?" asked Ed as he banged his chest, trying to recover.

"I didn't know you're both such flower enthusiasts and no, I don't think it's a Spring Gentian," she said forcefully, taking another sip of tea. "We call that Hags Wail," she said. "I have it around the house. You'd know if you ever called over," she said, staring at Ed. "It grows beside a small lake or Turlough called Poll an Chillaigh."

"What does that mean?" asked Ed.

"Hags Hole," she replied.

"Where is Hags Hole?" asked Neha quickly.

"Sure, it's not far from my house. A field or two away."

"I just don't believe it," said Ed as he slapped his hand to his head. "We'll give you a lift back now, Nuala," he said hurriedly. "The place is emptying out anyway. But you must show us that lake!" he added with desperation.

"Sure I will. An old recluse lives there, called Stuart. His brother died on the farm earlier this year."

As they got into the car, Nuala regaled them on how she played there as a child with her friends. She told them that it was called Hags Hole because a hag appeared at the side of the lake in the 12th century. The hag had apparently told a passing warring party of the O'Brien clan that they would all die in a coming battle. Then she disappeared into the air.

After a ten minute drive on the main road out of Ballyvaughan they took a right. Then a left. Nuala pointed to a green house at the end of the road. Ed drove down to it quickly and pulled up outside it. Neha offered to help Nuala out.

Ed knocked on the door. A man, maybe in his early eighties, opened the door. He was tall and thin. He wore an old grey suit, with a tie half done and had a grey cap on his head. And there… there in the breast pocket of his jacket was the flower… Hags Wail. Ed was sure he saw him before… he clicked it! When he arrived in Ballyvaughan the man was at the head of the funeral cortege, all those months ago.

The man gave Ed a dumbstruck look. He gave Neha a longer, more perplexed one. He looked towards Nuala. "Oh, hello Nuala," he said.

"Sorry to bother you, Stuart," she replied with a smile. "These men have a few questions about that flower – the Hags Wail," she responded as she made her way to the door.

Stuart held a confused expression. "Come in so… I'll make tea. It's been lonely since my brother Dan passed, anyway."

They were invited into the kitchen and sat down at the table. Neha and Ed were astonished – the flower was everywhere, inside vases, pots, jars…

Nuala and Stuart starting chatting. Stuart prepared a large teapot and Ed helped him pour. Stuart and Nuala stopped talking as they took a first sip of their tea. Neha gave Ed a stare.

Ed asked Stuart to tell them everything about his farm, the lake, the flower and his brother's death.

"It's all over me farm. Ever since we drained the lake. The cows love it! I even popped it around me house. Lovely sweet smell."

As Stuart took sips of his tea, he slowly but surely started to tell them everything he knew. Stuart and Dan had a very small lake out the back on their farm. In October 2018, they got a knock on the door from two lads. "They said they were from a mining company. One was South American and the other was a tall North American fellow. They said they were exploring for minerals and offered a large sum of money to drain out the lake."

Stuart said they couldn't believe how much the mining company offered. They both joked they would find pond weed! "Dan was keen to get more grazing land for the cows," said Stuart. "I liked the lake – it brought some peace. I was on the side of the ducks!" he joked.

Then Stuart explained that when they drained the lake a huge dolmen was down the bottom. Incredible looking thing. The tall US guy had arrived back with a young blonde Irish girl. She said she was an archaeologist. They did some small digs around the place for a few months. They were both gone by mid-November.

"Mendoza, the mining company, only showed back up earlier this year once the weather improved. The winter had prevented them doing much bar draining the lake initially. They started by doing some small digs around the place before bringing some bigger equipment down there. But then, they knocked the capstone off the Dolmen with their equipment. They stopped what they were doing instantly. Left a lot of equipment down there. Mendoza decided not to excavate further on the orders of the US guy. Dan had a bad accident the next day, the day of the great wind."

"I remember that. It was early May," said Nuala.

"He got caught under the cows. They stampeded. Never saw it before," said Stuart. Stuart stopped there.

Silence gripped the room.

"Anything strange happen around here since?" tried Ed softly.

"Not really," responded Stuart. "But I've heard lots of strange things from others over the last few months."

Ed said they were intrigued by the flower and asked if they could have a brief look out the back, at the drained lake.

"Sure, just down the very end of the field," said Stuart.

He led them down a corridor to a back door. He opened a clunky door. Neha and Ed walked through.

"You'll see the pumps are still on the edge. Don't go near them, they pumped the waters through into Lough Rask, a half mile that way," he said pointing to his right.

With that he closed the door.

Neha and Ed walked forward onto a small patio. Beyond that was an open gate. They walked into a green meadow, dotted with Hags Wail. It created a green and blue spectrum for the eye. A few cows walked across their path, happily feasting on the flower.

"I suspect that the man and his animals survived so long because of these flowers," said Neha.

"That or he's some lucky bastard!" Ed said with a smirk.

Neha chuckled at that.

They started up a slow incline, soon reaching the verge at the top. Ahead of them, around fifty metres on, there was a line of trees. Clumps of high reeds sat in between them. But in between the gaps, they could see it… Hags Hole. Neha went down on his front. Neha did the same.

The pump lines could be seen stretching back towards the glistening Lough Rask.

"Mother Earth did its best to hide this," said Neha.

"I'm not sure we should get too close," replied Ed with a whisper.

"We have no choice, Ed. We must take a look now in daylight, if we are to perform the ritual at night."

"Ritual–"

"I will explain later," said Neha as he began to crawl forward. Ed followed.

They crept up behind a large boulder. They both grabbed their pendants; they were shaking! They popped their heads just over the boulder and looked down. Hags Hole looked deeper than expected, around forty feet. It was around one hundred feet in diameter.

Ed's archaeology brain was mesmerised. The dolmen was big, at least head height. The capstone lay to the side, several metres away. It was a chunk of flat rock, at least a metre wide and five to six metres long.

"Heavy," whispered Neha.

Ed nodded in agreement.

One access point lay where the pump pipes went in. The ground sloped down gradually. The work of Mendoza, Ed thought.

They both looked on over the next few minutes, pointing out certain things to each other but saying nothing. Then Neha waved Ed back. They crawled back up. As they cleared the verge, Neha told Ed to grab as many of the Hags Wail flowers as possible. He did so. It added to their 'flower enthusiast' story whatever the real reason was.

Before Ed knocked on Stuart's back door, he saw the nose of a tractor, jutting out from the right hand corner of the house. He did a half run over as Neha knocked on the door. It was a decent and good sized tractor. Going up the two entry steps, he looked in the tractor door. He saw the keys in the ignition. He jumped in and got it started. It hummed nicely. He switched it off.

He got to the back door just as Stuart opened it. They thanked him but quickly made their excuses to leave. They made the short drive back to the cottage with Nuala.

*****

"We must perform a ritual," said Neha.

They sat at the table in the cottage. The wolfmoon was tomorrow night.

Neha described, as best he could, what he thought each of their roles would be. But he admitted that he simply wasn't sure his plan would work. This was different ground, he said, and he was not sure whether the two pendants would change the order of the ritual. He concluded that "much of tomorrow could be unpredictable."

Ed and Maria looked at each other. Each shared an alarmed expression. Maria said they needed to work together, as a team. That they should go through absolutely everything.

Ed agreed as he grabbed a pen and paper. "Let's start from the start," he said.

They agreed to work their way through it. Anything that could aid them for tomorrow night's big encounter. They started with their past experiences.

Maria went first, recounting her version of what happened both in Brazil and Ireland. All and every detail was encouraged, however irrelevant it might have seemed. Maria's encounter with the animals, her throwing of the spear and knife. They went down to a granular detail – how did she feel when she threw them? Did she have any kind of vision or image in her head when she did?

Ed jotted down the notes. He went next, handing the pen and paper over to Maria.

He discussed how he gotten the audit role, his trip to Dublin and then everything that happened in the Burren itself. They zoned in on his encounters with the dead. Barring Ed's encounter with Aine and the episode at Cormocroe Abbey, they could not find any link with the other encounters to the situation at hand. Ed also confirmed that he had never seen the dead before... let alone had supernatural encounters at this level.

Neha went next. He started way back when he first recused Karo, to the attacks on his village, to the journey he made with Maria and the others into the deep forest. Maria and Ed slowed him right down when he got to Volo and all their shared episodes within that village. They went meticulously through the vision he and Volo shared within that hut.

Then they discussed Neha's encounter in the forest, at the dolmen there. They again went through every detail in the most nuanced fashion. Maria, handing the pen and paper back to Ed, then quizzed her father several times on various aspects of the ritual there.

Finally, they asked Neha to remember and recount all his visions and dreams. Ed again jotted notes, scribbling down what he thought was pertinent.

Neha did his best to try to explain the intangible ways of Shamanism, the spirit world, the senses, the feelings…

Neha finished and Ed read through all the points they had written down.

"Does this help us at all?" asked Ed as he finished reading out the last point.

They asked Neha to tell them tomorrow night's ritual again. He did so and it didn't seem as laboured this time. Neha was able to put some definitive meat on the bone for one or two moments. His description of the ritual finished with him saying, "The water shall be a boundary between the two worlds." Neha stressed the importance of speed. They needed to complete the ritual as fast as possible.

"And that's it, Father? There's nothing else you need to tell us?" said Maria as she glared at him. Neha didn't respond but shook his head.

Maria suggested they take the morning off and then regather at the cottage in the late afternoon. Neha nodded as he said they needed clear minds for the task ahead. Maria then took the pen and paper back from Ed and started writing. She wrote the ritual out step by step, listing actions from one to ten. It included the preparation before the ritual as well as each of their roles during it. She read out the list and highlighted aloud what she had to do. Neha spoke about his role next.

Ed took the final list from Maria and read out his parts. "Are we sure this is all I have to do? I mean, I think we could be missing something?"

"You guided us to the dolmen and the knife," said Neha.

"You can drive the tractor," offered Maria.

Was that his big role, thought Ed. He could drive the tractor!? Ed felt like the actor who didn't like his lines…

Neha reached his hands out and grabbed a hand each from Maria and Ed. "I am proud of you both. We will succeed!" he added with conviction.

Ed let out a big breath. Yes, it would be unpredictable, dangerous, but at least they had a solid foundation to work off. "Well, at least we have left no… stone… unturned!" he said, with a small grin. Stoney faces was all he got in response.

Ed recognised the 'hanger' when he saw it. As his stomach rumbled, he suggested he pop to the shops to pick up some food. He did just that and came back with the rudimentary ingredients for spaghetti bolognaise together with two bottles of wine – one red, one white.

Ed did battle with the chopping board, pots and pans but eventually produced something edible. They tucked in by the fire that Neha had lit. Each had a full glass of wine. They enjoyed their meal in so far as none of them mentioned tomorrow. Ed found a classical music station on the radio. They left only one lamp on in the corner. They dumped their plates on the ground when they finished. The red wine and fire helped them relax. They started to drift, each looking into the fire.

As Ed poured out the last of the red wine, he saw Neha and Maria had stained teeth and lips. He realised his must be the same. They shared a small laugh before Neha downed his glass, excused himself and went to bed.

Maria suggested the bottle of white as she retrieved it from the kitchen. As Ed finished his red off, she poured the white into his glass immediately.

"You can tell a lot from a person who does that." He smiled.

"Sure," she said hiccupping. "I'm not fussy!"

Ed moved the conversation on. He asked about Brazil. More about what she did.

She only gave him concise, matter of fact answers as she twisted part of her long hair through her fingers. She poured herself more wine as Ed started to describe where he was from. Stuff about North England, his family, University. She agreed she must visit there as she yawned.

Then she went to the loo. Ed gently drank his wine. She came back and Ed noticed the mascara and lipstick.

She slowly leaned in towards him. "We may all die tomorrow night," she whispered.

Ed leaned in…

A strong gale buffeted the cottage. Ed looked around sharply.

So did Maria.

It died away.

Ed was fairly sure he had a serious look on his face. Maria certainly did. "Time for bed, then."

Maria nodded.

Ed got changed quickly and got in under the covers. He turned out the light and drifted off.

Ed heard a knocking noise – it was pitch black. He shot out of his bed and turned the light on. There was the light knocking noise again.

Was it Aine!?

The knocking noise came from his door. He walked over and yanked it open. It was Maria. She put a finger to her lips as she walked in without asking. "I couldn't sleep," she said stepping towards him.

There was a pause before they both lunged and kissed.

She kicked the door closed behind her.

Chapter 30

Sometimes they talked… sometimes they didn't.

Maria didn't know where they were, for most of the morning. Her father led the way as they criss-crossed paths, fields and small hills.

He would randomly pick up a flower here or a flower there, smell it and hand it to Maria. He selected a number of good sized sticks also. She put them in the bag too.

They had gotten up early, grabbed a bag and left the cottage. Neha was focused on their task. Maria found it secondary in her list of priorities. In the early afternoon, she had wrapped her arm around his and his priorities seemed to change. He became more chatty, about his life, her life. He told stories that mattered and stories that didn't. Maria didn't mind. They had shared the morning together… they had shared the day. They had shared each other. And she was ever so thankful for it.

They reached the bottom of a hulking mountain, 'Cappawalla', she thought Ed had called it.

Neha turned and looked at Maria. "Come, Maria. Let us sing a song to the sinking sun."

Maria looked at the sky as grey clouds moved overhead. The wind began blowing around them. "But Father, the weather is starting to pick up. We must get bac–"

Neha reached out his hand and gently took hers. He smiled at her and she smiled back. They started walking and ascended slowly. Neha held her hand all the way up. They reached the top, following a well beaten trail. Neha quickly scanned the bottom of several bushes, finding leaves and small branches. He had a small fire going in minutes.

He sat beside it and crossed his legs. Maria sat beside him and did the same. They sat in silence as Maria watched the sun going down in front of them. Grey clouds streaked past it.

Maria checked the time. "The sun is dying quickly, Father. We must–"

"The sun lives in our world for only a time, before it lives in another. We must sing so it comes back." Neha turned and looked out at the ocean. His song lilted slowly to life. It became more powerful with each intake of his breath.

Maria listened as she felt his hand grab hers tightly. She heard his words more clearly now. She began to sing softly beside him. She shut her eyes as the words flowed through her…

They finished the song together, in harmony.

Neha stood then… as she did.

"I like the height here," said Neha. "Closer to the sky spirits."

Maria stood and stared at the scenery in front of her. She heard her father walk behind her. He sounded as if he was rooting through their bag. Before she turned around to check, two hands went over her head. A necklace was placed on her neck and fastened.

She examined it. "This is Karo's!"

"It belonged to a leader, but now it belongs to another one. The leader of a tribe," Neha replied.

Maria was speechless for an instant, as she continued to touch it with her right hand. She noticed the time on her watch. "Father."

"It is time!" he said. "There is something else I must show you."

*****

Ed walked down Fanore beach. It was late in the afternoon. He placed his hood back over his head for the umpteenth time. The waves to his left crashed ashore. The water stretched further and further up the slanted beach, as if it were reaching, as if it were trying to escape. Beyond them, the white crests of the waves would emerge and dip in the sea as if they were racers doing the breaststroke. When the white crested waves did emerge, each had sea spray blown off their head. Ed looked up as he heard many cries of seagulls. A flock of them were fleeing inland.

He had picked up a newspaper this morning. The Cliffs of Cahir tragedy was described as 'a freak weather event'; the large wave was the result of 'unusual seismic activity'. How Ed wished both of those descriptions were true.

He woke this morning and there was no sign of Maria or Neha. He had picked up his phone to call her and then stopped himself making the call. They would be seeing enough of each other later, he thought.

He tried his best to clear his head. He had to resign himself to the fact that their plan probably wasn't 'the bloody good plan' that he previously mentioned they needed. It was just a plan. In reality, there probably was no 'bloody good plan' for tackling an evil spirit released in the wind.

Ed simply didn't know what to do with his potential last day on earth, so he had decided to come down here. But the weather wouldn't give him a break. Indeed, on the car radio, on the way down, warnings were being issued that a 'super storm' would be hitting them this evening.

Perfect fucking timing!

Ed sat in his car initially when he got down here. He tried to ring a few people. Many didn't pick up. One mate did but their conversation was on the dark side of the mundane moon. No news from either of them. He bored Ed with his family life story. Ed bored him with his archaeology audit. Ed could hardly tell him about him about the rest…

He walked back to the car in a zig zag manner as the wind pummelled him from his left and right. He needed to get the stuff that was part of his job… for the ritual. As he climbed back into his car and eventually won the 'battle of closing the door', his phone rang.

It was Bill, one of his mates from York University.

"Long time no see, or chat!" said Bill as Ed answered.

Bill's jovial tone was welcome. They exchanged pleasantries and a small chit chat.

Then Bill asked, "You hear about the professor?"

"No," said Ed. "Professor Barnes?"

"Yip," said Bill. "He got done for sexual harassment. Turns out he had been seeing a student!"

"Lisa?" Ed said with shocked disbelief.

"You guessed it! The professor's been suspended. Been booted out by the wife, too!"

Ed and Bill discussed the issue more before moving on. They agreed to meet for a pint when Ed got back. The call ended.

Ed drove back towards Ballyvaughan wondering if his life could become any more surreal.

As he drove through the village, everything seemed shut. Grey bulbous clouds raced overhead, like great battalions rushing towards a battlefield. He saw a small metal sign spinning in the wind on the bar it was connected to. It seemed that the world around him was preparing for a showdown. Ed sped back to the cottage, wondering if he was ready for his.

*****

Ed walked back into the cottage as a sheet of rain tried to follow him. He closed the door with his shoulder as he carried in the two full petrol cans. As he placed them down, Maria scooted past him in a towel, and on, into her room.

There were two large mixing bowls on the table. One looked like it contained Hags Wail, the other a variety of plants of and flowers. Neha was crushing the flowers in that bowl between his hands.

"Ed," Neha said handing him a bucket and small spade, "go out and collect as much mud and earth as you can in that." Neha turned towards the stove and started adding logs and turf inside.

Ed went back outside with the bucket and between sheets of rain and wind, collected as much mud and earth as he could. The light just died as he finished. He went back in with the bucket and placed it on the table. Neha was continuing to crush the multi-coloured flowers, using a mortar and pestle.

Ed saw a light smoke around him and noticed the stove lid was open. He walked over and placed his hand on the stove door.

"Leave that, Ed," said Neha without turning. "The smoke must cloud our vision here so we can see the spirit world more clearly."

"I haven't had much trouble with that lately," muttered Ed.

"Wash yourself now. We cleanse our bodies."

Ed went for a shower. When he was walking back to his room, he saw Maria ripping up an old shirt. She was tying the pieces of the cloth to the top of sticks, using some twine. She wore runners, small shorts and a light tank top. She wore a necklace too, that Ed hadn't noticed before.

Neha hummed a low song as he now mashed Hags Wail, water and mud in one of the bowls. Neha wore a single red tunic at his waist, nothing more.

Ed went to his room and dried himself. He chose a basic pair of swimming shorts and his crappiest pair of runners. "The men must go bare chested," Neha had said.

Ed coughed as he walked back into the living room. Neha was slowly chanting as he drew smoke from the fire over the two mixing bowls. One now contained a varied coloured powder. The other bowl contained what looked like blue coloured mud. Neha continued to chant as he grabbed some of the muddy blue mixture and began spreading it on Ed's chest.

He rubbed more and more on. Maria appeared to Ed's right, and began spreading the mixture on Ed's face. It was not long before he felt his whole body covered in the substance. He chanced a look in the mirror and a man smurf looked back.

Neha began rubbing the mixture on Maria and Ed followed suit, moving his muddied hands up slowly, so as to minimise wastage falling onto the floor. When she was adequately covered, Maria and Ed then rubbed the blue mud all over Neha.

As all three were now covered, Neha nodded to Maria and she retrieved Neha's cloak of eagle feathers. She placed it over Neha's shoulders and fastened it at the front. Neha then went to the kitchen and returned with a small bowl of some yellow looking paint, or dye. He went to the mirror and rubbed the yellow material around his eyes so they formed circles.

He told Maria and Ed to wait in the living room. He returned with a bag. Out of it he took the cloth parcel that held the knife. He began singing loudly as he unfastened the ribbon. The golden knife shimmered in the firelight as he removed the outer layer of cloth. The wind blew loudly around the cottage and heavy rain battered the windows. He took the knife by the stove and blew smoke over it, before placing it into Maria's out reached hands.

Neha began to walk around and roll his shoulders, twitching his hands and fingers outward. He made low and high noises. He reminded Ed of an opera singer who was preparing to go on stage.

Maria started to thrust her knife forwards, over and over.

Ed didn't know what to do…. so he started doing jumping jacks and press ups.

Neha ceased twitching and striding around. Maria stopped thrusting the knife. Ed stopped the jumping jacks. Ed put his arms by his sides and puffed out some air. All three exchanged a look – it was time!

Maria wrapped the knife back up in its floral laced cloth. Neha carefully poured the multi-coloured flower mixture from the bowl into a small pouch. He tied the ends and then attached it to the side of his tunic. Ed picked up the petrol cans and walked towards the door. Maria grabbed the bag that contained the sticks and slung it on her shoulder. Ed thought there might be something else in it. Something black popped out at the top… it looked like a garment of some sort, but he didn't ask.

Ed slowly opened the door. A howling wind screamed past. Rain pelted his face. It was dark, but Ed could see the tyre that hung from the rope on the tree was at a right angle in the wind. Ed tried to force the door shut… but he was losing.

"WE CAN'T GO OUT IN THISSS!" shouted Ed to Maria. Maria tried to push the door with him.

"WE MUST, ED!" shouted Neha from behind them.

Maria and Ed both turned their heads.

Neha held a lit candle with one hand while he protected the flickering flame with the other.

"GET BEHIND ME… HANDS ON SHOULDERS… AS WE PLANNED!"

Ed and Maria let go of the doorframe. It banged against the wall.

Ed managed to pick up the petrol cans in one hand while latching his right hand onto Maria's right shoulder. She in turn carried her bag on her left shoulder and placed her right hand on Neha's right shoulder. Neha began shouting words. He stepped towards the doorway as the candle flame flickered wildly. Ed and Maria took a step with him. Neha kept shouting the words.

The flame was going to be blown out, thought Ed.

Then Neha suddenly took his hand away from the flame… and blew at it. Instead of going out it steadied, dead straight. Neha's words became clear as he lowered his voice.

The storm outside made no noise, the rain and wind didn't hit them.

Neha took a step forward… then another. The other two instinctively followed as they fell into a slow rhythm. The flame stayed steady as did Neha's song.

Ed watched the silent horror show around him. Trees were nearly bent double in the wind. Streaks of rain flew past them or over them. But the three of them remained dry, untouched.

Their slow procession passed Lough Rask. Some water from the lake was driven up in the air by the wind. The remaining waters churned about. Their feet still moved in unison as they marched on.

They couldn't be far now, thought Ed.

Neha's song carried on. The flame remained strong and straight.

Then Ed heard a low sound. It started to get louder. The flame in Neha's hand started to flicker. The sound, no, the shriek, grew in intensity. It turned to a high pitched wail…

The flame snuffed out!

The wind and rain struck them as did the awesome noise. They were all pushed back, initially. Neha grabbed Maria's arm and Maria grabbed Ed's. Ed could still see Neha mouthing his chant. They began to slowly move forward.

The wind and rain suddenly began to ease off. Then it died off completely as they reached the edge of Hags Hole. They emerged soaked and weather beaten at the side of this drained lake. Neha kept his chant going a few seconds more, before stopping.

The clouds twisted above around a hole that revealed a bright full moon. It was eerily quiet. They were in the eye of the storm, Ed realised. As Neha and Ed looked at each other they saw big patches of the flower mud had been washed off both of them. But Maria's flower shield seemed in good nick.

Neha beckoned them forward and they slowly walked down the slope. As they had agreed, there was to be no talking. They chose their steps carefully. The moonlight left parts of the lake in shadow or complete darkness.

Neha quickly positioned himself in front of the standing stones. He started to lay the artefacts on the ground in a line – the oval ornament, the mask and the cup. Ed and Maria moved to different ends of the lakebed, petrol cans in hand. They began emptying the petrol cans around the edge of the lakebed, until they met in the middle.

Neha had already started a low chant as he moved from a crouch to a standing position. A slow wind began to gust around the perimeter of the lakebed. Its sound went up in pitch as it became stronger. As the wind began to shriek around the pit, Neha raised his arms above him, chanting loudly. That was the signal.

Maria and Ed, moving to different ends of the lake again, got their cigarette lighters and lit the petrol. Two flames streaked around the pit, following the petrol, soon forming a ring of fire.

A howl echoed in the air now as the wind blew around them.

Suddenly, something in the wind materialised above. It was the witch. She had a torn black cloak and skeletal hands. Her face, that contorted face, had no eyes and a hollow for a mouth. She looked at Neha and wailed.

Ed was terrified.

Neha kept his arms aloft. He was visibly sweating as he raised his voice amongst the noise. He had to keep the incantation going, he had told them, to keep her locked in position. He dropped his hand to his left.

Maria took the golden knife out of its floral cloth and threw it onto the ground with the other artefacts.

The witch laughed, or screamed hysterically, Ed could not tell which.

"WORSHIPPPPP!!!!" filled the air as she drifted down, and her bony hands reached down and grasped the knife.

Ed could hear her laugh now, it seemed more distinct, almost insane. She seemed to almost smirk at Neha as he looked to the sky and carried on with his chant.

Then, in one swift movement, Neha reached to the pouch at his side, pounced forward, unclasped his fist and blew hard at his open palm…

The powder shrouded over the witch, her cloak turning from black to a multi-coloured hue. The witch shrieked as her skeletal hands reached for her empty eye sockets and furiously rubbed.

"Now, Ed!" shouted Neha.

Ed stood beside Neha, took off his pendant and held it aloft in his left hand. Neha did the same, holding his up in his right hand. Neha began saying the same words over and over, as he and Ed brought their pendants slowly together. The two pendants suddenly snapped together. Ed knew that was the sign to step back.

Neha stepped towards the witch, repeating the same words, faster and faster. He held the combined pendant in his hand. Ed's heart beat furiously as Neha stretched the cord over her head. The pendant fell around her bony neck. She tore her hands away from her eye sockets and instead tore at the pendant. She fell to her knees clutching at it.

Neha looked upwards and held his arms horizontally at his sides, still chanting. He tilted his head forward and closed in on the witch, reaching his hands forward.

Suddenly, the witch stopped writhing; she stopped wailing. She stayed perfectly still on the ground, head bowed beneath her cloak.

Neha, for an instant, stopped.

Too late.

She raised her head and smiled. She had changed…

She was a person, a human almost, with long dark hair.

She stood, grabbing Neha by the wrist, and stabbed him in the chest with the knife. She arched the blade around quickly and stabbed him in the side. Blood gushed out of both wounds as Neha collapsed to the ground, landing sideways.

The circle of fire around them snuffed out.

"Father!" Maria screamed.

"Maria, get back!" Ed shouted as he got behind the witch.

She twisted around and bashed Ed in the side of the head with the hilt of the knife. He fell back. She turned back quickly and was already facing Maria. She closed in on her, grabbing Maria's wrist with her free hand.

Maria swung her arm at her…again, and again…and again.

But all her attempts went straight through the witch's body. "The power of two tribes!" the witch said in a gravelly voice. "The power of this world and the other!" The witch cackled as she slapped Maria and forced her to her knees. "This will be painful… this will be slow," she said with bulging eyes and a full smile. "You will be cut up, piece by piece, unless you say you worship me… say it and it will not be as tortuous," she added as she salivated.

Ed was groggy as he lay on the ground watching this disaster unfold. The ground was now covered in a heavy mist.

Then Ed heard a whisper in the wind…

An old woman's voice, '*You have a firm grip, Ed.*'

He recalled quickly, the old woman he had helped 'cross' the road!

He remembered Tommy and how he had slapped his hand away from his radio!

He remembered the coachman… who he had slapped on the back!

He remembered the warrior he had knocked over…

He remembered holding the greenhouse man's clippers…

Realisation poured through Ed's mind, his whole body.

He could see the dead, but he could also…

"I will never worship!" said Maria as tears welled up in her eyes.

"You will be sacrificed… and you'll beg," the witch said with glee. She raised the blade upwards…

But a hand suddenly caught her wrist. She continued to try to yank it down as she turned her head. The expression on her face was one of disbelief. Then fear, as Ed wrapped his other arm around her neck and held her fast.

He squeezed her wrist until she dropped the knife. A slow chant started up. No, thought Ed, it was more like a song. It sounded as if it was all around them. It got louder and louder, "*Yena Ha, Yena Ha, Yena ha, Yena ha ho*."

"NO!!" the witch shrieked.

The song grew louder again, *"YENA HA, YENA HA, YENA HA...*

"*YENA HA HO*!"

Maria and Ed looked down at Neha. He still lay on his side with his eyes shut. But the words came from his mouth again, "YENA HA HO!" Neha opened his eyes and stood.

"The only one who will be sacrificed today," he said as he walked towards the witch, "is you!" Neha, blood dripping from his mouth, looked at Maria and nodded. She sprinted back into the darkness.

Neha started singing… with passion and vigour. The ring of fire came back to life and soared into the air. Ed could hear drums around him now.

The witch's mouth was agape as she writhed in Ed's arms.

As Neha began to walk forward, Ed instinctively backed up, dragging the witch with him. Ed could see a line of people now on the right side of the lake – they looked like Neha. They stamped their feet as they sang with Neha. Ed stopped between the two standing stones as the witch carried on writhing in his arms. He lost his grip momentarily.

The singing around them… stopped.

The witch reached up one arm and a wind struck Neha and pushed him back. Then a new song started, this time, from the left side of the lake. Ed could see Celtic warriors, Celtic people. They sang as they too stamped their feet. The wind stopped as Neha began the Irish song. Ed yanked the witch back towards him and held her tightly. From behind Neha, Ed could see cat's eyes. They were moving.

Maria stepped out of the darkness. She wore the skin of an animal. Its head lay on hers and its skin covered her back. It was a large cat!?

No, it was a jaguar, Ed realised, as he remembered Neha's description of the vision.

The witch howled – a howl of fear, as Maria stepped forward. She carried a flaming stick in one hand, the knife in the other.

Ed grabbed the witch's wrists and pulled them back. He put his foot at the witch's back and pushed her forward.

The song reached fever pitch on both sides of the lake. It was a cacophony of voices. The chanting intensified. Then, as Maria reached the witch the singing subsided, and stopped. Neha stopped singing also.

A flash of lightning filled the lakebed.

Maria went nose to nose with the witch.

"PLEASE… NO… NO," she begged.

"I hope this is painful… I hope this is slow," said Maria as she plunged the knife into her chest. It snapped through the pendant and plunged into her.

The blade broke, at the hilt. The shard remained in the witch, a tip of the blade sticking out from her chest.

A clap of heavy thunder rolled around them now.

The witch cried in pain. Her form began to regress, to that old decrepit… thing.

Maria put the lit torch to her cloak and it was set alight. The witch shrieked and hollered as she was engulfed in flames, her remaining flesh beginning to melt off. Ed shouted as kept his grip on her but the flames didn't seem to touch him.

Maria stepped back.

Neha began chanting.

Ed thought he could understand the words. "And so you are cast down… forever… down to your tomb. Your forever, no escape!"

Lightning flashed; thunder rolled.

Neha broke from his chant, stumbling. Blood streaked down from his wounds and his mouth. "Ed, the capstone! Maria, the pumps! I can hold her here, but not for long." Neha chanted once more, although his words were slurred. He put his hands on the witch. He, like Ed, seemed unaffected by the flames.

Ed let the witch go and sprinted as fast as he could out of the Turlough and away to the tractor. Hardly able to breathe he got in; keys still there – thank Christ! He got it started and moved down towards the Turlough, as fast as he could go. As he reached the entry of the slope, Maria was darting from pump to pump, switching them on.

Ed saw Neha still had her trapped. The flames had disappeared, but she was glowing now with a red hue. Ed concentrated on his job, getting down the slope. He drove the tractor towards the capstone. He dipped the loader at the front and revved the tractor forwards until the claws at the loader front got in under the capstone. He moved forward slowly as he saw water starting to spurt out of the three pumps on the slope.

He lifted the loader and the capstone came up.

Then it dropped off.

Ed cursed as he reversed, the waters reaching the tractor tyres now. He went far slower this time as sweat poured down his brow. He got in under the capstone and lifted the loader up slowly.

The capstone stayed up!

It was finely balanced, but he reversed the tractor and then slowly moved into position, at the other end of the standing stones.

Neha's eyes were opening and closing as he swayed on his feet. His arms drooped at his sides.

The witch's wails and screams seemed distant now. The form of the witch seemed to be fading away. She was soon replaced by a glowing red ball of light.

Neha managed to lift an arm and waved his hand forward to Ed. Ed dipped the loader and the capstone began to slip downwards on to

Neha's end of the standing stones. The other end of the capstone was still balanced on the loader. Ed moved the loader control down to fully lower his side of the capstone.

But a shard of red light suddenly escaped the standing stones. It hit the tractor. The lift control on the tractor went sharply upwards. The capstone slid forward off the standing stones towards Neha!

"Father!!" screamed Maria.

"Neha!" shouted Ed.

Ed dashed out of the tractor and around to the other side. The water was up to his knees. He saw Maria's face held a surprised expression. Ed was equally star struck.

Neha held the stone in place, his arms outstretched. His left leg stretched back and his right one stretched forward.

Other faded forms started to appear to the left and right of Neha.

Ed looked on, in awe, as to his left a younger man appeared. He looked very like Neha. "Paka," Ed whispered in amazement. To his left, another indigenous tribesman man appeared. He was taller. "Karo," said Ed as he remembered Neha and Maria's description.

Two others held the stone to the right of Neha. A small, old indigenous tribesman. Ed guessed it was Volo. The other man he recognised already – King O'Brien from Cormocroe Abbey.

The water was at their waists now.

The red ball of light was whirring now as a wind started to swirl around them.

As the five men shunted the stone upwards, Volo turned to Ed. "*You must leave when the capstone is in place. There will be an enormous release of power!*"

They continued to heave the capstone upwards. Then the capstone fell into position on the two standing stones. The four men assisting Neha disappeared.

The red ball of light rotated faster as it also increased in size. The wind roared about them.

The water had reached their chests as Maria waded through it. "Come on, Father!" she shouted, as she tried to grab his arm.

He kept his hands on the stone, even though it was in place. He leaned back against the left standing stone. "No, Maria," he said softly.

As the water got higher, Ed had a sinking feeling in his heart.

"I lied," Neha managed through struggled breaths. "I lied," he said again.

"Whatever – come on!!" shouted Maria.

"Somebody of this world must hold the stone… at the end of the ritual. You see, it is all about balance in the end."

"Father, we can save you. You think you're dying but–"

"I'm going, Maria… not dying."

"No, Father!" said Maria as she tried to pull him away.

"Let me go. It is my time."

Neha looked at Ed. "Ed, thank you… thank you for everything!"

"Father!" Maria screamed, as the water reached their shoulders.

"I love you, Maria," said Neha. He managed to hold a hand up to her face. "Go now with Ed."

"No… No, No, No!"

"Ed," said Neha as he looked at him.

Ed grabbed her from behind. She kicked and tore at him as he pulled her back.

The red ball of light started to make a high pitched noise. It was becoming brighter and brighter.

"Goodbye, Neha!" Ed roared through the din.

Neha's head slipped beneath the water, a solitary hand remaining over the surface… still touching the stone. Ed waded through the water as Maria stopped fighting him. They began swimming to the side of the Turlough.

They got to the edge and started to climb the slope. Ed chanced a look around and saw the red ball convulsing wildly now, beneath the water. It seemed as bright as the sun. Its high pitched noise was almost deafening, as it continued to expand outwards.

Maria and Ed started running…

BOOOOOOM!!!!

They were flung through the air… falling into a ditch, as a red energy wave ripped overhead, carrying treetops with it. A mighty wind followed, blowing over them. Then the light dissipated, as did the noise.

Ed and Maria lay on the ground, heaving breaths in and out. They were covered in twigs, soil, and leaves, together with various other debris. They slowly stood. Ed could see more around him. The head of one of the water pumps smoked beside him.

Then he saw a glimmer of light in the distance…

The rising sun.

They stood in the same spot as the morning light imbued their surrounds. The cry of a bird broke the silence – the cry of an eagle. Maria stormed out of the ditch. Ed followed.

The Turlough was full, calm, static – peaceful.

They saw the eagle land on a branch at the edge of the lake. Below him, Neha floated in the calm waters of Hags Hole.

*****

Maria knelt down, holding her father's head as she lay him on her knees. Her head was dipped, her long black hair was streaming down, just like her tears.

Ed stood close by. He didn't know what to do, so he did nothing.

His body shivered but he didn't complain. It reminded him he was still alive.

Ed wasn't sure how many minutes passed by.

Then he saw the eagle circling above. It cried out before heading off in the direction of Lough Rask.

Maria looked up.

"Come on, Maria," said Ed softly as he crouched down. "We aren't doing any good out here."

He reached out and carefully untangled her arms from Neha.

She still sat though, her arms going limp at her sides.

Ed slowly lifted Neha up. He did it assuredly but as gently as possible. As he got Neha's body over his shoulder, he reached a hand down towards Maria.

She reached up…

And took the hand of her dead father instead. She stood holding onto it.

Ed began a slow walk, no, a trudge, towards Lough Rask.

Maria held onto her father's hand all the way.

The sun soon beamed down on them. A sense of calm filled Ed as he took in the dead calm around him.

As they passed Lough Rask, it looked half drained. Ed stumbled on over uneven ground until he saw them. Two bodies lay on the lower edge of the Lough. They were sprawled on a small ledge below the waterline. Their eyes were still open.

Ed recognised them. He tensed his back. They were the two hikers, the ones who had called to Ed's door the day he had arrived in Ballyvaughan.

Maria said nothing. She continued to hold her father's hand.

Ed marched on. Maria followed.

They made it to the path near the cottage. As they got there Nuala opened the door of her house. She blessed herself as her eyes took in the scene. She scooted out of her house, key in hand and opened the cottage door for them. She said nothing and offered no comment.

Maria let go of her father's hand as Ed reached the door. Ed walked in with him. He made a quick decision, laying Neha down on the kitchen table. Maria came into the room and Nuala was on her arm, balancing with her walking stick. She managed to sit Maria down and with her free hand grabbed a blanket and fluttered it over her. She placed a gentle hand on Maria's head and Maria tilted sideways. She lay down on the couch.

Nuala walked by Ed and gave his arm a soft grasp. She flung another small blanket from the couch into his arms before quietly walking out, closing the cottage door as she did.

Ed collapsed into a sitting position on the couch opposite Maria. Her eyes were closed.

He closed his and tilted his head back.

*****

Ed awoke with the sound of knocking. As he got up and walked to the front door, he saw Maria sitting silently beside her father, her hands cupping one of his.

Ed slowly opened the door. It was Ahern, Sheila, Nuala and Dr. Flynn. As they walked in, Maria continued to stare at her father.

The doctor stopped in front of the table. "I just need to check him," he said in a hushed tone.

Maria stood, making eye contact with no one. She stood in front of the stove with her back to everyone else.

The doctor gently began examining Neha.

Garda Ahern walked up to Ed, cap off, and lips pursed. "You did it?" she said.

"Yeah, but we lost the real hero," he said as he looked over at Neha.

"Found those two hikers," she said as they both watched Dr. Flynn. "Both had bullet holes in their chests."

"Mendoza!" spat Ed.

“No doubt,” she agreed quietly. “You hear what happened?”

Ed didn’t answer but stared at her instead.

“Mendoza lost their main cargo plane over the Atlantic last night. They have no idea where it is. That’s not all,” she muttered. “Come outside a second.”

Ed followed her outside. She led him to the boot of her police car and banged it with her fist. It sprang open. Ed was nearly blinded as the sunlight hit the shimmering objects inside. They filled the boot.

“I searched Flannery’s house as you suggested,” said Ahern.

“That bastard! What a hoard!” said Ed, as he picked up one of the golden artefacts.

“A lot of these will have to be handed in to the National Museum,” said Ahern, as she stared away from Ed. She coughed then. “But who’s to say that some of them were just found by you… on your own. Out on public land.”

Ed’s mouth fell open as he continued to stare at the hoard. “My audit… I don’t know whether this will fly with Deirdre, my boss.”

“I had a good long talk with Billy Joe about his ‘main investors’. I also talked to him about the media’s interest in knowing who they were, considering the two dead hikers that have been found. He’s pretty agreeable now. I’d say he can intervene on your behalf. I’m sure he’d be happy to make a few calls. You found the two hikers, after all. The reward you get won’t make you a millionaire… but it’s the least we can do!” said Ahern, as she smiled at Ed.

She slammed the boot lid down and patted Ed on the shoulder. They both turned and walked back inside.

Dr. Flynn looked as if he was just finishing his examination of Neha. Maria stood in the same spot, still facing away from everyone. The doctor stood back from Neha and looked at Ahern.

“He has passed,” said the doctor. “Can I just offer my condolences to you both,” he said, as he first looked at Maria’s back and then to Ed.

No one said anything for a minute.

"I suppose you'll want to repatriate the body. To where?" said Dr. Flynn. He directed the question to Ed.

"Brazil," said Ed.

"I can offer some assitan–"

"There is nothing in Brazil for him," cut in Maria.

"Well… maybe Fr. Donnelly could find a site and we could–"

"No!" snapped Maria.

The doctor opened his mouth, but then clamped his lips shut instead.

"That wouldn't be him… wouldn't be Neha," offered Ed sullenly.

There was a knock on the door. Nuala turned and opened it. As she came back, a flurry of people stood at her back.

Maria finally turned around. She began shaking her head and was about to say something when Nuala piped up. "Our tribe would like to pay our respects."

"Your father helped us!" shouted one person.

"He saved us!" shouted another.

With that, several people moved past Nuala and crowded around Maria. They each took her hand and shook it, and each, in their own way, said something nice about Neha.

Maria began to thank them. Although tears crept down her face, a slow smile rose up too.

More well-wishers called in. Some carried beer and others alcohol. Sheila stood by Maria throughout as the cottage soon became packed. Ahern excused herself and shuffled out the door.

Ed felt a slap on the arm as someone put a beer into his hand. A large whiskey was soon shoved into the other.

"Your father would surely have agreed to being waked," said Sheila as she forced a drink into Maria's hand.

The cottage was soon buzzing as people streamed in, paying their respects. They walked by Neha and blessed themselves.

Ed found himself speaking to people he didn't know, but the conversation was easy going; friendly. They wanted to hear about Neha on Mullaghmore, Neha in the Hikers Hotel when the 'great wind' attacked it, and Neha at Grainne's funeral when he sang his wonderful song. Ed happily told them what he knew. They hung on his every word.

Someone kept topping up his drink.

Ed heard Maria laughing at something an old man told her. She was smiling now as she shared a drink with Sheila.

A guitar started up in the back as a woman began gently singing. Somebody walked around with a tray of various hot snacks. Ed munched away as he traded notes with a local archaeologist. This carried on for… Ed wasn't sure how long. Then he saw Ahern back again. She grabbed his arm and pulled him to the side.

"I think I have an answer… a suggestion for Maria, about her father," she said.

Ed took her over to Maria. Ahern sat beside her and gently told her and Ed the plan.

Maria looked down for second, then back up. "That would be lovely," she said warmly. Then Maria added an idea. Then Ed added another suggestion. The plan was agreed.

"Brilliant!" said Ahern. "I'll sort it all now." With that she left the cottage with her mobile phone up to her ear.

Another hour or two passed.

A proper sing song broke out. It soon became serious, as a man took charge, taking names of those whose go it was next. Then each of them would take their turn as the cottage hushed down. "Order please, order please!" the man would say as the next participant took their turn.

The standard was high as Ed gave the best version of "The Owd Woman From Yorkshire" that he could.

Ahern walked back in as the late afternoon sun began to dwindle outside. She nodded at Ed and Maria. They both quickly got changed into the cleanest clothes they could find. When they walked back into the main room, it was empty except for Ahern, two men in black suits and an open coffin on the floor.

Maria and Ed carefully wrapped Neha up in his cloak of feathers. Ed, Ahern and the two men placed him into the coffin. Two more men walked in then.

Ed put his arm around Maria and they went outside. Nuala and Sheila stood on one side and Ed and Maria on the other, as the open coffin was walked into the hearse outside. Ahern opened the passenger door of her police car for Maria. She got in and Ed got into the back.

The procession took off at a slow pace. Ahern drove in front of the hearse with the blue lights of her car flashing on top.

The evening was peaceful, no sound… no wind.

As the cortege reached the edge of Ballyvaughan, other cars slowly crept along behind them. There were people on the streets on the left and right, hats lowered in their hands or hands clasped at their fronts. As they took a right towards the old pier, Ed could see the stream of cars behind them had gotten longer.

The sea beyond the pier was like a mirror of the world around it, a reflection of calm.

The cars soon moved past the pier and onto the coast road, towards Fanore. Ahern kept a steady but slow pace as the sun got lower in the sky.

They parked at the base of Slieve Elva mountain. They got out and Ed and five others were the first to lift the coffin up the path. A tap on the shoulder and then six others took over, then another tap and six others again. They made their way up the path in less than an hour.

*****

Maria picked the spot at Eagle Rock. Near the edge, overlooking the sea in front of them with Ballyvaughan to their right. The group carefully lifted Neha out of the coffin and lay him down. Maria selected the rocks, as the cairn was built up over her father.

Ed placed the last stone on top. The priest offered some brief words. As he finished, he waved incense upon Neha's cairn.

Ed and Maria stood in front of the cairn as the group went silent.

The setting sun hung from the distant horizon. The final strokes of its light turned the tips of the ocean to crystal. Below them, the waves gently brushed the sandy canvass of Fanore beach.

The eagle landed on top of the cairn. He fluttered his wings and looked to Maria.

Maria grabbed Ed's hand. She closed her eyes. She didn't know the words, she didn't know the song…

It started in her stomach and made its way up. Her Yine chant moved up and down in intensity and seemed to reverberate around the rocks themselves.

She finished as a gust of wind flew by the group.

The eagle cried beside them, cast out its wings and sprang from the cairn. It soared down the mountain side, quickly reaching the sea. It flew just above the waves, its wings spread wide. It sailed away on the wind, and on… into the distant setting sun.

"Where do you think he's going?" muttered Ed.

"Home," said Maria.

"He is going home."

Epilogue

Neha heard the sound of the forest around him. He stood up. The trees gently swayed in the wind at his back. A river flowed beside him.

Neha looked at his small scrawny arms.

He walked to the riverside and looked at his reflection in the water. A young boy peered back at him.

He heard someone shout from across the river and looked up. It was his mother smiling at him, calling him for dinner. His little brother, Karo, ran around at her feet.

Neha walked down the riverbank. And as he looked at his reflection again, he was now a teenager. He looked up and saw his father on the other side. He had his spear in hand. He was calling him over for a hunt.

Neha looked down again into the water and a young man stared back up at him.

He heard a voice shout his name, together with a laugh, it was… his wife, she was beautiful. She was carrying a little boy in her arms. He smiled at Neha and Neha smiled back. They waved at each other.

Neha looked down at the water and saw a middle aged man.

He heard another shout, his son, Paka, a tall large chested man. Paka called him over, they were to go fishing. "Father, come, come!" he said, waving him over.

Neha looked down once more; and saw… himself, older, wiser.

He looked across again. They were all there… waiting for him.

Neha stepped into the water.

He started to cross….

He crossed….

………….to his eternity.

About the Author

Ross Griffin is a debut author. He holds a bachelor's degree in History and Politics and currently practises as an in-house lawyer.

Ross was one of ten finalists of the 'First Page Pitch' competition at the Cork Book Festival 2019, where chapter 1 of The Haunted Wind was read out. He also won the 'Unlocking Potential' competition at the Dublin Writers Conference 2019.

He currently lives in Cork, Ireland, with his wife and two children.

CPSIA information can be obtained
at www.ICGtesting.com
Printed in the USA
LVHW021948280920
667305LV00005B/1145

9 781913 545505